Philip Gibbs

The Middle of the Road: Historical Novel

OK Publishing 2021

Philip Gibbs

The Middle of the Road: Historical Novel

Published by

MUSAICUM

Books

- Advanced Digital Solutions & High-Quality book Formatting -

musaicumbooks@okpublishing.info

2021 OK Publishing

ISBN 978-80-272-7294-5

Contents

I

For the twentieth time Bertram Pollard went to the door of the little room he called his "study" and listened. He heard nothing but the slow tick-tock of a grandfather's clock at the end of the narrow hall; that, and his own breathing which seemed loud.

The silence of the house in Holland Street, Kensington, was horrible to him; yet better than the rapid footsteps of a doctor, the quick rustle of a nurse's starched dress, the strange inexplicable noises of something being dragged across the room upstairs, water being poured out, a glass falling and smashing, and other sounds which had scared him when his wife was in pain.

He'd heard her moaning once or twice, had gone back into his room, shutting the door quietly, and saying, "Lord! . . . Lord! . . ." and nothing else but that again and again.

In that room of his-twelve feet by fourteen, as he knew by measuring it from skirting-board to skirting-board, as a mechanical occupation for his nerve-tattered brain-he had prayed, cursed, groaned, and even wept a little. He had paced up and down, sat down at his desk, put his forehead against the wall, gripped the mantelpiece, clenched and unclenched his hands, behaved with a ridiculous lack of self-control.

He was frightened by his own cowardice. "This won't do!" he had said once or twice, and then used the words which he had said to his own soul, not without effect sometimes, when men had lain dead about him and his chance of death had been as good as theirs. "Keep a stiff upper lip, my lad!"

That's what his father had said sharply to him as a small boy when he had taken a toss from a pony or cut his knees in a tumble. "Keep a stiff upper lip, my lad!" That was part of the family tradition, and it had served him pretty well at the war —a tradition of nerve-control, endurance of pain, hiding of fear, however frightened. It was no good now, when Joyce was suffering torture. No damn good.

His thoughts brooded over the last six months and more. What a brute he had been, and how frightful was life which caused women to suffer so much when this thing happened!

Joyce had not wanted it to happen. She'd had some foreboding of its agony, though she'd tried to hide it from him with her usual pluck. Wonderful pluck! This girl with "bobbed" hair, who felt that she was unfit to be seen if her nails weren't newly manicured, and who was as slim and fragile-looking as a Watteau shepherdess, had the spirit of all her family, and of many women in her crowd, as he'd seen them in the hunting-field, in canteens, once or twice in air-raids. He'd been more scared than this golden-haired "kid", as he called her then, when a bomb had fallen, smashing the door of a house in which they had been dancing, one night in London of war-time. His heart had given a thump, though he was a major of machine-guns, but Joyce had lit a cigarette with a steady hand, laughed without a tremor, and said, "Bad miss, brother Boche!"

That was the night he'd asked her to marry him, if he had the luck to get through the war. "The luck's yours, and my love will keep you safe!" she'd said, as he remembered now, and would remember always.

Well it had seemed luck then, though since, once or twice, he'd wondered whether the luck hadn't been with the men who'd gone out before the show was finished. They'd been saved a lot of worry-this worrying business of life after war, with its enormous disappointments, and the whole muddle and mystery of things.

Marriage was one of its mysteries. He'd gone into it as an escape from all troubles. Funny, that! It was to wipe out the memory of the things he'd seen. It would be the rest-cure for body and soul, both rather badly jolted and put out of gear by something like shell-shock. "Soul-shock," as old Christy had once called it.

This marriage with Joyce had seemed like getting by sheer, undeserved luck the ideal of beauty which old Christy used to say was the secret, unattained, and unattainable purpose of life.

"Beauty of life," said Christy-they were sitting together in a dug-out between Henencourt Château and the ruins of Albert —"is God's will on earth as it is in Heaven."

He used to talk like that though he was so ironical and blasphemous about all definite religion.

"Beauty is the most exquisite understanding of truth and happiness. Body as well as soul,
the material and the spiritual, must be given a chance of that, and when harmony is established
between 'em then Perfection, or God, is attained. But we're a long way from that at the moment,
Major, in this dirty little war of ours!"

That's what Christy had said, and Bertram had scoffed at him as a crawling Pacifist and
hot-air merchant, and made rude, insulting remarks about his friend's excuse for a face, which
departed abominably from beauty's line.

But he'd remembered Christy's words when he'd stood in St. Mary Abbot's church with
Joyce. She stood beside him-he could see her now like that, though she lay upstairs-slim, tall,
with gold-spun hair cut like a boy's, perfectly calm and self-possessed. "Isn't she beautiful!"
murmured the crowd of women outside the church, in High Street, Kensington, before they
drove away, and Bertram had agreed in his heart. She was the Beauty for which all his soul
had yearned during four and a half years of ugliness. She was the beauty of life which had
come to *him*!

He had called her that on the first night when they were alone together in this little house
in Holland Street which she had furnished out of her own money with reckless extravagance,
a delight in weird wall-papers and sham antiques, a passion for highly coloured cushions into
which she used to sink with little squeals of ecstasy.

It had been a great game of Life in those first few months of marriage —a year ago now.
Joyce had set the pace and kept it up with amazing resistance to all fatigue. He had pleaded for
"a quiet life," "time to love each other," "an escape from the crowd," but she'd jeered at him
as "an introspective slacker," dragged him out to theatres, dance clubs, other people's houses.
She'd filled this little house in Holland Street with an amazing collection of people whose
presence he'd resented sometimes with almost poisonous hatred-young staff officers who still
swaggered about Whitehall though the war was over, young clergymen who had been chaplains
at the front, young airmen who'd put up their wings some time after Armistice, girls who came
drifting back from canteens at Etaples, Rouen, Cologne, with a lot of army slang and a mania
for cheap cigarettes, a sense of boredom with peace, a restless desire for "a good time" and a
most embarrassing habit of discussing sex problems in mixed company with a complete absence
of reserve. They had come in and out of the house at all times of the day, even to late breakfasts,
where Joyce had joined them in one of her many dressing-gowns of Japanese silk and Futurist
colours, with her bare feet in bedroom slippers, looking like a sleepy boy, after dancing in some
overheated room until late night or early morning.

He had quarrelled with her for that. It was the cause of their first quarrel, "It doesn't seem
decent," he'd said, "and anyhow, I hate it." That was when she'd given breakfast in this way to
one of those Army chaplains of whom she knew so many-Peter Fynde, a young, good-looking,
conceited ass, with an exaggerated Oxford drawl, a slight stutter, and affected gallantry. He had
had the impudence to kiss Joyce's hand and to make some remark about her little feet, totally
unconscious of Bertram's hot flush and sulky discourtesy towards him.

Joyce seemed to have no regard even for the privacy of her bedroom, and there had been
another quarrel when Bertram had come back from an afternoon stroll and found Joyce, who
had complained of a sick head-ache, "giving audience," as she called it, to two young officers,
three girls, and Kenneth Murless of the Foreign Office-Murless, whom he detested most of
all her friends because he was too beautiful to live-one of those tall, curly-headed, Greek God
sort of fellows-and elaborately brilliant in conversational insincerities. He was sitting on a low
stool by Joyce's bed, feeding her with strawberries and cream, and telling some ridiculous story
about his life as a junior diplomatist at the Hague before the war, to the appreciative laughter
of the company, and Joyce's friendly smiles.

Bertram had made rather a fool of himself that afternoon. He admitted it now, in remembrance, with a groan of contrition. He had played the part of Petruchio in *The Taming of the Shrew*.

"I wish to God you people would clear out of my wife's room!" he had said, with violence. "Can't you see that she's suffering from head-ache and that all this chatter is the worst thing you can do to her?"

That second part of his speech had been clearly dishonest. It was not Joyce's head-ache he was worrying about-she seemed to have forgotten that-but his own jealousy, his hatred of this public possession of Joyce's room.

Of course she hadn't taken his explosion meekly.

"My dear Bertram," she'd said, in her pretty mocking way, "if you don't feel like a gentleman this afternoon, go and walk till you do. Anyhow, don't interrupt Kenneth's amusing story!"

Kenneth and the rest had laughed heartily. Bertram's desire for them to "clear out" seemed to them a delicious joke. It was he who cleared out, and later came back, when they'd gone, in a rattled temper, to say things to Joyce for which now he could have bitten out his tongue. She hadn't quarrelled. She'd been cool and smiling and sarcastic.

"My dear Bertram, surely you don't think marriage has given you the prerogative of tyranny? That's gone out of date. My love for you doesn't give you the right to insult my friends. Why you should get jealous and fussed because I receive them in my bedroom-look at all these bed-clothes and this heavy quilt! —I can't understand. I never heard anything so narrow-minded, so suburban! In any case, don't be disloyal to form. Our crowd doesn't behave like that."

"Our crowd!" Bertram had said bitterly. "I wish the whole crowd would go and drown themselves. I want you alone, to myself. You let these blighters into your bedroom, let them kiss your hand, but if I show any kind of emotion for you, you shrink from me. When I want to kiss you, as I always want to, you say I'm too 'beastly emotional'!"

"You must admit you are, Bertram!" Joyce had said. "I can't stand too much of it. It bores me. I prefer intelligent conversation, comradeship, laughter. What's wrong with that?"

"Marriage means more than that," he'd said gloomily, and then had made abject apologies for his sulkiness, and had gone down on both knees by her bedside, so that she had forgiven him, and tousled his hair with playful fingers. But there had been other quarrels of the kind, worse than that.

He was "nervy," he knew that. The War had left him all on edge. He was irritable with small things, the loss of a collar-stud, the slackness of a servant, the continual tinkle of the telephone bell-Joyce's friends suggesting some new "stunt." Some secret warfare was going on inside his brain, loosening his hold on old beliefs, and disturbing old checks and balances of mind, old loyalties of tradition. If he'd had some work to do, it would have been easier, but England had two million unemployed, and thousands of ex-officers like himself were wearing their boots out to find a living wage.

Joyce had been horribly distressed when she knew that a child was coming. All the tenderness which had overwhelmed him at that news failed to reconcile her to the idea, though she hid some fear that was in her. It was the inactivity forced upon her at the end which hurt her most; that and her loss of beauty for a time. "No more dances!" she had cried. "No more flying stunts at Hendon. Oh, Bertram, what a colossal bore!"

He had been angry with her again (and now cursed himself for that temper) because she'd insisted upon still retaining her crowd of friends about her to the last. She'd made no secret of her condition, even to Kenneth Murless, and Bertram had resented that candour with painful jealousy, shrinking from the thought that any one but himself should be in possession of their sacred secret.

"It's frightful!" he'd said. "It's like exposing yourself in the market-place."

"You're ridiculous!" Joyce had answered. "Anybody would think you'd been brought up at-Peckham. In the early Victorian era. Do you think people don't *know*?"

"Yes-but to talk about it to Kenneth Murless! That decadent waster!"

"A good friend of mine, whom I met long before I knew you." So Joyce had said, calmly and cruelly.

He had been violently angry. . . . How could he ever forgive himself for such brutality now that Joyce lay upstairs, between life and death! Lord! . . . Lord! . . .

The supreme moment of fear came when for more than the twentieth time he listened at the door of his study, and heard again the horrible silence upstairs, following those still more dreadful sounds of the activity of strangers busy with his wife. Did this silence mean death? He asked the question between two frightful heart-beats. Then the door opened at the top of the landing and there was the rustle again of the nurse's starched dress coming downstairs. Bertram went into his room and faced round as the woman came in after a tap at the door. It was the verdict of life or death.

"Is she all right?" he asked, failing to steady his voice.

The nurse seemed to be pitiful of his agony. His white face and haggard eyes were like those of many men she'd seen at such a time.

"Your wife's all right," she said; "no danger now!" She hesitated a moment, and then added nervously:

"The baby was still-born. I'm sorry."

She left the room again, and didn't see Bertram Pollard go to the mantelpiece and put his face down on his arms.

II

The child was a boy. It had perfect features, like a miniature Joyce, but after a glance and a whimpering cry, she wouldn't look at it again. Bertram knelt by his wife's bedside, trying to hide the wetness of his eyes. She put her thin fingers through his hair and caressed him, but after a short time said, "You worry me, rather," so that the nurse signalled to him to go away.

Bertram had felt an immense sense of relief at the sight of Joyce lying at peace after her ordeal. She was faintly flushed, and had all her beauty back, with a youthful, almost boyish look, touched by the character of her "bobbed" hair.

He turned at the door and glanced back at her, and when she opened her eyes again he kissed his hand to her with all his heart in that gesture of love, but she shut her eyes without response.

During his first reaction to the knowledge that Joyce was safe he had not worried over the death of the baby, except for Joyce's sake. It was only later that he began to think of the child. Something of himself lay dead in that cradle in the dressing-room to which it had been carried by the nurse. If it had lived —

His imagination wandered through the years ahead. There would have been a companion for him, a little pal. He would have taught the boy to ride, to play games, to face up to life, to be a gentleman. Not a snob! No, he would have taught him to be tolerant, and "democratic" in old Christy's way, with understanding of folk in the mean streets of life. He could have told that son of his something of the men he had commanded in the war, those Cockney fellows who had been all nerves and all pluck with a wonderful sense of humour. His son! . . . Young Bertram! . . . How fine that would have been! Life would have been less lonely-and, Lord! how lonely it had been with Joyce upstairs, and a nurse in the house, and the two maids whispering about the passages while he sat alone in his "study" with nothing in the world to study except his introspective thoughts! . . .

That night he went on tip-toe to the dressing-room, turned up the electric light, and drew back the coverlet from the face of the still-born child. His son! What a queer mite! Like a wax doll, with something of Joyce's look, and something, perhaps, of his own. He kissed the tiny dead face, and then drew back sharply because of its coldness. Not that he was afraid of death. He had seen many men die, and dead. But this little thing was Joyce's babe. That was piteous! After all her suffering! Oh, God! . . . Was it for the best? Had God been kind? There was something in life now which seemed to spoil things. Some trouble seemed to be brewing for further tragedy. That was what old Christy thought. The old foundations were slipping away. The War had shaken them too much. The next generation might have to go through worse things than their fathers. Fathers who had been good soldiers but not much good in time of peace, and found it hard to get a decent job!

Bertram Pollard covered the face of the still-born child, switched off the light, and went downstairs again. He wrote out an advertisement for *The Times* —Joyce's friends would want to know-and then, for hours, sat brooding until he fell asleep, and was only wakened by the "Lor', sir!" of the parlourmaid, Edith, who came in to tidy his room. She was very sorry for him, and said so in her chatty way.

III

It was the nurse who told him how to arrange for the child's burial, and he went round to an undertaker's in Church Street, Kensington, jostled by smart women, very bright at their morning's shopping so that he hated them. The undertaker's clerk was respectful but surprised when Bertram explained his errand.

"It's not usual, sir, to have a funeral for a still-born infant."

"What then?" asked Bertram.

The man coughed.

"As a rule we just fetch them away."

"Damn it!" said Bertram, with astonishing violence, "I want you to arrange a funeral."

He arranged for an oak coffin with a brass plate, on which the name "Bertram Pollard" was to be inscribed.

Before the little coffin was closed, Bertram carried it into Joyce's room, according to a wish she had whispered to the nurse. It was like a toy coffin with a doll inside. Joyce's eyes filled with tears but she turned her head away and did not speak a word.

"My dear! My dear!" said Bertram. Although he had walked with death so long he was distressed beyond all words by this little corpse. His own name on the coffin startled him when he first saw it. It seemed symbolical of something that had died in himself, his spirit of youth; his hope.

"If I were you, I'd get about a bit and see your friends," said the nurse, as they sat together in the carriage with the coffin on Bertram's knee.

She was a nice human soul, who had been a nurse in the War and had learnt pity for men.

"Most of my real pals are killed," said Bertram.

The nurse laughed, not heartlessly but to cheer him up.

"See those who are still alive. It's no use brooding. Carry on!"

It was the old rallying word of the War. It had some effect on Bertram even now. He straightened up.

"I wish I could get a job, nurse!"

"We want another nice little war," she answered.

He looked at her sideways.

"Do you mean that?"

She smiled back at him.

"You know you've thought so, sometimes! So have I. War's hell, of course. But there was something about it —"

"It's the impulse that's gone," said Bertram. "There doesn't seem to be any kind of purpose —"

"Love, life, work," said the nurse.

Bertram said, "Yes. Yes, of course!" and then, "I can't get the hang of things, quite. I'm just floundering, aimless. And anyhow, there's no work for my type. I was all right with machine guns. They're not wanted now."

"Men are wanted, and always will be," said the nurse. "Proper men, like you."

That cheered him. He said no more until the tiny coffin was lowered into the earth and the nurse and he were on their way back.

"Nurse," he said, "I'll get a job if I die for it."

"Get a job and live for it," answered the nurse. "Here's luck!"

IV

Joyce was sleeping —"as sound as a bell," said the nurse. Bertram had finished his dinner alone, hating his loneliness, and the deliberately cheerful way in which he had to answer the chatty remarks of Edith, the maid, who waited on him with a sense of drama in the house, and a desire to express comradeship. In his heart, though he liked the girl, he wished her at the devil, because of his fretted nerves, and refused a second serve of fruit jelly with an impatience which he tried to disguise by a "Thank you very much, Edith. Nothing more-for goodness' sake!" Then he went into his study, shut the door, and tried to settle down at his desk to some writing. He had no concentration of mind. The ticking of the clock on the mantelpiece annoyed him desperately. It had been playing tattoos in his brain during those hours when its fast little ticking seemed to be hurrying Joyce's life away. Well, she was all right now, thank God, unless the nurse and doctor were lying to him. He went over to the mantelpiece, took up Joyce's photograph, and kissed it. He would try to be less irritable and get a grip on that absurd temper of his. Then he swore softly because the telephone bell rang again. That was about the tenth time in the last hour. Joyce's friends desired to know how she was getting on. Why the deuce didn't they have the decency to leave him alone, and to leave the telephone alone, at such a time?

"Is that Mr. Pollard? Oh, forgive me, but can you tell me how dear Joyce is getting on?"

That was the usual way of putting it. His answers were brief. "Quite well, thanks!" then a slam down with the receiver. He wasn't going to give them any details.

A man's voice had spoken to him on the 'phone. "That you, Bertram? . . . Oh, I'm Kenneth Murless. How's Joyce?"

What right had Kenneth to ask such a question at such a time? It was like his impertinence! . . . And yet, somehow, because of Joyce, who liked Kenneth, he felt constrained to give a civil answer.

"Getting on well."

"Give her my love, old man," said Kenneth's voice on the wire; "say I'm frightfully sorry about her loss."

His love! Bertram's face flushed deeply as he stood by the plaguey instrument. That was going a bit too far!

"I'm afraid she's not well enough to get anybody's love just yet," he said icily.

"All my sympathy to you, old man," answered Kenneth.

This time Bertram had slammed down the receiver. He had no desire whatever for Kenneth's sympathy. He wished the fellow would get his Grecian nose down to his job at the Foreign Office and keep it there. Otherwise it might be in danger of getting broken one day.

That last ring he had answered took the frown off his forehead after he had listened to the first words over the wire.

"Oh, is that you, mother? Yes, Joyce seems out of danger now. . . . Come round? . . . Well, is the governor at the House to-night? . . . The Irish debate? Oh, yes, I forgot that monstrous farce. All right. I'll come, then."

He remembered there were other tragedies in life besides his own, more death than that of his still-born child when he bought an evening paper at the Underground station in the High Street, Kensington, on his way to his father's house in Sloane Street.

"Six deaths in Dublin to-day. Serious Ambush. More reprisals."

Those were the headings on the front page, and he felt sick at the words, and wouldn't read the details. The same thing as usual. British officers fired at and killed by boys in civilian clothes. Young Irishmen dragged out of their beds and shot in cold blood by "unknown men, said to be in uniform." Irish homes burnt by the military. Raids, bomb outrages, searches-the usual daily record of anarchy in Ireland which was becoming intolerable in his soul because of his divided allegiance as half an Irishman and half an Englishman, half a democrat and half a Tory, half a Protestant and half a Catholic, at least, he hoped, a Christian. He opened the paper as he sat in the district train, and saw his father's name on the centre page:

"Great Speech by Mr. Michael Pollard, K.C.:
Defends Government Policy of Reprisals."

end poetry block end rend

Bertram crushed the paper in his hands, and dropped it on the seat by his side. It was his father's field night. He would enjoy himself vastly upholding the "absolute necessity of putting down these murders with the firm hand of British Justice," appealing to the old Mosaic law of an eye for an eye, a tooth for a tooth, denouncing those who would treat with rebels to the Crown and "shake hands with murder."

Well, it would keep the governor late at the House. That was the only comfort. He would be able to see his mother alone, and avoid a savage altercation with his father, who treated him as a traitor to the British Empire-Bertram Pollard, D.S.O., M.C., who had been three times wounded in the Great War, and loved England with a kind of passion.

"Mother!"

She met him in the hall of the house in Sloane Street, and at the sight of her little figure and sad face, his jangled nerves, so tautly drawn during Joyce's long ordeal, gave a kind of snap, and when he put his arms round her he dropped his forehead on to her shoulder, and his eyes filled with tears, as in the old days when he came home from school, or left her after the holidays.

"My poor boy!" she said soothingly, "I understand. . . . I'm sorry about the poor little baby."

She took him by the hand into her small sitting-room and asked him to tell her all the details of his ordeal.

"Joyce's ordeal, mother!" he said, but she shook her head, and said, "It's worse for the men, if they're sensitive. The agony of waiting —"

There were many things he wanted to tell his mother, this little woman with her thin grey hair, and her worn face and kind brown eyes, to whom, as a boy, he had told all his secrets, confessed all his peccadilloes, and had no worse reproof than "Oh, darling!" She had spoilt him as she had spoilt all of them, Dorothy, Susan, young Digby, and himself, shielding them from their father's harsh and hasty temper, his Irish impatience, his old-fashioned Protestant intolerance-he was Southern Irish, but Protestant-with any license of youth. She had even told "fibs" to shield them, and they had loved her for it, and traded abominably on her fear of "the governor" and his sudden rages.

She was more afraid of him than they had ever been. Even as small children they had defied his authority. Dorothy had been the greatest rebel, long before her marriage to a Prussian officer whom she had met at Wiesbaden, in 1912, when already there was a whisper of war with Germany-pooh-poohed by Dorothy, as by many others who knew nothing in those days about international politics, and cared less. That was her last rebellion. Michael Pollard, K.C., M.P., had wiped his daughter out of his mind and heart. He hated "the Hun" worse because of her.

And Susan! . . . She took a pleasure in braving his wrath —"our Ogre," as she called him. She never tired of maintaining her right to breakfast in bed, which he denounced as "the slum-mocky instinct of her wild Irish blood."

"Your blood too, father, and no fault of mine!" was her answer to that particular argument, to which "the governor" would answer, "Thank God the Norman strain is stronger than the Celtic, as far as I'm concerned." She had ridiculed his Protestant austerity, flouted his parental commands as "Early Victorian tyranny," and had become a Suffragette with a joyous assertion of "liberty" which meant for her late dances and no questions, rather than Votes for Women, at a time when Michael Pollard, M.P. (not K.C. then) was a violent antagonist of Women's Rights.

Bertram had taken Susan's part in these domestic scenes, but Dorothy had been his favourite sister, his best comrade, and her German marriage, and long exile and silence during the years of war had made a gap in his heart.

He spoke of her now.

"Have you heard from Doll lately?"

Mrs. Pollard looked nervously at the door and pulled out some letters from a little bag by her side.

"Your father doesn't know I hear from her. You know he forbade all intercourse."

"Rubbish!" said Bertram.

His mother confessed to a sense of guilt in having this secret from her husband, but it was more than she could bear to be cut off for ever from her first-born.

"She writes lovingly. Her marriage-and the War-have made no difference, except that she defends Germany a little."

Bertram smiled at that, and said, "I suppose it is natural, but it takes a lot of doing, as far as the war's concerned." He asked about his other sister.

"What's Susan's latest game?"

Mrs. Pollard looked distressed. Again she gave that frightened glance at the door, as though her husband might come in at any moment.

"I'm afraid, Bertram! The child is devoted to the Sinn Fein cause! It's a passion with her, like Votes for Women used to be. Your father threatens to turn her out of doors if she says another word on the subject. There was a dreadful scene yesterday morning."

Bertram could imagine it. Susan delighted in dreadful scenes. She was an Irish rose, with many thorns, sharply pointed. No Norman coldness in *her* blood! None of her mother's Devonshire softness.

Mrs. Pollard revealed more than an ordinary anxiety.

"I'm afraid Susan will get into trouble. There was a policeman here a few days ago."

"A policeman? Sounds like melodrama!"

"He wanted Susan to give him the address of a young Irishman named Dennis O'Brien. Susan denied all knowledge of him, but I know she has been corresponding with the boy."

Bertram said, "My God!" and then begged his mother's pardon. He hid from her his own reason for alarm. He knew Dennis O'Brien. The boy had been in the machine-gun corps with him, and he had heard news of him from Ireland. It was not news to be talked of lightly. He was up to the neck in Sinn Fein.

"Where's Susan now?" he asked abruptly.

Mrs. Pollard's hands fluttered up to her forehead.

"Do I ever know? Modern mothers aren't taken into their daughters' confidence. They come and go as they please, and resent all questioning. It wasn't so in my young days."

Bertram smiled at the last words. How often he had heard them! How often he and the two girls-rebels three-had laughed at them, years back, as children. His brother Digby, now a "Black and Tan" in Ireland-horrible thought! —had been too young to enjoy the joke.

He lingered on, forgetting Joyce a little, and his dead baby, feeling a boy again with this mother whose love was restful, and all-understanding. They talked of old times, and she wept a little because so much was altering and she felt so much alone, now that Digby, her baby boy, had gone to Ireland in the midst of all that terror.

She made no allusion to Joyce's share in her loneliness. Joyce did not seem to like her much and kept Bertram away from her more than was quite kind.

Bertram guessed her thoughts.

"When Joyce gets better, we'll see more of you, mother."

"That will be nice, dear," she answered quietly, but not hopefully.

He left her before midnight, and was back again in Holland Street before the Houses of Parliament had finished a long debate on the Irish situation.

He saw by next day's papers that his father's speech was reported *verbatim*, but he didn't read it.

V

Joyce was slow in getting about. "Wants cheering up," said the nurse who still stayed on. "But I can't allow visitors yet. It's up to you, Major!"

Bertram did his best to cheer her up, and went in and out of the bedroom bringing flowers, books, illustrated papers, and making bright remarks about the weather and things in general. But he was not a great success. Joyce seemed to be fretting, and was in low spirits. She brightened a little when the nurse manicured her, and when a Truelove's girl came to curl her "bobbed" hair. She was also amused by the number of callers who came to enquire about her health, sending up messages and so many flowers that Bertram's gift of bloom looked insignificant. Every time she heard the bell ring she wondered which of her friends it might be-Billy Simpson, Nat Wynne, Peter Fynde-Kenneth Murless —?

"Has Kenneth called yet?" she asked Bertram, and when he said, "Half a dozen times, I should say!" she looked at him in an amused, challenging way, and said, "Nice Boy! I think nurse must let me ask him to tea."

Bertram restrained a sudden pang of jealousy. He mustn't get back to that absurdity. After a short silence which Joyce understood, he suggested meekly that it might be as well to see members of the family first-her mother, for instance, and his, and Susie, his sister. They would be rather hurt if others were let in while they were kept out.

Joyce made a comical grimace.

"What a boy you are for the conventions! Of course I must see Mother-though I don't see why I should see mothers-in-law and sisters-in-law. It would be far more fun to have Kenneth, and some of my own set. A rowdy little tea-party to celebrate my return to Society!"

"Lord! Don't return to that sort of thing," said Bertram hurriedly.

"What sort of thing?" asked Joyce, coldly.

He avoided a direct answer.

"Let's be quiet for a bit. You and me. I want to think things out. I must get some kind of work —"

"My tea-parties won't prevent you," said Joyce.

She sat up in bed, and her cheeks flushed.

"Don't let's get back to the old arguments, Bertram. I give you a free hand. I'm not jealous of any of your friends-though I think that Socialist creature, Christy, has an evil influence on you. I insist on having my own friends, and meeting them when and how I like. If you don't trust me, it's an insult to my sense of honour."

"My dear Kid!"

Bertram spoke with profound humility and compunction. Of course he trusted her. There was no harm whatever in anything she did. He knew perfectly well that her comradeship with Kenneth Murless was straight and clean and sweet-although he hated it because of his jealous love of her, hated all the people who surrounded her and edged him out of that absolute monopoly for which he craved.

"I shall ask Kenneth to tea to-morrow," said Joyce in a determined way, "and, then, any of the crowd who want to see me. I'm tired of this sick-room business. Never again, I hope, after this experience!"

"Ask any one you like," said Bertram. He bent over to kiss her, but she turned away from him fretfully.

For a moment he stood looking down on her, hurt by her quick movement to avoid his caress, and by the words she had spoken, but filled with tenderness because of his love for her. He stood like that in silence, when there was a tap at the door, and the nurse came in with Joyce's mother, Lady Ottery, who went quickly to the bedside and embraced her daughter.

"My poor darling!"

"Oh, mother," said Joyce, "my poor little baby!"

It was the first time Bertram had heard her mention the baby, and it touched him poignantly.

Lady Ottery said, "If only I'd been with you!" and Bertram wished in his heart that Joyce had permitted that, but she had resisted all his persuasion to have her mother with her.

"Mother is too dominant in time of sickness," she had said. "Besides, it's not fair to her, after the War, with Rudy and Hal both killed. If anything happened to me, she would die."

That was like Joyce. If she had to suffer, she would suffer alone and not drag others in. But Bertram wondered if Lady Ottery would have died "if anything had happened" to Joyce. He thought not.

He had been with her when the news of Hal's death had come from the War Office. That was a year after Rudolf's. Ottery had handed his wife the telegram without a word. He had been hit hard, and breathed heavily, plucking his reddish beard and staring at a distant tree with watery eyes. It was a July afternoon, and they were all standing in the gardens of Holme Ottery, watching the girls playing tennis on the lawns below the terrace. Bertram had come up to get a drink. He remembered now the look on Lady Ottery's face, her thin, sharp-featured, powerful face. Only for a moment did her lips and her eyelids quiver. Then she smiled at her husband, a strange, proud smile, and said, "For England's sake! . . ." After that, when she moved towards her husband and took his hand, she said: "Poor Hal has done his bit! Rudy will be glad to see him."

Bertram had marvelled at her courage, her hardness, her love of England, so great that she was ready to give all her sons for its safe-guarding. He remembered telling Christy that, when he went back from leave, and he remembered the rage with which he heard Christy denounce Lady Ottery's point of view and sacrificial patriotism.

"Its hellish!" he said. "We'll never stop War as long as women like that think their noblest duty is to breed sons for the shambles; as long as they rejoice in the death of their well-beloved for England's sake, or Germany's. It's making a religion of the foulest stupidity in human life. It's upholding the tradition of war-right or wrong-as the supreme test of virtue in a noble caste, and its blood sacrifice as a necessary, inevitable and sacred duty. How are we going to get peace in the world with that spirit in women?"

So he had argued on, until Bertram had told him roughly to "shut up, for God's sake!"

Lady Ottery had turned her house into a hospital during the War, and for three years or more had nursed badly wounded men, never shrinking from sights of blood or death, doing dirty and disgusting work, though never before the war had she soiled her hands, except in the garden, among flowers, or come in touch with the coarse and tragic aspects of life. That was the spirit of patrician women in England, however delicate and sheltered. It was the spirit of an old tradition. Joyce had it still, though in many small ways she had broken with tradition, and belonged to a new world of womanhood, careless of conventions, free of speech, in revolt against the old code of manners.

Mother and daughter! Bertram watched them as they talked together. How immensely different, yet how alike! Lady Ottery, with her rather awe-inspiring dignity, plainly, almost dowdily, dressed. Joyce, with absurd little bows on her night-dress, excited, thrusting off the bedclothes, stretching out for a cigarette, saying "Damn" when she dropped the match, laughing when her mother fastened up a little button which revealed too much, announcing her intention of having a tea-party for her "best boy," careless of shocking this old-fashioned mother. Yet,

Bertram thought, with the same steel, the same hardihood underneath her softness, and the same family tradition.

Lady Ottery directed her attention to Bertram for a moment, having previously ignored him. She disliked him, as he knew, disappointed with her daughter's marriage to a penniless young officer, and suspicious of his political views after one or two heated conversations. This afternoon, however, she was unusually gracious, and remarked that he looked worried.

Joyce told her that he was always worrying. He was suffering from some soul complex, which she could not fathom—an uneasy conscience, or a craving for the Higher Life.

"Too much sick-room, I expect! Husbands always get the worst of this sort of thing. Ottery fretted unreasonably."

She alluded to a lecture she was going to deliver in London, "The Religion of Revolution," and trusted (that was her word) that Bertram would go to hear it. It would explain the cause of social unrest and might clear up some of his little difficulties.

Bertram took the ticket she gave him, and suppressed an inclination to groan or laugh. He could not imagine his "difficulties" being dissolved by anything that his mother-in-law might have to say.

"I expect I'm suffering from the strain of peace," he said with a smile, when Lady Ottery fixed him with her lorgnette and said he looked "hipped."

"London's enough to depress a laughing hyena! But I'll take a walk in it while you and Joyce have a private chat. I expect she's heaps to tell you."

Joyce said she had nothing to tell. She wanted her mother to give her the latest social news, the inside of the political situation, and the state of the world generally. Was the Prime Minister still licking the hands of Labour? Had Evelyn got her divorce yet?

VI

London had a lowering influence at this time on Bertram Pollard, and filled him with such intensity of gloom that he began to hate the place which as a boy he had loved with romantic sentiment as the city of endless adventure where life's drama was rich and full.

He remembered but vaguely the tall brick house in Merrion Square, Dublin, where he had lived in his early boyhood, until his father had brought all the family to England. From their house in Sloane Street, during holidays from St. Paul's School, he had gone exploring the mean streets and slum quarters of London, lounging about the bookshops in the Charing Cross Road, peering into old churches, strolling around the markets in Covent Garden and Smithfield, listening to the cheap-jacks in Leather Lane, venturing into the Italian quarter at Hatton Garden with a sense of adventure, going as far afield as the London docks and the back streets of Stepney and Bermondsey, where he looked out for types of men who belonged to the novels of Jacobs and Conrad.

Then, in his first year at Oxford, he'd come down to London for "binges" on boat-race night, when there were wild rags at the music halls and tumultuous encounters of undergraduates in Piccadilly Circus, rather drunken, but joyous, dinners in Soho restaurants.

There had been no second year for him at Oxford, because of the war which changed everything, but as a machine-gun officer London still pulled at his heart-strings with a tremendous tug, and made him desperate for the seven days' leave which came so rarely.

"Good-bye, Piccadilly, good-bye, Leicester Square —" The silly old words yelled by crowds of men in khaki going to the mud and fire of Flanders for the first time-the second-timers didn't sing it so lustily, unless they had been drinking-always stirred his old sentiment for London. He repeated the words as he lay in his dug-out at night, twelve hundred yards from the Boche line out from Mailly Mailly on the Somme-his first pitch-and old Christy, who lay beside him chaffed him because more than once he spoke the word "London" in his sleep.

London! He used to whisper that word with a kind of ecstasy when he came out of Charing Cross station from the boat train which brought swarms of leave men in those old days of darkness and air-raids and mass emotion. The taxi drive through Piccadilly to his father's house was a journey of enchantment. Back again! London! What luck! Because it might be for the last time, every minute of it was precious, every dimly lighted lamp was a beacon of delight; the smell of the streets, the rushing swirl of taxis, the beat of rain on the empurpled pavements, the damp and fog of a winter's night, the wet crowds outside the theatres, the dear damned dismalness of London, drugged him, made his senses drunk with gladness.

The old town had been good in those days. Now when he went out into its streets, while Joyce was ill, he found no comfort in it. Perhaps that was his fault. Perhaps it was he that had changed, not London. . . . It was the world that had changed, and all men in it, and England that had seemed unchanging. As Bertram wandered about the streets, diving down some of the old highways, walking into the outer suburbs to tire out a brain that did not sleep enough at nights, he found that pessimism closed about him. He couldn't avoid it, for its gloom was in every face he passed, on every newspaper placard, in every group of men at every street corner, in long processions of out-of-works whom he met in mean streets.

These processions of unemployed men, all ex-service, hurt him horribly. They carried banners with the proclamation, "We want Work, not Charity." They were men whom he'd seen marching up the Albert-Bapaume road and the Arras-Lens road, and the Ypres-Menin road, when England and the world had needed them. They were the heroes who were fighting in a war to end war, the boys in the trenches for whom nothing was too good. Now they were shabby and down at heel, some of them in the old khaki with buttons and shoulder-straps torn off, all of them downcast and wretched-looking. "Not charity!" they said, but they had scouts out, shaking collecting boxes in the faces of the passers-by, in an aggressive, almost hostile way.

Bertram could never pass one of these boxes without putting a few coppers inside, until one day he remembered that it was his wife's money, not his own, that he was giving away. The thought made him flush in the street, and walk on with a quicker, restless pace as far as Upper Tooting. It was absurd for him to give to the unemployed. He was one of them, with less chance of work.

At many street corners there were groups of seedy-looking men of all ages, lounging aimlessly outside buildings on which the words "Labour Exchange" were painted. Bertram had only a vague idea about the service done by a Labour Exchange. The fantastic thought came to him that it would be a good idea to put his own name down for any job that might suit a man like himself, pretty good at handling men, or at any kind of organising work. That was a good word, "organising" —and he would use it to the fellow who ran the Labour Exchange.

It was in High Street, Marylebone, and he said "Sorry," as he elbowed a group of men hanging round the swing doors. One of them, after a glance at him, pulled himself up, as in the old days of soldiering, when an officer passed, but another lad snarled at him, and said, "No officer swank now. We've finished with that," and the sentiment seemed to please the crowd, as Bertram judged by the laugh that followed.

He was kept waiting in a bare room without chairs, while a boy scout took one of his old cards, "Major Pollard, D.S.O., M.C.," into an inner room.

A tall man, dressed in pre-war clothes which had been smart when new and still had style, though frayed about the cuffs and button-holes, stood with his back to the fireplace, and nodded to Bertram when he came in.

"Bloody weather!" he said.

"Not good," said Bertram.

"About as good as our delightful government!" said the man, ex-officer certainly, gentleman undoubtedly. He twisted up a black, and obviously dyed, moustache, with a fierce gesture.

"What's the government been doing now?" asked Bertram, by way of making himself civil.

"Still continuing to destroy the Empire, that's all," was the answer, delivered with a quiet ferocity. "Look at India, seething with revolt and delivered over to a Jewish conspiracy. The only man who dealt with things with a firm hand, condemned, dismissed, and disgraced. Look at Ireland. Anarchy and murder! What's the Government doing there? Surrendering to traitors who ought to be shot like dogs. Look at England-public money being poured out like water, Government offices squandering millions, the Government cringing to Trade-Unionists and Bolsheviks. Look at Germany! By God, sir, Germany will win the war yet! The Hidden Hand is still at work among our politicians. Where are the fruits of victory? The Government is allowing the Hun to escape the price of defeat. It's a damned conspiracy, sir!"

"It's all very difficult," said Bertram.

He had heard this very conversation before. Almost in the same words his own father had made a grand indictment of the Government and all its works. Queer that this shabby fellow, "down on his luck," as the men used to say, should be talking in the same strain as his high and dry reactionary father, whose sentiments when repeated by Bertram to Christy made that son of the people pour forth ironical blasphemies.

His new acquaintance began to tell of his own woes. After honourable service to his country, he had been reduced to living in a common lodging-house, seeking work in a Labour Exchange. A horrible humiliation!

"Why?" asked Bertram. "I take it that a Labour Exchange is to exchange labour? A pretty useful thing."

The man with a dyed moustache stared at him blankly.

"I hope you don't think I'm a damned labourer?" he asked, aggressively.

"I wish I were!" said Bertram. "Anything rather than lounging."

He was saved further argument by the boy scout, who called his name and opened the inner door.

The Labour Exchange secretary rose as he entered the office, and said, "Take a seat, won't you, Major?"

Bertram saw that he was in the presence of a man about his own age, twenty-five, and a pleasant-looking fellow, typical of the "temporary officers" who had poured out in their thousands to France.

"Anything I can do for you, sir?" said the secretary, offering a box of cheap Virginia cigarettes.

Bertram explained that he was looking out for a good job of any kind, and was disconcerted when the Labour Exchange man laughed, dropped the "sir" hurriedly, and said, "No good coming here, old man! Surely you're not so hard put to it as all that?"

"That's just what I am," said Bertram, "devilish hard put to it."

"What can you do?"

Bertram mentioned the blessed word "organising," but again the secretary smiled and shook his head. Then he asked a series of questions, like a machine-gun opening rapid fire.

"Do you write a decent hand? No? Can you type? No? Any good at figures? No? Shorthand? No? Knowledge of engineering? book-keeping, surveying, —any business, trade, or profession? No?"

"I was at St. Paul's School," said Bertram, "and one year at Oxford. I'm a jolly good gunner, and I was brought up as a gentleman. Hasn't England any place for my sort?"

He was resentful of the smiling ironical look of the man interrogating him.

"Not any kind of place at all, old man" —Bertram wished he wouldn't "old man" him so much —"unless you have a social pull. That's still some good for jobs in Government offices and that kind of thing, but it's getting less valuable as time goes on. Without it, fellows like you-and me-haven't a dog's chance. How do you think I got this job when I became demobbed?"

"Haven't an idea," said Bertram.

"Why, my pater is Chief Clerk of Marylebone. Social pull, my boy! Nothing else. There are thousands of young officers, ex-airmen, ex-everything, who'll have to emigrate, or starve to death. There's no alternative. . . . Well, there's one!"

"What's that?"

"Join the Auxiliary Force in Ireland. 'Black and Tans,' as they call them. Does the idea appeal to you?"

"Not in the least," said Bertram.

The Labour Exchange secretary laughed, and touched his bell for the boy scout.

"I don't blame you neither. A rotten game! Good day and good luck."

Bertram had winced over that "neither." He had been taught to speak pretty well, but though he would not say "I don't blame you neither," he hadn't learnt enough, it seemed, either at St. Paul's or Balliol, to get any kind of job in England.

"Not without a social pull," said the Labour Exchange fellow. As a matter of fact, he had a social pull. His father was Michael Pollard, K.C., M.P. —with a considerable pull on the Tory crowd. His father-in-law was the Earl of Ottery, related by cousinship to most of the old blood in England. His brother-in-law, Alban, was in the Foreign Office with Kenneth Murless and other friends of Joyce, his wife. But none of them had offered him anything, or suggested anything, or gone a yard out of the way to help him.

Joyce's people had no use for him. He didn't belong to their caste, though they tolerated him coldly, for Joyce's sake. He didn't speak their language, as it were. He didn't look at things from their point of view. He was an "outsider." How could he bring himself to ask them for a job? The supercilious Alban, for instance? He could not even go to his own father, with whom he was hardly on speaking terms, because of a hopeless divergence of views on the subject of Ireland. "Join the Black-and-Tans, like Digby," would be his father's most genial suggestion, just like this secretary of the Labour Exchange.

Yet for Joyce's sake he would have to humble himself and ask some of his exalted relatives to put him in charge of some department for wasting the tax-payer's money. A financial crisis was bearing down on him with the enormous and imminent pressure of the Germans in March of 1918 against the British line. He had come to the end of the money he had put by out of his pay during the war-the very last pound of it. Henceforth it was Joyce who would do the paying until he grabbed at a job, or begged for one.

"I'm getting dishonest," thought Bertram, as he walked through High Street, Marylebone, observing the mournful look of the people he passed, and turning his eyes away from a blinded man playing a piano organ.

"Old Christy's intensive education in idealism is wearing off. Lord, if only I could do some-thing worth doing-lift the world a little out of its mess-make it safer for the kids coming along-prevent more blinded men playing piano organs as payment for heroism! . . . Was it worth while, their sacrifice?"

The question that came into his brain seemed to him like a kind of blasphemy —a treachery to his own code, and to all the crowd who had fought for England. If that sacrifice had not been worth while, and so many men had died for false beliefs and hopes, then nothing in the world was right, and all that men were taught in faith was just a lie. Christy had said it *was* a lie, the whole make-up of civilisation, the code of his sort of people, patriotism itself. They had argued over that, almost savagely, and he had told Christy to shut up or clear out.

Yet how explain those newspaper placards which stared him in the face from newspaper shops in the Marylebone Road?

More Unemployed Riots.

Crime Wave Spreads.

No Houses for Heroes.

Is Europe Doomed?

Reprisals in Ireland.

France Insults England.

Not easy to keep cheerful, to retain a fair and sturdy optimism, to see the blessing of the victory, even after the slaughter of the world's best youth, when those facts were on the placards, between High Street, Marylebone and the lower end of Baker Street!

Yet Bertram Pollard, ex-officer and unemployed, did not despair. He felt something "inside him," as he used to say in his childhood, which promised some kind of revelation of all this mystery. He seemed to be waiting for a light that would make things clear to him in his own life, and in life. He was certain, beneath his deep uncertainty, that he would find some job to do, some job worth doing. God, or the great powers, or his own instincts, would give him a chance, a new impulse, some decent object in life. After all, he was only twenty-five, with health and strength and desire to find the right place.

Impossible that he should be useless and unused!

VII

A man came up in the dusk that was creeping into the streets of London, and walked alongside Bertram. He said something about no work, a sick wife, children, the war.

Bertram had heard it all a hundred times from other men, and tried to remember whether he had any money in his pocket. Then something in the man's voice stirred an old memory. He halted and stared into the man's face, and saw that it was one of his old company, Bill Huggett, the Cockney fellow from Camberwell.

He spoke his name, and the man was startled, and then shamefaced.

"Good Lord, Huggett! Have you come to this?"

Bertram was distressed. This man had been with him in the dirtiest places, on mornings of great battle, in the dreary old routine. He had always "groused," but had never failed in pluck, and always cheered his comrades by his grim humour when things were bad, and death neighbourly.

"Well, what else?" asked the man, in a hostile voice. He wanted to know what a bloke could do on twenty-five shillings a week, out of work pay, and food prices rising every day, and a family of brats to keep. After saving the blasted country!

Bertram suggested that other men had helped to save the country, and were in the same trouble.

"Not you, anyhow," said the man, with an ugly rasp in his voice.

"Me too," said Bertram. "Let's go and get a drink and talk things out. . . ."

They went through the swing door of a dirty public house somewhere behind Baker Street station, and Bertram sat opposite his former corporal at a table wet with beer dregs. At the bar a number of seedy men, some of them in khaki trousers under old overcoats, were drinking beer in a gloomy way, without much conversation.

Huggett asked for a glass of stout, which he said was food as well as drink. He was a thin-faced fellow, with a battered bowler hat and an old trench coat still stained with the mud of Flanders and the Somme, and the later grease of low class eating houses in London. By trade, as Bertram remembered, he was a French polisher, but according to his tale, there was "nothing doing" in French polishing.

It was at the end of a second glass of stout that he became talkative, and Bertram did not like his kind of talk. He liked it less because it expressed crudely and violently some of the ideas that had been creeping into his own mind-the rough deal that was being given to the men who had fought and come back, the inequality of reward for service done, so that while the front line men were unemployed, the slackers, the stay-at-homes, the artful dodgers, had captured all the jobs.

"Look at all the Generals in Whitehall," said Huggett. "Still strutting around as though the war was on, with flower gardens blooming on their breasts. Did they ever stand in the mud up to their knee-caps, serving a blarsted machine-gun under a German barrage? Not on your life!"

"They did their job as well as they knew how," said Bertram. "It had to be done. Somebody had to do it."

Huggett did not see why his job had to be done. The war had not been to make life easier or better for ordinary folk. It had made it harder. He was pleased to admit, as he wiped his lips with the back of his hand, that if Fritz had won he would have mopped up everything and skinned England alive. He had to be beat. But after the war? What about all the promises about homes for heroes? A land for heroes to live in? He was one of the little heroes, well, he'd done his bit! —but his unemployed pay was not enough to keep a dog decent.

He lowered his voice, and spoke of the bitterness of men like himself. They were getting savage. He wasn't one to believe in revolution, but there were others who did. They wanted to tear down everything, drag down everybody, smash up the whole show, and then all start level. There were foreign chaps about, round the factory gates, in the pubs, putting those ideas into the heads of young chaps who were ready for them. There were a lot of little leaflets going about-very hot stuff-pushed through letter boxes, and into the hands of factory girls. All Huggett wanted, and steady fellows who didn't hold with wild stuff, was decent wages for decent work, but there were numbers who weren't out for work at all. They were out for Red Revolution-bloody red-said Bill Huggett. "And can you wonder, sir, when there's nothing like a fair deal for honest working men. It's just asking for trouble."

Bertram listened gloomily. He seemed to hear in the words of Bill Huggett, this thin-faced Cockney, the voice of the underworld, not heard in Parliament or in the Press, the murmur of masses of men, discontented, bitter, restless, out of work, wondering, as he had asked himself, whether all the sacrifice had been worth while.

He switched the conversation on to another line, less worrying to his troubled mind.

"How's your wife, Huggett?" He remembered the man had kept his wife's photograph in his tunic during his time with the machine-gun company, and had shown it to him once with pride-the photograph of a plain-faced girl, in a cheap blouse and hat with "fevvers." Huggett took it out of his pocket now, and dropped it in the beer-dregs on the table.

"She ain't like that now. You remember I showed it to you one day at Mally Mally, down on the Somme? It was after that she went clean off her dot. After an air raid. They took her away, and I'm alone with the kids. Christ!"

The man's voice broke, and he drew his hand over his eyes.

Bertram said something in sympathy. What was the use? Presently he paid for the beer, and then took off his wrist watch and pushed it over to Bill Huggett.

"You might get something on that. It might help a bit. I've no money to give you."

Huggett stared at the wrist watch. It had been synchronised for zero hour in many mornings of battle. The young Major had worn it day and night, was always shooting his cuff to look at it. Huggett pushed it back.

"I wouldn't take it, not if I was starved to death."

"All right," said Bertram. He slipped the watch into his waistcoat pocket and then rose from the table to go.

"Come and see me, now and then, Huggett. We ought to keep in touch, as 'Comrades of the Great War,' eh?"

As he passed out of the public house, Huggett stood up stiffly and saluted with his hand to his battered bowler hat.

VIII

Bertram was surprised to meet Joyce's father in the Charing Cross Road on a day when he thought his elderly relative was at Ottery Park, deep in Domesday Book, or the Manorial system of England, or the Rights of Villeinage, or some other musty historical work in which he seemed to find much interest and drama, in spite of the more exciting events of contemporary life. Bertram wouldn't have noticed him but for the remarks of two passers-by.

"Do you know that old buffer?"

"No. Who?"

"The Earl of Ottery. You remember? Colonial Secretary before the War. The most reactionary old swine —"

Bertram was intending to take a slogging walk up to the north of London, to avoid one of Joyce's tea-parties to Kenneth Murless and his crowd-he was not in a mood for Kenneth's brilliant repartee-but he decided that it might be well to have a word with his father-in-law.

Lord Ottery was staring in at the window of a clothier's shop in which a number of garments were labelled "Ready to Wear" and "Hardly Soiled."

He was a heavy, broad-shouldered man, with a ruddy face, rather freckled round the eyes, and a reddish, unkempt beard and moustache. The professional sharper would have "spotted" him as a simple farmer up to London for the day, and an easy prey for the gold-brick story. And the sharper would have been extremely disillusioned.

"What are you doing here, sir?" asked Bertram, touching him on his arm.

Lord Ottery stared at him in a vague way for a moment, as though wondering who the deuce he might be, and then greeted him with fair geniality.

"Oh, it's you, Bertram. Thought it might be one of those young ex-officers who want to touch one for half a sovereign. Why the devil don't they enlist in the Black-and-Tans and knock hell out of Ireland? Far more useful than lounging about without a job to do."

Bertram did not reveal his thoughts on that subject, which were distinctly hostile. He merely repeated his enquiry as to what brought Lord Ottery to town.

His father-in-law chuckled, and said he would reveal a secret which he didn't want all the world to know. He was doing a little shopping to replenish his wardrobe. He had discovered that instead of paying fabulous prices to his tailor in Air Street, he could get excellent clothes, ready to wear, at exactly one-sixth the price.

He had already bought two lounge suits which fitted him like a glove, except for slight alterations needed in the back and under the arm-pits. He had also found a shop in the Tottenham Court Road where he could buy first-class boots, suitable for country wear, at a saving of two pounds on those he had been in the habit of buying at Croxteth and Trevor's in Pall Mall.

At one time, as he admitted, he would have shuddered at the idea of wearing ready-made clothes. In the old days, away back in Queen Victoria's reign, he had been a regular Beau Brummell, and never wore a pair of trousers twice in the same week, or a neck-tie more than once after he bought it, but now things had come to such a pass that economy was the order of the day. Besides, what did it matter? It used to be fashionable —de rigueur, even-for the French émigrés after the Revolution to wear ragged lace ruffles. With super-tax at two shillings in the pound, land tax a frightful burden, and investments paying no dividends, people like himself would be reduced to taking in each other's washing.

He mustn't go too far, however, in cutting down his tailor's bill! The other day an awkward thing had happened to him. He had bought a wonderful second-hand overcoat at a Jew dealer's in Covent Garden, astrachan collar, silk-lined, a wonderful bargain-twelve pounds, ten shillings. Dunstable would have charged him forty for it, at least. But when he was about to hang it up on his peg in the lobby of the House of Lords, old Banthorp came up and said: "Curse me blind" —everybody knows how the old ruffian swears —"if that isn't my old overcoat! There's the very hole I burnt with the stump of a cigar, just above the third button!"

"Of course I had to tell him I had bought it from a Jew dealer, and he laughed so much I thought he would have a stroke. But the real cream of the jest is that he was wearing a ready-made suit himself, as he afterwards admitted. It was he who put me on to that shop in the Charing Cross Road. Lots of us are doing it now."

Bertram laughed, and enjoyed the joke as much as was possible to a young man who had not yet come down to "cast-offs," but was unpleasantly in debt to his tailor.

"Things seem to be getting pretty bad," he remarked.

Lord Ottery stopped in the middle of Trafalgar Square and pointed his stick towards the clock tower of Westminster.

"The trouble is there," he said. "Those fellows in the House of Commons have sold themselves to the devil. They're not thinking of their country, but of how to keep their jobs and their votes. Promise the people anything-the Kaiser's head, German gold, doles for unemployed, perpetual peace, luxury for all, and no need to work. I'm afraid of the future. The Empire is getting into the hands of the Jews. Look at India! The Government is pandering to mob-law. Look at the Trade Unions! Whitehall is swarming with place-men, and England is governed by a corrupt bureaucracy. Other Empires have passed. If we don't face realities, rule with a strong hand, cut out corruption, get the people back to work, and stamp out the spirit of revolution among the masses, we shall lose our old place in the world. I shan't live to see it, thank God. You may."

Bertram glanced sideways at him as he passed sturdily down Whitehall, touching his broadbrimmed, badly brushed, silk hat to passers-by who saluted him. It seemed to Bertram that his father-in-law was a type of old England that was passing. The war had thrown up new men, more liberal in ideas, perhaps, at least less bound to old traditions, of nimbler mind, quicker to adapt themselves to new conditions; not so rooted in the soil of England, not so faithful to the old code of honour, not lifted above political temptation like those men of the old nobility, not so stupid and conservative, but not so strong and straight in their sense of duty, however wrong. They had served England well in the past.

"I'm a weakling to this man," thought Bertram. "I'm pulled two ways, by old tradition and by new ideals. I haven't the faith of either. I'm a rebel against the old caste, but doubtful of democracy. I hedge. I'm a blighted hedger. But he stands fast on his own side of the hedge, and will stand there, squarely, until something breaks through and finishes his type for ever. How soon will it be before something breaks through?"

Ottery seemed to answer his thoughts.

"Our day is done. I mean the day of the old quality of England. A little man in there, speaking the language of Billingsgate and Limehouse" —he pointed again to Big Ben —"began the invasion of our rights, led the great attack. The War and its costs have finished us. Profiteers are buying up the old estates. We can't afford 'em. We've been hit too hard by taxes and death duties. Look at Holme Ottery. Why, it's bleeding me to death, though I'm letting it go to rack and ruin."

He sighed heavily, and changed the conversation.

"How's Joyce?"

Bertram gave a good account of her, making no reference to anxieties in his own heart, private, secret things which disturbed him horribly-some change that had come over her after the death of the baby, a dislike of his caresses, a feverish desire for pleasure, a kind of hostility towards him because of certain ideas of his about silly political questions-Ireland! —and the rights of workingmen to a living wage. What absurd cause of quarrel between husband and wife! But, for the moment, anything seemed to serve as a cause of jangle between him and Joyce. It was her health, poor kid, and his aimlessness in life.

He suddenly blurted out his desire for a "job" to Lord Ottery.

"I'm one of those ex-officers you spoke about, sir! I must get a decent billet of some kind, for Joyce's sake. Can you put me in the way of anything?"

Lord Ottery stared at him vaguely, as though he were a long way off. He always put on that look when asked for anything.

"Eh? Put you in the way of anything? Why don't you join the Black-and-Tans? Knock hell out of those Irish blackguards!"

Bertram laughed, awkwardly.

"I'm sick of war. Besides, it doesn't mean much pay. Not enough to help Joyce with her house in Holland Street. I want to keep my end up."

Lord Ottery halted at the entrance to the House of Lords, touching his old hat to the policeman at the gate who saluted smartly.

"Why not go into business?" he said, as though "Business" were an open gate, easy to enter. "People are doing it now, I'm told."

He nodded to Bertram and then ambled into the courtyard of the Palace of Westminster.

"A social pull!" thought Bertram. "The old ruffian wouldn't lift a little finger for me!"

IX

It had been a regret to Bertram-almost a distress-that Luke Christy had not been in London lately, and he was glad to see his signature under some article in "The New World," showing that he was back again.

There was something in Christy's exalted pessimism, in his bitter and almost savage irony, in a queer humour darkly shaded by a sense of tragedy, which acted in an inexplicable way in Bertram as both an irritant and an opiate.

His own moodiness, his private doubts and difficulties, even his bigger apprehensions of political troubles at home and abroad, were made trivial by the intense world-ranging analysis of social disease threatening civilisation which Christy brought back from his journeys abroad.

He was seldom in London, and after a few days, or at most, a few weeks, in his rooms over-looking the river from Adelphi Terrace, would set out again for Paris, or Berlin, or Vienna, or Rome, with an insatiable desire to "see how things were getting on" in the spirit of peoples and in their social conditions. The results of his inquiries could be read in Radical weeklies under the heading of "Our Special Correspondent," in articles written with a cold scientific touch, over-crammed with facts and statistics, and unemotional. They revealed nothing of the flame at the heart of this man, none of his whimsicality of expression in private conversation, not a gleam of his philosophy, but Bertram believed that they were valued as important contributions to knowledge by international groups of men and women outside his own set, and unknown to him except by references in newspapers and in satirical comment by men like Kenneth Murless.

Kenneth called them "long-haired idealists," "Crawling Pacifists," and "home-bred Bolshevists." He had even referred to Christy once or twice by name, and had denounced an article of his as "a challenge to all established authority. The fellow ought to be shot."

"He's a friend of mine," said Bertram.

Kenneth Murless raised his eyebrows in languid surprise.

"That so? Then you're entertaining an enemy unawares. A viper in your bosom, old man. Christy and his crowd have declared war against our set and our ideals."

"What ideals?" asked Bertram.

"Preserving the good old order of things," said Kenneth. "The Stately Homes of England, our Prerogatives, our Very Pleasant Way of Life, which is already seriously threatened by tax-collectors and the greedy clamour of an insensate mob."

Bertram objected violently.

"The mob did most of the dying in the Great War, and now ask for a decent living wage!"

"For high wages and no work!" answered Kenneth in his best unimpassioned, smiling, and supercilious manner, which had made him successful as President of the Union, during his third year at Oxford.

He begged Bertram not to be led astray by the snobbish witticisms of his friends in a pampered democracy, not to be spellbound by their facile and foolish catchwords. He disliked the suggestion that the mob did most of the dying in the great war. The gently of England, the old aristocracy, poured out their blood like water in a prodigal way at the outset as at the end, while crowds of lazy young hooligans had to be coaxed and bribed to do their duty, and then conscripted.

Even then they took refuge behind "special trades," "essential occupations." There were no essential occupations as an excuse for staying at home by boys from public schools and universities and county families. They just went out and died, if need be, without a whine.

"That's true," said Bertram; "they played up all right. None better."

"I'm glad you admit that, Bertram!" said Joyce in her satirical voice, which Bertram knew was a challenge.

She was in the drawing-room of their house in Holland Street, lying back on the sofa among a heap of flaming cushions, with her legs tucked up, revealing her long silk stockings. A charming, slim, golden-crowned figure in a close-fitting jumper, so young and fresh that it was difficult even for Bertram to believe that she had been the mother of a child. How beautiful she was! How good to see her well again!

"Why shouldn't I admit it? Why should I even 'admit' it? It's an historical fact!"

"You're always taking sides with the common people. Backing up Labour with a big L. It's disloyalty to Us."

Bertram shifted moodily in his seat —a low window seat looking out to the street where a Punch and Judy show was being performed to a small crowd of children and nursemaids.

"For God's sake don't talk about the common people as though they were dirt, Joyce! They saved England. England owes them something. Those fellows in my company —"

Joyce flicked some cigarette ash into the fireplace and put her hands round her knees.

"Those fellows in your company! I can't think how you kept your authority, hob-nobbing with them so much!"

Bertram said in a low voice that they had saved his life more than once.

"That's ancient history," said Joyce. "You're always harking back to the old war! Let's forget it. We're talking about the present situation. The working people are thoroughly lazy, utterly demoralised, and infected with Bolshevism. They ought to be kept in their places with a strong hand."

"I agree!" said Kenneth Murless. "They've become tyrannical and snobbish."

"Snobbish!" said Bertram, laughing, and making an effort to keep the temper that was rising in him.

"Yes," said Kenneth, observing a paradoxical argument from afar; "the snobbishness of the working classes is disgusting. Because they don't wear collars and ties, they won't associate with men who are afflicted with stiff linen round their necks. Because they're illiterate, they make a caste of illiteracy and condemn the Intellectual as a parasite and a pariah. Their Trade Unions are more exclusive than West-end clubs, more intolerant than mediæval Star Chambers. Their Labour leaders are enemies of the liberty so hardly won for England by English gentry-freedom of speech, equality before the law, justice for rich and poor alike, religious toleration, taxation according to wealth. Why these fellows are all for the suppression of liberty. Anybody who ventures to disagree with them is called a damned reactionary. If they had their way, as in Russia, they would prevent the free exercise of religion, and stifle all intellectual opposition with the hangman's rope. Even now in England the working class is the only one exempt from taxation, getting their education for nothing, and blackmailing those who have accumulated a little money by hard toil."

"Like you," said Bertram.

"Like me," answered Kenneth, calmly. "I confess my little job at the F.O. is not exacting, but don't I toil over my sonnets-on official stationery —? Don't I agonise in labour to produce a gem of thought for 'The London Mercury'?"

"You ought to go into the House, Kenneth!" said Joyce. "Your eloquence would overwhelm Lloyd George himself. And I will say there's a lot of sense in your head, in spite of your devastating beauty, and supercilious conceit."

She spoke in the usual vein of irony with which she set her wit against Kenneth's, yet with an underlying admiration which he perceived and liked.

His face crimsoned a little, and he laughed affectedly.

"For that tribute, dear lady, my heart's thanks! But don't tempt me to sully my bright soul with the dirt of politics. Diplomacy, yes, the higher Machiavellism, but, please, not politics! It's impossible to keep clean within the precincts of Westminster."

Two of Joyce's girl friends called, followed by the Reverend Peter Fynde and an Italian countess who spoke detestable English and made enormous eyes to Kenneth Murless-enormous black eyes in a dead white face. Bertram noticed that her hands were dirty, though they glistened with wonderful rings. She called Joyce "*Carissima.*" —It was an opportunity for him to slip away and see old Christy again.

X

Luke Christy answered the rap of a little brass knocker on a door up three flights of stairs.

"Hullo, Major! I had an idea you'd come. You can't keep away from my sinister influence."

He saluted in an ungainly fashion, like a drunken Tommy, and then gripped Bertram's hand in his long, bony fingers. He was a tall, thin, loosely-built man, with a clean-shaven face singularly ugly because of its long, lean jaw and bulging forehead. "An ugly mug," as Bertram had often insulted it, but with a bright light within, shining out of dark, humorous, brooding eyes.

He was in his shirt sleeves, unpacking some hand-bags amidst a litter of dirty shirts, collars, socks, pyjamas, newspapers, and paper-backed books, and other salvage from a long journey.

"Just come back from Poland," he said, "by way of Berlin. Put on a pipe and tell me all about life and London, while I stow this wreckage away. How's Lady Joyce and the British aristocracy?"

He looked up at Bertram with the whimsical smile which always twisted his face when he chaffed Bertram about his close relationship with "bloated aristocrats." His own family kept a little shop in a Warwickshire village.

"Joyce is pretty well," said Bertram. "She had a baby . . . but it died."

Luke Christy's twisted smile left his face, and his eyes shone with sympathy.

"Oh, Lord! That's tragic. I'm sorry."

Bertram sat watching him "tidy up," a process which seemed to consist in heaving his dirty linen into a cupboard, and flinging the paper-backed books on to a shelf already crowded with papers.

The whole room was framed in books, badly assorted in size, and mostly of tattered bindings. Above them were some rather good etchings and caricatures torn out of foreign newspapers, fastened to the walls with drawing pins. On the mantelpiece were photographs of several young soldiers, one of Bertram himself, and a "homely" elderly woman with grey hair, exactly like Luke Christy-who, as Bertram knew-was Christy's mother.

A door opened into an inner room into which Christy plunged now and then with pairs of trousers, boots, and other bits of clothing. It was from this inner room that he began a monologue to which Bertram listened through the open door.

"Hard for a girl to bring a life into the world, and then see it flicker out. I'm sorry to hear that, Pollard. It's the saddest thing for you and that exquisite little lady of yours. Good God, yes! But for myself, I couldn't risk it, anyhow. I haven't the pluck. I should be filled with dreadful forebodings."

"About what?" asked Bertram.

He could not see Christy, but heard him moving about the inner room.

"Why, to bring a new life into the world. Was it a boy?"

"Yes," said Bertram, "it was going to have my name."

"A boy, eh? Oh, Lord, no! I couldn't bring a boy into a world like this. It wouldn't be fair. Not yet awhile, until we see how things are going to shape out. Major" —he still kept to Bertram's old rank —"I'm afraid I'm becoming a coward."

He came to the half open door, and leant against the frame of it, looking in at Bertram, who sat in a low leather chair with his back to a long casement window through which the dusk of a grey day crept from the darkening Thames below. So Christy had often stood in the entrance of a dug-out when he and Bertram lived in the earth not far from an enemy's line.

"What are you afraid about?" asked Bertram, with a curious thrill, like the sensation he had had as a boy when his nurse told him ghost stories.

"I'm afraid of this civilisation of ours, and of all sorts of forces creeping up to destroy it."

For an hour or more he talked of the things he had seen.

He had been to Eastern Europe, from which civilisation was passing. Poland was poverty-stricken, disease-stricken, and utterly demoralised.

Austria was no more than the corpse of a nation which had once been a mighty Empire, and now was a bulbous-headed thing without a body.

Vienna was its bulbous head, a great capital of over two million people without the means of life. He described the dance of death there, the starvation of women and children, the misery of the mean streets, the ruin of the intellectuals and the professional classes. In the hotels and restaurants and café concerts, foreigners were gathering like vampires to feed on the mortality of that old centre of civilisation. Austrian Jews and international gamblers, making paper fortunes out of the fluctuations of paper money, guzzled and gorged in an orgy of vice with girls who sold their smiles for the sake of a meal or an evening's warmth.

The old palaces of Vienna still stood, the great mansions and cathedrals and churches and art galleries and museums remained as the heritage of a splendid past, but the life that made them had gone. When they began to crumble there would be no money to repair them. No man or woman could follow the pursuit of beauty and truth, painting or music or science, as in the old days. They must either get back to the land, and grub a sparse life out of the soil, or starve to death. So it was with other countries, the little new nations of the Baltic, the great Empire of Russia.

He'd not been into Russia-it pulled him tremendously, he must get there somehow-yet out on the frontier he'd met the refugees, and heard their tale of misery. In Russia civilisation was passing, had almost passed.

He would have to go to Russia before long to see the truth of things. There was a famine coming which would destroy millions of people. Disease was already rife, amounting to pestilence. Again, there, the only people who could live at all were those who stayed close to the soil, and were desperate in defence of their own produce.

Was Europe, a large part of it, going to return to the Peasant State? That might happen. That would be something to cling to, though not civilisation as it had been built up through centuries of struggle. But worse than that might happen.

He'd been to Berlin and other German towns. What was happening there? An immense industry of a people over-strained by war, crushingly defeated, beaten to the earth in pride, but desperate to regain their place in the world and defend their national existence. They were working with an astounding energy, adapting their immense genius to the necessities of this peace and its penalties. Krupps' which had made great guns, were now turning out sewing-machines, reapers and binders, cash registers, razors, anything of metal for the markets of the world. But the indemnities put upon them by the victors made all their energy fruitless. The mark was dropping in value week by week. Every time they paid their indemnities it dropped lower with a rush. The printing presses poured out new marks. That enabled them to undercut their rivals in every market of the world, but at the same time they were bleeding themselves to death.

Meanwhile France was putting on the screw, goading the Germans to hatred again, making them vow vengeance, some time, some day, in the future, however far ahead. France was ready to ruin the whole world rather than let Germany get up again, and the whole world, and England first, would be ruined, if Germany were to go the way of Austria and plunge over the precipice into national bankruptcy.

There were evil forces at work everywhere, forces of cruelty, and greed, and stupidity, and hatred. The men of the Old Order were keeping a grip on the machinery of Government, arranging new balances of power, making new alliances for an "inevitable" war. Hostile to them, were those out to destroy all civilisation, at any cost, the revolutionaries for revolution's sake, the fanatics allied with the murderers and the cave-men of life.

In between those two extremes, poor patient people, desiring peace, were bewildered by the non-fulfilment of all their hopes after so much sacrifice, and in their ignorance turning this way and that, to false gods, to those who appealed to their lower passions, to those who doped them with the greatest falsehoods. There was no truth-teller to whom the masses would listen. No high and noble leadership, but only corrupt and unclean men, holding on to power, or little men, honest in a little way, clinging to their jobs.

Other forces were at work, biological, evolutionary, and mysterious forces, which no man could understand or govern. There was a new restlessness in the soul of humanity. Some great change was happening, or about to happen. The old checks and balances had become unhinged, in the minds of men, in the spirit of peoples, in great races. The coloured peoples of the world were stirring. Some yeast in them was rising. Some passion of desire. India, Egypt, Africa, Mesopotamia, were seething with the spirit of revolt. He had been in the East. He had seen something of it. The white races would have to take care. There were other races waiting for their place. Japan and China were changing in "the unchanging East."

What of the British Empire? Little old England, dependent on overseas trade, on world markets which had failed, on a mercantile marine which could not get its cargoes, would be hardest pressed of all. . . . And the spirit of revolution among men embittered by war, disillusioned by false promises, beaten back to a low standard of life, had touched even England, at last.

"Major," said Luke Christy, "I wouldn't care to bring a son into the world."

Bertram rose, and did not answer for a while. He went to the window and stared out into the darkness creeping over the Thames. From Christy's windows he could see the curve of the river, and the lights of the great old city gleaming through the purple dusk, and the red fire from the engine of a train passing over Charing Cross bridge, and the head-lights of motors and taxi-cabs streaming along the Embankment-all the glamorous life of London in the hour between dusk and darkness of an evening in May. A scene in modern civilisation as he knew and loved it.

He turned round to Christy and said: "You old ghoul! You make me shiver. It's not as bad as all that!"

Christy laughed, and switched on the electric light, breaking the spell of darkness.

"It's my morbid temperament! P'raps I'm all wrong. But I'm just watching, and trying to find out the drift of things."

He'd found one curious thing wherever he went, in whatever country; he found men and women talking anxiously, analysing civilisation, uncertain of its endurance. Was that a good or a bad sign? The intellectuals of Greece and Rome used to talk like that before the "decline and fall."

"Let's drop the international situation and get down to home politics. What are you doing with yourself, Major?"

"Looking for a job," said Bertram.

Luke Christy advised him to get a soft job, in one of the Government offices, with good pay out of the rate-payers' pockets and no more work than an office boy could do without knowing it.

"I want to be an honest man," said Bertram.

Christy seemed to find that uncommonly amusing.

"My dear Major! The only honest men in the world are those who are dying of starvation. All who have more than that are rogues. I'm one of the worst of hypocrites, for while I bleed at the heart for suffering humanity, I get a good price for the articles in which I describe its torture and disease."

Bertram suddenly flushed a little, and spoke in a nervous way.

"Christy, I believe I could write, if I tried. In the old days at St. Paul's, I had a notion-anyhow, I feel I might do something if I had a shot at it. What do you think?"

"You?" said Christy.

That word and its emphasis of surprise were not encouraging, and Bertram found it hard to confess to his friend that he had been writing a book, and believed that at last he had found his object in life, and the impulse he'd been seeking.

"What kind of book?" asked Christy.

"A book on the War."

Christy groaned, and cried "Kamerad!" with raised hands.

XI

Joyce had gone out to a dance, leaving Bertram alone to write his book. She had made him a fair offer to come with her, telling him that it was his own fault if she had to rely on other company as an escape from boredom.

"What company?" he asked, and looked up sharply from his papers.

She shrugged her shoulders.

"Some of the usual. The two Russian girls and Jack Hazeldeane, Kenneth."

Bertram pushed his papers on one side.

"What's the use of my coming? The two Russian girls bore me to death with their tales of the old régime and stories of Bolshevik atrocities. And I hate to see you dancing with Kenneth. He dances like an amorous ballet master. Besides —"

"Besides what —?"

"If there's any dancing to be done, it's I that want to dance with you."

"All the time, Bertram?" She smiled at his greed.

"Yes. You're *my* wife."

His damnable jealousy had got the better of him again.

"Not your property, my dear!" said Joyce.

"Not other people's property," grumbled Bertram. "I'm old-fashioned enough to object to your doing that jazz stuff with any fellow who likes to put his arms round you. It's disgusting."

"It's you that are disgusting!" said Joyce.

Her face flamed with sudden anger, and Bertram saw the steel glint in her eyes. She was standing by the doorway in her evening frock, a thing of blue silk, showing her white neck and bare arms. The light of the electric candles on his desk played with her gold-spun hair. Bertram loved the look of her, and yet knew that temper was creeping up into his brain because he could not stop her from dancing with a man he loathed, nor hold her to himself alone, nor get from her the absolute love he desired, hungrily.

"That's not a good word from any wife to any husband," he said, heatedly.

"Your word!"

She laughed and lingered at the door, looking at her husband with a queer, half-scornful, half-enticing smile which he did not see because he was staring at his papers. There was even a little pity in her eyes.

"Better come! That book of yours is getting on your nerves."

"It interests me," said Bertram.

"I know I shall hate it anyhow. I want to forget the silly old war."

"Everybody wants to forget it," said Bertram, with a touch of passion in his voice. "The Profiteers, the Old Men who ordered the massacre, the politicians who spoilt the Peace, the painted flappers. I'm damned if I'm going to let them!"

"Painted flappers?" said Joyce. "Meaning me?"

"Not meaning you," he answered.

"Thanks for that!"

She left the room, and Bertram heard Edith say the taxi was waiting. He rose and made a step towards the door, as though to join her after all. He wanted to go, in spite of Kenneth and the Russian girls. He wanted Joyce's beauty, though he would have to share it with her friends. But it was too late. The door had clicked behind her, and he heard the taxi-cab drive away.

He was too rough with Joyce. Why shouldn't she dance with other men? Was it some strain of his father in him that made him hate it so-his father's harshness and intolerance. Or was it the passion of his love which Joyce seemed to deny him-did deny him-after the death of her baby? She did not respond to his endearments, and made no disguise of her dislike of his caresses. Or was this constant wrangling between them-becoming rather serious at times-due to an intellectual challenge between their different points of view-her patrician philosophy of life, his democratic leanings? Anyhow, it was all very difficult. He would have to be more careful, get a better grip on himself, rise to more selfless heights of love, if need be, and if possible, make a sacrifice of his very passion for Joyce's sake. It was all very difficult!

He constrained himself to get to his writing again, now that he had refused her offer of companionship. Soon he lost himself in his task, glad of the swift flow of his pen and his savage strokes. It was strong stuff. It was a bitter indictment of the stupidities, the blunders, the unnecessary slaughter of men, which he had cursed in time of war because his own men had been the victims, with the others. Those orders from Corps Headquarters! Inconceivable! Unbelievable in their imbecility!

He had written for several hours, utterly absorbed, when he heard the electric bell ringing in the hall. Joyce back already? Hardly. The clock said midnight, and she was not back then, as a rule, from one of her dances. Edith had gone to bed, as Joyce had taken a key. He would have to open the door. Confound it! Who on earth —

It was Susan, his sister, and she had a man with her, standing back a little behind her in the darkness of the porch. She came into the hall with a "Hullo, Bertram!" and the man followed her and shut the door.

She leant against the wall, breathing in a hard way, as though she had been running. The man by her side was Dennis O'Brien whom Bertram had known in France. He kept his felt hat on his head, and his hands in his pockets, and stood looking at Bertram in a careless, quizzing way. But he was pale.

"Rather late for an evening call," said Bertram.

Susan asked whether the servants had gone to bed, and when Bertram nodded, led the way into his study with her friend.

"Shut the door, Bertram, old boy."

Bertram obeyed her. He had a sense of apprehension. There was something strange in his sister's look and manner.

"What's the game?" he asked.

Susan took one of his cigarettes and lit it by a spill from the fire before answering. O'Brien sat down in Bertram's desk chair, and held his hat between his knees. He was wearing a trench coat, and looked shabby.

"It's like this, Bertram. Dennis, who, by the way, is my man-we married a week ago-is 'on the run,' as they call it. He's very much wanted by the English police, and I'm going to ask you to be sport enough to put him up for a day or two. He'll stay close and give no trouble."

She looked over at Dennis, and laughed in a low voice. Bertram noticed that one lock of her dark hair had come loose beneath her hat. Her brown eyes had a kind of liquid light in them, or some leaping flame, and her cheeks were flushed. She looked more Irish than he had ever seen her. Perhaps it was excitement that had set that part of her blood on fire, or the marriage she mentioned "by the way." Susan married! To a fellow who was "wanted" by the English police! And the crisis in the family.

Bertram laughed, but mirthlessly.

"So O'Brien is 'wanted,' is he? And you've married him, Susan? Any more announcements?"

"That's all for the present," said Susan. She watched her brother anxiously, saw his face harden a little, and then went to him and clasped his arm with both hands.

"Bertram! You and I were always pals. You've helped me out of many a scrape, and never said a word. This affair is my worst scrape, and Dennis's. It's a question of life and death. Play up to the old tradition!"

"I want to know more," said Bertram. He spoke sharply, and looked over at O'Brien, who was silent, with a nervous smile about his lips. "What game have you been up to in England? That arson business?" He remembered that several timber yards had been set on fire at the London docks, with Sinn Fein warnings of further damage.

Dennis O'Brien shifted his felt hat round, and stared at the brim.

"I'm not answering questions," he said.

"Perhaps it's worse than arson," said Bertram. "Were you in Dublin last Monday?"

There had been an attack outside the Castle. Two British officers in a motor car, and three Sinn Feiners lying in ambush had been killed. Others had escaped.

Dennis O'Brien became more pale, and Susan drew in her breath sharply.

"I was in Dublin," said Dennis O'Brien. "The point is whether you're a friend or an enemy."

"I'm a friend of Ireland," said Bertram, "but an enemy of those who drench her with blood, and drag her into anarchy."

"The English," said O'Brien.

"Irish too, by God!" said Bertram.

O'Brien shrugged his shoulders, and said something in a low voice about the right to liberty.

Susan threw her cigarette in the fire and put her arm round Bertram's neck.

"Brother o' mine! It's no time for argument about Irish liberty or English tyranny. Don't you understand? Dennis is my husband and his life's in danger. You must hide him here, for my sake!"

Bertram thought hard and rapidly. Susan's words called to his chivalry. She was this man's wife. And it was not easy to turn a hunted man from his door, anyway. But what about Joyce? In hiding O'Brien he might drag her name in, and her father's name. —'The Earl of Ottery's daughter shelters an Irish rebel.' The newspapers would make a fuss of that! And his own father's name? Michael Pollard, K.C., who defended the policy of reprisals! A family scandal all round, and damnably dangerous!

"Can't you find another place?" he asked Susan, weakly.

Susan laughed.

"The police were pretty close. We dodged 'em by the length of a street."

She held his arm again, and said: "Big brother! Sportsman and gentleman! For the Irish blood that's in you!"

"With English loyalty," said Bertram, sharply.

"In that case," said Dennis O'Brien, in a sullen way, "I'll just slope out into the streets again. I take no favour from English loyalty. To hell with all its loyalties!"

He stood up and went towards the door, but Susan ran round the table to him and caught hold of his coat.

"Dennis, my dear! Bertram is all for Irish liberty. And don't forget I'm half English too!"

"All Irish now!" said Dennis, in a low, passionate voice.

Bertram watched them. His face was flushed, and he had thrust his hair back so that it was all tousled.

"This is a devilish affair," he said, "but if O'Brien cares to stay here, he can have that sofa!"

"Well played!" cried Susan softly, and with those words she kissed her brother, and her eyes were wet and shining.

"It's not a very cordial invitation," said O'Brien, with sarcasm, "but if your brother gives his word —"

"Do you doubt me?" asked Bertram. His voice had a savage note.

"I'm in your hands," said O'Brien, more humbly.

Presently Joyce came in. They had not heard the front door open, so that her appearance in the room was unexpected. She stood for a moment in the doorway, her fur cloak half slipping from her shoulders. Then she spoke to Susan, not hiding her surprise.

"Hulloa! Anything wrong?"

Perhaps it was their silence, some look in their eyes which suggested to her that something was "wrong."

"You're looking splendid again, Joyce," said Susan, in her best "society" manner. There was always a sense of armed truce between the two girls. Bertram's sister resented what she called the "haughty condescension" of Bertram's wife. Joyce had not disguised from Bertram that in her opinion Susan was "a dangerous little spit-fire —with atrocious manners."

"I'm quite well, thanks."

Joyce glanced at O'Brien, who had risen from his chair as she had come in.

"Won't you introduce me?" she asked Susan.

Susan said, "This is Dennis O'Brien, my husband." It was very calmly said.

"A surprise!" said Joyce. "Congratulations to both of you, and all that, I suppose. Rather sudden, wasn't it?"

She failed to shake hands with Dennis O'Brien. As she had told Bertram many times, sometimes amusing times, and sometimes not, she hated all the Irish except half an Irishman.

She sat in Bertram's low arm chair, yawning a little, with her long white arms behind her bobbed hair.

"A cigarette, Bertram!"

Bertram gave her the cigarette, lit it for her, and mumbled something about the late hour, and bedtime. He had a foreboding that Joyce didn't intend to go to bed until Susan and Dennis had gone. And Dennis was not going. There would have to be an explanation. There would probably be a row.

It came half an hour later, after strained and unnatural efforts at bright conversation by Bertram and Susan, while O'Brien sat gloomily silent, and Joyce yawned with increasing carelessness, and asked occasional questions without listening to the answer. The crisis happened when she sprang up and stretched her arms above her head.

"Haven't you people got any home? I hate being inhospitable, Susan, but you and your new-found husband had better go. Bertram and I sometimes sleep o' nights."

There was a moment's silence before Bertram answered:

"O'Brien is staying. He's going to use the sofa to-night."

There was another silence.

"Sorry," said Joyce, "but I can't allow that."

"Why not?"

Bertram knew the "row" was coming.

"It's not in my contract with the maids," said Joyce very calmly. Then she spoke another sentence which seemed to reveal a knowledge, or at least a guess of the inner meaning of this visit from Susan and Dennis.

"Besides, my house is not going to be made a hiding place for Irish rebels. I'm English, and play the game accordingly."

Yes, undoubtedly, there was going to be a row!

Bertram decided upon a frank explanation. Joyce had the right to know.

"Look here, Joyce, O'Brien is Susan's husband, and the police are after him. You know how I stand about Sinn Fein. . . . Anyhow   I've given my word. O'Brien stays here to night."

"He does *not* stay," said Joyce. "This is my house. If that man is not out of it in two minutes, I'll telephone to the police."

She walked quickly to Bertram's desk and caught hold of the receiver.

Bertram followed her, still explaining, rather desperately. He had given his word. He quite understood Joyce's point of view. He sympathised to some extent. This Sinn Fein business was criminal folly. But O'Brien had been a friend of his in the War. And he was Susan's

husband. Did she understand? His own brother-in-law! He was in real danger, and it was
not in the code of their crowd-was it? —to hand over a hunted man. —A criminal? Well,
he didn't know. O'Brien had told him nothing. He asked no questions. Besides-that was all
beside the argument.

"I've given my word, Joyce-my honour's pledged."

"What about my honour?" asked Joyce. Her voice was very cold and hard. "My father's
name? Our honour to England?"

She turned to Dennis O'Brien, still holding the telephone.

"Are you going? Time's up."

Dennis O'Brien smiled at her, and his Irish eyes paid homage to this girl's beauty as she stood
facing him, so hostile. He had been smiling all through Bertram's monologue. It seemed to
amuse him, this altercation between the English girl and his wife's brother.

"I'm going," he said. "Don't worry at all. It's what one expects of English women! They
would turn a starving dog out of doors."

"Mad dogs," said Joyce. "With a whip."

It was Susan now who intervened, ragingly.

"Joyce! You're a damned cat! No wonder Bertram has a hellish time with you. I'd like to see
the Bolsheviks playing with your bobbed hair, and your lovely white neck."

Joyce picked up the telephone receiver, and said, "Police station, please."

"No!" said Bertram.

He took hold of Joyce's wrist and wrenched it from the instrument, conscious of his own
violence.

"Joyce, I forbid you. I gave my word. Surely you respect that? By God, you *must* respect it.
If you touch that telephone again, I'll —I'll carry you upstairs."

Joyce looked at him squarely, and their eyes met and searched each other. She saw more
anger in his eyes than ever before. She saw that he meant to use his strength.

"I surrender to force. Three to one, and all enemies."

She laughed on a high note, picked up her fur coat, and went out of the room. They listened
to her light steps up the polished stairs, and to the sharp slam of her bedroom door.

"Poor old Bertram!" said Susan, dabbing her eyes with her handkerchief.

He turned on her fiercely.

"How dare you speak of Joyce like that? She was perfectly right, apart from my pledged
word. If O'Brien plays the rebel, let him take the risk of rebels, without crawling into English
houses for a hiding place!"

Susan paled.

"*Et tu, Brute!*" she said in a low voice.

She spoke a whispered word to Dennis O'Brien. He nodded, and buttoned up his trench coat.

"Yes, let's be going. —Good-night, Pollard."

Bertram did not answer.

He made no move, as he stood planted on the hearth-rug by the fire, staring moodily at a
cigarette holder which Joyce had dropped, while his sister and her Irish husband went out of
the room, and a moment later left the house, as he heard by the quiet click of the front door
lock. He stood there for half an hour after they had left, and then summed up his thoughts
in his usual sentence:

"It's all very difficult!"

After that he went up to Joyce's room, which was locked. There was no answer to his tap
on the door, and he crept miserably to his own bed.

Joyce was perplexing to Bertram after that midnight scene with Susan and Dennis. He had expected a painful quarrel on the subject, a denunciation by Joyce of his behaviour, a defence on his part, an argument beginning with generalities and ending with personalities, always dangerous between a young husband and wife, both inclined to passionate temper. But Joyce declined to discuss the matter. She had stayed late in bed next day, and had come down to luncheon with her wrist bound up. He did not understand the cause of that bandage until he enquired and received the answer:

"You nearly broke my wrist over the telephone last night. Perhaps you're not aware of the violence you used."

No, he was unaware of it, and made abject apology, horribly ashamed that he should have used physical force to his wife. It was a coster's way of argument.

"Joyce! I'm immensely sorry and ashamed. But you see my difficulty last night. I had given my word —"

"I refuse to discuss the affair," said Joyce. "You know my views. If you say another word about it I'll leave the house."

That was that. She was not even curious to know whether O'Brien had spent the night in Bertram's study. Perhaps she had enquired from the maids and had satisfied herself on that point. Yet Bertram was certain that the incident was not regarded as trivial in her mind, and that it had caused something like estrangement between them. She went her own way, deliberately shutting him out of her plans, or, at least, not consulting him, nor giving him a chance of joining her. She was rarely at home to luncheon during the few weeks that followed Susan's visit, and generally returned only in time to dress for dinner. Even then he had no chance of private conversation, for she invited friends to dine night after night-was it with the deliberate intention of avoiding intimate contact with him? —and afterwards filled her drawing-room with a miscellaneous crowd, or went out with a party to the theatre or the dancing clubs.

Bertram was lonely whether she stayed at home or not. He was beginning to feel lonely in body and soul. Joyce answered him when he spoke to her, but no more than that. She was quite gay at times-nearly always-but it was not into his eyes that she laughed.

Kenneth Murless used the house as his own, "dropped in" for dinner, or after dinner, always civil to Bertram, never disconcerted by Bertram's sulky manner, always bright and paradoxical, and entertaining to everybody but Joyce's husband, who hated him-for no reason but that Joyce liked him.

There were other men whom Joyce liked, and who liked to be liked by Joyce. The Reverend Peter Fynde, who came from the church round the corner, was what Bertram called a "parlour cat," and came purring round to tea, or at nine-thirty, after "Evensong," with gossipy anecdotes about Lady This and Lady That, and soulful sayings about the "Healing Power of Faith," the "Beauty of the Unattainable," and communication with the "Dear Remembered Dead." At dinner, when the ladies had left the table, he was inclined to tell somewhat Rabelaisian stories, drawn from his experience as an army chaplain. "A human fellow," was the general verdict about him, "a perfect dear" by the women. Bertram thought him a perfect ass, but did not tell them so.

He had nothing in common with the people who gathered round Joyce. They irritated him. Listening to their conversation, he found their point of view "poisonous," if not idiotic. It was at least-and he wanted to be fair-hopelessly reactionary. They still had a habit of talking about the people of England as "the mob" or "the masses," and they spoke about "Labour" as if it were a sinister, evil, destructive monster, and not a class of men, quite human, for the most part rather decent, many of them the real heroes of the war-keen to earn a living wage, desperately anxious not to be forced back to the edge of the poverty line, or over the edge. Millions of Bill Huggetts, and better men than Bill-rather neurotic, always a "grouser" —but not out for blood and terror, or anything beyond food and shelter for a family left on his hands by a poor mad wife.

Labour? Bertram had been going about London getting into touch with some of the men of his old company —"Comrades of the Great War," as they called themselves, in barely furnished clubs where they gathered at night, because of their craving for the comradeship which had been the best thing in war. They were still restless and unsettled. Some of them were still hardly better than "shell-shocks." Their minds were groping towards some solution of their present distress-unemployment, high prices, a sense of broken faith with them by the nation they had served. Some of them talked glibly, as Huggett had said, about Bolshevism and Communism. The frightful experiment in Russia-what was the truth of it? —held some lure for them. There were some who believed "it would do London a bit o' good."

Bertram didn't believe there was much of a real revolutionary spirit among them. They were sick of war and bloodshed, and the "crime wave," as the newspapers called it, was only the work of a small minority of young men unhinged by the cheapness of life in war, and by war's brutality. Bertram marvelled rather at the patience, the essential patriotism, the commonsense of the majority of men he met about. Any hankering after the Russian way of revolution was but a vague vision of some system of society which would give men greater equality of luck, and a sense of security.

That was not the opinion of the people in Joyce's drawing-room. They confessed to fear about the future. It was, perhaps, the presence of two Russian girls of the old régime, and some of the men they brought with them of their own caste and country, which suggested the possibility of revolution in England. They were never tired of telling tales of Bolshevik atrocities, none of them from first-hand evidence, but likely enough, and dreadful in detail. The elder of them, the Countess Gradiva-Lydia, as Joyce called her-had set up a hat shop in Mount Street, Mayfair, where Joyce had met her and made friends. The younger-Paula-played the violin, wonderfully, at recitals and concerts. They were both tall, ugly, elegant girls, speaking half a dozen languages with equal facility and passionate gesture.

"Why doesn't England send an army and rescue my poor country from its tyrants?" asked Lydia one night of Bertram. "I cannot understand your English policy, your dreadful inactivity."

Bertram had heard many remarks of the same kind by the Russian girls. They enraged him.

"Why don't your Russian men do a bit of their own fighting? Why do they lounge about the capitals of Europe, and expect other people to liberate Russia and restore Czardom, and get back their wealth?"

"You're a Bolshevik, then?" asked Countess Gradiva, staring at him with black, challenging eyes.

"Not in the least," said Bertram. "But I'm dead against these fatal expeditions in which England has poured out gold she can ill afford-with what result? More bloodshed in Russia. Another disastrous retreat of incompetent generals, more suffering and horror, and harryings of poor Russian peasants. That's how it seems to me. I may be wrong."

The Countess Gradiva called out across the drawing-room, which was crowded with Joyce's friends. She had a high, harsh way of speaking, and a shrill laugh.

"My dear Lady Joyce! Your husband is a naughty bad Bolshevik! He's saying the most dreadful things, *ma chérie!*"

"He makes a habit of it," answered Joyce.

Bertram flushed angrily at her retort, though Joyce had spoken with a smile. He knew by the tone of her voice that she intended to hurt him, and it hurt.

"I tell the truth, occasionally, and that's dreadful, I admit," he said to Lydia Gradiva.

"Not the truth about Russia, you wicked man. You do not know our poor Russia!"

"I would go even as far as Russia, to get the truth," said Bertram. "Does anybody know?"

"You mean I lie to you?"

"There are many lies about," said Bertram, "but I'm not referring to you, especially."

She whipped his hand with the end of a long necklace of amber beads, so that they stung him. Then she called him a revolutionary monster, a Jacobin.

"I can see you leading the English mob and hoisting the Red Flag over the House of Commons!"

The English "mob!" There it was again. Always the talk came round to the chance of an English revolution. Those people were afraid-even of England!

It was General Bellasis who revealed a new cause of fear which took hold of the imagination of London society at this time. Bellasis was one of the men who liked to be liked by Joyce. He was still on active service-in Ireland-but seemed to spend his time travelling between Dublin and Whitehall, and always came to Holland Street with flowers for Joyce, theatre tickets for Joyce, and homage in his eyes. He looked more gallant than any hero could be-at all times-in his uniform with many decorations —a tall, lean fellow, with a hard, clean cut face, blue, sailor-looking eyes, and an empty sleeve where his left arm used to be. But he confessed that he was suffering from blue funk (he exaggerated his symptoms) because of an incident that had happened to him in St. James's Street, outside the club, that very afternoon. A wretched-looking fellow had come up to him, offering to sell some bootlaces. "Thanks, no," said Bellasis. The man had followed him, whining something about a wife and children, and thrusting the bootlaces under his nose. "I've said I don't want 'em," said Bellasis, as he related. "Get off with you, my man." He had not spoken roughly, though he disapproved of begging, especially when every out-of-work was getting a Government dole. But then the man had pulled something out of his pocket and given it to Bellasis, saying, "Well, take that for luck!" Bellasis supposed the company could guess what it was.

Kenneth Murless guessed right, first time.

"The silver slipper!"

"Yes," said General Bellasis, "the silver slipper! And I can tell you, I don't like it!"

The Reverend Peter Fynde claimed that he had been given one at Ranelagh, three weeks before. Exactly in the same way. He had refused an importunate beggar and received the slipper "for luck."

Kenneth Murless took precedence of Fynde, in point of time. It was two months at least since he had been given the slipper. That was outside the Carlton. A typical incident. A paper boy had tried to make him buy his last copy of *The Pall Mall Gazette*. Murless had seen it already, read every line of it. The boy had persisted until Murless had told him to run away or he would get a box on the ears. "Take this for luck!" said the boy. So he had the sign of the slipper.

"Has everybody gone mad?" asked Bertram. "The silver slipper! The sign of the slipper! What on earth are you all talking about?"

It was Murless who explained, in his best diplomatic style, after expressing surprise that Bertram should not have heard of the sinister thing. It appeared that in the time of the French Revolution, secret agents of the Free masons and Jacobin clubs presented silver slippers to people whom they particularly disliked. It was not a good thing to get one. Most of those who did perished on the guillotine. *"C'est l'histoire qui se répète, mon vieux!"* Kenneth Murless spoke lightly, with a smile, but there was a hint of fear in his voice, and in the room silence for a moment, after he had spoken.

Bertram laughed loudly and harshly.

"Of all the old wives' tales! And you highly educated and extremely modern people believe such stuff as that!"

Joyce lit a cigarette, and puffed out a little wreath of smoke, daintily.

"I hate to tell you I've had the silver slipper! But if the worst comes to the worst, I hope I'll go scornfully to death!"

Bertram looked at her, and though he did not believe the ridiculous explanation of the silver slipper, he could not resist a tribute of admiration in his eyes. Joyce had more pluck than any man in the crowd. If the impossible happened, she would go "scornfully to death!" With patrician pride. She read his thoughts, and a wave of colour rose to her forehead, and for a moment her eyes softened to him. Then she turned away, with a word about the boredom of the subject.

"Why not some Ouija board?" she asked. "Peter, you're a wonder with the spirit world!"

It was the Reverend Peter Fynde who took the centre of the room. He hoped that if they experimented a little it would be with reverence. He deprecated the frivolous way in which some people approached the world beyond the veil, as so many were doing it in society now.

Bertram groaned.

"I call it blasphemy. To me, there's something horrible and indecent in this attempt to 'call up' the dead."

"I don't agree with you," said Joyce. "The other day we were in touch with Hal and Dudy. They spoke as they used to-the old home slang. One could not doubt."

"It was all being drawn from your subconscious mind, Joyce. But I object to the whole business. It's unhealthy. It's rotten and decadent."

"You needn't stay," said Joyce.

Bertram did not stay. After his altercation with the Reverend Peter, he went out to see some of his own friends, whose ideas he liked better than those of Joyce's crowd, whose point of view was more like his own than Joyce's.

Alas, for that! Alas, for many things. How was it going to work out between him and Joyce? Were they drifting apart? Were they going to add one more to all those broken marriages which had become an epidemic in English life, after the War? No, by God, not that! It was only the inevitable strain of early marriage. They would have to readjust themselves a little. More patience on his side. More understanding on hers. Tolerance. Give and take. Politics barred. Religion barred. A sense of humour. Success. Yes, if his book succeeded and he could establish a literary career, paying his Scot and lot, it would make a deal of difference. Joyce would be proud of him, and the book would help her to understand his point of view. Thank Heaven for the book! It kept him busy. It gave him an object in life. It was the expression of the truth that was in him. It was a cure for loneliness. . . . Oh, the curse of loneliness!

XIII

Luke Christy was still in town. It was when the sense of loneliness was in Bertram that he found himself drifting towards the Adelphi to Christy's rooms. The time of day or night didn't matter. Christy was always glad of a "yarn," and an excuse to drop his work awhile, when Bertram called, if he happened to be in. And he was mostly in, not going out much to meet his friends but expecting his friends to come to him.

"That's the test I put 'em to," he said. "If they come, I know they love me. And I've never learnt how to behave outside my own rooms. I break their china, or eat with the wrong fork, or scandalise the servants. I'm a plebeian, a coarse-mannered loon, hopelessly ill-educated."

Christy's friends accepted the condition he imposed. There were often several in his room when Bertram called, smoking innumerable cigarettes, talking, talking. Remarkable men and women, most of them, new in type to Bertram, and wonderfully interesting. They were literary people, journalists, social workers of one kind and another, professional idealists. There was also Janet Welford, at times, more interesting than any of them, and more alarming. Now and then came a foreigner —a Russian, an Indian student, a Belgian poet, a young Czecho-Slovak, an Austrian musician, an American professor, even a full-blooded Red Indian, once an officer in the Canadian flying corps, and a brilliant young man, speaking perfectly good English, and liberal in ideas.

They were all liberal in ideas. Rather too liberal, some of them, according to Bertram's way of thinking. He was startled by the boldness with which they accepted the necessity of change in the whole structure of social life and international relations. While he was worrying out of old inherited instincts and traditions, with some travail of doubt, they had jumped clean beyond to more advanced ideals than he could accept. They put no limit to their conceptions of liberty. If Ireland wanted a Republic, then it was her right to have it. They only questioned the wisdom of wanting a Republic, and the political possibility of obtaining it, with England hostile to that idea. They believed that national independence was less desirable, less "advanced" than federations of free peoples, linking up into ever widening groups, until the United States of Europe and the United States of America, and other associations of peoples would become the United States of the World. A distant vision!

Bertram's mind refused to follow them as far as that. He balked at the first obstacle, and insisted that Ireland had no right to greater freedom than that of Dominion Home Rule. He believed in the link between the two countries. England had rights as well as Ireland, her own need of security and freedom. He did not see how England could be safe or free, with an Irish Republic on her flank, able to cut her communications at sea. An Irish Republic would be a mortal blow to the old historical pride and sentiment of England.

Christy laughed at that argument of his.

"England's old historical pride and sentiment are going to be rudely shocked before long, my child! She can't afford those antique treasures. She's got to keep pace with the new needs of a world ruined by those dangerous possessions of old castes. It was historical pride and sentiment which caused the German ultimatum in 1914, and led to the massacre of the world's best youth. All that's in the Old Curiosity Shop now. Such stuff and nonsense must be replaced, lest we perish, by a spirit of comradeship and commonsense between peoples. Not "My country, right or wrong," nor "Kaiser and Fatherland," but "Service to the Human Family.""

"I believe in patriotism," Bertram had said, stubbornly, and that confession of faith, which he would never have stated in Joyce's "set," because it was taken for granted as the very air they breathed, seemed to astonish and amuse some of Christy's friends, as though he had uttered some ancient heresy in an outworn creed.

"Patriotism has been the curse of the human race," said Henry Carvell, the war correspondent, who had seen more of wars, big and little, than any man in England, and had been a knight-errant of the pen in most countries of the world. A heavily-built, square-shouldered man, with white hair and a ruddy face, he spoke with a kind of smiling contempt for Bertram's simplicity of ignorance.

"It's a survival of the old tribal rivalry which replaced the cave-man law when every old ourang-outang defended his lair and his females from all others of his species. 'This is my patch of earth. I've drawn a line with my club. It marks my territory. Cross it if you dare. I'm stronger than you. Yah!' That's patriotism. I've seen it working out in bloodshed and brutality from the Zambesi to the Rhine."

Bertram made a violent protest against that line of reasoning.

"I utterly disagree. If you deny patriotism, you rule out human nature and one of its strongest instincts."

"I don't deny it," said Henry Carvell, with a touch of impatience. "I denounce it. What virtue do you see in it?"

"Love of familiar things in life. Loyalty to the ideas of one's own people, their code of honour and all that. Men will die in defence of those things, in the last ditch."

"Why die?" asked Christy, grinning at Bertram in a friendly way. "Why get into ditches? Why not talk it out with the other fellow whose ideas, most likely, are exactly the same?"

Hubert Melvin, the novelist, took up the argument. He was a chubby little man with a bald head, a great expanse of brow, and a plump, good-natured face, like Shakespeare without his beard and dignity.

"Our friend, Pollard, is enlarging the definition of patriotism. He seems to be talking about sacrifice for the ideals of life. They reach beyond frontiers. They're not limited to a particular patch of earth hedged round by jealousy and governed by a small group of rascals calling themselves patriots! Of course men will die for what they believe to be the true faith."

"Quite so," agreed Henry Carvell. "Unfortunately, all national education-in a South African tribe or a European state-is intensive suggestion to primitive minds that their community, alone in the world, is in possession of the true faith. Their tribal custom becomes the only code of honour. They are encouraged to impose it, with missionary and murderous zeal, upon the rest of humanity. German 'Kultur,' for example, British 'Justice,' French 'Liberty,' and so on."

"British Justice is a pretty good thing," said Bertram. "We believe in fair play."

"In Ireland?" asked Christy, and Bertram was silent. No, somehow, for five hundred years, British Justice had rather fallen down in Ireland. It had been dragged into the mud since the War.

These conversations in Christy's room were altering his whole outlook on life, drawing him further and further away from the ideas of Joyce and her people. He resisted some of the extreme doctrines put forth calmly, as though they were accepted platitudes, by Christy's friends, but he found himself agreeing more and more with their fundamental principles, and leaning heavily to their side of life's argument.

These men, Henry Carvell, the war correspondent, Hubert Melvin, the novelist, Arthur Birchington, the critic, Nat Verney, the Labour member, W. E. Lawless, the political economist, and Bernard Hall, the editor of *The New World*, —to name but a few of those who came to Christy's rooms-differed from each other in a thousand ways of thought, never agreed in detail, engaged each other in endless controversy, over words, quotations, facts, ideas, philosophy, but Bertram, as an outsider and a younger man, seemed to discover in them some common denominator of character and quality.

What was it that bound them by invisible threads? Not any party creed, for some called themselves Liberals, and others Socialists, and others Individualists, and others declined all labels. Not any code of caste, for they belonged to different strata of English life, by birth and education.

Henry Carvell had been a Balliol man and a rowing Blue, before he disappeared into the wilds of Central Africa on his first expedition.

Hubert Melvin, who wrote satirical novels, had never been educated at all, according to his own account, and belonged to that vague, ill-defined middle-class which stretches around London from the mean streets of Brixton to the garden suburbs of Wimbledon, and treks northward from the artistic seclusion of St. John's Wood to the outer wilds of Golders Green and Finchley.

Nat Verney, the Labour member, had wielded a pick in the mines of Lancashire before taking a course, out of Trade Union Funds, at the London School of Economics.

W. E. Lawless, the economist, had been President of the Union at Oxford, his father was the well-known Judge, and his mother the beautiful Gwendoline Ashley, daughter of the actor.

Bernard Hall, whose editorship of *The New World* had founded something like a new school of English journalism-critical, scholarly, pledged to international peace, scornful of popular clamour and political insincerity, had been educated in France and Switzerland, and his swarthy face, his dark, brooding eyes, and the passionate temperament which he tried to hide under a mask of irony, came from a French mother and a Colonel of Seaforth Highlanders, his father.

A strangely assorted crowd, not more like each other in experience and heritage than others who drifted into Christy's rooms. What, then, brought them together, and inspired them with some common quality and purpose?

Bertram thought he had found the key to the puzzle in the word "Tolerance." These men were wonderfully tolerant of things that divide other men-religion, race, social environment. Henry Carvell had been brought up as a Catholic, Christy was an advanced sceptic on all religion, Lawless, a Christian Scientist. They had no race hatreds. At a time when the English people, and especially English women, continued to keep the hate fires burning against "the Hun" who had caused such agony in the world, these friends of Christy's denounced the Peace Treaty as an outrage, because of its harsh terms to the beaten enemy, raged against the continuance of the blockade which had forced the Germans to accept its "humiliations" and "injustice" —

"It's new in our code," said Carvell, "to make war on women and children," —and they believed that by generosity the German people could be induced to abandon their militarism and link up with a peaceful democracy in Europe.

There were times when Bertram, listening to this talk, felt uneasy, guilty of something like treachery. These men were too tolerant. They seemed more sensitive, sometimes, to the sufferings of the German people than to the sacrifice of their own. He quarrelled with them for that, and was beaten every time in argument because he found himself yielding to their sense of chivalry, to their belief in the "common man," to their faith in the ultimate commonsense of an educated democracy, to their hatred of cruelty.

No, it was not tolerance that he found the binding link between them, for they were violently intolerant of those whom they called "reactionaries" —all men not in agreement with themselves-arrogantly intolerant of ignorance and stupidity in high places. What seemed to bind them in intellectual sympathy was hatred of cruelty, to humble men, to women and children, to primitive races, even to animals and birds. They were instinctive and educated Pacifists, believing in the power of the spirit, rather than in physical force, in civilisation rather than in conflict, in liberty and not in oppression, in free-will, and not in discipline.

"Discipline is death," said Christy, and when Bertram cried out against that as blasphemy, he consented to modify his statement by admitting the necessity of "self-discipline," based on understanding and consent, but not imposed by external authority.

"We must kill the instinct of cruelty in the human brain," said Bernard Hall, of *The New World*, and the flame in him leapt through his cold mask. "We must give up teaching our children the old cave-man stuff, about soldier heroes and hunters of beasts. We must make it a public shame for women to be seen wearing the plumage of lovely birds."

This hatred of cruelty was at the bottom of their arguments about the Peace Treaty. It coloured their views on India, Ireland, Egypt, the exploitation of Africa, the Negro problem in the United States, the unemployed problem in England, the relations between Capital and Labour, even the question of Divorce.

It was all very difficult. . . . It would be more difficult with Joyce, if he allied himself definitely with this group of men and their philosophy. He felt they were trying to "convert" him, to win him over wholly to their side.

"You ought to join us," said Nat Verney, the Labour member. "Labour has need of lads like you. The younger Intellectuals."

He spoke with a North country burr in his speech, in spite of the London School of Economics. He was a sturdy, youngish man-thirty-five or so-with a shock of brown hair and a Lancashire face, hard as teak, square-jawed, with deep-set eyes in which there was a glint of humour, in spite of the light of fanaticism now and then, when he was bitter against "the classes" and his great enemy "Capital."

"Why don't you write occasionally for *The New World* —?" asked Bernard Hall. "You have the gift of words, if I may say so."

Bertram's heart gave a thump at that compliment from Hall, distinguished editor, fastidious critic. Was he serious or only sarcastic?

"A realistic novel on the War," said Hubert Melvin, raising his Shakespeare brow, and a little plump hand. "Nobody in England has come up to Barbusse. You could do it, Pollard! It's burnt into you. Give it 'em hot and strong —'The Old Gang!' Put the heart of England into it."

Bertram had glanced at Christy. He had pledged him to secrecy about his book, and Christy kept the pledge.

"Pollard may surprise us all!" So Christy said, and then spoilt his speech for Bertram by a grin and a jibe. "But we mustn't forget his aristocratic connections! It's hard to break with one's caste."

"That belongs to the wreckage of war," said Henry Carvell. "I'm glad of the smash. Think of the entrenched snobbishness of England in 1913! Thank Heaven that heritage of stupidity has been blown to bits."

Christy was not so sure that it had been blown to bits. In time of war there had been a little mixing up. Patrician girls had been dairy-maids, hospital nurses, canteen women. Public school men had gone into the ranks, now and then. Now they were all dividing again, getting back to different sides.

Bertram agreed with Christy, thinking of Kenneth Murless, General Bellasis, and others. He agreed more with Christy than any of the others. He was glad when they went away, leaving him to "jaw" with this old comrade of his. Christy was of simpler stuff, dead true in his estimate of facts. What was it in Christy that caught hold of him so? Perhaps his intense sincerity and his harsh realism. He did not deceive himself by illusion, however pleasant and idealistic. He told the truth as he saw it, unsparingly, to himself as well as to others. He had revealed Bertram to himself.

"You're pulled two ways, old man," he had said one night, as they had sat each side of his fireplace, here. "There's a tug of war between two opposing ideals in your brain. You're a traditional Conservative, trying to make a truce, or Coalition Government, with Liberal ideals. A foot in both camps."

"A Jekyll and Hyde!"

Bertram laughed, but he had been touched by this sword point which had pierced his armour.

"A Hamlet in Holland Street," said Christy. "You want to murder your old uncle, Tory Tradition, but you can't bear to 'kill him at his prayers.' You're still under the spell of Caste."

"It's my caste by proxy. It's my wife's."

"True," said Christy; "and out of chivalry to her, you will deny the light that sometimes gleams in you-the fierce, white flame of truth."

He quoted Scripture. It was a habit of his, though no Churchman.

" 'He that loveth father or mother more than me is not worthy of me; and he that loveth son or daughter more than me is not worthy of me. And he that taketh not his cross and followeth after me is not worthy of me.' "

"A harsh doctrine, if harshly interpreted," said Bertram. "It sometimes leads to the cruelty which your friends hate so much."

"One must be hard for honesty's sake."

Christy spoke of the secret in his own life which only once before he had revealed to Bertram-on a night before a morning of battle.

"When I found that my wife was dragging me down into the dirt of lies, into the squalour of self-pity and spiritual impotence, I left her-with my blessing. It was hard-because I had loved her."

"Hard on her," said Bertram.

"For a time," Christy agreed. "Afterwards she was glad. We had nagged at each other for five years, before the war. That gave her relief. She was sorry I didn't get killed. Of course I ought to have been, for her sake-perhaps for mine. After the Armistice life became intolerable. She had changed and I had changed-or rather, developed on separate lines. We were worlds apart. She hated my Socialistic tendencies. I hated her damned little suburban philosophy. You see, she'd married beneath her. A clergyman's daughter. Think of that-with me!"

Bertram remained silent for a while. Was Christy's story to be repeated in another sphere of life; in another quarter of London? Joyce had married "beneath her" —a peer's daughter to a lawyer's son.

"Christy, old man," he said at last, "I believe in Loyalty. It's my central faith. Loyalty to one's country, one's wife, one's code of honour. Without that life, to me, is unlivable."

Christy puffed at his old burnt pipe for several minutes before replying.

"Loyalty's good," he admitted presently; "but to the highest and not to the lowest. Loyalty to lies is disloyalty to truth. That's one of life's little ironies. A damned nuisance, sometimes!"

The conversation was broken by Janet Welford, who came in to see Christy, whom she loved.

XIV

That lady, Janet, —Janet Rockingham Welford, as her name was given in full on the title pages of several novels and below the columns of articles in *The New World* —was an old friend of Bertram's. Not old herself, for she was on the vital side of thirty, but they had played together and pulled each other's hair at a kindergarten in the Cromwell Road, read fairy tales together under the trees in Kensington Gardens, and, years later, had met each other at "parties" in the wonderful remote days before the War-was it a thousand years ago, or in another life. After that they had not met until, surprisingly, one night, in Christy's rooms.

While Bertram had been in the trenches, Janet had been at Boulogne, with more buttons to her uniform than Bertram could boast, driving ambulances and maimed men from the railway to the "clearing stations," after a wild three months with a convoy in Belgium, when she was often under fire in Dixmude and Pervyse, more reckless of danger than the Belgian officers and English stretcher-bearers.

Now she was living in a little flat in Overstrand Mansions, Battersea Park, writing audacious fiction (Bertram blushed when reading it), pacifist articles (rather too bitter!), and occasional verse-very mystical-for evening newspapers. She also found time to play the companion and guide to blinded soldiers in Regent's Park, to act as secretary of a Socialist club, to speak at Labour meetings, to give evenings at home to young men and women of advanced views, and to call on Christy for inspiration, advice, and intellectual refreshment.

She was what she called "decidedly Left but not extreme." Bertram, after some conversational enquiries and experiences, found her so extreme that he could see no further way "Left" than instant and bloody onslaught against established order. Her political, social and moral views made him feel that his hair was rising on his scalp. She frightened him. She also attracted him by an irresistible gaiety and audacity-by an overflowing good nature and joy of life.

The first time he'd met her in Christy's rooms, she had come in like a gust of south wind, calling Christy absurd, newly-invented names because he had failed to come to one of her "receptions."

"You reptilian, hypersensitive Bohunk! You self-absorbed, psychoanalytical Pumpdoodlum!"

Then she had seen Bertram, with an instant recognition met by a slow-dawning remembrance in his mind. Those big, brown eyes, that short, straight nose, that whimsical, biggish mouth-in what former life had he seen this girl, kissed her, if he remembered well, pulled that mass of coiled hair, not coiled so neatly then? — Why, yes, Janet Welford!

She made a dart at him and seized him by a coat lapel.

"Bertram Pollard, by all that's romantic! My boy lover of Cromwell Road! My dream knight of Kensington! He whom first I kissed, and would gladly do again, but for maidenly modesty and Luke Christy! Lord, how my little heart throbs within this silken bodice!"

Of course he was utterly embarrassed, shy as a schoolboy, red-faced as a cut beetroot.

"Don't mind me," said Christy. "Only I ought to warn you that Bertram's a married man. And his wife's a real lady."

"That makes the operation safer and more delicate," said Janet Welford. "Bertram, for old time's sake? To catch again the fleeting impress of youth's delight? How say you?"

She offered him her cheek. The invitation could not be refused without default of chivalry, but he was awkward and restrained in his salute.

Janet Welford rubbed her cheek with the back of her hand and said, *"Quelle violence! Qu'il est féroce, cet Anglais, et formidable!"*

She sat on the arm of the old leather chair, and put her arm round Christy's neck and her cheek against his cheek, and called him a beautiful pterodactyl, and a most wise old plesiosaurus.

"Don't you come vamping me too recklessly," growled Christy, with mock resentment. "I may be ugly, but I'm human."

"You're impregnable in virtue," said Janet Rockingham Welford. "Alas for amorous womanhood in a world of surplus women!"

She sighed deeply, and then pulled Christy's ears, left the arm of his chair, and sat demurely opposite Bertram.

"Tell me," she asked, "are you one of Us?"

Bertram enquired in what way, and she explained she meant the Only Way, the Far, Far, Better Way. Was he one of those who had turned their back on an old and wicked world, full of old and wicked men (and women) and marched forward with youth to the New World of equality, brotherhood and universal peace?

It was Christy who murmured with a grin:

"Pollard's groping towards the light."

"Let me take him by the hand," said Janet Rockingham Welford. "I'll lead him into such a blaze of light that his young soul will be dazzled. He will see the vision of the glory of light and the bright coloured garments of radiant humanity. . . . Will you come, my friend?"

"Is it far to walk?" asked Bertram, "or must I take a 'bus?"

She told him that it was no further than the Charing Cross Road, over a bookshop, on Tuesday and Friday evenings, at the club meetings of the "Left Wing." She was secretary, and would make him a probationary member. Fee, two shillings and sixpence. Including coffee.

She made other enquiries as to his political and philosophical mentality, and found him doubtful. She diagnosed him as a case of psychic suppression, with a political complex. His instincts, she thought, were healthy, but his opinions idiotic. If he would leave himself entirely in her hands, with placid faith, she would undertake to root up his inherited and developed prejudices, and turn him out a fresh young soul of the Left Wing, eager for exalted flight.

"Your marriage, Bertram dear?" she enquired presently; "are you fretting at the yoke, or have you acquired that technique which makes it possible for two human beings to dwell under the same roof-tree, day after day, even week after week, without agony of boredom and a nerve strain beyond endurance? Tell me frankly. I can help you."

Bertram flushed to the roots of his hair, said "Hang it all!" and then laughed heartily. Janet Rockingham Welford was really the most remarkable specimen of modern young womanhood that he had yet met.

She seemed glad to amuse him.

"That laugh will do you good," she informed him. "You've been worrying about things. You've secret fears. I expect your dreams ought to be regulated. Laughter is the great remedy of fear. I know that from my blind men."

"Are you ever serious?" asked Bertram.

"I never leave laughter far behind," she answered.

And that was true, as he found, not in Christy's rooms but in hers, to which he went rather often, after that first meeting, and in little restaurants around St. John's Wood or in the "Zoo," where he met her after her work with the blinded soldiers of St. Dunstan's.

She was serious sometimes, passionately serious about the state of civilisation, the hatred between nations, the nation's forgetfulness of boys who had been stricken in the War, and the objects for which they had fought, the indifference of the lucky classes to the growing poverty, the increasing despair of ex-soldiers, crippled men, nerve-broken women, the cruelty of the world to starving Russia-oh, yes, she admitted the secret spell of Bolshevism! —the brutality of England to Ireland, the refusal of the United States to enter the League of Nations, the trickery, the wickedness, the corruption of European Governments who poked up the worst passions of the crowd, and lied to them, and played the old game of international rivalry so that the world was being staged for another war.

She dropped her fantastic way of speech in talking of these things, and scared Bertram by the violence of her language, and by the red flame of her spirit, reckless of all restraint, impatient of delay, eager for "direct action" to cure the evils which she saw and loathed.

But laughter came quick upon her passion. She laughed wholeheartedly at Bertram's fears, his loyalty to old traditions, his hatred of violence, his moderate views, his moralities. She called him a Queen Victorian Englishman, an 1880 Jingo, a trimmer, a hedger, a Girondin, a disciple of Samuel Smiles, a John Halifax, Gentleman, a Tory Democrat, and in a moment of exasperation, a Poor Damned Soul.

He caught a glimpse of her now and then, pacing rapidly round Regent's Park with a blinded soldier on each arm. They laughed continually as she talked to them. They looked happy. They chatted brightly, and they turned their faces to her sometimes as though seeing the way in which the wind blew a brown tress across her rose-flushed cheek, and the brightness of her eyes.

Bertram had hated to see those blinded soldiers, groping their way about the Park, tapping the kerb-stone with their sticks, standing, and listening intently, as the taxi-cabs swirled by, afraid, melancholy, stricken. The sight of them made him curse the war again, and go back to his book, to write more bitterly of its anguish.

But Janet Rockingham Welford was at her best with those blinded men, and he had no argument with her in that part of her work, though in all else.

He went often to her rooms.

XV

Not a word of news had come from Susan or Dennis O'Brien, and Bertram's anxiety had been allayed for a time because of the argument he used to his mother, and to his own sense of uneasiness-that no news is good news.

His mother was fretting miserably. It seemed to age her, and he noticed that she was weak in health, and no longer had that placid resignation to the worries of life which had made her so comforting as a mother to unruly but devoted children.

A greyness had crept beneath her skin, so white and transparent in the old days. She seemed to have lost her interest in the little duties of domestic life which had filled her time in all the days and years of Bertram's remembrance, and it came as a shock to him, greater than any other sign of distress in her, that on his last visit some withered flowers remained unchanged in the vase on her table, and her writing desk was disorderly with many letters and household bills hopelessly mixed up, as he remarked when she tried to find a letter from his brother Digby. She had made a religion of "tidiness." Susan's rampageous carelessness had been a source of constant annoyance to her sense of order. This litter in her desk, and those unchanged flowers, were signs that something had broken in her spirit, and Bertram was shocked by that, and by the grey sadness of the little woman who had given him life, as she sat, with restless hands in her lap, and a kind of hidden fear in her eyes.

She was afraid because Susan hadn't written one word to her about her secret marriage or her present whereabouts. That marriage, which Bertram had revealed, was like a blow to her. She had prayed that Susan might marry a "nice" man, so that she would settle down and have babies, and be happy. She'd even asked God to let her live until she had that sense of security in Susan's happiness-her wild, beautiful, reckless Susan. But now this secret wedding with a young man who was in conflict with the law, and had done dangerous and dreadful things, was worse than anything she had feared.

"What does the governor think?" asked Bertram.

Mrs. Pollard's eyelids quivered as she looked at her son.

"Your father thinks it's all my fault."

"He would!" said Bertram, bitterly.

"First Dorothy. Now Susan. One married to a German, the other to an Irish rebel! It makes him feel like King Lear, he says. He forbids me to mention his daughters."

"What a man!" cried Bertram. "What colossal intolerance!"

His mother reproved him, timidly.

"Your father's a good man, my dear. You must be patient with his point of view. Those dreadful politics —"

Bertram raged inwardly against his father, with a storm of anger at the unyielding, deep-dug, inhuman prejudice of his attitude to life, but for his mother's sake he swallowed the bitter words that rose in him. He tried to comfort her by reminding her of news she'd received from young Digby. The boy was coming back from Dublin on leave. He might have heard something about Susan and Dennis. Anyhow, it would be good to see him. He had been very lucky.

But his mother shook her head, and refused to be comforted.

"Digby is my chief anxiety. I lie awake at night thinking of him in the midst of all those raids and searches and murderous attacks. I can hardly forgive your father for letting him join the Black and Tans, as they call them. He's so young. Such a child!"

Bertram growled that it was a disgrace to the family, anyhow. The Black and Tans were dragging England's reputation in the mud. They were no better than hooligans. The scum of the Army that had fought for Liberty.

Again his mother reproved him. They were doing their duty In upholding law and order, she said, and Bertram laughed bitterly, thinking of what old Christy would say to that, and Janet Welford. But how could he argue with his mother, so wan-looking, so melancholy? She had withered like the flowers in her vase. He had been tempted to tell her about his own troubles, to ask her advice about Joyce, who was so "distant" from him now, so unresponsive to his love. . . . But he could not burden his little mother with more family tragedies. He rose and kissed her forehead, and said, "It's all very difficult!" It was his old familiar jest.

She smiled at him, and seemed to brighten.

"You've always been good and true," she told him. "How's dear Joyce?"

"Splendid," he told her, and then left her, to get some news of Susan, if he could, by way of Dennis O'Brien's sisters.

He'd been reminded of those girls by Janet Welford, to whom he had told the story of Susan and Dennis. Janet knew everybody, it seemed to Bertram, and he was not surprised when she said, "Dennis O'Brien? Of course! And his three sisters in Maid of Honour Row. Don't you remember how they learned dancing with us in the old days at the Kensington Academy?"

Yes, he remembered now, three little girls with pigtails down their backs and an Irish way of speech, and a habit of dropping rosaries out of their pockets when they danced. They were Irish Catholics, and he and Janet, alone together in her rooms, had discovered them at the old address in the telephone directory, under the name of their father, Sir Montague O'Brien.

No news is good news, as Bertram found when he went to the O'Briens' house. They had received news of their brother Dennis, and it was bad. He guessed that at once, when the maid showed him into one of the rooms of their house in Maid of Honour Row, a little Queen Anne house with panelled walls and a powder closet, where once the waiting ladies of a Stuart Queen had lived, not far from the old red-brick palace in Kensington Gardens.

The three O'Brien girls suited the house, and the panelled room, painted white, with little chintz curtains in the casement windows, and gilt-framed mirrors on the walls, and miniatures of Irish gentry in old-fashioned dress.

The girls whom he remembered with pigtails, had their dark hair coiled high, and their frocks were cut low at the neck, showing their full white throats, not unlike the portrait of a Georgian lady over their mantelpiece. Bertram remembered their names now, long forgotten, as he thought, though tucked away in his subconscious storehouse of old memories-Rose and Betty and Jane, in order of age.

A young priest was with them, and Bertram, as he entered the room, saw at a glance that they'd been praying on their knees, for they had risen hastily at the maid's tap on the door. The young priest held his beads. They had been reciting the rosary, as Catholics do, for the dying or dead. The girls had red eyes, and tried to hide the sign of tears when Bertram announced himself as "a kind of brother-in-law" and asked for news of his sister Susan.

A letter lay open on the table, and Rose O'Brien, the eldest sister, handed it to him without a word, while another gush of tears came into her eyes. It was in Susan's handwriting and was but a short message. Dennis had been arrested near Dublin, and taken to Mountjoy Prison.

She was in hiding with friends they knew. It would not be safe for her to write any more. She sent her love, and ended her letter with the words, "God save Ireland-and my dear Dennis!"

There was silence in the room while Bertram read the letter. So Susan had crossed to Ireland with the boy, as he had guessed. Dennis had been taken to Mountjoy Prison. On what charge?

He asked the girls that.

"What has Dennis done?"

None of them answered. It seemed to Bertram that they weren't sure of trusting him.

It was the young priest who answered.

"Does it matter to the Black and Tans what an Irishman has done, or not done? It's only surprising that they didn't kill poor Dennis at sight. It's a Reign of Terror, without law, without justice, without mercy."

"On both sides," said Bertram, sharply. "I see no distinction in murder-Sinn Fein or Black and Tan."

The priest laughed uneasily, but into his large dark eyes leapt a little flame of passion.

"Sinn Fein does no murder. It fights in self-defence for the liberty of Ireland, and executes spies and murderers-the British soldiery and their bloody rabble, the Black and Tans."

Bertram groaned with a kind of anguish. He had used the same arguments with Joyce, with Kenneth Murless, with all that crowd. But when the priest spoke them his mind refused to admit this one-sided view, this assertion that Ireland had no guilt.

"It's all madness," he said. "Madness and murder. Insane anarchy. Black-hearted crime. How can you defend it as a Catholic priest-even as a Christian?"

The priest shrugged his shoulders.

"You're an Englishman. How can you understand the Irish point of view? The divine passion of a people fighting for freedom against ruthless oppression? It's not in your mentality."

"I'm half Irish," said Bertram, bitterly, "and sometimes I wish, by God, that I hadn't a drop of Irish blood in my veins! But because I'm half English as well as half Irish, I say that England cannot surrender to Irish gun-men. You're fighting with the wrong weapons in a dirty way."

Rose O'Brien had whispered to the priest, and he answered as though he had gained new understanding.

"I don't argue about Ireland with a son of Michael Pollard, K.C."

It was a shrewd blow, and Bertram was silent under the thrust of it. He turned from the priest to the three girls.

"Your brother's wife is my sister," he said. "What's to be done?"

Rose O'Brien answered him.

"There's nothing to do but pray."

Betty O'Brien saw something else to do.

"I'll go to Dublin to-night. If the dirty Black and Tans touch me with a little finger —I'll lay a whip across their faces. I'm Irish, body and soul."

"Hush, Betty, for the love of God!" said Rose, and Jane, the youngest, said, "Be quiet, darling!"

It was Jane who showed Bertram out of the house, after he had written a line to Susan, in case Betty saw her.

The girl touched his arm, and whispered to him:

"I'm not Sinn Fein, like Rose and Betty. I'm sure our Lord wouldn't like it. But I'm Dennis's sister, and he's the noblest boy I know. Dear God! what will I do if they take him from us?"

She leant up against the door-post and wept bitterly but very quietly.

"They'll send him to prison for a time," said Bertram; "it's not so terrible."

He kissed her hand, to make her understand his sympathy.

"God help Ireland-and England!" he said, and then lifted his hat and walked away. If he had been wholly Irish, he would have been Sinn Fein too. His passion would have flamed out for Irish liberty. But he was the son of an English mother, and loved England first and best. Why was he always pulled two ways? Why did this infernal tug-of-war go on in his heart and brain, between the extremes of thought? Most men walked on one side or the other, on their own side of life's hedge. He tried to keep to the middle of the road, and both sides flung stones at him.

XVI

That night young Digby came to see him. The boy was not wearing his uniform in the Black and Tans. It was not popular in London, and the authorities kept it out of sight.

They greeted each other in the usual way.

"Hulloa, old man!" from Digby. "Hulloa, young fellow!" from Bertram.

They were alone together in the "study," Joyce having gone out to dinner again.

"How are things?" asked Digby.

"How's yourself?" asked Bertram.

"I feel good to be in England again, after that hellish place, Ireland! One feels safe in the streets. No need to keep an eye over one's shoulder. A knock at the door doesn't make one jump out of one's giddy seat!"

And yet, a little later, he started and looked towards the door when there was the double rat-tat of a postman's knock.

"Sorry!" he said, with a queer grin, as he fumbled for his pipe and lit it.

He was barely twenty, and had escaped the Great War by a year or two, though he had been in training as an officer-cadet before the Armistice; a fair-haired boy, with clear-cut, delicate features, almost girlish, and something of his mother's look. But altered, thought Bertram. Something had changed in him. There was a loose look about his mouth, and his eyes were shifty. He had developed a slight stutter in his speech.

"Any whiskey, old man?" he asked Bertram, after some preliminary conversation about his father and mother, Joyce, and the right thing to see at the theatre.

Bertram produced the whiskey, but raised his eyebrows when Digby poured out half a glass and drank it like water.

"I say! That's a stiff dose, isn't it?"

The boy said it was nothing. He had got into the habit of it. Everybody drank like a fish in his crowd. Nothing else to do in the old barracks. It was rather encouraged by the "Officer commanding." Even the men could drink as much as they liked before going out on search parties and raids. It made 'em a bit fierce and kept up their spirits. Otherwise they would be too easy with the Irish, especially the Irish girls, who were damn pretty, many of them.

It wasn't a pleasant thing to search girls' bedrooms at night. At night? Yes, of course. All search parties went out at night, drew a cordon round certain streets, then banged at the doors, or bashed them in, while an officer, with a sergeant and five men or so, went through the house looking for rebels, and fellows on the run, concealed arms, and all that.

A rotten job for a gentleman.

One night he had a lot of trouble with his men. They routed out three girls in their night-shirts —ladies, too, and amazingly pretty-and started mucking about with them. One girl had her night-shirt torn off, and screamed enough to pull the house down. It was the sergeant's fault. He was drunk that night, and beastly amorous. Digby had threatened to shoot him, and did actually knock down one of the men. That sobered them up, and they left the girls alone, but it made them savage, and in the next house they shot a young boy-just a kid-who tried to shut a door in their faces.

"Killed him?" asked Bertram in a strangled voice. This narrative made his blood feel like boiling lead. Hot and cold waves passed up his spine to the top of his scalp.

"Oh, Lord, yes! Plugged through the head."

On another night there had been a hell of a scene. They had run to earth a young rebel in Collin's command. He had been in the ambush at Black Rock where five Scotties had been killed. O'Callaghan by name. His mother and sister had hidden him in a linen cupboard. Of course, they found that pretty quick, but the sister stood between his men and the cupboard, with a red-hot poker, and threatened to burn the eyes out of the first man who tried to pass her. The sergeant drew his revolver, but the mother flung herself at him and he had to shoot her. Then the sister attacked, and one of his fellows ran her through with a bayonet, to save himself from the red-hot poker. What else could he do?

It was worse when the women started screaming and praying round their men folk. It put the fellows' nerves on edge. Their nerves were always on edge. They couldn't walk a yard without the chance of getting a sniper's bullet in the brain, or being plugged in the back of the head by some fellow who had just passed, in a busy street, or a lonely lane. That sort of thing gave a man the jim-jams. It was worse than real war, he imagined.

No wonder the men treated the Irish "rough" at times or got out of hand and shot up a village in which some of their pals had been killed. Killed without a dog's chance. What did it mean, exactly, "shooting up" a village? Oh, just driving through in an armoured car and spraying the windows and door-ways with machine-gun bullets. Women and children killed like that? Often, of course. A rotten game, but guerrilla warfare was like that. . . .

"Any more whiskey, old man? Oh, thanks."

He went on talking, describing raids and ambushes and reprisals, for an hour or more, until Bertram could listen to no more of this narrative by his "kid brother" as he used to call him. It made him feel physically sick. It seemed to drain him of all vitality, so that he trembled at the knees when he began to walk about the room.

"It's frightful! It's devilish! After the Great War and all our sacrifice for liberty! Two English-speaking peoples, bound together by blood, by Christian faith, by heroic memories! My God! Digby, I implore you to chuck it. Hand in your papers. Resign. Cut your right hand off rather than do that dirty work! It's dishonouring. It's filthy. It's murderous."

Digby's face flushed. He gulped down some more whiskey, and lit a cigarette.

"It's got to be done," he said, sullenly. "Somebody's got to do it. It's what happens in this bloody world."

He was less than twenty years old, and all his memories were of war, and blood, and death. He was annoyed by the emotion of his elder brother. He was also a little drunk. Presently he said, "So long, old man, I think I'll go and do a show."

Bertram had not asked him about Susan and Dennis. When the boy had gone, he raged about the room again. He remembered this boy, Digby, when he was a little fair-haired thing to whom he used to tell fairy-tales in bed. Their mother used to come and kiss them and tell them to go to sleep. Now this! Bertram was overwhelmed by a sense of pity for the mothers of the world.

XVII

Tucked into the frame of the Jacobean mirror (sham antique, but rather good-looking) over the mantelpiece of Bertram's "study," was the card given to him by Lady Ottery for her lecture on "The Religion of Revolution: Past and Present." He had glanced at it several times from day to day with a sense of annoyance, as at the notification of an impending menace, such as a date with the dentist or any distant disagreeable and inevitable duty.

APRIL 10.
THE RELIGION OF REVOLUTION:
PAST AND PRESENT
BY
THE COUNTESS OF OTTERY
CHAIRMAN
HIS GRACE, THE DUKE OF BRAMSHAW, K.G

Once or twice he had murmured, "Oh, Lord! I suppose I'll have to go!" and then, as familiar objects lose their force of impression, he'd forgotten the lecture and its date. It was Joyce who reminded him one morning, at the breakfast table, to the music of an early piano organ in Holland Street,

"I suppose you're going to Mother's lecture?"

He said "Oh, Lord!" again and "When is it?"

It was on the following afternoon, and Joyce was naturally annoyed with him when he showed signs of shirking the engagement. She couldn't understand, as she said, fretfully, why Bertram disparaged her Mother's intellectual ability-Joyce always spoke of her Mother with a distinctly capital M —to say nothing of her historical knowledge. Lady Ottery had studied considerably more than Bertram, who was a desultory reader, and had read a good deal at the British Museum last winter, as well as belonging to the London Library, which allowed her to take out eleven books at a time on serious subjects.

"The amount of knowledge Mother has amassed is stupendous," said Joyce. "Whether you agree with her or not, I think you ought to respect her research work."

Bertram muttered something about not believing much in book-knowledge, but retreated on that line of argument as the author of a book which soon he hoped to present to Joyce with love and homage, as the first-fruits of his new-found gift. In the end, he capitulated, and agreed humbly to go to the lecture and behave himself with due deference to his exalted Mother-in-law. He tried to give a touch of humour to the surrender, and obtained the glimmer of a smile from Joyce. But she froze him by saying that she hoped her Mother's lecture would convert him to more reasonable views, and make him see the frightful danger of the opinions held by his revolutionary friends at a time when England was threatened by mob-law.

"My dear Kid!" he said, making light again of her over-serious mood. "In the first place my friends aren't revolutionary" —he had to make a mental reservation of Janet Rockingham Welford —"and in the second place, I don't agree that England is threatened by mob-law."

"Not by the coming strike?"

He hesitated for a moment, and then said: "The men call it a lock-out."

She called that hair-splitting over words, and though he would not consent to that-it made all the difference to the argument-he agreed that there would be a serious situation in England, dangerous, even, if all the miners left their pits, and millions of unemployed and idle men were added to the two millions already without work. The stoppage of coal would gradually strangle all industry, and the railways, which were the vital arteries of the nation.

"There may be Civil War," said Joyce, calmly, and Bertram answered sharply, "Nonsense! Who suggests that?"

"General Bellasis. As the Home Office man, he knows."

"I wish to goodness he'd keep his precious knowledge to himself!" said Bertram angrily, "and not come round here mixing scaremonger politics with tea-table dalliance!"

Joyce's colour rose slightly, as a hint that she was "vexed."

"He's one of the best. If you weren't so unreasonably jealous, I'd ask you to make a friend of him."

"Why?"

All Bertram's nerves jangled at this suggestion of friendship with a man he detested as one of the professional warriors of Whitehall, with Prussian instincts and supercilious manners.

"Because he can put you in the way of a job. In fact, I think he's going to offer you one."

"Did *you* ask him?"

"More or less. Don't you want a job? It's time you began to keep your end up."

Bertram rose from his chair, walked to the window, and tossed a blind tassel to and fro.

Presently he spoke, in a low, emotional voice.

"I was hoping you wouldn't say that! I'll pay you back for board and lodging when my book's published."

She followed him to the window, and put her hand on his shoulder, with a caressing touch, which surprised him. It was some time since she'd done that.

"Bertram, I'm not playing the spiteful cat. You know it's not my style of play. I'm not flinging anything in your face, or any rot of that kind. But you know you want a good job. You've said so a hundred times! Now General Bellasis is ready to offer you one. Why get huffed?"

He was melted by her words, by the old comradely tone of them, by her hand on his shoulder. If she only knew how a touch from her could kill his temper!

"Give my book a chance," he said. "I believe I can do something at the writing game. Meanwhile, if Bellasis has anything to offer, I'll think of it, seriously. What sort of a job, do you think?"

"Organising," she told him, and he liked the word. "Something to do with the home defence of England-in case of trouble."

"Trouble?" He looked at her vaguely.

"The strike."

"Oh, Lord!"

"Why not?"

He didn't tell her why not, and indeed, she couldn't wait to hear why not, for some friends called with a car to take her to Brighton for lunch and tea. But his mind went quickly to recent conversations with some of the people whom Joyce didn't know and didn't care to know-Bill Huggett, down in Lambeth, Janet Welford, Luke Christy, Nat Verney, the miners' leader, Lawless, the economist, Bernard Hall, editor of *The New World*. They also had been talking about the coming strike, which they called a lock-out, and had seriously disturbed his mind on the subject.

Christy and his friends declared that the ultimatum issued to the miners was the first challenge of Capital in a conflict which they intended to wage with Labour, until the spirit of the workers was broken and they were reduced again to the cheap standards of pre-war wages upon which the prosperity of British industry had been developed-for the employers.

While the Government was squandering millions of money on maintaining overstaffed departments filled with "limpets" pouring more millions into Imperialistic adventures in Mesopotamia, and the East, giving immense financial support to any Russian ruffian of the old régime who gathered together bands of bandits to invade the Republic, and generally ignoring the realities of financial ruin in Europe, following the War, they were engineering a systematic assault on Labour, in order to weaken its political power and reduce it to economic subjection.

The heroes of the War, "our brave boys in the trenches," were already being branded as "Bolshevists" by Government spokesmen. The men who had fought at Ypres, on the Somme, and across the Hindenburg line, and whose patient courage in years of mud and misery and devouring death had won the War, in spite of the stupidity of generals, and the personal intrigues of politicians, were now to be denounced as revolutionary rascals, unpatriotic "blighters," who must be "taught a lesson," and forced back to a low standard of wages, and of life.

That was Christy's way of thought about the ultimatum to the miners. It was supported with facts and figures by Nat Verney, the Labour member. He took the trouble to analyse the proposed scale of wages at a little conference of writing men in Christy's rooms, brought there by Bernard Hall, of *The New World*. He seemed to prove that they were less than a living wage, so grotesquely out of scale with the prevailing cost of life that if the men accepted the ultimatum-hurled at them suddenly without previous warning or discussion-they would surrender their very birthright-the right to exist.

Verney spoke quietly, with a smouldering but masked passion.

"We shall fight them to the last ditch. The Government, in league with the mine-owners —that's certain-have forced an issue which we're ready to accept. We're not afraid, for the judgment of the people will be on our side."

Bernard Hall admitted that, personally, he *was* afraid. There was a sense of bitterness among millions of men who had fought in the war and now were disillusioned with the promises made and betrayed by politicians. With so many men idle-lack of coal would shut down every industry-there might be a violent conflict. The Government was prepared to use force. He understood they were calling out the Army reserves. Some act of hooliganism, some shot fired accidentally, or otherwise, by any fool, and frightful things might happen.

"Supposing the soldiers refuse to fire on their own crowd?" asked Verney, and something in his eyes showed his hope for that.

There was silence in Christy's room, until Christy himself broke it.

"That means Revolution-and the end of England as a world power."

"We're not out for Revolution," said Verney, in a low voice. "We're out for a decent rate of wage-nothing more than that."

Then he raised his voice a little, and it had a thrill in it.

"If the Government asks for Revolution, if it arranges it, the blood guilt will be on its head."

Bertram spoke for the first time. He was irritable, because all this grave discussion had come as a surprise to him, and suggested unpleasant possibilities which he hadn't imagined, and didn't believe.

"Don't you think we'd better drop all mention of the word Revolution? It's an ugly damn word, and oughtn't to be in our English vocabulary. It isn't in our English character, if I know England."

The company had been startled by Bertram's intervention, all but Christy, who understood his silences and his outbursts, and the working of his mind.

"Do any of us know England?" asked Bernard Hall, after a slight pause. "The men who went out to the war-to France, Palestine, Egypt, Salonica, Russia-have come back again. We don't understand what's going on in their minds. They don't understand themselves. We're dealing with uncertain, unknown forces."

"I know the men pretty well," said Bertram. "I keep in touch with them."

They paid some heed to that, and admitted his claim to give evidence, acknowledging their own distance from the labouring classes, their theoretical guesses.

"You don't think they're out for trouble?" asked Hall. His dark, Celtic face, with its brooding eyes, was heavily overcast by the shadow of anxiety.

"They want peace," said Bertram, "and enough to eat, decent house-room, and a little pocket-money for the fun of things."

It was Bill Huggett who had given him that view of the situation. He used Huggett as a guide to the mind of the London crowds, the average mind of the dreary processions of men, marching with trained step through London with banners saying, "We want work, not charity," and the point of view of the seedy-looking groups lounging about the Labour Exchanges, and of other assemblies of men listening on Sunday afternoons to political orators in Hyde Park. Bill Huggett was his interpreter.

The man had succeeded in getting back some of his work as "French polisher." He was earning about two pounds ten a week, out of which he paid eighteen shillings for two miserable rooms in the slums of Walworth. With the rest he could manage to get food for himself and his four children, in spite of high prices. Getting back to work had changed his whole aspect. He was more alert, and less inclined to "grouse," and he'd regained some of the old Cockney humour which had made him popular as a company sergeant in France and Flanders.

Bertram spent half an hour with him, now and again, in his lodgings, or in a public-house round the corner, and Hugget, though always embarrassed by this comradeship of his former officer, and somewhat suspicious of its motives, was not ungrateful or unfriendly.

It amazed him that Bertram seemed pleased to sit in his dirty little room for a few minutes, not bothering when the youngest "brat" began a howl in the next room, and dozens of other children, sickly, ailing, underfed some of them, joined in a chorus of wailing in this block of "workmen's dwellings."

Women railed through open or broken windows, looking into a courtyard filled with "washing" —and threatened to break the jaws of small children, if they didn't "be'ave," or insulted each other for certain grievances connected with the water supply on the common stairways. Doors banged, cheap gramophones blared out jazz tunes. Somewhere a violin was being scraped like the crying of a soul in agony, by a diligent practiser of finger-exercises. Shrill laughter of coarse-voiced girls rang out in the passages. Oaths floated up from the courtyard. The noise of distant domestic quarrels came vaguely into Huggett's room, where he sat in his shirtsleeves, smoking Woodbine cigarettes and answering Bertram's questions with a queer, nervous grin.

" 'Omes for 'Eroes!" he remarked once when the strange medley of noises in the Workmen's Dwellings became more than usually discordant.

The "silver slipper" story upon which Bertram questioned him, excited his sense of humour.

"Silver my foot!" he said; "white metal at sixpence the gross! A Bolshevist emblem? Well, if that ain't the funniest yarn! Strikes me there's no more sense in some of them so-called Toffs than in the long ears of a coster's moke."

He had a realistic mind, and was something of a philosopher, like others Bertram knew, who had risked their lives in the war, and escaped by a hairsbreadth chance of luck. In their billets behind the line, in dug-outs, in shell-holes where they had lain wounded, these men, or some of them, had thought starkly of the meaning of things, had talked with each other in a kind of short-cut language, incoherent, yet understanding. Now they thought of the Peace they'd helped to make, and the life they'd come back to find.

"It's like this, Major. We're fed up with lies. The blarsted lies of newspapers. The muck them politicians say. The rotten stuff some of our own leaders say. In the old days we used to believe what we was told or what we read. Now we've found out. We've been kidded, all along! That's made us think. We know a bit of truth ourselves. We know what 'appened to us. The things we did. The things we've seen. We can't be kidded any more. That makes a lot of difference!"

"What do the men want?" asked Bertram. "What are they looking for?"

"Not over much," said Huggett. "There's some that talk a lot. I did a bit myself before I found my job again. Communism. Bolshevism. Bunkum. More kidding! Most others are out for peace-no more bloody war, not at no cost-decent 'ouse-room —not this dog 'ole for eighteen bob a week —a bit of pocket money for the fun of things. See?"

Bertram thought he saw. He believed that Huggett knew the truth of things about the spirit of the men. He marvelled at this fellow's commonsense, his soundness of judgment, his sense of humour, his patience. Those had been the qualities of the men in the war. They were still there. If all the men were like Huggett, or most of them, England was safe. The menace was only in the minds of men like Bernard Hall of *The New World* —intellectually morbid-and in the minds of Joyce's crowd, who were obsessed by the bogey of Bolshevism-that strange foreign growth, so alien to English ideas.

XVIII

"Joyce's crowd!" To some extent his own crowd. He saw it, not for the first time, but peculiarly defined in his imagination, and in all its glory, on the afternoon of Lady Ottery's lecture. He drove in a "taxi" with Joyce from their little home in Holland Street to the Wigmore Hall, and by the time they'd reached Cumberland Place, at the top of the Park, fell into line with a steady stream of automobiles of highly expensive kinds.

"The New Poor aren't so beastly poor yet," said Bertram, thinking of Huggett in his squalid rooms with the four squalling brats.

Joyce tapped his hand sharply.

"They've saved a little out of the wreckage. Precious little, and we're all going 'broke.' "

Joyce had two reserved seats towards the front of the hall. Bertram saw that she wore a new hat for the occasion, a little blue thing, with an osprey plume (Bernard Hall would hate her for that!), and the short ermine cloak which Lady Ottery had given her for "going away," when they were married. She looked splendid in health again, and exquisite to his eyes as she stood up looking round the hall and smiling to many friends who waved hands to her, or programmes. The two Russian girls-the Countess Lydia and her sister-were a few seats behind, and called out over the heads of other ladies:

"So glad you could come, *chérie!* Your husband too! *Merveilleux!*"

That last sentence was a dig of spite from the Countess Lydia.

"How d'you do, Lady Joyce?" This very gallantly and formally from General Bellasis, who nodded affably to Joyce's husband, and said, "Going strong, Pollard?"

Kenneth Murless sauntered in (his arduous duties at the Foreign Office didn't prevent afternoon outings of this kind) looking elegant, as usual, in morning dress with a white slip beneath his waistcoat, and immaculate spats. Bertram hated him unendurably.

"Well, Joyce! Is Lady Ottery in good form? Not nervous, I hope?"

"Mother is never nervous," said Joyce. "It's not a family failing."

She held a kind of reception, standing there by her seat, and Bertram was aware of some extremely pretty girls, and many ugly old ladies. The old ladies interested him most. God, how ugly they were! Many of them wore black silk with beads. He thought such costumes had departed with Queen Victoria. Others were youthfully dressed in the latest style, with odd little hats and short capes like Joyce's, and low-necked bodices. They were fat and old and hard and wrinkled. He did not blame them for that-poor old darlings! —but only observed them. He knew some of them by sight. He'd had the honour of shaking hands with some of them-little old hands with many rings-at various receptions to which Joyce had dragged him. There were two Dowager Duchesses, like caricatures of themselves by Bolshevik artists. The Lord alone knew how many Countesses. The old Régime had rallied up.

The men were in a minority, but those present were full of quality-old gentlemen whom one sees in profile deep sunk in club chairs, white-haired, bald, with bags under their eyes, with side-whiskers, with hawk noses; and middle-aged men who, one day, would be the exact replicas of the old gentlemen, but now straight-backed, with close-cut hair, firm mouths, alert eyes.

Bertram recognised Lord Banthorp, Viscount Risborough, the Duke of Berkshire, old Brookwood of Banstead, Morton of Greystoke, and the new Earl of Winthorp. He also observed the entry of several Major-Generals and Brigadiers in "civvies," as Bill Huggett called his old pre-war clothes, and not so terrifying as when his machine-gun company had been reviewed by them before and after battle.

His mother-in-law had certainly drawn "a good house." It represented the aristocracy of England in its oldest and crustiest tradition, with only a thin sprinkling, he guessed, of the newer vintages. The old, ugly ladies had come out of their hiding-places in Mayfair to support England in "the hour of danger." There was something fine about them, in spite of ugliness, even because of it. He admitted that. He knew their spirit, indomitable, hard to themselves as to others, resolute in what they believed to be their duty. They were the grandmothers of modern girlhood in Joyce's crowd, those pretty, laughing, dashing-looking girls, and on the whole, perhaps, of stronger stuff. Well, perhaps not! Joyce and her crowd had come out well in the war, with some scandalous exceptions. His eyes wandered about, studying the faces in the hall with something like a new vision-Christy's angle of vision, Janet Welford's.

There were beautiful faces there, neither old nor young, of middle-aged women, rather sad, rather anxious, rather worn. They were the women who had suffered the strain of war most in their souls, with long patient agony. The mothers of fighting men, the wives of others. He could see in their eyes that they remembered things which he remembered, which others forget. Among them was the beautiful Lady Martock, in her widow's weeds.

The Duke of Bramshaw led Lady Ottery to her chair on the platform, and there was a clapping of hands, and a scuttling to places.

Joyce took her seat, and her face was eager and proud because of this public tribute to her mother. Her father, who had come in late, with Alban, sat next to her on her left hand. His face wore his usual vacant look, with slightly opened mouth.

"Your mother's marvellous!" he said to Joyce in a loud voice, which she "hushed" immediately, and after that rebuke, he settled himself deliberately to sleep. He had heard a good deal at home about the Religion of Revolution. It was not new to him, and he had acquired the habit of sleep in the House of Lords and during all speeches.

Alban, on his father's left, wonderfully good-looking, dressed almost as well as Kenneth Murless, kept awake, but appeared painfully bored. He too, was aware of his mother's theory. He avoided it as much as possible, while agreeing with its general thesis. Out of filial respect and devotion he had come to-day, at some personal sacrifice in the way of a game of real tennis at the Bath Club, which was a passion of his.

The Duke of Bramshaw opened with some general observations on the subject of Lady Ottery's lecture. He was a thin man, with a long, mournful face, a sharply curved nose, and a bald head. Caricaturists made him look like a diseased bird of prey. In the clubs he was generally known as "the greyhound," because he made a little hair go a long way.

In melancholy tones he referred to the honour he had in introducing the Countess of Ottery, who, indeed, needed no introduction to such an audience as he saw before him, well aware of her devoted work during the War, of her great virtue as a wife and mother, of her noble patriotism, and of her profound scholarship. They were to receive the benefit of her historical knowledge that afternoon.

He himself had been a student of history, as far as his duties in the House of Lords would permit, and other services which he had been called to do for his King and Country, but he confessed that he had been amazed by the revelations which Lady Ottery had discovered in relation to a continuous tradition of revolutionary doctrine, of a most subversive, destructive, and damnable kind-if they would permit him to use so strong a word-from the time of the Fourteenth Century to the present day.

Lady Ottery had made it quite clear to him, he felt sure that she would make it quite clear to the audience-that the revolutionary spirit which they found in the world around them, not only in Russia, but nearer home, in their very midst, he regretted to say, was due to the dreadful propaganda of a secret cult, mainly of German-Jewish origin, which had for its object the overthrow of civilisation, the downfall of Christian morality, no less than the destruction of all law and order. The members of that cult, the Initiated, as they called themselves, were but few, but they were powerful.

As Lady Ottery would tell them, they belonged to the tradition of Satan worship, that dark and evil blasphemy of the Middle Ages. It was an awful thought that men in England belonged to that secret brotherhood. They were working among the labouring classes of England. They were, he said so with a frankness which the gravity of the time demanded, endeavouring to promote at that very hour, a Strike which threatened to paralyse the life and industry of Great Britain. The Countess of Ottery was not, therefore, lecturing on an academic theory of history, unrelated to their present situation.

"In short, my Lords, ladies, and gentlemen, the lecture we are about to hear is a warning of the menace at our very doors. . . . Lady Ottery —"

With enormous melancholy he bowed to the applause of the ugly old ladies and the pretty young ones, and resigned his place on the platform to Bertram's Mother-in-law.

"For Heaven's sake!" said Bertram, aloud. Sheer rage was rising in his brain. What did all this mean? Did these people seriously believe all that dark and monstrous nonsense suggested by the Duke of Bramshaw? A sentence of Bill Huggett's came into his brain. He repeated it to himself, over and over again, as Lady Ottery began her lecture, and went on with it.

"There's no more sense in some of these so-called Toffs than in the long ears of a coster's moke."

And yet the Duke of Bramshaw was not a fool. He had been educated at Eton and Oxford. He had made many speeches in the House of Lords. He had held high office during the War. These people were not fools. They were highly educated. They helped to govern England. Good Heavens! They were, in their way, among the best types of English aristocracy. It was impossible for him to believe that such an audience could listen patiently to such a wild falsification of history and commonsense as that outlined by the Duke of Bramshaw, and elaborated by his mother-in-law.

Joyce had said, "Do behave, Bertram!" and he "behaved" while Lady Ottery read page after page of manuscript in a clear, hard, penetrating voice, perfectly self-possessed, strikingly handsome, utterly convinced of her own argument.

Bertram tried not to listen to her, but her words penetrated his brain.

With a kind of insane and dreadful logic she ranged through centuries of history, connecting the origin of all revolts, uprisings, passionate outbreaks of peasants-and peoples-from the Black Death to the French Revolution, from that to the Chartist Riots, from 1848 to the Liberation of Italy, from the Veto of the House of Lords to the Russian Revolution, and from Bolshevism in Russia to Trade Union strikes in England-to small groups of fanatical men and women, belonging, as the Duke had said, to a secret cult pledged to the overthrow of civilisation and religion.

She quoted old documents, newly discovered letters, ancient memoirs, journals, revolutionary pamphlets, political allegories and squibs, enormous tomes of German philosophers, French atheists, Italian free-thinkers, Russian anarchists. Her range of research, her immense industry, was wonderful, and she had hewn her pathway of argument with remarkable skill and clarity through a jungle of false evidence.

But she had entirely ignored the ordinary impulses of human nature-the savage instincts of men when they and their women folk are starving while others are fully fed, the passion of downtrodden peoples for the liberty of life, the long patience, breaking at last into impatience, of simple folk oppressed by corrupt and cruel tyrannies, the vision of a better human life in the minds of those who starve in garrets and languish over sweated labour, the righteous wrath of those who see their rulers growing rotten with luxury and vice, the divine rage at the heart of a people under the scourge of the knout, and the brutality of a secret police, the silent, ever-growing pressure of the Nobodies of the world for more joy in life, a wider margin of ease, a greater share of luck and opportunity, the claims of men who have done good service and expect a fair reward.

Bertram thought of all the men who had gone marching with him, and before him, and behind him, up the roads of war in France and Flanders, the men of England, Scotland, Ireland, Wales. They had seen the bodies of their "pals" blown to bits, but had not turned back. They had sat down with Death, smelt it, heard it scream above their heads, known the fear of it, seen the close horror of it, day after day, month after month, year after year, but had not surrendered some faith in them, some love of their soil, some heritage of the spirit. Were they now likely to be the victims of a "secret cult," urging them to overthrow civilisation? Were they in dark conspiracy, as the dupes of German Jews, to play Hell and Satan-worship in the country they had saved by the valour of their souls? They were restless, discontented, bitter. What wonder, when prices were rising high against them, and wages were going down, and unemployment was creeping up like a dark tide of misery into millions of little homes? This lecture of Lady Ottery's was an outrage to the men who had fought for England, though she had no idea of that. It was a perversion of all truth in history. It was putting morbid fears into the minds of an audience already obsessed by fantastic bogeys. It would lead to conflict and cruelty.

"Joyce, I can't bear it. This is mad and monstrous!"

So he whispered to Joyce, and she turned to him angrily, and said, "Be quiet, Bertram!"

Their movement, and Joyce's answer, awakened the Earl of Ottery. He smiled sleepily at Joyce, and said her mother was remarkable.

Presently Bertram rose in his seat, bent again to find his stick on the floor under some ladies' muffs, and whispered again to Joyce:

"Sorry, darling! I'm going. I can't breathe."

"You're abominable!" said Joyce, in a low voice, and turned her head away from him with an angry shake of her bobbed hair.

He strode through an audience that was hostile to his going. Old Brookwood of Banstead growled audibly as he passed, "Be quiet, sir!"

Outside, groups of chauffeurs were chatting beside their motor cars, and across Oxford Circus, as he passed through, came a procession of unemployed with their banners.

"We want work!"

XIX

Bertram was staking everything on his book, in spite of Christy's "hands-up" and cry of "Kamerad!"

It was going well, —amazingly well. He was astonished at the way in which words came to him. After the first agonies he had found himself writing easily, rapidly. It was as though he was just the instrument recording the dictation of some mind beyond himself. In reality, as he knew, he was drawing upon his memories, and emotions stirred up in his subconsciousness, repressed for a long time, and now liberated. He remembered things which, at the time he hadn't noticed much, or at all-smells, sounds, minute particular details of visual impressions. The pictures of war were as sharply etched in his mind's eye as when he stared for the first time across No Man's Land, or took his machine-gun up to Fricourt on the Somme and saw death busy on a day of great battle.

It was extraordinary how he could reach back to it all, from this little house in Holland Street, Kensington, within sound of the London 'busses passing up Church Street. When Joyce was out or in bed, and he was writing in his study, alone, late at night, the old life of war came back to him so vividly, with such intensity, that more than once when he lifted his head, he was startled to find himself, not in a dug-out, or leaning over the sand-bags of a trench parapet-he smelled chloride of lime! —but in his room, with Joyce's portrait over the mantelpiece, and peace outside the windows.

Here in the manuscript sheets before him, as far as he'd gone, he had told what war was like. The men who knew would say, "That's how it was!" He had paid the tribute of his soul to Tommy Atkins, who had not been given a fair deal. The book might do a bit of good. It would pass on the experience of those who knew the meaning of war to a generation which wouldn't know, unless some one told them. This was worth doing. Perhaps worth living to do. Had he been spared to live to do it? There might be something in that. He'd always wondered why he should go scot free-not a scratch all through the war, with other men dropping on every side of him. Anyhow, he would try to pay back for the grace of life-such as it was! —by this book.

It was the truth, in every line of it, in every word. He had found the gift of words. That was his buried talent, now revealed. That was what he'd been searching for, the meaning of that queer sensation of waiting for something to happen. This had happened! The gift of words-the greatest gift in the world, if a man pledged his soul to truth.

He hoped Joyce would like his book. It would be fine if she said, "Well done!" when he read it to her. She would be critical. She would hate some of the things he had written, brutal, some of them, but she would acknowledge the truth of it, the bigness of his achievement. For it was going to be big, with the spirit of the greatest war in the world, and of England's manhood.

He was telling it all, nothing left out, nothing shirked, in horror, courage, boredom, fear, filth, laughter, madness. Joyce had seen a bit of it in London hospitals. She wouldn't funk reading about it, and she would be generous in praise, if he had written it well, as she was generous to Kenneth Murless for his snappy sonnets. She would understand him better after reading it. She would be more patient with him. And she would see that he was going to keep his end up, and not sponge on her for everything.

With a bit of luck the book would make some money. That would make things easier in married life, and give him the independence which all men must have. It would make him less moody and humpy in his temper. Perhaps it would bring Joyce and him closer again, in the old relations of love and comradeship, which somehow had been interrupted.

It was with this thought in his mind that he gathered up a bundle of his manuscript and went up to Joyce's room. It was the morning after Lady Ottery's lecture, and Joyce was still in bed. She had a habit of lying late. Perhaps she would be inclined to let him read some of his stuff.

He was absurdly emotional, as all writers with their first creation. He'd been living with the book. He had staked his hopes on it. It was his mind-child.

Joyce was busy with the papers when he went in and said, "Good morning, darling!" She murmured a reply of some kind, and turned over another page of *The Morning Post*, which rustled loudly.

Bertram waited for a little while until she might finish the society news, or whatever it was that she was reading. She was sitting up in one of her Japanese silks with a ribbon tied round her hair, and a little frown on her forehead, like Marjorie Maude in "Peter Pan." He sat on the bed by her side and watched her eyes roving over the big printed sheet. She was reading nothing very important. Her attention was not fixed on any definite news.

"I've brought my book, as far as it's gone," said Bertram with preposterous nervousness. "Care to hear some, Joyce? I want your opinion."

Joyce didn't care to hear any of the book. She had something else in her mind. It was his hostile demonstration at her Mother's lecture.

"You behaved abominably yesterday afternoon," she said, ignoring the book altogether. "Even father accused you of bad form when you walked out like that."

"Oh, Lord!"

He confessed his contrition, said "Let's forget it, sweetheart!" and showed her the mass of manuscript he had written.

"I believe I've done the trick," he said, with excitement in his voice. "I'm certain it's the real thing. Spare me an hour before lunch and let me read a bit."

"It doesn't interest me in the very slightest degree," said Joyce. "Please go out of my room, and let me get up."

If she had struck him in the face with her clenched fist she couldn't have hurt him so much.

He didn't understand that he'd come at the worst possible time for a reading of his book, when Joyce was deeply mortified by his contempt of her mother's lecture, and more annoyed because of his casual regret and "let's forget it!" regarding an incident which seemed far from trivial to her. It was contempt for her, as well as for her mother.

Bertram's exasperated comments at the Wigmore Hall were another revelation of the wide gulf between her ideas and his. He was drawing further and further away from all the loyalties which she believed were the essential faith of an English gentleman, one of her class, one of those who stood for the things which belonged to her family and creed.

She had been irritated from the beginning by that book of his. It was ridiculous to think that Bertram could write! He had none of the brilliance of Kenneth Murless, and had shown himself plainly bored by the conversation of her friends on books and poetry. Even on that subject he had been hostile to their ideas, and had denounced the work of people like Stephen McKenna and W. L. George with contemptuous words as "unreal stuff."

That book he was writing had been a cause of secret irritation in her mind. He had preferred it to her company. He had deliberately isolated himself in its scrawled sheets, instead of joining her little parties, and making himself agreeable to her crowd. The book had been a barrier between them. It had made him careless of getting a decent job. It had caused him to brood over the beastly war while she wanted him to forget it. He was probing the old wounds again, deliberately intensifying his morbid outlook on life. She guessed it was filled with his bitter, democratic, anti-class views, which seemed to her like treachery to England.

And anyhow, he wanted to read it to her at the very hour when she was going to have her hair curled by the girl from Truelove's who was due at ten o'clock! Really Bertram was exasperating!

Perhaps that was what she had been thinking. Bertram worked it out in that way afterwards, some time afterwards, when he tried to analyse the reason for Joyce's unkindness. Because it was unkind-damnably. It took all the grit out of him in its immediate effect.

Knocked all the stuffing out of him, as he put it to himself when he went downstairs again, flung his manuscript on the desk, and said "Hell!"

He hadn't argued with her, just said, "Sorry I bothered you!" and then turned on his heel and went out of his wife's room. He passed the girl from Truelove's on the stairs, and thought bitterly that Joyce was more interested in her hair than in his book.

XX

It was not to Joyce that he read out his book when it was quite finished, but to Janet Rockingham Welford, author of "Mixed Marriages," "The Surplus Virgins," and other alarming works. With her usual desire for information, her habit of asking the most searching and intimate questions, she had gained his admission some time ago that he was no longer searching for a "job" because he had found his object in life-this book on the war, and the gift of words. He didn't call it a "gift" to her. He called it his new obsession, and was pleased with her excitement.

She was vastly excited. She vowed that she had seen "in the blink of an eyelid" that he had something to tell the world that the world should know.

"Don't be timid!" was her advice. She urged him to be brutal, to tell the truth in its starkness. She hated those little scribblers who still covered the filth of war with rose-water, concealing its stench. She wanted Bertram to be cruel to himself and to his readers, not to spare them a jot.

"Make their nerves jump," she said. "Take them by the scruff of the neck and thrust their noses into the horror, and say, 'Look at this! That's what it's like! And this is what it's going to be again, to your little snub-nosed boys, to your annoying but necessary husbands, to your best beloved, unless you're jolly careful.' "

Bertram said that was his idea. He'd been honest, anyhow. Not brutal for literary effect, but true to the things he'd seen.

Janet wasn't satisfied with that. She wanted him to be true to the things he'd felt as well as seen. She wanted him to remember his own agony in the worst hours, to get into his book all the agony of all the men, blinded, crippled, shell-shocked.

"Make it a masterpiece!" she implored. "Write it to revenge my blinded men."

Bertram told her she expected too much, and warned her that he was only a beginner at the writing game. He needed criticism.

"You'll get it, little one!" promised Janet Welford. "Read it out to me, and I'll make your flesh quail if you haven't been honest with yourself."

That was her invitation, and he accepted it with the sensitive, wistful, urgent desire of all beginners in the art of Literature not for criticism-which is terrible to suffer-but for encouragement, interest, understanding, praise.

Night after night he went round after dinner to Janet's flat in Overstrand Mansions, Battersea Park, one of a long line of tall blocks of dwellings mostly inhabited as Bertram found, by the poorer "Intellectuals," the "Surplus Virgins" (as Janet called her own class of unmarried women), and newly-wed couples on modest means, with room for one perambulator in the little "hall." Some novelist had once written a book about this street, called "Intellectual Mansions, S.W.," and the name had stuck.

She barred out all other visitors until the reading was finished, by the simple plan of putting an envelope under the door knocker with an inscription in her big, bold handwriting, "Out of Town." Several times as he read, Bertram heard footsteps faltering on the landing outside, and then going down the stone staircase again, dejectedly.

"Poor wretches!" he would say, and Janet would light another cigarette, or puff out a wreath of smoke, and say, "Absence makes the heart grow fonder! Get on with it!"

She was helpful to him. She didn't spare criticism. She made him "quail" all right! She found mistakes in grammar, split infinitives, frightful faults in style. She cried out at such times as though he'd touched her with a red-hot poker: "Oh, my little sensitive soul!" —"Oh, my æsthetic Aunt!" —"Oh, ignorant and nerve-shattering soldier-man!" Such absurdities of ejaculation warned him of dreadful blunders, which then she corrected like a stern "school-marm," so comical in her caricature that Bertram laughed while he quailed. A hundred times she stormed at him because he'd "shirked" the uttermost reality, turning away with cowardice from the obscenity of war's torture-chambers.

"Stronger!" she would say. "Stronger! That's weak. Let the Truth come right out and show its bloody face to those who still believe in the glory and splendour of war's adventure-the romantic women, crudest in all the world, the hundred per cent patriots who would engage in world war for a nice point of honour or to avenge a pin-prick!"

There were times when Bertram felt the cold chill of failure on him. This book, then, was no good! He had failed! He had fooled himself into the belief that it was the Real Thing.

But these moods did not overwhelm him, because of Janet's emotion, rage, laughter, tears, as he went on reading. She loved what he had written about the men. She knew them. She had nursed them. They had wept out of blind eyes in her arms. They had "groused" and cursed and laughed and joked and agonised, and revealed nakedly the secret of their souls to her. She knew, and Bertram had written what she knew.

After each reading he asked her anxiously for her opinion. Was it any good? Did it have the slightest chance? He wanted her to tell him frankly.

She teased him a little. She said: "I reserve judgment," or "I've read worse stuff," and then when he was tortured by doubt, she laughed in her full-throated way, and told him to be con-ceited because she wasted so much time upon him. Christy would be jealous of him, if he ever knew.

"Christy jealous?"

He looked at her searchingly, to see how much truth there might be in that, but he could not guess the meaning of the whimsical look in her eyes, nor of the sudden blush that flamed into her cheeks after those careless words of hers.

After the reading of the last chapter, he asked his usual question: What did she think? Any good? Or had he wasted his time, and his hopes?

She did not answer for a little while, and then suddenly took both his hands.

"It's good! . . . Not all the truth, but all true. . . . A good book, soldier man, and almost great! Thank God, you've written it!"

These words warmed his soul. He was enormously grateful for them. A wave of emotion swept over him because this praise, so simply spoken, so generously, by this girl who understood, was a reward for his labour.

He raised her hands to his lips, and kissed them.

"Whatever happens to the book," he said, "your sympathy and help have been tremendous to me. How can I pay back?"

She let her hands linger in his, not deliberately, but carelessly. She laughed at his suggestion of "paying back," and called him by the absurd nickname which she had invented for him.

"No fee, Sir Faithful! I'll be satisfied for service done when you abandon the Halfway House and come over to the Left Wing!"

"Not likely!" answered Bertram. "I walk in the middle of the road."

XXI

After that reading of the book, there wasn't the same excuse for Bertram to go to Janet's flat in Battersea. Not the same reason. Yet he went. The truth was, as he admitted, that he could not keep away because he craved for the laughter, the audacity of thought, and the free comradeship which he found with Janet and her friends, and not in his own house. Decidedly not in his own house in the week or two that followed Lady Ottery's lecture and Joyce's refusal to interest herself in his work.

Even Edith, the parlourmaid, showed by various little signs of sympathy meant in a kind spirit, but frightfully embarrassing, that she was aware of Joyce's unkindness.

"Aren't you going with her ladyship to-night, sir?" Or, "Seems a pity you don't like cards. Her ladyship is that fond of Bridge!"

Deliberately Joyce involved herself in a series of bridge parties which ignored Bertram's claim to companionship and included, every time, it seemed, Kenneth Murless or General Bellasis, generally in the rooms of the Countess Lydia in Whitehall Court. Now that his book was finished, and in Christy's hands for professional advice about the way to get it published, Bertram felt loneliness closing about him with a greater chill. Sometimes he thought Joyce was teasing his jealousy. She talked of Kenneth in terms of affectionate comradeship, and then glanced at Bertram to see whether she had piqued him. She confessed that she owed Kenneth a good deal of money for Bridge debts —"but of course he could wait." Kenneth had been in particularly good form that night. His stories about Lady Speelman's ball had made everybody laugh. She was going to the Opera with Kenneth and the Russian girls.

Bertram didn't disguise his feelings, but he restrained the expression of his temper. Something had happened in him worse than ill-temper. It was a coldness that was creeping into his heart, a sense of some complete and terrible misunderstanding between Joyce and himself, beyond all petty quarrels.

He had a dreadful apprehension that something in the very quality of his character was alien, offensive, and intolerable to the fastidious and delicate mind of his young wife. Perhaps he was of a coarser fibre than she was. He was afraid the war had brutalised him more than he was aware of. He had certainly "learnt to swear abominably in Flanders," like English soldiers of Smollett's time, and his nerves had been frayed so badly that he didn't always check his tongue in the presence of Joyce. But it was deeper than that, and worse than that. Joyce seemed to find him a vulgarian, a common fellow. There were times when her eyes seemed to say so. . . .

Janet Welford did not make him feel like that. She called him "Sir Faithful," and once "did homage to him," so she pretended, in her jolly way, as "a very parfit gentil knight." By that name she introduced him to her friends, those queer, free-spoken, amazingly audacious girls who seemed to be the advance guard of Social revolution in England, and played intellectual games of skittles with the old traditions of English life.

He sat dumb among them at times because of their wild talk. They were pretty Bolshevists, who frightened him with their revolutionary ideals. The Russian experiment had not been revealed yet in all its ghastly failure, and they spoke lightly of Lenin as "the Master-mind," and had a sentimental affection for Trotsky as "the new Napoleon," and refused to believe a word of the atrocity stories manufactured, so they said, by propagandists of the White Armies at Riga and Helsingfors.

Bertram wondered what would happen to his exalted Mother-in-law, if she were suddenly to be transported from Holme Ottery to that flat in Battersea Park, and heard such discourse. He wondered what would happen to himself, if she saw him there, surrounded by these pretty witches. Not pretty all of them! Janet's best friend, Katherine Wild, was a snub-nosed woman, with short hair cut like a man's, but with courage and comedy in her grey eyes. She and Janet made the pace in conversation, egged each other on to new extravagances, made one great jest of life.

It was but verbal flippancy. Bertram remembered Janet's devotion to the blinded soldiers of St. Dunstan's. From Janet he knew that Katherine Wild devoted all her life to the starving children of the devastated countries in Europe, as the organiser of relief. She had been working in the soup kitchens of Vienna, and knew, as few others, the agony of Austria. It was the knowledge of life's tragedy that made her seize at any of life's jokes, and make a religion of laughter. Her great hope was to get into Russia and to extend the work of relief to that country, which was still blockaded by the rest of Europe because of the menace and fear of Bolshevism.

"I shan't have seen the depths of human misery," she said once, "until I've crossed the frontier into Russia."

"Do you want to see the depths?" asked Bertram.

"The uttermost depths. Until then my knowledge of life won't be complete. You must go there too, Mr. Pollard!"

"Why?" asked Bertram.

She told him that Janet had spoken to her about his book on the war. The last chapter couldn't be written until he'd been to Russia. There was the aftermath of Armageddon. After War, Famine, and after Famine, Pestilence. The Four Horsemen of the Apocalypse had ridden through Russia, and the noise of their hoofs could be heard in Western Europe, coming closer, closer. In Russia Europe might read the writing on the wall.

"It's the key to the riddle of the New World," she said. "By what happens in Russia, and the world's reaction thereto, we shall know our fate."

Strange how he could never escape from talk about Russia! In Joyce's crowd he had listened constantly to tales of Red Army atrocities, the sufferings of the old régime. In this crowd he listened to denunciations of White Army cruelties, and the sufferings of Russian peasants.

Once he lost his temper, and flared out into violent speech which might have forfeited him the friendship of Janet Welford, if she had not been enormously broad-minded, with an all-embracing sense of humour.

With her women friends he could be patient, whatever they said, for they had a sincerity of idealism which was proved honestly by service in some human way, with sick children, or suffering men, as nurses, guardians of the poor, workers in University settlements, guides to blinded soldiers. But some of Janet's men friends seemed to him poisonous.

They were members, mostly, of that club, "The Left Wing," into which she had desired, vainly, to beguile him. But he saw the types in her rooms, and didn't like the look of them. They were egoists, conceited with their own superior "idealism," *poseurs* of rebel philosophy, amateur Jacobins, without passion or sincerity.

Two of them were young men who had escaped service in the war by going to prison as Pacifists. No doubt that needed greater moral courage in a way than surrendering to the general tide of emotion and faith by getting into khaki. Theoretically he admitted the right, even the nobility of men who for conscience' sake, religious belief or spiritual abhorrence of war-like the Quakers-dared public contumely by refusing services at such a time. It was contrary to his own convictions, for though he hated war, and knew its insanity, he believed that when once a people had become involved, they must stand in defence of their own country and of their own homes. Still, he understood the reasoning of men morally and utterly convinced of the Christian command, "Thou shalt not kill."

But these young men who came to Janet's flat had been Pacifists when their country was threatened, and now were revolutionists, talking very glibly of Lenin's right to destroy the enemies of Russian liberty, and of the glorious prospect of a world revolution for the overthrow of the Capitalist system.

It was a young man named Lucas Melvin who aroused Bertram's rage. Talking in the affected accent of Christchurch, at its worst, and playing with a silk handkerchief which he had drawn from his shirt cuff, he proclaimed his belief that Labour was about to overthrow the Government by "direct action."

"This coming strike," he said, "will lead to a general paralysis of industry. All the Trade Unions will unite for general action. I anticipate the pleasure of seeing a number of Profiteers and *bourgeois* hanging on the lamp-posts in Whitehall. *Vive la Révolution Anglaise!*"

This speech was received with laughter and applause, and the company was surprised when Bertram rose slowly from his low chair by the fireside, and stood with his back to the mantel-piece, glowering at Lucas Melvin, as though preparing to knock him down.

"I can't pass that!" he said.

"Pass what, dear sir?" asked Melvin.

"That damned, insincere, and dangerous nonsense of yours."

Melvin protested that he didn't like those coarse words. He also objected to Bertram's method of argument. It was neither elegant nor polite.

"It's not so coarse as revolution," said Bertram, bitterly. "It's more polite than a revolutionary mob would be, if they caught you with a silk handkerchief up your sleeve. Don't you realise that if you and other young fools who play about with the revolutionary idea were ever to find yourselves in that state of things, your necks would be wrung first by a mob that's not out for elegance? They'd just wipe you out like midges. Don't you understand that if England were to go in for revolution, all Europe would be dragged down with her, and war would be child's play to that anarchy and horror?"

"I see you belong to the reactionary set," said Melvin, with an air of bravado, but his voice was not quite steady. "Doubtless you uphold the principles of *The Morning Post*."

"I try to see things with commonsense," said Bertram, "not like a child, ignorant of realities. I've seen war. I don't want to see revolution. I imagine it's worse."

It was Janet who poured oil on the troubled waters.

"Sir Faithful," she said, "verily you speak the words of truth and wisdom. This child has been well rated. But of your mercy, remember that this is a bower of fair ladies, and not a tilting-ground for angry knights."

"Sorry!" he said, and his rage died down. Lucas Melvin retired hurt, and soon the others went, leaving him last, and alone with Janet.

"I behaved like a 'muddied oaf,' " he said. "Do you forgive me?"

She forgave him so well that she sat on the floor by his side with her hands clasping her knees, talking about the queer complexities of life, the muddle in human nature, the mixed motives of men and women. Presently she told him that he had better go home. It was unfair to his wife to stay so late.

"Joyce won't be back yet," he said, "and I hate going home to a lonely house."

She looked up into his face searchingly.

"I'm afraid your married life is not all it should be. Whose fault?"

"Mine," he said.

She told him that if he weren't so beastly timid, she would get down to the secret of the trouble.

"I'd like to help," she said.

"You're helping," he told her, and then something seemed to warn him that this was not playing the game by Joyce, and that he was losing hold of the loyalties to which his soul was pledged. Janet was helping him too much. In a little while he might not be able to live without her help, her sympathy, her understanding, her comradeship. A sudden movement he made, drawing back from her a little, surprised her.

"What's the matter, Faithful?"

"I'd better go. After all, it's getting late."

But it was only ten o'clock, and not too late for a visit from Christy. The maid had let him into the hall, and they hadn't heard him enter, and were not aware of him until he came into the room.

"Hullo!" he said. "Where's all the party?"

"Faithful broke it up, with violence."

Janet rose from her seat on the floor by Bertram's side and held her hand out to Christy like a Princess. He kissed it with warmth, and said, "The Ugly Beast pays homage to Divine Beauty."

"The handsome Megatherium to the beautiful Pterodactyl!" said Janet.

They were acting in the usual way, but Bertram was aware of some state of tension in the room. Christy was not quite at his ease, nor Janet quite natural.

"Going so soon?" asked Christy, as Bertram went towards the door.

"I've been trying to go for half an hour."

"Then stay not on the order of your going, but go!"

Christy laughed at the old quotation spoken by Janet, but Bertram saw a queer look in his eyes, of shyness or distress. Was old Christy jealous of him, because of his comradeship with Janet?

Ridiculous!

XXII

Christy's criticism of Bertram's book was not devastating. He suggested merely the elimination of certain passages which seemed to him libellous against a certain General, and said simply, "You can't afford a law suit," when Bertram protested violently that he intended to libel the old scoundrel, but hadn't been half strong enough in his character study of a blood-thirsty Junker, ruthless of men's lives. His praise was limited to a few words, but magnificent to a man who knew him as Bertram did.

"You can write. You know the right words."

That was good enough from Christy, hard critic, and honest as death. He asked Bertram to let him send the book to Heatherdew, the literary agent, and his friend. He would find a publisher, if any man could, and take a personal interest in it, as a hater of war.

Bertram wanted to know how many weeks he would have to wait before the book appeared, and what payment he was likely to get, an impatience which amused Christy, who had more experience.

"It can't be out till the autumn, at earliest."

"Not till the autumn! Good Heavens!"

"It's not accepted yet, old man. Hang on to patience."

He conveyed a suggestion to Bertram from Bernard Hall of *The New World*. Why not write an article, dealing generally with the threatened strike? Hall suggested a title: "The Mind of the Men," on the lines of Bertram's talk about the Comrades of the Great War and their point of view. What Bill Huggett had told him, and so on. It would be a valuable contribution, with knowledge at first hand, not easy to get.

"I'll have a shot," said Bertram. "Do you think the strike is likely?"

"Inevitable, I'm told. Nat Verney knows."

For some time Christy discussed the possibilities of trouble. The Government seemed to be asking for it. It was true about calling out the Army Reserves. They also proposed to recruit the Middle Classes for self-defence. That would divide England into the Haves and the Have-nots. A short-sighted policy at such a time, when all such clear-cut distinctions ought to be avoided. Big Business, with the Government in league with it, was out to smash organised Labour. The plan was to defeat it in sections, first the miners, then the railway men, then the engineers, then the other great trades. It was to be a general campaign to bring down wages to pre-war rates. A sound policy, if prices came down to the same level, but there was about as much chance of that as of friendship between France and Germany!

"Low wages and sweated labour! That's the watch-word now. No 'Homes for Heroes,' and other fine cries which went very well in war-time."

Bertram thought it was unfair to the men.

"It's a damned outrage!" said Christy.

For some time the two friends were silent. They knew each other well enough for long silences. Christy's cheap clock on the mantelpiece ticked with a little staccato tattoo. They did not trouble to switch on the light, but sat smoking in low chairs on each side of the fire-grate in which a few coals burned in a heap of white ash. Christy drew hard at his pipe now and then, and a little red glow lit up his long, lean face with its deep sunken eyes and bulging forehead. Down below, in Adelphi Terrace, or its neighbourhood, some ex-soldier was playing a one-string fiddle, not badly, but with long-drawn melancholy. Cavalleria Rusticana-they all played that. Down the Thames, beyond the Tower Bridge, no doubt, a steamer was sounding its siren. The Batavia boat, off to Holland, or a river tug moving. The murmur of London, the voice of its enormous life and traffic, made the windows throb, and above its low-toned rhythm, the horns of motor-taxis bleated incessantly.

Christy stirred, and poked the dying fire with his boot.

"I'd like to see how this strike works out. I want to be in England if there's any real trouble. But I'm off again."

"Already!"

Bertram was distressed. He hung on to Christy's comradeship. Here, in these rooms, was a sanctuary into which he could take refuge from the worries of life, or at least could ease them, by unloading his pack awhile, and sorting it out with old Christy. It was not so much Christy's words which helped him, but his presence. They'd been together in dirty places during the war. They had sat in the same mud-holes, listening to shells overhead, and expecting death together. They knew each other's courage and fears. Christy had wept once, when his *moral* had broken for a while. He had just cried like a child when the sergeant was blown to bits, not because of any love for the sergeant, but because of the beastliness and unending misery of it all. Bertram had been on the verge of shell-shock once. He was afraid of being afraid. Supposing he let down the men, played the coward, or something? Christy had strengthened him then. They knew each other-in weakness as well as in strength. He hated to think of Christy going away again so soon.

"Where now?" he asked.

"Berlin for a start. Then-perhaps Moscow. I've asked for permits."

"Moscow!"

Christy grinned, and confessed it sounded like asking for the tiger's cage to be opened. But he wanted to get into Russia, and *The New World* had asked him to go. It was impossible to find out the truth of what was happening there. Everything one read was a manufactured lie. He wanted to know the truth. He would be restless until he found out. Was there anything at all to be said for the Russian experiment-Communism? It was no good talking about Bolshevik atrocities. They weren't Communism. He wasn't sure of them, anyhow, but if they'd happened, they belonged to the realm of that murder mania which overtakes people in times of war and revolution. He wanted to see how the system worked, whether it was any solution of Capitalist civilisation. It was absurd to pretend that Western civilisation was the last word in human wisdom and scientific organisation. The profiteer was in himself a denial of that! Perhaps, with all their blunderings and cruelties, Lenin and his crowd had caught hold of some sound idea. Perhaps it was the beginning of a new era in social history. He wanted to see for himself, to know. He had no preconceived ideas. He was out for the truth, whatever it might be.

"I'm afraid you'll go Bolshevik!" said Bertram. "If you do, our friendship ends."

He spoke the last words lightly, but not without sincerity and fear.

"I'll let you know," said Christy. "A post card will do. 'I've gone Bolshy.'"

He laughed at the thought of the postcard travelling from Moscow with its awful message to the outer world. Probably the censor would seize it. It would be burnt at the end of a pair of tongs, lest it should spread sedition. Bertram's world would never know. At some future date he might hear of his former friend leading a Red Army against Poland, or sitting with a long white beard, like Karl Marx, in the Kremlin, ruling Russia.

It was some minutes later when Bertram asked a question sharply:

"Have you told Janet Welford?"

Christy poked the fire, and put it out, with great deliberation.

"No."

"Christy, old man," said Bertram presently, "is there anything between you and Janet —I mean in the way of love and that sort of thing?"

Christy laughed, and rose to look at himself in the glass, and laughed again.

"With this ugly mug? Does the Neanderthal Man indulge in amorous dalliance with beautiful women of the Georgian era? What a horrible thought!"

"She loves you this side idolatry," said Bertram.

Christy suddenly flamed out in anger, and it was the first time Bertram had ever seen him lose control.

"Damn you, Pollard! Why can't you leave that subject alone? What right have you to talk of Janet at all? She used to come here often before you spent all your evenings in her rooms."

Bertram was astounded and overwhelmed by this sudden outburst. So Christy *was* jealous of him! Christy-of all men in the world! —whom he would no more hurt than cut off his own right hand!

He went over to him, and grabbed his shoulder.

"Why, you silly old ass! Do you think I wanted to barge in between you and Janet? What about Joyce, and my loyalty to her?"

Christy's gust of rage died down as quickly as it had risen, and he was pale and ashamed.

"Sorry, Pollard! Fact is, you touched the wrong nerve. I love that girl Janet like an infatuated Romeo. She sets my frog's blood on fire. That's one reason I'm off to Moscow. Running away!"

"Why run?" asked Bertram. "Why not tell her?"

Christy gave another whimsical look at his face in the mirror over the mantelpiece.

"Not in that mug, laddie! Besides-now we're talking —I've got a wife, too, don't you see, although I don't live with her? And anyhow, this damned old world of ours don't lend itself to love-making just now. It's falling into ruin, and I'm busy watching it. The human equation doesn't seem to matter, and the ghosts of dead boys, who were robbed of life before their time, mock at my senile passion. I ought to know better at my time of life. I'll be forty-five in Moscow!"

He made only one other reference to the subject. It was when Bertram left his rooms that night.

"Referring back," he said, "I might say a parting word, laddie. If you're not cut out for disloyalty-and it needs a special temperament-cut and run when loyalty's over-strained. It's the safest way. . . . And Moscow is an interesting place."

They gripped hands and wished each other luck. Luck to the book. Luck to the adventure.

"Dashed funny thing-life," said Christy, leaning over the staircase as Bertram went down.

"It's all very difficult!"

They both laughed. They had spoken the same words a thousand times in France.

All very difficult! Yes. Bertram, going home, wondered whether Janet Welford had more than a whimsical affection for Christy. How old Christy had fired up! He never suspected him of passion-and at forty-five! Time for the fires to burn out. . . . He also wondered whether Joyce understood the meaning of love. Something would have to be done to make her understand, or his life, and hers, would be utterly spoilt.

XXIII

Bertram had just read his first newspaper article, entitled "The Mind of the Men" —Bernard Hall's title-in that week's issue of *The New World*, when he heard his name called from the next room by Joyce. There was a note of emotion in the sound of that call, and he went to her quickly, wondering if she had hurt herself.

She was standing by the side of her writing desk, holding an illustrated paper —*Country Life* —with a look of amazement and alarm.

"What's the matter, Joyce?"

She pointed to a photograph, and said, "It can't be true!" He saw at a glance that it was a view of Holme Ottery from the west wing, with its stone, ivy-covered terraces, and broad flight of steps leading down to the tennis lawn and rose-garden. It was just there, coming up from the tennis court, that he had heard of Rudy's death, when Ottery had handed the telegram to his wife, fingering his red beard and staring across the grounds with watery eyes. There was the Venus with her broken nose, and the copy of the Goose Boy of Pompeii.

"Holme Ottery," said Bertram. "Why not?"

It was always being photographed for the magazines.

Joyce pointed to some words above the picture, and said, "Can't you see?"

The words were —"Historic House for Sale."

Holme Ottery for sale? No, impossible! It had been in the Bellairs family for four hundred years or more. It was a part of English history. Its beauty, its tradition, its ghosts, its very soil, belonged to the spirit of the family that had played some part, not insignificant, in the making of England-as soldiers, courtiers, statesmen. It was Alban Bellairs, Earl of Ottery, who had been one of Elizabeth's favourites before he died with Essex on the scaffold. Rupert Bellairs, fifth Earl, had been an exile in Holland with Charles II., and afterwards Master of the Horse at Whitehall. Joyce Bellairs, the great-great-grandmother of this Joyce, was the famous beauty to whom Steele wrote some of his sonnets. Holme Ottery was in the history books. It meant all that and more to this girl, his wife. Every fibre of her body belonged to that heritage. The tradition of her house was the corner-stone of her own spirit. In pride and faith she was a Bellairs of Ottery, this girl whom he —a young officer "without a bean" —had married when War had broken down for a time the strongest thing in English life, which was caste.

"Some mistake —" he said.

Joyce was weeping passionately. He had never seen her weep before, and it hurt him poignantly. He put his arms about her, trying to say words of comfort, but she shook herself away from him, and paced up and down the room like an angry boy. It was anger which dried her tears.

"Father's done this without saying a word to me! Even Mother hasn't written! It's treachery to the whole family. I won't allow it."

Bertram was silent. He remembered what his father-in-law had said to him outside the House of Lords-something about Holme Ottery bleeding him to death.

"Do you think Alban knows?" he asked.

As the eldest son, Bellairs must have been consulted, must have given his consent to sell.

"Alban is weak as water! Father may have talked him over. I'll go down this very day, and let 'em know what *I* have to say on the subject!"

Later she rang the bell, and told Edith to pack her bag.

"I'll come with you," said Bertram.

Joyce didn't seem to think there was any need for him to come.

"It's a family affair," she said, coldly.

A family affair? Oh, yes, he was outside the family. Merely the insignificant husband of a Bellairs. His voice would have no weight in the family councils. He was just a damned outsider, tolerated as an unfortunate *mésalliance* —Joyce's mistake. Perhaps Joyce guessed a little at those thoughts of his, as he stood silent, with flushed face, raging inwardly at the humiliation which her words made him feel.

"I didn't want to drag you into a family row," she said. "But you'd better come, after all."

It was in his mind to say that he would be damned if he went, that he had no intention of being patronised by the supercilious Alban, his detestable brother-in-law, or bullied by Lady Ottery, his exalted Mother-in-law. But the sight of Joyce's tear-stained face restrained him. The news that Holme Ottery was up for sale was a blow at her heart, as he could see by her unusual pallor. He would be a cad to quarrel with her now, and thrust his own personality forward in the family tragedy.

When she went upstairs, he turned over the pages of *Country Life*. Holme Ottery was not the only house for sale, as well he knew. Page after page was filled with the usual announcements of "Noble Estates," "Fine Old Country Mansions," "Historic Residences." Some of them belonged to people he knew, as he had seen many times before.

He remembered other words spoken by Lord Ottery. "Our day is done," he'd said. "The War and its costs have finished us."

These advertisements were only one more proof of the change that was happening in England, where the Old Order was gassing, giving place to-what?

It was no new revelation to him. He'd seen the boards up outside many old houses. Some of his own friends had abandoned their old places and come to live in the Albany, Belgravia, Knightsbridge, the Kensingtons, and other districts not immensely far from Mayfair, but outside its former sanctuary, now delivered over to the New Rich. They were not distressingly poor. They were carrying on rather well! But they'd lost the family roof-trees, the quiet parklands, something of their state in England. Profiteers, American millionaires, Jews, were taking over some of the old houses, though many remained unsold. . . . This news about Holme Ottery for sale brought sharply home to Bertram that silent, social, bloodless revolution which was happening in England. Well, it didn't matter very much to him. It mattered very much to Joyce.

She was silent going down in the train to Sussex, and seemed to have a chill. He wrapped his overcoat about her in the corner of the first-class carriage where she sat smoking cigarettes through a long amber tube. She wore her country clothes of rough tweed, and looked, he thought, "patrician" to her polished finger-tips. But amazingly young, and child-like, in a white Tam-o'-shanter, with a gleam of gold where her bobbed hair curled above her neck. He would have liked to kiss her neck, so delicate and white, so inviting, as she bent her head over the morning paper. He sat close to her for a while, and put his arm about her waist, which she suffered impatiently, until she asked him to give her elbow room and not to get into one of his "soppy moods."

That sent him to the other side of the carriage, moodily, and he sat staring out of the train at the passing meadows, all silver and gold and green, on this day of Eastertide. The sunlight of an April sky chased across the thatched roofs of little old cottages, touched their tall twisted chimneys, gleamed on church spires, chased the shadows in feathery woods. Little old England! So snug, and ancient, and sheltered, and peaceful. He'd only learnt to love England properly when he was out of it, fighting for it, —with only a thin chance of getting back to it. Ireland was his father's country, his own birthplace. England was his mother's land, and it was England, not Ireland to which his soul gave allegiance.

Lying in the earth of France, he had thought back to England, yearned for it. Not only and always for London, its mighty heart, which he'd loved, but for the smell of fields like this, for the sight again-once again-of an old village like one of those, with a square church tower, and walled gardens, and orchards white, as now, with blossom. He had tried to get something of that into his book-the inarticulate, half-conscious love of England which had come to country boys, Cockneys, young louts in khaki, so that some instinct in them, some strain of blood, some heritage of spirit, had steeled them to stand fast in the dirty ditches of death, whatever their fear.

Perhaps in a few days the safety of England would be threatened again by social conflict. As the train crawled slowly through Robertsbridge, he saw the newspaper placards, "Strike Certain. Notices Issued." Bad, that. Perhaps the railways might close down. They'd have to motor back from Holme Ottery. Christy had just got away in time. He wondered if his article on "The Mind of the Men" would attract any kind of notice. It might do some good. He'd been fair to the men, tried to make people understand their point of view, their reasonable claim for a living wage.

Joyce spoke for the first time from her corner.

"I'm going to give father hell. He ought to have consulted me."

Bertram suggested that perhaps his father-in-law had wanted to save her from the worry of it, while she was unwell.

"Nonsense!" she said, impatiently. "It was just cowardice. He hadn't the pluck to tell me."

Probably Joyce was right. So Bertram thought when they met Lord Ottery, beyond the lodge gates, strolling towards them, with a little white dog at his heels. He'd come to meet his daughter in answer to a telegram she had sent from Victoria station.

"Well, Joyce!" he said, holding out his hairy cheek for her to kiss. "Glad to see you looking so strong again."

He was obviously ill at ease. He pretended not to be aware that Joyce had failed to kiss him, and that her answer of "Well, father!" to his "Well, Joyce," was decidedly hostile and challenging.

"Your Mother's not very bobbish this morning," he said. "Sick headache, or something of the sort."

"I'm not surprised," answered Joyce, with a little sarcastic laugh which plainly suggested that Lord Ottery was the cause of her mother's ill-health. She walked with a long, swinging stride up the avenue of elms which led towards the old house, so that her father lagged a little behind her.

He remarked that the crops were coming along well, in spite of the dry weather. He also expressed annoyance because the villagers had been breaking down some of the fences on the south side of the park.

"The spirit of Bolshevism," he said. "All those young fellows back from the war are socialists and lawbreakers. I can't understand it. They weren't like that after the South African War."

Joyce continued walking in silence. Bertram, stealing a glance at her, saw that there was a bright spot of colour on each cheek-danger signals. It was when she reached the lawns outside the house, and saw its old grey walls and mullion windows close to the terrace, and the sloping banks with their clipped hedges, that she turned on her father and revealed her anger and her anguish.

"Father! I can't believe it's true! You couldn't bring yourself to do it!"

"Do what, my dear?"

Lord Ottery put on his vacant look, and opened his mouth a little, like a stupid rustic.

"Put the house up for sale!"

"Oh, the house! Oh, Lord! Who told you that? *Have* they put it up for sale? I've seen nothing about it in the Press."

Joyce clutched her father's arm, and shook him a little.

"Father! Tell me the truth. You're not going to sell Holme Ottery?"

"Sell it, my dear? Who would buy it? It's most unlikely that any one in the world would buy it. It costs a fearful lot of money to keep up. Look at it now-going to rack and ruin. A white elephant, Joyce. What with income tax, land tax, death duties, price of labour —"

"Have you put it up for sale?"

Joyce stamped her foot, and her blue eyes looked piercingly into her father's grey ones. His were less courageous. He looked sheepishly at Bertram, of whose presence he had previously taken no notice at all.

"My dear Joyce," he said, "I wish you wouldn't be so imperious! I'm an old man now. I'm getting devilish hard-pressed in my old age, and I have the right to a little domestic peace."

"Father, have you put it up for sale?"

He hesitated, shifted a little from one foot to the other, and poked up a stone in the path with his thick cudgel.

"Well, my dear, I suggested to those damn fellows, Huxted and Wells, that they might get an offer some time."

It was the confession that Holme Ottery had been put up for sale. Joyce accepted it as such.

"It's a treachery!" she cried; "a treachery to Alban and all of us. We won't allow it. We ought to starve rather than let the house go. All our history is there. It's what we mean and are. Without that we're nothing."

"It will be a great sacrifice, my dear," said the tenth Earl of Ottery. He, too, looked up at the old house which his forefathers had built, in which they had lived and died and played their part in English history. There was a little mist before his eyes.

"A great sacrifice!" he said in a broken way.

"I'll talk to Mother about this!" said Joyce, savagely.

Lord Ottery smiled at her, and patted her hand.

"Yes, go and talk it out with your Mother. She's in her room reading *The Times*."

Joyce ran up the terrace steps, without waiting for Bertram, and the two men watched her slim, boyish figure disappear through the doorway of the west turret.

"Women like talking," said Ottery. "It doesn't alter things, though. Talking never did."

He thrust his fingers through his red beard, and then put his hand through Bertram's arm, leaning on him a little heavily. It was the first time he had ever done so, and Bertram thought it was a sign of weakness.

"No amount of talk will bring back England to its old state," said Lord Ottery, gravely. "Only hard work and good will, and honest government, and wise leadership, can help towards that. The war has robbed us of our old prosperity. We're going to be poor. We must steel ourselves to poverty."

He whistled to his little white dog.

"Hi, Clincher!"

Then he asked Bertram whether he was an authority on the Black Death. He found that subject wonderfully interesting. It threw a great deal of light on the wage-system in the Middle Ages.

XXIV

Joyce spent the rest of the morning in her Mother's room, and Bertram was left to amuse himself alone. It was not very amusing. He was aware of a sense of isolation, not for the first time, in this distinguished household. Lord Ottery, after some minutes of almost intimate conversation, and that episode of holding on to Bertram's arm, became absent-minded, and then, as though dismissing a footman, gave Bertram to understand that he wished to be left alone in the library, while he pursued his studies on The Black Death.

Bertram strolled round the stables, where most of the stalls were empty, though Ottery still kept a few hacks, and Alban had his hunter, "Lightning."

He passed a few words with the grooms, and found himself reminiscing on the war. One of them had been with "his lordship," meaning Alban, Viscount Bellairs, in the Grenadier Guards, and had been hit on the same day of July '16 in the attack on Morval and Lesbœufs. Afterwards, for the second time, at Fontaine Notre Dame, below Bourlon Wood, in November of '17. Remembered the great Tank attack in November '20? Lord, yes! Major Pollard was there with his machine guns? Fancy that! . . . Well, it seemed a long time ago, and like a dream.

"Care to go through it all again?" asked Bertram.

The two men laughed, appreciating some hidden joke, not to be put into words.

Something was said about the strike.

"Them Labour chaps ought to be mowed down by machine guns," said one of the men. "Dirty tykes!"

He was amazed when Bertram said he thought they had some justice on their side. It struck him "all of a heap." They were all bloody Bolsheviks, begging his pardon.

Bertram himself was astonished at this point of view of men who had fought in the War and were of the same class as those in the world of "labour" they denounced. As he sauntered away, after a few light remarks, he supposed they were survivals of English feudalism. Their outlook was limited to the horizon of this old house. They belonged to the Family. They were for the maintenance of the Old Order which paid their wages, gave them perquisites, belonged to their tradition of service. The War hadn't changed their mentality much. Strange!

He strolled round to the lake, and found Alban sitting on the end of the punt, smoking a cigarette and reading the *Sporting Times*, with his back to the wind. He was in an old heather-green jacket and grey, moss-stained trousers, with a cap at the back of his head, and looked better like that, to Bertram's yes, than in his town clothes, with white spats and all.

"Good morning!" said Bertram, with more geniality than he quite felt, not having much affection for his brother-in-law.

Alban glanced over the top of the *Sporting Times*, and allowed himself to show a faint surprise.

"Hullo! Come down with Joyce?"

Assured on this point, he became absorbed again in his pink paper.

Bertram waited a little while for the condescension of another remark. Not obtaining that favour, he strolled away again, cursing inwardly at the incivility of his brother-in-law.

"A damned cad!" he said to himself. "An insufferable snob!"

And yet, as he had to admit to his sense of fairness, there was no reason why Alban should have engaged in chatty conversation. He himself resented fellows who were always "yapping." Alban wanted to read the *Sporting Times*. There was heaps of room in the park for Bertram.

"It's the Irish strain in me," thought Bertram. "I'm always suspecting uncivil treatment when none is meant. It's the 'persecution' mania. I'll have to check it."

Yet, in spite of all these arguments, his moodiness was increased at the luncheon table because of the almost complete ignoring of his presence by Joyce and her family. Not a word was said about the sale of the house-servants being present-and there was some general gossip, mostly by Alban and Lady Ottery, of a social and political kind. The Prime Minister had gone to Chequers Court for Easter, with his usual gang. The War Office had drawn up a complete programme in case the strike led to any rioting. General Bellasis was organising a Home Defence Corps. All ex-officers would be asked to join.

"Doesn't it seem unnecessary?" asked Bertram.

Alban looked at him coldly, as he might have stared at a junior subaltern of the Guards Mess, after an impertinent remark.

"Extremely necessary," he answered.

Lord Ottery put in a remark.

"Bellasis is coming down for the week-end, he tells me. We shall hear all about it."

Bertram glanced at Joyce, and wondered whether she had suggested this visit. He detested Bellasis. Joyce seemed to be aware of his look, for she flushed, ever so slightly, though she did not meet his eyes. She had been crying again, he thought. Most unusual for Joyce. He felt very sorry for her. Sitting there at the old dining-table, under the portrait of Rupert Bellairs, fifth Earl, by Lely, it was impossible to believe that Holme Ottery was up for sale.

How like Joyce was to that fellow! He hadn't noticed it before. Although Charles II's favourite had a plump pink face, softened by long ringlets, he had the same kind of eyes and nose as Joyce's, with the same glint of steel in the eyes. She sat next to her Mother, crumbling her bread and looking thoroughly "vexed." He had seen her in such moods of late, at his own breakfast table, when she came down to breakfast.

Lady Ottery had given Bertram a wintery smile, and permitted him to kiss her cheek. He felt as though he had kissed one of the marble pillars in St. Paul's Cathedral.

"A sharp frost last night," she said, and as this statement didn't call for much of an answer, she seemed to forget his presence, and engaged Alban in an argument on the subject of Mrs. Asquith's Memoirs, newly published, of which she disapproved strongly.

"An outrage!" was her opinion, and she also believed they would be used as propaganda by radicals who desired to destroy society, and delighted in all such revelations of corruption in high places.

"It seems to me an extremely witty, harmless, and entertaining book, Mother," said Alban. "My only regret is that it contains such little scandal. Think of all the things she might have written!"

"If we must have scandals, let us keep them to ourselves, my dear," said Lady Ottery, firmly. "In my young days we hushed up anything that might prejudice our position in the public mind."

"Most dishonest!" said Alban lightly.

"What do you think, Ottery?" asked Bertram's mother-in-law.

"Entirely as you do, my dear," said Lord Ottery, somewhat vaguely, having been thinking, perhaps, of The Black Death.

Bertram expressed an opinion upon Mrs. Asquith's portraits of "The Souls." He thought it would be quoted centuries hence as a picture of English life in the 'eighties. His opinion did not seem to impress his wife's family or Joyce. There was no reply to his remark, and Alban switched off the conversation to the character of his new terrier —a cunning little devil with a hell of a lot of pluck.

"Doing anything special this afternoon, Joyce?" asked Bertram, towards the end of this meal which had been a silent one for him.

"I'm talking business with Alban," said Joyce, in a most determined voice, as though announcing an ultimatum to Alban himself.

He took it as such, and groaned a little.

"Certainly, old girl, much as I hate such palavers."

Talking business with Alban. Not for Bertram to intervene. He had no right to "barge in" upon such discussions, though Joyce happened to be his wife. Well, he might do a slope down into the village, and buy an afternoon paper, or perhaps tramp over the Common, and watch the village boys starting the season's cricket. Holme Ottery was not very sociable to-day to an outsider like himself.

That was what he did, and he recovered his sense of humour a little as he watched the game of cricket between the youngsters of Ottery. He even laughed aloud at the argumentative interruptions of the game, with wild and angry shouts of "How's that?" "That ain't fair!" . . . "Who's umpire?" . . . "Umpire be blowed!" Youth didn't change, in spite of social upheavals, the passing of the Old Order, houses to let, falling Empires, ruin in Europe, threatened strikes, any damn thing. Boyhood survived, with its laughter, its quarrels, its passionate excitement, its game of life. Survived, in spite of war's massacre! Many of those kids must have lost fathers and brothers. The shadow of the War had been over their childhood. They'd seen women weeping at the news of death. But it had not spoilt the spirit of youth. They'd forgotten the shadow. Bertram wondered if any of them would live to see another Great War, would live to die, as fathers and brothers had died, in the same old battlefields, blown to bits, sliced by flying steel, gassed, plugged with machine-gun bullets. Not if he could do anything to save them. Not if his book had any luck.

How wonderful was the fruit blossom this year! The little orchards round the Common were snowed under with white and pink petals. The April wind was laden with scent of apple-blossom, cherry-blossom, pear-blossom, and drenched with the stronger perfume of lilac, splendid in the cottage gardens. It stole into his senses like an opiate. Why worry? This beauty of England endured through the centuries, through civil strife, foreign wars, all kind of trouble, soon forgotten. Spring had come again, with its English loveliness, calling to his heart, putting its spell upon the senses. Romance and love should go hand in hand in little old villages like this. So they had gone hand in hand, a year ago, when he and Joyce had wandered through Ottery village, not caring because the village folk smiled to see their love, glad of their friendly, smiling glances. A year ago! They didn't go hand in hand just now. Something had come between them, some coldness. Perhaps with the coming back of spring again, their love would come back. He would woo Joyce again, as a humble lover, as a passionate but patient lover. This very night he would sue for her kisses, as once she had kissed him with sweet lips. He would entice her down to the little wood beyond the lake where one night they'd stood listening to a nightingale, with their arms about each other, like children, like Adam and Eve, like any man and any woman in the spring-time of life, with pulses thrilling to the tune of love, freshly heard.

Sentiment! Romantic stuff! Well, why not?

XXV

He stood outside a quaint kind of shop on the edge of Ottery Common, and wondered if he could get an evening newspaper with late news from London.

It was an old thatched cottage converted into a shop by the simple plan of using the front garden as a show place for antique furniture, brass warming pans, old china on old tables, wooden toys —"made by Blinded Soldiers" —queer odds and ends from attics and lumber rooms —a violin without a bridge, silver spurs, a spinning wheel, a portrait of the Prince Consort by Winterhalter, an oak cradle.

In one of the cottage windows, with its little panes of knobby green glass, was the notice, "Tobacco, Eggs, and Ferrets." In another window were the words, "London Papers; Lending Library; Home-made Jams." A useful kind of shop! Anyhow, here was a chance of getting an evening paper.

Other people thought so too. A pretty girl, whom Bertram dimly remembered as one of Joyce's friends-the Vicar's daughter, perhaps, —rode up on a bicycle, left it against the garden wall, and stepping over the oak cradle, cried out in a merry voice:

"Papers in yet, Mr. Izzard?"

A voice from the cottage answered as cheerily:

"Not a damn one, Miss Heathcote!"

"Well, I'll wait. I want the latest news about the strike. Is there going to be Civil War, do you think?"

The girl-it *was* the Vicar's daughter, as Bertram remembered-asked the question as lightly as she might have enquired about the chance of a shower. As lightly it was answered through the open doorway of the cottage.

"Not as far as I'm concerned. Having been a little hero once, I've turned Pacifist. No more naughty strife for me! Live and let live is my philosophy."

"No good hedging like that!" said Miss Heathcote, who was sitting on an iron-bound chest, turning over some old engravings. " 'He who is not with me is against me.' Our wicked Bolshevists will demand allegiance or hang you up to one of your own oak beams."

"Oh, I'll sacrifice to the false gods!" said the voice inside. "No martyr stuff for me. Thrice was I wounded in Flanders. . . . Peace! Peace!"

"Caitiff!" cried Miss Heathcote.

Bertram went into the shop, and said "Hullo, Izzard! What on earth are you doing here?"

He'd remembered in a flash-that name and that voice. Major Arthur Izzard, D.S.O., and a double bar to his M.C., the most reckless fellow he had ever met in a front line trench, and one of the most comical. They'd spent some merry and memorable evenings in old Amiens, down from the line, between one "show" and another. Izzard had been a great lad for the eggnogs in Charlie's Bar, and proclaimed his passion for Marguérite in the restaurant of "La Cathédrale." Now he seemed to be proprietor, serving-man, and shop-boy in this village storehouse.

When Bertram hailed him, he was sitting on the counter with his legs dangling, arranging some eggs in a basket. Deliberately he let one of the eggs fall and smash, as a sign of his astonishment and delight at seeing Bertram.

"Great Scott! My old college chum!" (This had no foundation in fact.) "My trusty comrade-in-arms! My fellow-consumer of cocktails behind the lines of Armageddon!"

He gripped Bertram's hand, and pump-handled vigorously, and called in the Vicar's daughter to be introduced to another "little hero."

"What's the game with this shop?" asked Bertram.

Captain Arthur Izzard, D.S.O., said it was no game, but the real business. Like thousands of other officers of the Great War, he had worn out many boots, seeking a job in London. Vainly. England was surfeited with home-coming heroes. She'd nothing to offer them, after they'd won the dear old war. She wanted to forget them. They were a damned nuisance. So in a moment of brilliant inspiration, he had set up this business for himself. It amused him vastly.

It also provided him with something to eat. It also enabled him to do good to his fellow beings, by spreading spiritual and intellectual light. He was the centre of village culture. Mothers came to him for advice upon the feeding of babies, maidens desired information on the comparative merits of Ethel M. Dell and Zane Grey. Farmers consulted him on insecticides. Miss Heathcote discussed with him auto-suggestion and the Freudian theory. He bought old furniture from Sussex cottages and sold it, at outrageous profits, to the New Rich, and occasionally Americans. He was a beneficent influence in Sussex, and all the ladies loved him.

"Some of the foolish ones," said Miss Heathcote, laughing and blushing in a way that suggested affectionate familiarity with this good-looking fellow and his whimsical ways.

"What about social caste?" asked Bertram, and his question amused young Izzard vastly.

"Caste? The damn thing has broken up like a jig-saw puzzle! Not even the Countess of Ottery, poor old darling-your mother-in-law, by the way! —can keep it going nowadays, when Younger Sons are drifting into trade. Why, Billy Wantage-Lord William of that ilk-is keeping a pub at Wadcombe, and doing very well."

The conversation was interrupted by a red-haired boy who rode up on a bicycle with a bag slung round his shoulders, which he dumped into the cottage.

"You infernal young scoundrel!" said Arthur Izzard, "I believe you've been watching the cricket-match."

"Train late," said the boy, grinning.

Izzard seized the papers, and disregarding his customers, read the news for himself.

"Hell!" he murmured to the company, which had increased by two ladies, and an old gentleman of Mid-Victorian aspect, with white whiskers.

"What's the latest?" asked Miss Heathcote.

"Strike officially begun. Two million men 'out' already. The Triple Alliance will probably join."

"What will that mean?" asked Bertram.

Arthur Izzard gave him a queer look.

"It may mean something like social revolution in little old England. No trains, no supplies, no industry anywhere. General paralysis until something smashes."

"Abominable!" said the old gentleman with white whiskers. "We must smash the Trade Unions. They're the curse of the country. I'd flog every man who comes out on strike."

"Five million, maybe," said Arthur Izzard, and he winked at Bertram, as though with secret understanding. He said something else, under his breath.

"The Comrades of the Great War."

"I'd turn the machine-guns on to them," said Miss Heathcote. It was the opinion of Lord Ottery's groom.

Arthur Izzard smiled at her as he sat on the counter and swung his legs.

"I wonder if that would be wise-or kind-or safe?"

He waved his hand, as Bertram left the shop.

"Come in again, old man! I've excellent tobacco, new-laid eggs, home-made jam, young ferrets, old instruments, any old thing! And a private room for pals!"

"I certainly will!" said Bertram.

He walked back to Holme Ottery, thinking a little about the Strike, but, strangely enough, not very much. He was thinking more about Joyce. Something had stirred his senses, this breath of spring, this countryside, this scent of lilac and apple-blossom and wet earth. The memory of his love-making, here, a year ago, recalled to his mind and heart the joy of it, and his boyish ardour. London had put his nerves on edge, and made him impatient, irritable, moody. Perhaps Joyce had suffered too, in the same way, from the artificial life, the depressing and lowering atmosphere of London after war. It was better here. They might put themselves straight again, recapture their former gladness in each other, thrill again to the touch of each other's hands, and lips, to the warmth of body and soul. He would talk to Joyce and woo her here back again.

Holme Ottery was wonderful in the dusk of this April day, with a silver streak, through a pile of dark clouds, above its many gables and high chimneys, and shadows closing about its grey walls. Through some of the windows in the west wing, lights were gleaming, in a homely way. Joyce was in one of those rooms, with her gold-spun hair, and slim body, and all the beauty of the Bellairs women-like that Joyce whom Steele had loved-and all their pride and quality.

A pity the old house was up for sale, but Joyce's beauty belonged to him.

XXVI

It was impossible to get a private word with Joyce before dinner. Her "palaver" with Alban was still in progress when Bertram returned, as he found when he went searching for her in the morning-room, her bedroom, at the end of the gallery, and at last in Alban's little room on the other side of the great stairway.

Alban called "Come!" sharply in answer to his tap at the door, and did not look friendly when Bertram went in, smiled at Joyce, and said, "Any chair for a mere husband?"

Joyce's face was flushed. She and Alban were seated at the table, which was strewn with papers. The brother and sister were wonderfully alike, Bertram thought, as they sat together, side by side. Joyce had the same profile as Alban, though softened and more delicate, the same line of forehead and nose, finely cut, like a Greek cameo. She took no notice of Bertram's entry, but went on talking to her brother.

"Then it comes to this: You insist on bleeding father to the extent of four thousand a year, and Holme Ottery must go to some horrible Profiteer!"

"That's the position, apart from the word 'bleeding,' " answered Alban irritably. "You can see for yourself. The Governor is paying taxes out of capital, borrowing for upkeep, wages, and interest on mortgages, and breaking into capital again for my little bit, and yours. When he pegs out, death duties will swallow most of what's left."

"It's disgraceful!" said Joyce. "It's a damned disgrace!"

She rose from the table, flinging back the papers, and went over to the window, staring out into the dusk of the park.

Alban laughed, and drummed on the table with his finger-nails.

"It all comes of having a democratic government, pandering to the working-classes, bribing them with doles, and ruining trade and capital by excessive taxes."

"Somebody must pay for the war," said Bertram.

Alban became aware of his presence again, and answered him gloomily.

"Not in that way. The Germans ought to pay."

It was Bertram's turn to laugh.

"Even Germany can't pay for the ruin of the whole world, after her own losses."

Joyce swung round from the window seat.

"For Heaven's sake, Bertram! Don't go pro-German, after being pro-Irish, pro-Bolshevik, and anti-everything that's English and patriotic!"

"Quite so!" said Alban, associating himself with his sister's protest in a somewhat pompous manner.

Bertram felt a sudden warmth in his blood creeping up the back of his neck. He was not annoyed with Joyce, because he could understand her sense of tragedy about the old house. He was not angry with her, though her words hurt him hideously, after his thoughts about her beauty and the chance of re-capturing her love. But he had no use for that "Quite so!" of his brother-in-law.

"I fancy I did my job pretty well in the war," he said quietly. "If England ever needs me again . . ."

He checked himself. What was the good of arguing? Joyce and Alban were both on edge because of this family crisis. Anyhow, he would be an idiot to proclaim his love for England. It might be taken for granted after his service.

"Oh, bother all that!" cried Joyce.

She dismissed the need of argument on that score by another attack on her brother.

"I'm not going to let this business end in mere talk, Alban! If there's any chance of saving Holme Ottery —"

Alban's temper mastered him for a moment, and he interrupted his sister harshly.

"Haven't I told you there's no earthly chance? What's the good of playing about with unrealities? Facts are facts. Figures are figures."

"Yes, and your four thousand belong to the facts and the figures," answered Joyce, just as angrily. "If you gave up gambling and racing, you could put some back into the family pot."

Alban stared at his sister with that hard look which sometimes came into his eyes, as Bertram knew. But he answered icily, after a moment's hesitation:

"Don't let's have an altercation, or get down to personalities. Four thousand is not too much for my position. I'm extremely economical. I might remind you that father settled two thousand a year on yourself. What about that?"

Joyce spoke in a low voice.

"I'd cut every penny of it to save Holme Ottery."

Alban leaned back in his chair, regarding his finger-nails, and laughed more amiably.

"Heroic, and all that, but utterly useless, little sister. Besides, what about your own home? Bertram isn't making a fortune just now."

"He'll have to get a job," said Joyce.

So the attack had come round to Bertram now. He was to be made responsible, perhaps, for the necessity of selling Holme Ottery! Perhaps, after further conversation, he might be accused of instigating the Strike, and would be saddled with the sins of the Government!

"I don't think I'll get dragged into this family discussion," he said, with a desperate effort to be patient and calm. "Anyhow, it's time to dress for dinner. Coming, Joyce?"

"Presently," said Joyce. He didn't wait for her, and went up to his own room on the north side of the gallery, and having shut the door with a bang, sat down on the bed with his knees hunched up and his face in his hands.

"He'll have to get a job' " Joyce had said.

Well, he'd found his job, and written his first book, now in the publisher's hands, and his first article, already published, in *The New World*. Not much, but a good beginning. He objected to Joyce's way of speaking that sentence —"He'll have to get a job!" She had spoken it harshly. Did she imagine that he hadn't tried to get a job, that he had been a slacker, an I-won't-work? He had gone the round of all his friends, answered advertisements-even gone to a Labour Exchange! —in the hope of finding some decent kind of work. He had agonised because of his idleness, until he had sat down to write a book and found himself writing it.

Not one of her precious Family had offered to help him. Ottery had just stared vaguely at him when he had asked for his influence. Alban wouldn't walk a yard to get him anything. Not all the crowd in Joyce's set had put anything in his way, though some of them pulled the social wires. He must have a straight talk with Joyce before the day was out. He must put himself right with her and bring her back to him. Impossible that things should go on in this way-this frightful, soul-destroying way.

So he brooded, and was late for dinner, and received the rebuke of Lady Ottery's frigid glance.

XXVII

There were several people from the neighbourhood to dinner, and Bertram was amused to find himself next to Miss Heathcote, the Vicar's daughter, whom he had met in Izzard's oddity shop.

They talked a little about that, and the girl seemed nervous of owning friendship at this table with a man who kept a shop.

"Lady Ottery doesn't approve of such new-fashioned ways," she whispered, glancing with amusement, and a little fear, at the handsome lady at the head of the table.

Bertram was less amused to see General Bellasis sitting next to Lady Ottery, and Kenneth Murless on the other side of Joyce. They had both come down for Easter as old friends of the Bellairs family. The conversation at their end of the table seemed to be about the Strike. General Bellasis, handsome and florid as ever, was doing most of the talking. Bertram heard only bits of sentences, disconnected threads of his discourse.

"Serious challenge to Government authority. . . . War against Law and Order. . . . We must knock the stuffing out of Labour! . . . Rank Bolshevism!"

The Heathcote girl on his left was prattling about a play she had seen in London-one of Galsworthy's. Jolly good! Very daring, though. Her father was shocked when she told him the plot. Parents were so easily shocked these days. They didn't realise the difference war had made to the outlook of women. Everything was discussed. The realities of life and death. Marriage.

Bertram endeavoured to play up to her remarks, but his glance kept wandering back to Joyce.

She wore an evening frock of white silk, as simple as a child's, with a necklace of pearls, and in this old dining-room, with its panelled walls and timbered roof and high-backed chairs, looked in her rightful place. She belonged to the house. The house belonged to her, not in timber and stone, but in spiritual heritage. She was Joyce Bellairs of Holme Ottery. The son of an Irish lawyer had no right to her. She belonged to a different stock. She'd been bred by centuries of "selection." Bertram was but a clodhopper to this child of Caste. So he thought, gloomily.

Kenneth Murless was more of her kind. He too belonged to a Family-the Murlesses of Warwick, with a genealogical tree intertwined with branches of the Bellairs, Charringtons, D'Abernons, Courthopes, Grevilles-all the proud old stock. He kept Joyce amused at this dinner table, as he always amused her, with absurd fantasies, word-play, anecdotes, satirical verse, social caricatures, all charmingly told, lightly, with ease, in a way unaffectedly, though he had conceit.

Bertram observed him closely. Never by a single word had Murless been uncivil, in the slightest degree discourteous, in his relations with Bertram, though he must have been aware of jealousy. Once or twice he went out of his way at this dinner to smile at Bertram, though he was too far down the long table to bring him into his conversation. Once he raised his wine glass in friendly salute. Bertram answered it, with a sudden sense of compunction for his habitual sulkiness with Kenneth Murless. He was a gentleman, and more genial than Alban Bellairs.

Lady Ottery rose from her high-backed chair, with her usual dignity. Dinner, even at home, was to her something of a ritual.

"Don't talk too long, Ottery," she said to her husband. "Some of us would like a game of bridge."

Lord Ottery hated to be hurried over dinner, and said so. Besides, Bellasis was talking about his plans.

"I want to hear them," said Joyce. "I'll join you later, Mother."

She lit a cigarette, and sat on the arm of one of the oak chairs, and took a sip out of Kenneth's wine glass.

General Bellasis shifted his chair round, so that he faced the little group left at table-Lord Ottery, Alban, Kenneth, Bertram, and Joyce. He had told them most of what the Government had in mind. There was no doubt the Strike was a threat to the whole authority of Parliament, to the social order of England. The men's leaders were fairly sound, he thought, moderate in their ideas, on the whole. But behind them was a real revolutionary agitation. Underneath, undoubtedly, a lot of dirty work was going on by paid agents with foreign gold. Bolshevists, pure and simple.

"Say rather, impure and artful!" said Kenneth Murless.

General Bellasis laughed, and waved his cigar at the interruption.

His point was that the time had come when Labour had given them the chance for a straight fight. They had challenged "Us."

"Meaning the Government?" asked Alban.

"Meaning the Decent Crowd," said the General. "Anybody with a stake in the country, including the unfortunate Middle Classes. All of us. Well, we accept the challenge. We're ready to knock hell out of them."

Lord Ottery expressed his view. He did not believe in arranging a clash. He always avoided clashes, if possible. The history of England, he thought, was in the main the successful avoidance of the real issues. That was our genius.

"I agree," said Bellasis, in a tone which showed clearly his disagreement. "But this clash has got to come. It's inevitable. We must get the working classes back to their kennels. Back to cheap labour. Back to discipline. Otherwise we're done."

"What's your plan?" asked Alban.

"Yes, that's the point," said Ottery. "Has the Government thought out a plan? I doubt it. They never think out any plan."

"This is all taped out," said General Bellasis. "The War Office has been working it out."

Lord Ottery mumbled something to the effect that this didn't inspire him with confidence. General Bellasis laughed again, rather irritably.

"Oh, of course the War Office gets a lot of kicks. But some of us aren't such fools as we look."

"Nobody would accuse you of looking a fool, Bellasis," remarked Ottery in a kindly way, and he stared vaguely at Kenneth Murless because that young man laughed loudly at the remark, and even Joyce gave a little squeal of protest.

It seemed, after other conversational interruptions, that the War Office plan, in the event of a General Strike was to recruit a Defence Corps, divided into various districts of England. Ex-officers and men would be invited to join for a three months' service. They would take over the transport system, work the railways, organise lorry columns, ensure the vital supplies of material life, meat, milk, bread, and so on, and defeat the purpose of the strikers, which was to strangle national industry and activity. If there were any attempts at violence, intimidation, picketing, the Defence Corps would be ordered to do their duty, relentlessly.

"Fire on the mob?" asked Lord Ottery.

"Fire on any ruffian, or body of ruffians, endeavouring to hold up national life."

"Naturally," said Alban.

"I hope there'll be a lot of shooting," said Joyce, heatedly. "A good opportunity to get rid of our Bolshevists."

Bertram stiffened uneasily in his chair, and thought of making a protest, but decided to keep his thoughts to himself. He hated Joyce to speak like that. He was thinking of Huggett, and his "Comrades of the Great War" in the slums of London and other great cities, so many of them out-of-work, despairing, rather bitter, but not Bolshevists. This new Defence Corps might not be quick at distinguishing between honest men and ruffians. Some chance shot, any hooligan fool, might lead to bloodshed of a terrible kind. This plan was to divide the nation into two classes. It might come perilously near to civil war. He agreed with old Ottery. Better avoid the clash. Better not to ask for it. He wished Joyce had not spoken those words.

General Bellasis had swung further round in his chair, and now faced Bertram with a friendly smile.

"Joyce tells me you want a job, Pollard? If that's so, I can put something in your way. How would it suit you to help me run this show, as Deputy Director for the South Coast?"

Bertram felt a sudden chill down his spine. He was conscious that all eyes were turned upon him, Joyce's, Alban's, Kenneth's, Lord Ottery's. He was aware that they expected him to look "pleased," eager to accept this offer.

"Bertram-how splendid!" said Joyce. "A chance at last!"

"What exactly does the 'show' mean?" asked Bertram.

He endeavoured to show polite interest, but his voice was hostile, in spite of his effort.

General Bellasis explained that it would mean a recruiting campaign, then a certain amount of drill, to "lick the men into shape" —and then the business of defensive patrols.

"Military police work?"

General Bellasis said "Exactly!" and added his opinion that it was a splendid opportunity for Bertram. It would bring him under the eye of the Government-very useful-make him a public character of some importance, and lead undoubtedly to a good place later on in some Government department. As Director of Home Defence, he could appoint any man he liked for the post, and he had the greatest pleasure in offering it to Bertram.

The offer was handsomely made, in the General's best style of good fellow and gallant soldier. It was received with a chorus of congratulations from Joyce, Alban, and Kenneth, with an expression of approval from Lord Ottery.

"It'll suit Bertram down to the ground," said Joyce. "He knows how to handle men, I will say that for him!"

She was a little excited, and slipped off the arm of her oak chair, standing with her hands clasping its high back, and looking at Bertram.

"Good for you, Bertram!" said Kenneth Murless. "I'm glad for Joyce's sake as well as yours. I can think of no better stepping stone to a sure place."

Alban concurred.

"An admirable post. Service to the country. Good pay, not bad fun."

Lord Ottery agreed. He thought it "Very handsome of the General."

Joyce was watching her husband. She could read his face better than the others. She saw how first he flushed and then paled a little, while a tuck gathered his forehead into a frown. He was thinking hard, and not certain of his answer.

"Exceedingly kind of you, General," he said, slowly. "Many thanks. But somehow, I don't like the job."

There was silence for a moment or two in the big dining room where many generations of Bellairs had sat at table, discussing events of history, more unfortunate than this, quarrelling, laughing, feasting, drinking.

"You don't like the job?"

General Bellasis smiled, not good-humouredly.

"What's wrong with it?" asked Alban, icily.

"Tell us!" said Kenneth Murless, raising his eyebrows in a quizzical way.

Joyce spoke more emotionally.

"Bertram! Pull yourself together. If you don't accept this —"

The last words seemed to hold a threat.

Bertram thrust his hands into the pockets of his dinner jacket, and leaned forward in his chair, staring at the carpet.

"It's like this —" he said, groping for the right words; "I don't like to see people of our class-your class, if you like! —organising their forces to beat down poor devils who want to keep up a decent standard of life, after a war they helped to win. I've looked into the question of this Strike. It's really a Lock-out by the masters-but, anyhow, the men are being offered wages which aren't quite good enough, they think. Not a fair deal for men who helped to save England. They may be wrong, of course, but that's how it seems to them. This Defence Force-it sounds all right. I'm ready to serve on the side of law and order. But it looks like a Snob Force for giving Hell to working-men who want a living wage. Aristocracy versus Democracy. Middle Classes against the Mob. Yes! If necessary, I quite agree. But I fought with the Mob. I saw it going over the top on mornings of battle. I walked through its dead bodies afterwards. I learnt to know its spirit, and liked it, on the whole. I'd hate to shoot down fellows who used to salute me in the trenches, and whom I saluted as the salt of England. Of course order must be kept. I understand that. No body of men must be allowed to blackmail a nation, and there may be a bit of that in the minds of the Labour leaders. But there seems to be an idea-General Bellasis hinted at something of the sort-that a little blood-letting wouldn't be a bad thing. Some idea of forcing the clash, so as to teach Labour a lesson, with machine-guns, and so on. I know something about machine-guns. I served 'em in the Great War. I'm not inclined to turn them against my own men-unless Hell breaks loose. . . . And I don't think Hell is going to happen. It's a newspaper scare, and nothing else. It's not going to happen, unless it's made to happen. I'll see myself damned before I help to make it. . . . Do you see my point, General?"

They had let him speak out, without a single interruption, in dead silence. He had been aware of their faces about him. Joyce had become quite white. She was still standing with her hands on the back of the tall chair, and her eyes were fixed on Bertram with a look of amazement, at first, and then anger. Once or twice she smiled, in a queer way, as though some of his words seemed to her too ridiculous. Alban sat with his head bent, glowering. Kenneth Murless was watching him, with a look of extreme interest, as though at some new phenomenon of human nature. Lord Ottery sat back in his chair with closed eyes, fingering his red beard. The General had become restless, crossed and recrossed his legs, shifted a wine glass, flushed angrily, and then met Bertram's eyes with a hard, hostile look.

"I regret my offer has been refused with such a distasteful —I may say, disgraceful-expression of opinion, sir."

That was his answer to Bertram's argument, and he spoke it harshly, in a court-martial manner.

Joyce moved away from her chair, and stood by the great fireplace. Bertram knew by a glint in her eyes that she was deeply emotional at that moment, but she spoke to the General quietly, with a smile.

"It's not refused. Bertram permits himself a certain amount of hot air. Why not? But he accepts."

"Is that so?" asked the General, looking first at Joyce and then at Bertram, with perplexity. "That's so, isn't it, Bertram?"

Bertram's eyes met Joyce's. He saw in them a kind of entreaty, and behind that a kind of command.

"I'm afraid not," he said. "I hate the idea of it."

Joyce moved away from the fireplace. She still spoke quietly, but there was a new thrill in her voice.

"I apologise for my husband, General! But if Bertram doesn't accept, I shan't think much of his loyalty to me-or to England. Meanwhile, I'd better join Mother, who's probably fuming at my absence."

She left the room with her head held high, and a little smile about her lips, but Bertram, who knew the play of light and shadow in her face, saw that she was passionately distressed with him.

There was silence for a moment after her going, until it was broken by Alban Bellairs.

"I think you're a damned fool, Bertram. Have you gone Bolshie or something?"

"I've explained my views," said Bertram, coldly; "I don't expect you to understand them."

Kenneth Murless thought a little tact might help, and spoke in his agreeable voice.

"I see his point of view. It's extremely interesting as a study in sentiment. I don't agree, of course, being a hopeless Reactionary, thank goodness, undisturbed by any liberal or revolutionary thought."

Lord Ottery was about to utter a judicial opinion, but decided that it was hardly worth while after dinner, —and dozed a little with his red beard on his shirt front.

General Bellasis cut short all further discussion, in his hard, matter-of-fact way when dealing with men. He had another manner in the presence of women he liked.

"For your wife's sake, Pollard, I make the offer again, for 'yes,' or 'no,' without argument. Which is it?"

Bertram did not answer for a second or so, but in that time he reviewed his life with Joyce, and saw with tragic certainty that this was the crisis. Acceptance meant surrender of his ideals, such as they were, and definite allegiance to opinions and acts which would put him for ever on the side opposed to liberal thought.

He was to decide between Joyce's "crowd" and the labouring classes of England, or at least between the philosophy of men like Bellasis, summed up in the phrase, "Give 'em Hell!" and that of Christy who believed in human brotherhood. This job, offered by Bellasis, would kill the friendship of men like Christy, Lawless, Bernard Hall. They would put him with the Junker class, and turn their backs on him.

Not that that would matter, if he did the right thing. But this was the wrong thing. It would be a surrender to stupidity. It would be the sale of his intelligence for the sake of position, and peace with Joyce —a sin against the Light. Peace with Joyce? Joyce's love and favour? It would be worth while to surrender a good deal for that-everything in the world, but a man's honour to himself.

These people, Bellasis, and Alban, and Kenneth Murless, and all their kind, extremists in reaction, were asking him to betray his sympathy with the men who had been his comrades in the lousy trenches. To go right over to the Bellasis side-one day to give an order to shoot, perhaps-would be to break faith with Bill Huggett and all poor devils like him.

He saw Huggett now as a Type, the Cockney soldier back to civil life, back to his slums, trying to keep his "kids," uncertain of work from one week to another, begging "bobs" from passers-by when there was no work. It was to bring such men to heel that the Bellasis band were organising their forces, recruiting University boys, and unemployed officers-the way to conflict! What had old Christy said? "Loyalty to lies is disloyalty to truth."

So in that second or two, these thoughts rushed into Bertram's head, and he made his decision.

"No, General. Thanks very much."

General Bellasis rose from his chair, and flung the end of his cigar into the fire.

"Let's join the ladies," he said sternly, as though dismissing a battalion on parade.

Lord Ottery awakened from his dose.

"Yes, a game of bridge, eh?"

Kenneth Murless opened the door, and waited until the General and Ottery had left the room, and then Alban looking black-tempered. For a moment Kenneth lingered, glancing at Bertram, who was standing by the chimney-piece, staring into the redness of the log-fire.

"Speaking as an Egoist," he remarked in a genial way, "I'm distressed by your violation of self-interest, Bertram, but uplifted by your idealistic faith."

"Much obliged for your favourable opinion!" said Bertram, kicking a burning log.

Murless smiled, and followed the others to the drawing-room.

Alone in the great dining-room of Holme Ottery-up for sale-Bertram used his old catch-word.

"It's all very difficult!"

His face was lit by the warm glow of the fire as he stirred the embers with his boot, and there was a look of pain in his eyes when he raised his head and glanced at the portrait of Joyce Bellairs whom Steele had loved. He spoke her name, but it was of his wife he was thinking.

"My poor Joyce!" he said.

XXVIII

When Bertram went to the drawing-room, he found a foursome at bridge in progress-Lord and Lady Ottery, Joyce, General Bellasis. Kenneth was making himself agreeable to Miss Heathcote and presently suggested a game of "pills," so that they left the room together.

Nothing doing for Bertram, who felt that he was frozen out. Joyce deliberately avoided his glance, or, at least, never looked his way, though he tried to entice her eyes by wandering around, shifting a little porcelain figure on the mantelpiece, and rattling a few coppers in one of his pockets.

He wanted her to look at him. He had a foolish idea that he might send her a message with his eyes, asking for her understanding, and for her comradeship. But she seemed to be absorbed in her game, and was gay in altercation with her partner, General Bellasis. Bertram's endeavour to establish communication with her was answered only by Lady Ottery.

"Don't fidget, Bertram! My partner is sufficiently trying."

Her partner was her husband, Ottery, who resented this slight upon his ability at bridge by a mild protest of "That's unfair, my dear!"

The situation was ludicrous as far as Bertram was concerned. He knew that for him this was a night of crisis. He had made the great refusal, for what he believed to be conscience' sake. He wanted passionately to talk it over with his wife. Some long emotional strain had reached its breaking point to-night in his relation to Joyce. His heart must speak to hers now, urgently. This polite, distant, unnatural way between them must be broken by plain talking, by the rough reality of human nature. He couldn't wait any longer for that. They must have it out, once for all, and now. . . . But meanwhile Joyce played bridge with Bellasis, and without looking at him.

He would make her look.

While Bellasis was writing down the last results of play, Bertram went to their table and bent over Joyce with his hand on her shoulder. She gave a little shrug, which he knew meant to say, "Take your hand away," but he kept it there, heavily, and spoke to her.

"I want to speak to you, Joyce, presently. After your game."

"Hasn't there been enough talk?" she asked, impatiently.

"No," he said, "there's got to be more. I've something important to say."

Lady Ottery tapped his hand with a card case.

"My dear Bertram. Please don't interrupt. Can't you find something to read?"

"Sorry!" said Bertram, "but I wanted to have the favour of a few words with Joyce presently."

"The night's young," said Ottery, impatiently. "Don't spoil the game, sir."

"Your answer, Joyce?" said Bertram.

She looked at him now, straight in the eyes, with a challenge of will.

"After the game, and when I'm ready. Not before."

"Right!"

He went out of the room, and out of the house, and for more than an hour wandered about the park.

It was a warm night on the last day of April, with a three-quarter moon, so that the branches of the trees were silvered and the lawns flooded with a milky radiance. The old house with its tall chimneys flung black shadows across the terrace paths, and the broken Venus gleamed white above the flight of steps to the rose gardens. The night air was still fragrant with the scent of flowers and damp grass, and warm earth. In the long avenue down which Bertram paced, a nightingale was singing to its mate, with little trills of passion.

Bertram remembered the last time he had heard a nightingale singing like that. It was in Notre Dame de Lorette, after a battle at Lens. The red flash of gunfire made a regular pulsation of light through the shell-gashed trees and the roar of bombardment shook the very earth. But the little bird in the tree went on singing to its mate. Queer! Even with men, love and the mating business of passion went on and would not surrender its claim though half the world was in ruins and civilisation was menaced by many dangers, and the individual had no sense of security.

That was the best philosophy, the only way of life. It was ridiculous to worry over much about the future. Old Christy was always worrying, and trying to put the world right. Better, perhaps, to carry on, like peasants and plain folk, for self-preservation, for the essential needs and appetites of self-existence —and let the world take care of itself. Holme Ottery was in ruins, like half the world. This old house, so stately in its hushed gardens and wooded parkland, so beautiful in this moonlight, as at noonday, had reached its last phase of life, at least as the roof-tree of the family which had built its beauty. Did it matter very much? Not if the life of the family went on to new development, following the thread of fate through changing ways-not if Joyce still loved her mate.

Bertram felt the stir of passion in his blood, as several times this day. Joyce challenged him. She disapproved of his ideas, and was angry because he had decided something against her wish. She put her will-power against his, tried to coerce him to her way of thinking, spoke with satire, irritably, harshly. That was all nonsense! Life was bigger than that. Love was bigger. He would make Joyce his mate again, not by argument, and intellectual duels, but by passion, by the emotion that stirred in him on this night of April, as it stirred the little creeping things of the warm earth there, and was astir in the hedges and ditches, and bushes and woods, of this Holme Ottery and all other places, and had been stirring since life began, because this was life.

When after an hour Bertram went back towards the house by way of the rose-gardens, and the long pergola, through which the moonlight crept, he heard Joyce's voice. She was speaking quietly, and he saw her figure in a black cloak sitting at the top of the steps on the parapet. She was in the full white light of the moon, though not sharply outlined, because of its filmy glamour. Below her, sitting on the top step, with his knees tucked up and his hands clasped round them, was a man's figure, his shirt-front gleaming very white. It was Kenneth Murless's long and elegant form, as Bertram could see by his very attitude. Their voices sounded clearly across the garden, though they weren't speaking loudly.

"It'll break my heart to leave Holme Ottery," said Joyce.

"Sad! Horribly sad!" answered Kenneth. "It's a tragic world altogether for our little lot. We belong to the past. You and I, Joyce, are prehistoric survivals. Awful thought, that!"

"We needn't surrender without a fight," said Joyce.

Kenneth Murless laughed with his soft musical note.

"God is on the side of the big battalions, my dear! The mob is moving out. We haven't a chance."

"To Hell with the mob!" said Joyce.

Kenneth laughed again, pleasantly.

"Your husband would hate to hear you say that!"

Joyce didn't answer for a moment, and then spoke harshly.

"Bertram's a traitor to our side of things!"

"Hush!" said Kenneth.

It was when Bertram walked out of the pergola and came up the terrace steps and stood quite close to them.

"Joyce," he said quietly, "you and I must have a talk, if Kenneth will permit."

Kenneth stood up, and smiled rather nervously at Bertram.

"I'm off to bed, old man. Good night, both." He walked quickly back to the house, leaving Bertram to Joyce.

"I'm for bed too," said Joyce. "It's too late for talk. And you heard what I said, I presume?"

"That word 'traitor'?"

"Yes."

She drew her cloak closer about her shoulders, and moved towards the house, but Bertram took her by the wrist.

"We've got to have it out, Joyce. Shall it be here, in the garden, or indoors?"

She tried to release her wrist-the same wrist which he had hurt over a telephone-but he held her fast.

"Indoors," she said.

"All right."

He held open the door of the little turret for her, and as two could not pass together, released her wrist as she went in. She slipped away from him then, and ran lightly up the stone stairs which led to the gallery round the great staircase, and her bedroom. She had the door of her room almost slammed in his face before he reached her, and held the door-handle.

"Not quick enough!"

"No."

They stood facing each other rather breathlessly inside her room. Joyce laughed a little, but in a baffled, angry way, like a thwarted child.

"It's the first time I've been in this room," said Bertram. He looked at the smallness of it, and the neatness. It had been Joyce's room since she had left her nursery in the house. Some of her girlhood's treasures and toys were there; a doll's-house in the corner, a pair of skates hanging over a cupboard, a horse-shoe, tied up with ribbon, over the mantelpiece, photographs of herself and Alban on Shetland ponies, a pair of foils crossed on one of the walls, and a fox's brush-her first-over the narrow wooden bed.

"I hope you won't stay here long," said Joyce.

She slipped off her cloak and sat in an old wicker chair by the stone-piece where a small fire had almost burnt out. She still had the look of a rebellious child —a King's page, with curled, cropped hair.

"Joyce," said Bertram, "have you forgotten that I'm your husband, and you're my wife?"

"Is that what you've been waiting to ask me all the evening?"

She teased him with her mockery.

"By God, it is!" he said quickly. "And I want an answer."

She answered him in the worst way.

"I wish I could forget a most unfortunate fact!"

Perhaps she didn't mean to be quite brutal with him. It's likely that she was just trying his temper, and yielding to her own. But it hit him hard, and he reeled under the blow, not only in a mental way, but physically.

"You mean that?" he asked, staring at her.

"Isn't it true? For you as well as for me? Surely you see the misfortune of our marriage? You don't like my ideas, my character, my whole outlook on life. That's unfortunate for you. I detest yours. That's unfortunate for me. We belong to different sides. That's unfortunate for both of us."

Bertram marvelled at the cold way in which she could speak these things. Had she forgotten, utterly, how she had loved him once, and all his devotion to her? Did it mean nothing to her that she had been the mother of his dead child? Was she so heartless that she could see herself divided from him by that sheer gulf of which she spoke, and not agonise at its tragedy, nor weep, but talk so calmly, so coldly of its happening? No, he didn't believe that. Heart and soul refused to believe.

"My dear!" he said. "My dear! Don't let's say bitter and frightful things because we're out of temper. I know it's so easy. It's a question of nerves, little irritations, small rotten differences that mean-just nothing. They don't matter more than passing shadows. What does matter is our love, above and beyond all that. I want to tell you that my love for you is unaltered, and unalterable, although you have been pretty rough on me lately, and not given love, or anything like a fair deal. . . . But I want to wipe out the remembrance of that. I want you and me to get together again, as comrades and mates. Nothing else would matter then. Our different points of view? Oh, Lord! how trivial! Joyce, take me back to your bed and your heart, and your beauty, and let's make a game of life again!"

He leaned over her, put his arms around her, tried to draw her close to him, as she sat there in the wicker chair by the little fire that had almost burnt out.

She drew her chair back on the polished boards, and sprang up, beyond his reach.

"What's all this stuff you're talking?" she said, angrily, two spots of scarlet on her face. "You say you love me. Why do you always jeer at my friends and my ideas? Sulk in my drawing-room? Behave like a boor to my crowd? Ally yourself with Pacifists and pro-Germans and revolutionaries? You say you love me, and talk sentiment. Less sentiment, please, and more honesty. That offer to-night! It was a test of loyalty. To England in a big way-certainly to me, as far as I mean anything in your life. Yet you refused it. You failed to pass the test. Why, from the lowest point of view, you ought to want to keep your end up, and pay your own way, like an honest man! You remember the word I spoke to Kenneth? I use it again now, to your face. You're a traitor to the things I stand for, to all I am. Until you do something to put yourself right again, I won't live with you. It's dishonouring."

"By God!" said Bertram.

He was white to the lips now, with anguish and rage. This girl used her tongue like a lash. She cut his heart open, flayed his soul. And yet, as she stood there, facing him, he loved her with an extreme passion, and her beauty was a torture to him.

He acknowledged the truth of some things she said. He had jeered at her friends, often enough. He had sulked in her drawing-room. He had behaved like a boor to her crowd. All that was true. But the rest of it was not true, and it was cruel. She called him traitor-he who loved England as he loved Joyce, hungrily, so that the smell of its earth, as the fragrance of her hair, excited his senses, touched him with spiritual emotion. It was damnable that she should use such words. "Dishonouring!" she said. She wouldn't live with him because it was dishonouring!

He strode a pace towards her, and caught hold of her right arm.

"In the old days a man would have flogged his wife for such words. I've a damned good mind to box your ears."

"Have a try!" said Joyce, breathing hard.

He didn't box her ears, but let her arm go and dropped his hands to his side, and stood there with his head bowed, staring at the floor. There was silence between them for at least a minute, which seemed like an hour. Joyce for the first time was weeping, with her face turned away from him.

Presently he spoke again.

"It rather looks as though I'd made a mistake. I thought you still loved me, in spite of drifting away a bit. It seems any love you once had is like that little fire of yours-not much ever, and now burnt out. Why, God alone knows, not I! But it's a pity. Perhaps it's my fault partly. I may come to see that one day. Now, to-night, I think you've been hellish to me. I'll clear out to-morrow. . . . If you want me ever, I'll come."

He stood at the doorway, looking back at her. She stood by the side of the little bed where she had slept as a child, with her face turned away and her body shaken by sobs. He hated to part from her like that, and this was the parting.

He spoke her name once more.

"Joyce!"

She didn't answer him, and he left her room and shut the door. Next morning he left Holme Ottery before breakfast, and went back to town, but not to the little house in Holland Street.

He went to his mother's house in Sloane Street, and asked for his old room.

XXIX

Mrs. Pollard was astonished and distressed when her son told her that he wanted to use his old room for a few weeks. She guessed, in spite of his carefully vague explanations, that something had gone wrong between him and Joyce.

His "explanation" left much to be explained. He suggested that Joyce was immensely upset by the proposed sale of Holme Ottery, and might stay down there a while to see the last of the old home. But that was no reason why he shouldn't stay with her, or go back to the little house in Holland Street. He countered that by saying he hated loneliness, and as he had to keep close to town for his literary work, preferred to take up his old bachelor quarters. Besides, it would be good to see so much of his mother again.

"Aren't you pleased, little mother?"

He had the humiliation of asking her to lend him some money, but to her it was a pleasure, and she wrote him a cheque for more than he could use in a twelve-month, and said, "With my love and blessing, dear!"

She knew he was concealing some secret from her. His face, which she could read like an open book-so much like her own! —told her that he was suffering a hidden wound, which hurt him horribly. He couldn't hide much from a mother who lay awake at night listening to his footsteps pacing up and down in his room overhead-would he never go to sleep? —and who heard him groan now and then, like a tortured soul.

"I'm afraid you had a bad night, dear," she would say in the morning, and wouldn't believe him when he said, "Oh, no. I slept all right after thinking out a few things."

She accepted all his explanations for her husband's benefit. Michael, to whom she announced the news of his son's home-coming, did not see any mystery underlying it, but only inconvenience to the servants who had been reduced in number since the break-up of the family. He had a respectful admiration for Joyce Bellairs as the daughter of the Earl of Ottery, and sympathised-he said-with her sentiment about the old house. Doubtless she would wish to stay there before it was bought by some American millionaire or some war-profiteer. Most natural and commendable. As for Bertram, he hoped the boy would spare him political altercations-they seemed to disagree on most subjects-and any reference to more painful episodes which he had entirely removed from his mind. By that, as Mrs. Pollard knew, he referred to his eldest daughter's German marriage, and Susan's Irish adventure.

Bertram "spared" him everything with regard to these forbidden subjects. He met his father only at breakfast, and exchanged a few commonplace remarks over the eggs and bacon. Their first greeting had been characteristic of the somewhat strained relations existing between them.

"Hulloa, father! Here's the Prodigal back. Don't bother about the fatted calf."

"Good morning, Bertram. Putting in a bachelor week? I shan't see much of you as I'm desperately busy."

"Don't worry about that, sir."

Bertram's father became absorbed in *The Morning Post*. After breakfast he retired to his study for an hour. At ten o'clock he drove down to the Temple. Occasionally he returned for dinner, but Bertram generally dined out, if he knew that his father was expected. At midnight, or thereabouts, Mr. Michael Pollard, K.C., M.P., having completed a day of arduous toil on behalf of law and order and the good governance of a great Empire, came home again, and retired to rest.

Bertram, at that time of night, was generally in his own room, pacing up and down, not aware that every footstep was heard by his wakeful mother. He was "thinking out a few things," as he told her.

They were not pleasant things, nor easy. Since the war he had made a complete failure of his life. He had made a hopeless mess of his marriage. Here he was back again, in his bachelor state, in the little old room where, as a boy, he had lived in a dream world of hope and ambition. How many times he had sat on this bed, generally with one boot off and one boot on, looking into the unknown future with a boy's impatience for its coming, thinking of love and its mystery, wondering about the girl who somewhere was waiting in the world to be his mate, to fulfil the vague and wonderful promise of life which as yet he saw only as on the threshold of its glory. Now he knew! He had met the girl of his vision, and she had abandoned him.

He had never thought of that possibility, when he had sat with Romance as his source of knowledge in this little room. That was before the War had come crashing into Romance with terrific realism. That was in old quiet days when it had seemed adventure enough to wander through London on journeys of exploration, and when books of travel, history, drama, were more exciting than anything that really happened in modern life.

He used to put his head out of this window looking down on Sloane Street, listening to the rush of traffic, after theatre time, until it was very quiet, and only a late hansom-the last of their kind-came with a klip-klop up the street, or a primitive "taxi" honked its horn. The sky was always quivering with the lights of London, above the chimney-pots, as high as the stars. The boy Bertram used to stare at that radiance, with his room all dusk behind him, so that his mother would be worried by his keeping awake —"reading in bed" was her passionate dread! —and it seemed to him like a mirage of life itself, with all its mystery and enchantment.

Ten years ago! Not more than that, though a whole life-time in experience. Four and a half years of war had intervened, awaking Bertram and the world out of false dreams and beatific visions. Four and a half murderous years, crammed with death, and horror, and heroism, and laughter, and boredom, and fear, and filth. Then a year of marriage-worse than war. More difficult than the technique of war, more nerve-racking, and more terrifying than death in the results of failure.

Here he was, after complete failure, back in his bachelor room, as Joyce was in hers! Yet not back again as before. Impossible to get back to the boy who was here in this room ten years ago. Those books on the shelves which had meant so much then, meant nothing now, had no comfort in them, no romance, no thrill of any kind, no wisdom. Not even Shakespeare, in the old Leopold edition, could give Bertram any solution to his problem of marriage with Joyce. Shelley, Browning, Laurence Housman, Kipling-all the poets he had loved-what could they tell him now? "Damn all!" as the men used to say in war time. Conrad, Stevenson, Quiller-Couch, Barrie, —Lord! he could hardly bear to look at them.

Over his mantelpiece were photographs of Dorothy and Susan, and a small boy-Digby-in knickerbockers and an Eton collar; Dorothy as a girl of eighteen, with her hair "up" for the first time, wonderfully pretty in an evening frock of a style now hopelessly old-fashioned; Susan as a girl of sixteen, with a short white frock, and long black stockings, laughing like a tomboy. The last few years of history had made a difference to them. Dorothy was Frau von Arenburg, a "Hun's" wife; Susan the wife of an Irish rebel now in prison; Digby, the boy in knickerbockers, a Black and Tan. And Bertram, their brother, staring at these old photographs, touching his old books, sitting on his bed with his head in his hands, was ex-Major of machine guns, now unemployed, and ex-husband of Lady Joyce Bellairs, of Holme Ottery, in the county of Sussex.

He had received one letter from Joyce since that night at Holme Ottery. He had read it ten times or more, and then torn it up into small pieces.

My Dear Bertram:

The scene you made last night was inexcusable, except on the score that you are still suffering from shell-shock or some war neuritis. It's impossible for us to live together while you continue in that mental state. I suppose your sudden departure this morning means that you are of the same opinion. Whether we ever come together again depends on you. When you can afford to keep me, and when you prove your loyalty to my ideals, I shall be glad to live with you again. Not till then. I've decided to give up Holland Street and stay here with Mother until Holme Ottery is sold, which I pray will not be soon.

I know you think I've been hard and "unsympathetic," and unkind. Of course, there's something to be said on your side. I know you've loved me in your passionate, emotional way, as much as any man could. I'm grateful for good times we had in the beginning. But that's only one side of love, the animal side which I dislike. I want the other side of love, which is, surely, communion of ideas, comradeship in understanding, the same faith and code. That you've not given me. However-it's past argument now.

Yours,

Joyce.

Past argument now! Well, he was not going to re-open the argument. So he told her in his answer to that letter. Perhaps he'd been a fool to write so much-sheet after sheet, revealing the secret things of his mind, the strain and stress of his nature, pulled two ways by two strains of blood, a conflict between old tradition and the new hopes of humanity, resistance to extremes of thought, so that he might plod along the Middle of the Road.

The strain and stress of his nature! He had made her understand, if words were plain, that she was the cause of his irritable temper, so much of his impatience. His love for her was passionate, as she said, and a man couldn't suppress passion too long, without nerve-storms. Long before the child was born, and ever since, she had made no response to his emotion, and kept him at a distance, coldly. Her presence, the scent of her hair, the turn of her head, the touch of her finger-tips, made his thrill to her, but though she had been so close to him, always putting this strain upon his senses and his vital nature, she had repulsed him, resisted any intimate contact with him, deliberately held him in exile. She hadn't played the game by him. She had shirked her marriage vows. She had made his married life an agony-and intolerable, because of the very greatness of his love! She wrote about communion of ideas. Yes, he agreed with that, utterly. But communion means exchange, give and take, a little yielding on both sides, tolerance, understanding. She had never troubled to get his point of view. She had never stood on tip-toes to see over his side of the hedge.

She had taken her stand with the Old Caste and the least liberal part of that, the extreme high and dry section of it, left behind by the great tide of changing life, now in England, at last, after the opening of the sluice gates by the shock of war.

He was not intolerant of her ideals. He was pulled back to them against reason, even, by old sentiment, the romance of history, by the very ghosts of England. He could understand her resentment of change which meant the downfall of Holme Ottery, as one symbol of a passing era. He understood and grieved with her, because he loved the old stones of England and every brick in every wall. But he saw the inevitability of change, the need and right of it.

He stood with his face to the future, not weeping with his head turned backwards to the past. He had tried to make her understand his view of life. She'd not troubled to understand. Because he had not agreed with abject submission to her ideas, her old-fashioned, out-worn creed, she'd used that word "traitor!" and cut his heart open.

As for his being able to keep her, he had understood that she wasn't in a hurry for him to pay his board and lodging. They'd had that argument out before, and she had promised to give him time. She'd broken that promise —a week or so too soon! A little more patience, perhaps, and he would have proved his quality as a writing-man, by getting a fair price for hard work.

He had not been a slacker. He had slaved over his book, late into the night. He would have gone on slaving, joyously, to earn a decent living, to pay for the things she liked, to take his share of life's costs.

Well, "it was past argument now!" Agreed! No further argument should come from him. Nor did he intend to crawl to her, whining, to be "taken back." By God, no! If she wanted him, she would have to ask for him. She would have to beg him to return, without conditions, on equal terms, acknowledging his right, and persuading his of love. Otherwise, never. And perhaps never, even then, if she waited too long, for even loyalty couldn't suffer too great a strain, though now he sent her his love. . . .

So he had written, or in some such way, all night, with spells of thought when he had laid his head down on his arms, and, even, had wept a little like a weak boy. She hadn't answered the letter. It was "past argument, now!"

His mother worried him by trying to get at his secret. A dozen times a day she spoke about "dear Joyce," and he had to fence with her until about a week after his coming back she broke down his guard, and he told her everything, or nearly everything. Then he was put into the absurd position of defending Joyce.

His mother was indignant with her son's wife, called her a "selfish creature," and a "heartless hussy," and couldn't understand at all how any wife could so behave to any husband. It was, she said, "the moral breakdown caused by the war." English girls seemed bereft of their senses, judging from the daily papers, and all the dreadful divorce cases. Joyce was another example of that. She wanted, like all the others, nothing but pleasure. Duty never entered her head. Self-sacrifice for love's sake was not acknowledged these days. She was merely an empty-headed creature, with bobbed hair and short skirts.

"Mother!" said Bertram, "I can't let you speak of Joyce like that! She's not in the least empty-headed. On the contrary, she's stuffed full of knowledge and ideas. As for her bobbed hair, it's the fashion, and a pretty one."

Absurd-to be defending Joyce who had given him Hell! Yet he did so, time and time again, until at last he became angry, and said, "Let's give up talking about it, mother, for goodness' sake! You don't understand Joyce's point of view, or mine. It's impossible to explain. I can't explain it to myself. I only know that it's a frightful tragedy."

He hated to talk roughly to his mother. The love she had for all her children, now departed from her, was concentrated on Bertram who had come back for a little while. She could hardly bear him out of her sight, and often, when he went up to his room he heard her quiet footsteps outside the door. She was listening to his movements, standing near him, though outside the room. She was happy, or almost happy if he sat with her, holding her hand, or if she could watch him from the other side of the fireplace, while he sat back in a low chair, pretending to read the paper, and thinking, thinking of Joyce, and his loneliness, and what the devil to do with his life. Never quite happy, for always in her heart was grief over the exile of Dorothy in her German home, and anxiety about Susan who only sent post card messages from Dublin, saying nothing, and fearfulness on behalf of young Digby in the midst of civil war.

"It's a dreadful world, Bertram," she said, once. "As a young wife I was so happy with all my babies, and never dreamed of all the horror ahead-war, revolutions, famines, plague, endless strife. If only Queen Victoria could have gone on living, we might have been saved all that. She kept things safe by her virtue and wisdom."

Bertram tried hard not to laugh, yet he laughed aloud at the idea of the poor old Queen "keeping things safe" in a world that was making ready for convulsion even in her time, by great natural moving forces that no mortal could restrain; not King Canute with the advancing tide, nor Queen Victoria in a changing era.

"Why do you laugh at me?" asked Mrs. Pollard.

He patted her hand.

"You still belong to the Victorian Age!"

"We felt safe in that time," said his mother. "Now I don't know what new terror will happen from day to day. There's an awful uncertainty, everywhere."

"It's Reality breaking through Illusion," said Bertram; but his mother, as he saw, did not understand him, and he did not try to make her understand. He was pitiful because of the troubles that had overtaken her in the last phase of her beautiful and faithful life.

Tears came into her eyes when he told her that he was spending the evening away from home. He had promised to call round again at Janet Welford's flat in Battersea Park.

"I know it's dull here alone with me," said Mrs. Pollard, "but you hardly know the comfort it gives me to see you back again, now all my other dear birds have gone from the nest."

"Never dull with you, little mother," he said, bending to kiss her forehead. "But I like to see my friends at times. I'll be back before you go to bed."

But he stayed rather late with Janet, and wasn't back until his mother had tired of waiting. She heard his step passing her door, and called out, "Good night, my dear!"

XXX

Janet Welford —"Janet Rockingham Welford" of fiction fame-was a source of comfort to Bertram at this time. She had a courage regarding life, a natural and unaffected buoyancy of character, whatever might happen in a world of tragedy, which shook him out of his morbid brooding while he was in her company. She carried over the audacity of her war-time spirit, when for a while she had driven an ambulance into the Belgian zone of fire, to that after-war period when most men and women felt drained of vitality, and suffered miserable reaction.

It was, perhaps, her daily service to the blinded men of St. Dunstan's which kept her soul tuned to the old key of "carry on!" which had inspired masses of people during the years of conflict so that they forgot, or put on one side, their own griefs and cares, because of the great sufferings of others, and the common need of sacrifice.

That was her explanation.

"My blinded boys keep me healthy and vital and brave," she smiled. "How the devil can I indulge in the megrims, sit down and sob over my woes of thwarted passion, gloom over the possible downfall of civilisation, or six shillings in the pound for income tax, when those blind boys have to be kept merry and bright to save them from despair and suicide? They just knock one's egotism stone dead."

"It's splendid of you!" said Bertram.

Janet wouldn't allow any kind of splendour to herself.

"Punk! It's only another form of selfishness. They're my soul-cure. If I didn't laugh for their sakes, make up the most ridiculous and risky stories, to get a smile out of them, coerce myself to look on the bright side of life, so that I can reflect some sunshine into their sightless eyes, I should probably suffer from sex-complexes or other forms of beastliness. I serve them to save myself. That's what I tell them, and they think it an excellent joke. 'Have we done you good this morning, Miss?' they ask, and I say, 'You're my Salvation Army, my lads!' and that keeps us laughing round Regent's Park."

Bertram wondered sometimes whether Janet's philosophy was not founded on tremendous pessimism rather than on unbounded optimism. A queer thought! Yet he had seen that kind of psychology working out to the same result, in France and Flanders, among the civilian folk.

French girls who had seen their little homesteads go up in fire under the enemy's guns, peasants who had lost everything in the world, except life, by the invasion of the "Boche," women who had lost fathers, husbands, lovers, brothers, acquired an astonishing serenity, even a gaiety of mind. Nothing seemed to matter to them now. Death itself was a "bagatelle."

He had seen girls laughing as though at some fantastic joke, when they poked about the ruins of their cottages and found bits of old furniture, the wheel of a baby's perambulator, the relic of some old familiar thing. It seemed to give life a different sense of proportion, annihilating its vanities, its greeds, its fears, its illusions. They were down to the bed-rock of frightful realities, and nothing worse could happen to them, and they were all "in the basket" together. Their fate was no worse, and perhaps a little better, than that of their neighbours.

So, in a way, it was with Janet. At least, he sometimes thought so. Her father, and then her young brother, had been killed in the war. Her mother had died of the anguish of these shocks. She herself had spent the years of war nursing mutilated men. It gave her that strange serenity of vision which for a time had come to many of those most stricken by war, though afterwards, when peace came, they collapsed.

She hadn't collapsed. It seemed simply silly to Janet that English people should worry because trade was bad, and get alarmed about the prospect of social revolution, or excite themselves about the downfall of exchanges. She stared forward to the future with audacious vision, and demanded not a hark back to the old standards of comfort and tradition, but root and branch changes, bold experiments in social legislation, tremendous endeavours towards the building of a new world.

Anyhow, she was not afraid. Not of Bolshevism, not of poverty, not of any new tragedy that might emerge out of the chaos of a Europe convulsed by the effects of war.

"It's all frightfully interesting," she said, "and, anyhow, worry won't stop the working out of Fate. Why be afraid of Fate? We shall all be dead quite soon. Let's play the game out, and see it through, and pass the ball on to the next players, when we've had our innings."

"That sounds good," said Bertram, "but it doesn't cure the heart-ache of a woman left alone because her man was killed in the war, or give any comfort to an unemployed man, hanging about Labour Exchanges in search of jobs that aren't there. Your philosophy of devil-may-care won't stop another bout of massacre in Europe if the Old Gang are allowed to play the fool again, or save the next generation of boys from being blown to bits in lousy trenches. We *must* worry. It's our duty to worry and find a scientific way of escape from all this madness."

"I don't call that worrying," she answered. "I call that thinking straight and acting with courage. That's our point of view in the 'Left Wing.' "

"Oh, Lord!" said Bertram, "Your parlour Bolsheviks think all crooked, and have no more courage than lop-eared rabbits."

Janet laughed without a trace of annoyance.

"Some of them are disgusting little egoists," she admitted. "But, anyhow, they're educating themselves, and frightening the Reactionaries. I like to see the Enemy getting scared."

She used the word "enemy" to represent the Tory crowd-Joyce's crowd-more especially the Countess of Ottery's audience at the Wigmore Hall.

These political conversations ranged over wide fields of discussion, and Bertram seemed to amuse Janet by his efforts to moderate her extreme views. She became more violent to tease him into argument, and when he called her a Jacobin, who would knit below the scaffold when heads were falling, she retaliated by calling him a Girondin who would try to make revolutions with rose-water.

All this talk seemed to have relation to things happening, or likely to happen, away beyond Battersea Park, through the length and breadth of England.

The Coal Strike had begun. The railways had cut down their service of trains to a bare minimum. Factories were closing down in all the industrial towns. Millions of men were idle and living on strike pay. The Army Reserve had been called out, the Middle Classes were being recruited under the scheme of General Bellasis, and the Miners were in daily conference with the Engineers and Transport Workers, who were discussing the question of a general strike. If the "Triple Alliance" voted for that, not a wheel would turn in England, and civil strife would certainly break out, unless something like a miracle intervened.

So far no violence had happened. The miners had come up from the pits, and were white-washing their cottages. They had made a fatal mistake already, alienating public opinion, which, until then had been steadily in favour of their side of the argument. The Pump men had been withdrawn from the pits, and some of the mines were already being flooded.

"A logical act," said Janet. "The Pump men received their lock-out notices with the others. The mine-owners must take the responsibility."

"Rotten tactics and bad morality," said Bertram. "The men ought to safeguard their own means of life."

So they argued, as all other men and women in England then, in every household where opinions differed on one side or the other, and where there was a sense of imminent disaster to the old foundations of civil life.

But of more intimate and poignant interest to Bertram was Janet's frank talk about his private disaster-the failure of his marriage. She had asked blunt questions about his relations with Joyce, amazingly indiscreet and fearless questions, and after fencing with them awhile, he had told her the truth of things, with reticence and reservations, and a sense of loyalty to Joyce, so that he put down most of the cause of failure to his own stupidity and lack of patience.

Janet listened, cross-examined, probed his mental wound, with the skill and ruthlessness of a psychoanalyst.

"Very interesting!" she remarked, more than once, like a doctor diagnosing a difficult case.

"The inevitable clash of opposed temperaments," was another remark of hers, delivered with an air of superior wisdom, and an amusement which she did not try to conceal.

"You're not very sympathetic!" complained Bertram. "Not very helpful. What's my way out of this mess?"

Janet said, "Forget it. Shove it away into your subconsciousness, and go on as though it didn't exist. You'll find that it all straightens out."

She gave him the benefit of her diagnosis.

"It's a case of sex-repression on your side, and of fear-complex on your wife's side. Yours is a simple case. Perfectly ordinary. Nothing to worry about. Your wife's case is more complicated."

In response to Bertram's plea for enlightenment, and his heated protest that he *was* worrying, most damnably, Janet elaborated a thesis regarding Joyce.

Bertram's wife, she said, was the victim of an early environment which had caused abnormality. She'd been sheltered since babyhood from all contact with the realities of life. She was never allowed to speak with "common people" on equal terms. They'd pulled their forelocks to "the little lady" when she had passed in her perambulator. They'd curtsied at the lodge gates every time she went in and out. She was made to believe that she was superior to the rest of the world, with the exception of other people like herself, who lived in other houses like Holme Ottery.

The rest of mankind, to her child mind, was entirely taken up with the duty and honour and delight of providing a pleasant life to those born in the higher sphere-mowing the lawns, grooming the horses, clipping the hedges, polishing the floors, waiting at table, bowing silently when rebuked however unjustly, utterly dependent upon Lady Joyce Bellairs and her exalted family. She'd had no notion, as a child, that outside the parkland of Holme Ottery the world had moved on. The portraits of her ancestors in their silks and laces seemed to prove that her world, and theirs, had always been the same, and always would be, sheltered, protected, served, admired.

Then the war had come, breaking through the quietude of Holme Ottery, but not, for a while, smashing the old illusions. Joyce's father had still played the great game of ruling the county as Lord Lieutenant. Alban had played the diplomatic game in the Foreign Office. Joyce's friends had been officers, saluted by all men as they passed, holding authority even more firmly than of old.

It was only after the war that Joyce had been frightened.

She saw that Holme Ottery and all that it meant was threatened, that stupendous taxation was killing the old way of life for people like herself, destroying their sense of security, their power, their pleasaunces. And she had become aware of other perils; the bogey of Bolshevism, social "unrest," a new insolence of men back from the war, no longer quick to pull their forelocks when the lady passed, but talking bitterly about their "rights," their claim to work, and a living wage.

Joyce Bellairs was afraid of brutal forces threatening all that she had loved as a child, all that she had believed as a child. Her behaviour to Bertram was on account of that. It was a fear-complex. She loved him, but the very strength of her love made her brutal to him when he seemed to ally himself with the powers that made her afraid.

"It sounds all right," said Bertram, listening a little impatiently, "but it's all wrong! Joyce doesn't understand fear. She has more than the courage of men."

"Physical courage, yes. Not mental courage."

"Besides," said Bertram, "that doesn't solve my problem. How am I going to live a single life, apart from Joyce, who is still my wife? How am I going to persuade her to withdraw that word 'traitor'?"

"Give her time, and don't worry," was Janet's answer to his conundrum. "A little separation will do you both good. Heavens alive! The constant companionship of marriage would be a strain on two archangels. I couldn't bear it."

"You've borne my company patiently for three evenings a week," said Bertram.

"Yes, but not for three breakfasts! It's breakfast that's the test of love. Most people break over it, like boiled eggs."

Bertram wasn't sure how far Janet's talk was sincere, how much she believed in her own absurdities. Perhaps she was behaving to him as she did to her blinded men, talking "any old thing" —to get a laugh out of them, to "keep their pecker up."

He accused her of that once, and she blushed a little, as though found guilty.

He made her blush another time, when he spoke of Christy's love for her.

"I suppose you know Christy worships you?"

She veiled her eyes with her long brown lashes, and said, "Yes, I know. . . . Poor dear old Plesiosaurus!"

"Why don't you fix it up with him?"

A little smile played about her lips.

" 'He's never asked me, sir, she said.' And, besides, I haven't told you that I requite his gloomy passion!"

"He's one of the best in the world," said Bertram.

She agreed, but said that the best were almost as difficult as the worst when it came to board and breakfast with them.

"Aren't you human?" asked Bertram, half jestingly, half in earnest. "Don't you need love, and the passion of life?"

She talked so frankly to him that he could speak like that.

That doubt about her humanity amused her exceedingly.

"Man!" she cried, "I'm a living Cleopatra without her Antony! If I were to ease up an instant on blinded men, political meetings, 'Left Wing' committees, audacious novels, and all manner of work, goodness knows what I should do in the way of amorous adventure. I go in for what the psychoanalysts call the sublimation of sex."

"What the deuce is that?" asked Bertram.

"Transferring the emotion to intellectual aims. Producing books instead of babies. Reforming society instead of yearning for a kiss. Keeping busy on foolish, futile things, instead of wasting one's energy in amorous dalliance. That's my advice to you, young fellow! Cut out the emotional stuff for a time. Forget Joyce and marriage, and all this morbid love-agony. Life's bigger than that. It's only a little messy side of life. We make too much fuss about it, exaggerate the importance of the damn thing by always thinking and writing and talking about it. Go and make a revolution somewhere, or lead an expedition to find the living Megatherium, or write a book to 'bust' the falsity of things, or cut down trees in Canada, or convert cannibals to Christianity, or Christians to a decent code of honour, or make some plan for a higher civilisation, or some plan for destroying the civilisation we have-any good, straight, clean, manly job that's not mixed up with the eternal soppy and sickly question of love and Louisa. Give it a miss, O Knight of the Rueful Countenance."

Bertram shook his head.

"Human nature is human nature. It doesn't give one any peace that way. It keeps on nagging."

"Don't let it nag. Crush the little devil down. Say, 'Avaunt, you vampire!' Look at me! A Cleopatra, yet beyond reproach, as Cæsar's wife!"

She cheered him. There was something in her point of view. He must put the problem of Joyce out of his mind and heart as far as possible. Get busy! Well, he was writing some more articles for *The New World*. They helped him to forget.

And yet this girl, Janet, so gay, so kind, so wise, even in spite of her extravagance of thought and speech, was beginning to trouble him in the very way he wished to avoid, in the very way she derided and denounced.

She troubled him one night when she said suddenly, "A pity, Sir Faithful, that you didn't marry me instead of Joyce! I understand you better. We think more on the same line. And you were my first Dream Knight, in the days when you kissed me in Kensington Gardens."

It was just like her to come out with a startling thing like that, in a matter-of-fact way, as though it were nothing out of the ordinary, and undisturbing. He was strangely disturbed, and hardly knew what to say.

"Too late now!" was all he could say, and then laughed uneasily.

She troubled him again by the way she used to sit on a little low stool by his side when they were alone together in the evening or even when Katherine Wild was with them, leaning her head against his knees. He liked it very much because it was so comradely and sisterly, but he was human and separated from his wife, and not a disembodied spirit.

He was troubled more than all one night when he was leaving her and she put her face up to be kissed and said, "A chaste salute, Sir Faithful? Why not?"

He kissed her, and it was good in his loneliness. And yet not good in his conscience. For he had faith and loyalty, to Joyce who was his wife, though unkind to him, and to Christy who was his friend, and the lover of this girl.

As he went back to his mother's house in Sloane Street, he spoke aloud the old catchword which was his usual comment on life:

"It's all very difficult!"

XXXI

A thunderbolt struck the house in Sloane Street at half past eight one morning. It came, as other bolts had fallen upon men's and women's hearts during the time of the Great War, in a little pink envelope. This one was addressed to Bertram Pollard, and it came from Dublin.

Dennis condemned to death execution Wednesday. Implore father's influence. Susan.

Bertram was sitting at breakfast opposite her father, who was reading *The Morning Post* as usual at this meal. His mother was pouring out coffee, and was aware instantly of his sudden indrawing of breath.

"Oh, Bertram!" she said, in a low voice. "Is it bad news?"

She slopped some coffee from the pot over the edge of a cup.

He was tempted to lie to her and say "Nothing much! A business matter," but before the words left his lips he knew that honesty was best. She had seen his look of dismay, if he prevaricated, she would guess that the news was worse than this, though this was bad.

"It's not good," he said. "It's about Susan's husband."

"That young scoundrel!" said his father, glancing over the top of his paper; "what infamy is he mixed up in now?"

Bertram read out the telegram, and saw his mother's face change to a new tone of pallor, and the look of anguish in her eyes for Susan.

" 'Implore father's influence.' " These words caused his father to drop *The Morning Post* in which he was reading a terrific indictment of Sinn Fein with a sense of fierce enjoyment.

"I wouldn't use a hairsbreadth of influence to save my own son from the hangman's rope, if he were a Sinn Fein murderer."

"He's your own daughter's husband," said Bertram. "The relationship is fairly close."

"Too close," said Michael Pollard. "Susan dishonoured her name by that secret and shameful marriage. I'll never forgive her. I've already given orders that her name will not be mentioned in my presence."

He picked up the paper again, and pretended to read, very calmly. But his hands trembled, so that the paper rustled.

"My dear!" said Mrs. Pollard; "for our dear Susan's sake, I implore you, as she implores you. I've been a faithful wife to you. I beg you now to use any power you have in a plea of mercy for that misguided boy."

She had risen from her chair, and Bertram saw that she was more excited than he had ever seen her. She had a tragic look, and age had crept into her face suddenly, so that she seemed an old, old lady, very frail and broken.

His father lowered his paper again, and he too was startled, it seemed to Bertram, by his wife's look and speech.

"My darling," he said, "trouble falls heavily upon your poor soul, because of our children's folly. But I can do nothing in this matter, even if I would. If the fellow has been condemned by court-martial, it's clear that he's guilty of murder. He must suffer the punishment of murderers. No power of mine can save him."

"You can have an enquiry made. At least postpone this dreadful sentence! Michael, if you have any love for me, in my old age, and my weakness —"

She faltered forward to him, and would have fallen if Bertram had not sprung towards her and held her close.

"Mother! Courage!"

"My poor Susan!" she cried. "My dear little daughter!"

Mr. Pollard rose, pale now, like his wife, visibly distressed.

"I'll see if there's anything to be done," he said. "I'll make enquiry. Hush, Mother! Hush, now!"

She put her hand on his shoulder and wept miserably, and said, "For God's sake, dear. I can't bear it! This is the worst that's happened yet."

Bertram took her to the sitting-room, and left her there later, when she seemed more composed, though still trembling. He went to his father's study, and entered without knocking, and saw his father standing with his hands behind his back, staring at the floor with a heavy frown.

"Father," he said, "something's got to be done about this. You must get to work quickly. It's not long till Wednesday."

Michael Pollard stared at his son with anger and suspicion.

"How much do you know about this?" he asked. "Did Susan tell you how many murders her precious husband has committed? How many of your fellow officers he has shot in cold blood?"

"I know nothing," said Bertram. "Don't talk to me, father, as if I were an accomplice of Dennis O'Brien."

"You're sympathetic with Sinn Fein," said his father. "You sheltered this very man in your own house, I'm told."

Bertram wondered how he knew as much as that, but didn't ask.

"He was with me an hour or two. Susan brought him. But that's nothing to the point. For mother's sake you must do what's possible, and quickly, sir!"

"There's nothing possible," said Mr. Pollard. "I know all about the case already. This man O'Brien has been found guilty of leading an ambush against British officers, two of whom were killed. He was captured on the spot, a week ago, tried yesterday, and condemned. I have the full report."

So he knew before the telegram came! He had not thought it worth while to tell Bertram before or to guard his wife against the shock of the news.

Bertram begged him to put in a plea for mercy. It wouldn't be ignored, because of his name and service to the Government. It might save O'Brien's life, at least, and Susan's life-long misery.

Michael Pollard's face hardened.

"I speak to you more frankly, Bertram, than to your poor mother. For her sake I've already done as much as I can in honour. I've enquired into the proofs of guilt, into the Court Martial procedure. There's no doubt of guilt, no flaw in the conduct of the trial. The Chief Secretary has favoured me with a private consultation. I told him, as I tell you, that I wish for no mercy on behalf of an Irish rebel who has fired on forces of the Crown, and killed men in British uniform."

Bertram groaned, and quoted, not lightly, but in anguish, the old Shakespearean line,

"The quality of mercy is not strained."

"Sinn Fein has no mercy," said his father. "It's ruthless and bloody and cruel."

"Need we meet cruelty by cruelty?" asked Bertram. "Wouldn't chivalry gain more for us?"

"Never!" answered his father harshly. "The Irish Catholics don't understand the meaning of chivalry. These Sinn Feiners would stab a man in the back who held out his hand in friendship and forgiveness."

"You're Irish of the Irish!" said Bertram. "Your Irish blood is in my veins. We of all people should understand the passion of our race for liberty, their remembrance of old crimes against their faith and land, their frightful heritage of memory. I loathe this guerrilla warfare, but I understand its motives and impulses. In their spirit it's as much a fight for liberty as that of any people who strive to free themselves from a foreign yoke. O'Brien's deed was not real murder, at least in his soul and conscience, because it was an act of war-armed men against armed men, and ours with no right in Ireland, except that of ancient conquest. Surely there's a difference. Surely as an Irishman, you see there's no moral baseness in what O'Brien did? Except the madness of argument by blood and force for an ideal of liberty which might be gained by other means."

"Every word you say convinces me that you're on the side of the rebels," said Michael Pollard. "You're a traitor in my own household. I'll be glad when you leave my house before I have to turn you out."

It was the second time that Bertram had been called traitor. Once it was his wife who called him that. Now it was his father. He went white to the lips at the sound of it, and that last sentence of his father's put passion into his brain.

"Did God make you without humanity?" he asked. "Is it for nothing that you've lost the love of all your children and now risk the love of the woman who bore them, and is stricken by your harshness in her old age?"

Michael Pollard's face became ashen in colour at these words from his son. He took a step forward, and then raised his hand sharply.

"Silence, sir! I have one son who is a comfort to me, and to his mother. Digby does his duty and is loyal. I find no loyalty in you. I don't wish to hear more of your rebellious insolence."

"Then you refuse to raise a little finger to help Susan in her grief, or mother in her agony?" asked Bertram.

His father turned from him.

"Leave my room!"

Bertram left the room, and that night crossed over to Ireland from Holyhead. In his mind was the thought of three other people stricken by this tragedy-those three sisters of Dennis O'Brien, who would be weeping for him now, and praying still to God, who didn't answer their prayers. The youngest of them-Jane-had said, "What'll I do if Dennis is taken from us?" She'd had a foreboding of his fate, perhaps a knowledge of his guilt.

Guilt it was. Bertram sickened at the thought of that guerrilla warfare which he had tried to defend to his father, but couldn't defend in his heart because of loyalty to England and hatred of cruelty. It was all madness and murder, though with some spiritual value behind it, and not ignoble passion. Those young men, mostly boys, who fought for Irish liberty, were willing to die for Ireland, went to their death on the scaffold like martyrs. Yet they adopted methods of war which were Red Indian in their savagery. On the other side, the British Government had abandoned all sanity, all statesmanship, all decency. By a series of stupidities, falsities, betrayal of pledges, they had maddened Irish manhood into this state of rebellion-at least had reopened old wounds, and revived old passions. Now they could find no other policy than that of coercion, meeting Terror by Counter-Terror, trying to break the spirit of the Irish people by raids, searches, shootings, burnings. God! What a horror, after the Great War! And what a mental agony for a man like himself, hating the methods of both sides, seeing the point of view from both sides, divided in sympathy, trying to keep to the middle of the road, between the two extremes. Once again he was called traitor, and felt the word like a wound in his heart. Traitor, though he was loyal to the truth as far as he could see it. Traitor, though he had pledged his soul to loyalty!

XXXII

It was a rough passage from Holyhead, and he felt sick in the smoking saloon, crowded with officers of the Royal Scots, among whom, silent and absorbed in thought or prayer, sat two Irish priests. There was a battalion of soldiers on board-mostly boys of nineteen or so-and most of them were horribly sick as they lay among their kit and rifles. They cursed Ireland, the War Office, Lloyd George, and other powers which had ordained this night passage across the Irish Channel and the "bloody job" at the end of it.

Bertram spoke a few words to one of the officers, a captain with a row of decorations. He had been on service in Ireland before, and was going back from leave.

"What's it like over there?" asked Bertram.

"Like nothing on earth," said the officer. "Worse than France, barring barrage-fire. One never knows when one is going to be sniped, or blown up by a bomb thrown from a side street. Not a gentleman's job! A rotten dirty business."

"What's going to be the end of it?"

The young officer shrugged his shoulders.

"They'll go on with this guerrilla game for centuries, unless we wipe out the whole lot. Another Cromwell show! Of course, I'm not supposed to hold opinions, but speaking privately, I'd give them anything less than a Republic, clear out British troops, and let them stew in their own juice. They'd fight like Hell among themselves. That would make less Irish in the world, and save a lot of trouble. What's your view?"

Bertram's view was much the same, with regard to "clearing out," though he believed they wouldn't go in for civil war among themselves if they had Dominion Home Rule.

"You don't know them," said the Captain of Royal Scots.

"I'm half Irish," Bertram told him, and the officer said, "Oh!" suspiciously, and after that was silent and moved away.

The railway journey to North Wall was uneventful. The line was guarded by troops, and there were many soldiers in the train, wearing steel hats and full fighting kit. Boys again, sullen-looking, and with shifty, nervous eyes.

Then Dublin.

Bertram walked through the streets like a *revenant.* Dublin belonged to a former life. He had forgotten it for a thousand years-or was it only sixteen? He found his way to Merrion Square, and stood outside his father's old home-Number 23 —and gazed up at its windows through dirty lace curtains.

Inside one of those rooms he had first seen the light of day. Half-forgotten incidents of his childhood came back to him, vividly, with astonishing sharpness of detail. He remembered putting his head once through those railings and not being able to get it out again. That was when he was four years old, or thereabouts. Good Heavens! There were two of the railings bent, where his Irish nurse had pressed them apart with a cry of "Holy Mother of God!" Betty was her name. He remembered now. And there was the ring and wrought iron lion's head of the door-knocker which he had just been able to reach on tip-toe, later in that early life of his.

He remembered "the Move" —the frightful excitement of it-when, at nine years of age, he had left this house with all the family, for England. He had wept bitterly at leaving, especially when his broken rocking-horse had been cast on to the scrap heap, with other wreckage of nursery life. He could remember the mangy tuft of hair on that wooden beast, and the smell of red paint which had once represented a saddle. He had kissed its wooden nose, and howled when it was taken from him for ever.

Betty had frightened him about England. "The English will skin you alive if you make a noise in their London town. . . . The English know nothing but hate for the Irish. . . . The English are a bad-tempered set of spalpeens, and there's no truth in them at all."

Dublin! . . . It was strange to be here among his own people, a foreigner among them. He had the English way of speech, the English way of mind. Some of them, especially the young men, scowled at him as he passed down Sackville Street. They knew him as English by the cut of his clothes, by the look in his eyes. They didn't see the Irish strain of blood in him.

He looked at their faces as they pushed by. What was wrong with them? They were people haunted by some hidden fear. There was fear in their eyes. They kept glancing about them, uneasily, watchfully. Some men were nailing boards outside a shop window, and one of the planks fell on to the pavement with a slight crash. Instantly a group of people gathered round a shop window scattered and ran into neighbouring doorways. The men with the boards laughed. One of them called out, "No danger at all, at all!" —and in a moment or two men and women emerged from shelter, smiled at each other, and went their way again, with that nervous glance to left and right.

Haunted! Yes, that was the word. Many of the women had haggard eyes, drawn, pallid faces, little lines of pain about their mouths. They looked as though they had lost their sleep for nights or weeks. Their nerves were tattered. It was easy to see that by their sudden shrinking from any little noise, like the crack of a jarvey's whip, or a boy's shrill whistle.

They greeted each other like women Bertram had seen in French villages after mornings of great battle when the wounded had gone streaming by.

"Dear God!" said one woman to another as he passed.

"Mother of Mercy!" said another.

There was no mystery about it. Here, in Sackville Street were outward and visible signs of conflict, old and recent; the ruins of the Post Office and public buildings bombarded during the Rebellion of Easter Week in '16, and new bulletmarks on the walls of shops, and through plate-glass windows. Many shops were barricaded. Others were shut up and barred. Women did their shopping through narrow entrances of stacked timber. It was a city of Civil War.

Worse than Civil War, thought Bertram, for here there was no knowing who was friend and who enemy. Any of these young Irishmen strolling by might have a bomb in his pocket, and hurl it at any man he had marked down, rightly or wrongly, as a spy, a detective, a Government official, a British officer in mufti. From any window or any roof might come the crack of a sniper's bullet.

An armoured car passed, with its machine guns poking through the loop-holes, and people stared at it sullenly or fell back on the sidewalks as it went by. Many of them ran quickly into side streets when a lorry full of soldiers came at a rapid speed down the street. It was covered with a wired cage in which young soldiers wearing steel hats, like those boys with whom Bertram had crossed, sat with rifles on their knees, looking down on the crowd in Sackville Street with unfriendly eyes, smiling ironically when they saw them running.

Dublin in time of Peace, after the Great War! In that former life of Bertram's —how many years ago? —it had been a gay, careless old city, if he remembered well. Young as he was, he had walked up that very street alone, or hand in hand with Susan, without any fear, or sense of peril.

Somewhere in the city was Susan now, weeping because the man she loved was to be hanged on Wednesday morning, which was next day. He must find her, and stand by her in this time of trouble. But first he must find Digby.

It was to find Digby that Bertram had come to Dublin. He had a last wild hope that Digby might help to get a reprieve for Dennis O'Brien. A word from him to his commanding officer, from that officer to the Judge Advocate in Dublin Castle, might have some result. The condemned man was Digby's brother-in-law, Michael Pollard's son-in-law. Surely, surely it might lead to mercy.

Digby was in barracks somewhere on the north side of the city. Bertram found the place by enquiring of a group of soldiers, halted with stacked rifles in a street off Fitzwilliam Square. They were suspicious at first, and would not answer his questions. The sergeant went so far as to tell him to "clear off, unless he wanted a hole through his head." He became civil and informative when Bertram gave him his card, showing his old rank of major in the British Army.

"Sorry, sir! But we have to be careful. These damned Irish —"

The barracks where Digby was quartered were a good mile away, and difficult to find. No good asking the passers-by, and quite dangerous. They didn't like people who paid friendly visits to British barracks. He had better be careful, walking alone. Not pleasant to be shot in the back of the head!

The sergeant drew a little map on the back of an envelope. He seemed to know Dublin blindfold.

"I've searched every street in that district. Two of my lads were killed in Donegal Street, not two weeks ago. Not a health resort in that quarter!"

With the map, Bertram found the barracks, and was glad to get there. As he walked up dirty narrow streets where "washing" was hanging out of the windows, sullen glances, and sometimes foul words, greeted him from people lounging in their doorways, or slouching by. A young girl spat as he passed, as though he were a living stench. Two youths with caps drawn over their eyes followed him a little way, scowling when he turned to glance at them, and searching him with suspicious eyes. They dropped back at a corner saloon. A frowsy woman sitting on a doorstep smoking a cutty pipe, while some bare-legged children played about the street, raised her voice and cursed him.

"May the divils of Hell strike you dead for an English blackguard!"

"I'm as Irish as yourself, mother!" he answered her, not liking the way in which windows began to open and heads come out, at the sound of her shrill voice.

"Irish are ye! Then why the divil d'ye look like an English cut-throat? Holy Mother o' God! May the English soon be driven into the sea and all drowned with the spawn of Hell!"

At the barrack gate, the sentry fell back with his bayonet on guard. At the sight of an unknown civilian he looked thoroughly scared, and the point of his bayonet trembled.

"It's all right, my man," said Bertram, in his best army style. "I'm Major Bertram Pollard. I've come to see my brother, Mr. Digby Pollard."

"No civilians allowed, sir," said the man. "Nobody in civil clothes," he added, as a concession to Bertram's rank.

"Send a message up to the O.C. It's important."

The message was sent, and an orderly came down to take him to Colonel Lavington. It appeared that Digby was out on a search party and would not be back until the following day.

"Sorry!" said the Colonel pleasantly. "Anything I can do for you, Major?"

Bertram was utterly depressed by this stroke of evil luck. By the time Digby came back, O'Brien's execution would have happened. He revealed the tragedy of his mission to the Colonel.

"I'm here on a forlorn hope, sir," he said. "It's to make a plea for a man condemned to death. My sister's husband, Dennis O'Brien."

Colonel Lavington sat up in his chair, and did not hide his surprise.

"That man O'Brien! Your brother-in-law?"

"Didn't my brother Digby tell you?"

"Not a word!"

The Colonel was sympathetic. He made no concealment of his hatred of the whole show in Ireland.

"I ought not to say so —I'm a Regular, you know! —but the politicians in England seem to be bungling frightfully. I don't approve of these executions. They only inflame passion still further, and make martyrs of the condemned men. The scenes that go on round the prison on the morning of execution are hair-raising!"

There was no doubt about Dennis O'Brien's guilt. He had been captured in the ambush, after shooting a British officer-poor young Stewart-MacKey. He'd been tried by Court Martial and condemned to death for murder. Of course, in a way, it wasn't murder. The Irish argued that men captured like that ought to be treated as prisoners of war. As a soldier, he saw something in that. Still, as long as the present policy continued, he could not criticise. It was all a dirty business. Dreadful! Worse than war!

He would ring up the Judge Advocate. He might go as far as that.

Bertram listened while he "rang up." He listened with a sense of Fate in the disjointed words spoken at last over that little instrument in a white-washed room furnished with a table, two chairs, and a map of Dublin on the wall.

"Is that the Judge Advocate? Oh, Colonel Lavington speaking. About that man, Dennis O'Brien, in Mountjoy Prison. Yes, to be hanged to-morrow morning. Yes. I have his brother-in-law here, Major Bertram Pollard, son of Michael Pollard, M.P. His brother-in-law. Yes. You knew? Telegrams from London? Oh, yes, special report! Well, then, you don't think-No. Not a chance? Must take place? Reprieve impossible? I understand, sir. Yes. Yes. Sorry to have troubled you. Oh, of course. At six o'clock to-morrow? Thanks. Quite so. Yes, Major Pollard's with me now. Yes. I'll explain. Your regrets? Yes. Thanks again, sir. All right. Good-bye."

"Not a chance?" asked Bertram.

The Judge Advocate had explained fully. Bertram could hear the crackle of his voice on the telephone. The Colonel's words had been said between long bouts of speech from the Judge Advocate-that hoarse crackling in the receiver of the instrument.

"No. You understood by my answers? The Judge Advocate has been in communication with the Chief Secretary about the case. It has been thoroughly considered. Their decision is definite. Justice must take its course, and so on. Well! . . . I'm extremely sorry for your sake, and for your sister's."

He was wonderfully courteous, charmingly sympathetic, not at all a Black and Tan in his political opinions, but it would make no difference to Dennis O'Brien.

The execution was at six o'clock? Yes, at Mountjoy Prison. There would be strong guards outside. Sure to be a public demonstration.

Bertram thanked Colonel Lavington, gave him the latest news about the English Strike, shook hands, and went. His coming to Ireland had been in vain. He might as well have remained in London, except for the knowledge that he had done his best, for Susan's sake.

He had no idea where his sister was living in the city, and perhaps it was better so. What could he say to her? How could he give her any comfort?

XXXIII

That night he slept a little in his chair in a bedroom of the Shelbourne Hotel. At four o'clock in the morning he awakened, cramped and chilled. It was the morning of execution. Something called to him to go out to Mountjoy Prison, though overnight he had no such intention. "The scenes that go on round the prison are hair-raising," said the Colonel. What kind of scenes? He would go and see for himself. It would help him to understand the spirit of the Irish people, the spirit of half his own blood.

He found a jaunting car, and bargained with the jarvey to take him to the prison.

"They're hanging Dennis O'Brien," said the man. "God's curse on them!"

All round the prison were strong forces of troops. Several armoured cars were drawn up, and a search-light was turned on a dense black crowd of people waiting there through the night, for the coming of dawn. They were mostly women and young girls, with shawls over their heads. Some bareheaded, some well-dressed with hats of the latest style. They were of all classes and ages, and with them were some priests who moved about among them, leading the recitation of the Rosary.

Again and again, with endless repetition, the crowd, kneeling on the cobble-stones, murmured their prayer:

> Hail, Mary, full of grace,
> The Lord is with thee,
> . . . . .
> . . . . .

Holy Mary, Mother of God,
Pray for us sinners
Now and at the hour of our death,
    Amen

Between each prayer there rose another sound, the strangest, most terrible sound of a human kind that Bertram had ever heard beyond a battlefield. It was the wailing of women. It was like the cry of the Banshee, as he had imagined it with horror in childhood. It rose and fell in rhythmic anguish, from all those shawl-covered women, kneeling with bowed heads, or raising their heads and hands like a Greek chorus, to the heavens above. The search-light moved above them, touched their white hands, searched along the line of upturned faces, seemed to search their souls and reveal their passion. Between the "decades" of the Rosary, and the wail of the women, other voices rose, crying out ejaculatory prayers and sacred names.

"Holy Mother o' God! . . . Sweet Jesus, have mercy on him! . . . Christ be with him to the end! . . . Saint Joseph, comfort him! . . . God help him!"

The soldiers in their shrapnel helmets and field kit stood motionless. Their helmets-the old "tin hats" of France and Flanders, —were touched at times by the white finger of light, and their faces were sharply illumined in those moments. Young, square-jawed, English faces. Now and again one of them pushed back some one in the crowd with the butt-end of his rifle, sharply, but without brutality. An officer passed down their lines, occasionally spoke a word of command. Bertram was edged amidst a group of women. When they knelt, he felt himself isolated and too prominent, as the only man among them, and standing. He decided to kneel, and he too bowed his head when the prayers rose again for a soul shortly to be hurled into eternity at the end of a hangman's rope. Frightful thought! That man had been a comrade of his in the war. They had touched hands. Only a few weeks ago he had sat in Bertram's study in Holland Street with Susan, his young wife, Bertram's sister. Now this!

Holy Mary, Mother o' God,
Pray for us sinners,
Now and at the hour of our death,
    Amen.

For the hundredth or thousandth time the words of the Rosary came from the kneeling crowd. A woman close to Bertram fell all huddled in a faint on the cold stones. Other women bent over her, loosened her shawl. A girl was sobbing loudly, with her face in her hands. A boy —a mere child-ended his prayer with a curse. "To Hell with England!"

Somewhere, perhaps, in the crowd was Susan, weeping and praying for her man. When the search-light passed Bertram stared closely at some of the women's faces, but did not see his sister, though more than once his heart gave a thump because he thought some girl was like her. The light of dawn crept into the sky, above the prison walls. Presently a silver streak broke through the black clouds. The crowd perceived it, and because the hour of execution was coming near, the wail of the women rose louder, with greater anguish.

"Christ have mercy on him!"

"Lord have mercy on him!"

A bell began to toll. Bertram could see it wagging to and fro in the turret of a chapel above the prison wall.

A priest stood up on a box, or some small platform, and spoke some words to the crowd, which Bertram failed to hear. Somewhere in the crowd a woman shrieked, and then was hushed down. All heads were bowed, and a dreadful hush came upon them for what seemed like a long time to Bertram, before the patter of prayers rose again. The dawn was creeping up, and the sky was grey, and rain began to fall.

Bertram was conscious of stones cutting into his knees. He was faint with hunger, and felt a little sick. He found himself trembling, and a cold sweat broke upon his forehead.

Dennis O'Brien! Susan's husband!

What year was this? 1921! Nineteen hundred and twenty one years in the Christian era! After the Great War. . . . Civilisation! . . . Peace! . . . The Self-Determination of Peoples! . . . Liberty! . . . What was Joyce doing? . . . What was all this tragedy called Life? . . . Where was God? . . . Where was Susan in the crowd? . . . Oh, Christ!

The silver streak broadened, and the top of the prison wall was clear cut against the sky.

The bell tolled. A strange deep sigh came from the crowd. The bell stopped tolling. Above the prison wall a little black square fluttered.

A priest stood on the box again, and raised his hands, and spoke some more words. Bertram heard the end of them.

"May the souls of the faithful departed, through the mercy of God, rest in peace, Amen."

Another priest took his place.

"He died as a Christian martyr. His last words were, 'God save Ireland'!"

A frightful confusion of sound burst forth. No one was kneeling now. The women had risen to their feet, some wailing, some crying in shrill, fierce tones, some weeping noisily, some laughing, even, as one girl near Bertram, with hysteria. Men's voices sounded among the women's.

"God save Ireland! To hell with England! May God curse them for this day! The bloody tyrants!"

As in a kind of liturgy, prayers answered the curses.

"May his soul rest in peace!"

"Mother of God, pray for him!"

The soldiers were turning back the crowd with their rifles lengthwise. An officer shouted words of command. An armoured car moved, driving a line among the women. Bertram was pressed amidst a living mass, mostly women, forced along with them. The tress of a woman's hair, uncoiled in the night, flicked across his face. Hands grabbed at his shoulders for support. A girl swooned and fell against him, and he put his arm about her and helped to carry her. Presently, after a long while, as it seemed, he found himself with elbow-room, able to walk freely, following separate groups of men and women. . . .

In Sackville Street he came face to face with Susan. She was walking with a girl on each side of her, one of whom was Betty O'Brien, the sister of Dennis, who was hanged. Their clothes were wet and bedraggled, their hair wild, like all the women who had waited outside the prison.

"Susan!" said Bertram.

She stared at him without recognition for a moment, and then faltered forward, and clutched him, and wept with her head against him. But not for long. Some other passion shook her, not of grief but rage. She drew back from her brother, and took Betty's arm.

"Bertram," she said, in a hoarse voice, "for what has happened to-day I'll never forgive England. I'm Sinn Fein to the death. Body and soul of me for Ireland and liberty!"

In her tear-stained eyes was a wild light. She looked like a drunken woman of the streets.

A crowd gathered about them, and an English officer came up and said very politely, "Please pass away. Please don't make trouble."

"Get away yourself," said Betty O'Brien. "Out of Ireland with all your tyranny!"

"I must ask you to move on," said the officer.

Bertram tried to induce Susan to give him her address, but she refused.

"I want to be alone," she said. "And you're too English."

"I'm your brother, and the same old pal," said Bertram. "I want to help you, little sister."

She put her hand on his arm.

"Help me by leaving me. Don't you understand? I've been through Hell's torture."

She turned away from him, down a side street, with Betty and the other girl, and he did not follow her, because he understood.

That morning in the Shelbourne Hotel, he was called up on the telephone by Colonel Lavington.

"Is that Major Pollard? Oh, good morning."

There was a moment's silence, some hesitation on the telephone. Then the Colonel spoke again.

"I'm sorry to report bad news. Your brother Digby was killed last night. A sniper's bullet on the outskirts of Dublin. A splendid young man. Most regrettable."

Most regrettable! It was the old phrase used in the Great War when youth was killed. "I regret to report the loss of your gallant son —"

How was Bertram to face his mother with the news? How was he going to balance the tragedy of Dennis O'Brien with the tragedy of Digby Pollard? How was he going to get any sane judgment about this frightful orgy of death and outrage, hangings and shootings, prayers and curses and bleeding hearts?

Digby! That kid! A baby only a few years ago, to whom he told fairy-tales as he lay in bed! Now dead by a sniper's bullet. What year of the Christian era? Yes, 1921! Bertram in his room at the Shelbourne laughed aloud, harshly, and then wept.

XXXIV

One of the tragic moments of Bertram's life, which afterwards he could never remember without a shadow darkening his mind, was when he entered his father's house after that visit to Dublin.

His way back had been delayed by the Coal Strike. The fast train from Holyhead was cancelled, and he had to come by a slow train, crowded with men thrown out of work by the shutting down of factories for lack of fuel. "It's the end of England if this lasts long," said one of them, but Bertram thought only of his journey's end, and of his meeting with his mother, now that Digby lay dead, with a sniper's bullet through his brain.

The news had come to her, he found, through a report in *The Evening News*, confirmed, almost immediately, by a telegram to his father from the Irish Secretary. Mrs. Pollard was in her little sitting-room when Bertram arrived, and tried to rise from her desk when he bent and put his arms about her. She didn't weep very much, except for one brief agony of tears, but was quite broken. Over and over again she spoke the name of the dead boy, her last child, and said many times that she knew he was doomed. She was almost too weak to walk across her room, and complained that her heart had gone "queer."

Bertram carried her up to bed that evening, and sent for a doctor, who looked grave, and told Bertram that his mother was in a very feeble state of health, with a pulse far below normal. Nothing organically wrong, except a cardiac weakness, but general lack of vitality. She would need constant attention, and he would send a trained nurse round that night.

Bertram sat by his mother's side before the nurse came that evening. She clasped his hand almost like a child afraid to be left alone in the dark, as once he had held hers. Several times she seemed to be wandering in her mind, wandering back to the early days of her motherhood, when her children were young. She seemed to be worried because Dorothy had torn her frock, and a little later, told Bertram not to tease Susan.

"Do you hear me —?" she asked suddenly, after a long silence.

Bertram bent over her, and told her that he heard.

"You mustn't tease little Susan," she said. "You're getting a big boy now."

Then she fell asleep, still clasping his hand, and he listened to her breathing which seemed troubled, and sometimes came with a quick flutter.

Bertram sat cramped in his chair, while the room darkened as the evening crept on. All his love for his mother moved in him with poignancy, now that she lay stricken by this last blow of fate. After his boyhood, when his mother had been all in all to him, she had become not much more than a beautiful memory. Oxford, the War, Marriage, had thrust her out of his active interests of life. Weeks had passed, and he had not given a thought to her.

Now he remembered, and renewed the devotion of his boyhood to this little woman, so frail, but so brave, till now, who had never spared herself to give her children health, who had been so patient with all their woes, and so eager for their happiness. He remembered when he had been unwell, and she had tip-toed to his room at night, to feel whether his forehead was "feverish," to dose him with little white pills from her homeopathic chest, and send him to sleep with a few soothing words. They had taken all that for granted, as children. Now, in manhood, Bertram, sitting by his mother's bed, reproached himself at the thought of his ingratitude, accused himself of selfishness, was sharply touched with, pity, because of all this little mother of his had suffered in life, and with anger against life itself.

The War had been an agony to her. She could never understand the reason for all that massacre. It made her doubt even the goodness of God, which before she had never doubted. That so many boys should be killed, for "politics," as she said, sounded to her a terrible cruelty, due to some madness which had overtaken the world. She had submitted, doubtfully and silently, to her husband's fierce patriotism, and to Bertram's excitement when he first enlisted, and to all the war-fever of England. Perhaps Dorothy's marriage to a German, before the War, made her less inclined to desire the wholesale slaughter of the enemy than many mothers of England. She felt pity even for the German mothers, to the great annoyance of Michael Pollard, and the amusement of Bertram in the first ardour of his hatred for the enemy-quickly quenched after a few weeks of fighting, when he, too, lost all actual hate for the poor wretches on the other side of the barbed wire, sitting in mud, as he was sitting, with the same chance of being blown to bits.

She had rejoiced in the Armistice because it had saved Bertram, and Digby, who was getting ready to go out, and all other boys of a fighting world. An enormous burden of anxiety was lifted from her shoulders by the "Cease Fire" of the guns. She became young in spirit again, for a time, until gradually she came to suspect that there was no great security in this peace, and was aware of an orgy of blood and murder in Ireland, which came very close to her when Digby became a "Black and Tan."

Bertram alone there, in her bedroom, in the darkness that closed about him, thought of all the tragedy of life that hadn't ended with the war. It was still claiming its victims, though Peace had come. It had released human passions everywhere, unchained the primitive instincts of the human beast, weakened the nerve-power and controls of civilised life, made a wreck of many lives and hearts. Death was still busy. Famine and pestilence were ravaging many peoples. In the one letter he had received from Christy in Russia there were terrible words.

"Millions are eating nothing but grass and leaves, and not enough of that," he wrote. "Typhus is sweeping these people like a scourge."

England had escaped calamities like that, but unemployment was creeping up like a dark wave-millions were idle because of the Strike-and trade was at a standstill. What was the future? "Europe is dying!" said Anatole France, according to the papers, and Christy thought so too, in his blacker moods. Did it matter much? What was life, anyhow, to the individual soul? Not much of a game, except for a little laughter, some moments of love, some years of illusion! Here he was, sitting by the bedside of this mother whose children had gone from her-all but himself-and whose heart was broken by the death of her last-born in a foul kind of civil war. Susan's husband had been hanged. Bertram's wife had left him. A cheerful kind of family record! Not worse than in millions of other families in civilised Europe. Not so bad as in Russia, or Austria, or Poland, according to reports.

His mother wakened, and spoke to him in a feeble voice.

"Are you there, my dear?"

"Yes, mother."

She was no longer wandering back to the early years, but remembered what had happened.

"It's terrible about Digby."

"Yes, mother."

She was silent for a little while, and then spoke again.

"Bertram! Work for Peace. The world is so very cruel, and the future so dark! Work for peace, my dear. Peace is so beautiful. Promise me."

"Promise you what, mother?"

She drew his head down with her weak hands, and as he kissed her, he heard her whisper the word "Peace."

That was the last word he heard his mother speak. The nurse came, and the doctor, and his father was sent for from the House of Commons, where there was a debate on the Coal Strike, as Bertram saw by the next day's papers. It was at some time past midnight that his father came downstairs and entered his study, where Bertram was sitting, waiting for the doctor's latest word about his mother's health.

"Is she better?" he asked.

"She's dead," said his father.

He lurched a little as he walked across the room, and then sat heavily in his chair and put his arms down on his desk, and his head on his arms, and wept with a passion of grief.

It was the first time Bertram had seen him give way to any emotion, except that of anger, and at the sight of that grief all hostility to his father, because of so much hardness and intolerance, was thrust aside by pity. He had loved young Digby best of all his children, and the boy's death had struck him a frightful blow, which only his pride and his freshly-inflamed hatred of Sinn Fein enabled him to bear with self-control. But his wife's death, so sudden and so utterly unexpected, smote him beyond all endurance.

He had been hard with her sometimes, he had made her afraid of his temper, and many a time she had wept because of his stern way with "the children," but she'd never had cause to doubt his love for her. He had loved her, in spite of all tempers, perhaps because of it, with what he believed to be never-failing devotion. To him she was the perfect wife and perfect mother, and perhaps his intense egotism, his old-fashioned belief in the "mastery" of the husband, and the submission of the wife, were never shocked by the knowledge that his wife sometimes described him to her children as "very trying," and-regarding Dorothy's marriage-as "most unjust."

He had depended on her for his comfort, for his sense of security in home life, for the thousand little duties which she had done for him as a daily routine. Now that she had been taken away from him like this, after Digby had been killed-the boy he had loved best in the world-he felt fearfully alone, and was broken-hearted.

Bertram put his hand on his father's shoulder and said: "Courage, father!"

He remembered the better side of his father's nature now, the old days, before politics-the madness in Ireland-had so embittered their relations. Michael Pollard had not been always harsh. He had been playful when his children were young; humorous and comradely at times. Perhaps his children were partly to blame for the irascibility which had overtaken him in later years. They had been self-willed, deliberately rebellious of his authority, sarcastic when he had laid down the law, regarding obedience and discipline, stubbornly intolerant of his intolerance.

So Bertram thought now, in the presence of this stricken man, forgetful for a while of his own tremendous loss, his loneliness of soul, while he watched his father's agony, and tried to comfort him, and could not.

XXXV

It was after his mother's funeral that Bertram's courage failed him. He had a letter from Joyce which put all but the finishing touch to his sense of abandonment by any kindliness of fate. She wrote to him from Paris-the Hotel Meurice-where she had gone with Lady Ottery. She still called him "My dear Bertram," but her letter did not warm his soul.

She had been horrified to hear about Digby-that ought to kill his sympathy with Irish rebels, if anything would. She was also deeply sorry to hear about Mrs. Pollard's death, though not surprised, after so much worry and so much tragedy.

She wished to let him know that Holme Ottery was being bought by an American, and that, to avoid the unhappiness of seeing the old house pass into new hands, she and her Mother had gone to Paris, on the way to Italy-while arrangements were being made by Alban to warehouse some of the old furniture and family treasures.

Her father had taken a new house in town, rather bigger than the little old house in John Street.

They had sold the Lely portrait of Rupert Bellairs, and she had wept to see it go. It was the symbol of the great smash in the family fortune. England was doomed by a prodigal Government, playing into the hands of Bolshevism.

One passage in the letter stabbed him.

> . . . Kenneth Murless has shown me your articles in *The New World*. That one-the first? —called "The Mind of the Men" made me want to use bad language. No wonder you refused that offer from General Bellasis! Your words might have been spouted by a Hyde Park orator on an orange box to a mob of shifty-eyed hooligans. How can you, Bertram? How *can* you? To me it's incredible, after your war-service! It's nothing but rank treason. . . .

There was something in the letter about the beauty of Paris in May. Then another line or two about the hatred of France for Germany, and for the English Liberals who were playing into the hands of Germany.

> . . . The French won't tolerate any breach of the Treaty.
>
> They will force Germany to pay, or march across the Rhine and seize her industrial cities. I quite agree with them. After all, we *did* win the war, though some people behave as though it were a shame to do so. . . .

Well, well, Joyce's views on foreign politics didn't matter very much. Some other words in her letter mattered more to him.

> Kenneth Murless has come over to Paris in the Embassy-as First Secretary. I see a good deal of him and he keeps me amused. When are you going to be sensible and make a career for yourself? I'm a little tired of being a grass widow, though as a rest-cure it has done me good! I'm ready to forget and forgive, if you care to join me here. Besides, *it must be one thing or the other*. . . .

Those words were underlined.

At the end of her letter she signed herself "Yours affectionately," and Bertram laughed aloud at the words, but not with any merriment of soul. She had wept when the Lely had gone, not much when he had gone! . . . Kenneth Murless amused her. She saw a lot of him. . . . She was ready to forget and forgive!

He wrote a raging letter to her, and then tore it up. He accused her of damned heartlessness, told her that he would never play her lap-dog again, reminded her of the things she had said to him at Holme Ottery, and ended by saying that if Kenneth Murless amused her so much, she had better make it one thing or the other, as far as he was concerned. He would be glad to know her decision.

Having written all that, he heard, almost with physical audibility, the words his mother had spoken to him on her death-bed. "Work for Peace, Bertram!" She meant peace in Europe, between peoples, with Ireland, but the spirit of peace must begin in the heart of the individual, between one and another-even between husband and wife. He wrote another letter, less violent.

> Dear Joyce:
>
> I'm still trying to earn a living. I'm sorry you don't like my articles, because they're the way to that possibility. You say you're ready to forget and forgive. That seems to me hardly good enough. When you tell me you love me again and want my love, I'll come to you. I thought that was understood between us. . . .

He referred to her sympathy with his family afflictions:

. . . Yes, it's sad about Digby, and mother's death leaves me very much alone. . . .

That correspondence with Joyce didn't seem to alter much in their relations to each other. It left him in exactly the same situation spiritually, and physically —a husband "on probation," with a verdict of disloyalty against him, but an offer of pardon on recantation of faith.

No, not good enough! Hopelessly impossible on any basis of self-respect or decent comradeship, to say nothing of love. Yet tempting to a man who hated loneliness, and was alone; who, at the very sight of Joyce's handwriting, felt the same thrill of passion for her which had come to him always at the touch of her finger-tips, or the quick toss of her head, or the whiteness of her neck. It was a temptation to his weakness, but he was stubborn as well as weak, and wouldn't yield to such a miserable compact as this surrender would mean to his manhood.

He was in a wretched state of mind, which Joyce's last letter intensified in wretchedness. Susan's agony, Digby's murder, his mother's death, his father's grief and rage-for he was raging now with more personal passion against the Irish rebels-had smitten him at a time when Joyce's desertion would have been enough to cast him into the blackest depths. It seemed as though God, or fate, had a special grudge against him, and kicked him when he was down.

The last blow —a feeble tap, perhaps, yet overpowering for a while to his moral strength-befell him in a letter from a man named Heatherdew, into whose hands, as literary agent, Christy had placed the war-book.

My Dear Major Pollard (he wrote):

For our friend Christy's sake, as well as in the usual way of business, I have spared no trouble in trying to find a publisher for your book, "The Machine Gun Company," which I may say I have read with the greatest interest and admiration. It has now been to eight publishers and all of them, without exception, express the opinion that, at the present time, there is no market for war books. The public, they say (I think incorrectly) wish to forget the war. My own opinion is that they are tired of war books which do not go to the heart of the business which you and I know. However, I consider it useless to make further effort, and I therefore return the manuscript, advising you to hold it for a year or two, when it may have a better chance.

It was a vital disappointment. Bertram had always clung to the hope of this book as a compensation for his failure to get "a job," as a justification, even, of his life. He had put everything that was in him into this book, his secret agonies and fears, his quality of courage, his love of England, his understanding of the men, the ardour that was his in the beginning of war, the joy in comradeship, the later disillusion, the final disgust.

This was the war as it had passed through his own soul, and through the souls of all the men he knew. It was the Absolute Truth, as he had seen it and known it. It was, above all, his defence against Joyce's accusations, and the general suspicion of her family and friends that he was a "slacker," unpatriotic, and careless of his country's honour. Janet Welford had spoken well of it. "It's good!" she had said, and had praised it as "almost great." Well, here it was back again, soiled by publishers' readers, scrumpled through the post, condemned.

Bertram flung it into a drawer of the little old desk where, as a boy in his father's house, he had written secret verses, youthful essays about London life, and, later, love-letters to Joyce Bellairs.

An immense gloom closed down upon his spirit. What was the use of anything? He had tried hard, and failed utterly, in every way. He had made a frightful mucker of life. His luck was out. Why kick against it? Why not face up to the futility of life-for him, anyhow? He hadn't even had the decent luck of going out with the men who had met a bullet or a bit of shell. Those things had passed him by, though he hadn't dodged them. That was a decent way of death, and honourable, the easiest way out of all difficulties. Even now, a bullet would solve a lot of problems, and answer that alternative which Joyce had put: "It must be one thing or the other." He wondered if she would weep as much for him as for the Lely portrait of Rupert Bellairs. She might like the sentiment of being a widow for a little while. She would look beautiful in her weeds, with a little bit of white lace under the black round her gold-spun hair, almost as beautiful as Lady Martock. Kenneth Murless would say all kinds of consoling things in his gentlemanly way. All her friends would write, wire, send messages, flowers. The two Russian girls would utter extravagances in broken English, and the Countess Lydia would enquire whether Joyce's husband had died a Bolshevik, or suggest that he had killed himself at the bidding of Lenin and Trotsky, "who have agents everywhere, *ma chérie*!" Well, he would provide a lot of pleasure to all kinds of people, and end his own misery at the same time.

He had left his old service revolver in the study at Holland Street. Quite easy to get, if Edith were still there, as parlour-maid.

Chatty Edith! She would be glad to see him again. He would have to invent all kinds of lies to explain his absence and his visit, unless he told her straight out that Joyce had deserted him and he'd come to find his revolver to blow his brains out. He could hardly do that! She would scream, or send for the police, or swoon away. Then he would have to fetch the doctor, or throw water at her, or some nuisance of that kind.

Anyhow, he could get his revolver. He had killed a German with it once. That was in a raid near Bullecourt. He remembered the jump into the German trench, after the long crawl across No-Man's Land and the long wait every time a Verrey light went up and he had to lie doggo trying to look like a sand-bag. The German sentry tried to stick him with his bayonet, and he shoved the revolver into the fellow's face and fired it. It was the only thing to do, but he was sorry afterwards. He had searched the man's pockets for letters and post cards-the Intelligence wanted them for identifying a German division. They were all letters from a girl named Lisa. She was dying to see Karl again. She pined for his dear kisses. She was a lonely little Lisa in Magdeburg. If only the cruel war would end! So, in a dozen letters, and a score of closely scribbled postcards. He was sorry he'd killed the fellow stone dead, with that revolver in Holland Street. Now Karl would be revenged by the same weapon that had killed him. Ironical that! A sort of Greek fate business.

Bertram took the 'bus from the top of Sloane Street to High Street, Kensington, and walked up the narrow passage to Holland Street by the west side of St. Mary Abbot's. That was where he had married Joyce. "Isn't she beautiful?" said the women outside, and he agreed and thought her the most beautiful thing on earth, and marvelled at his luck. A little more than a year ago!

Newspaper placards were filled with Strike news.

"Drastic Train Cuts." "Sensational Scene in House of Commons." "Nat Verney States the Miners' Case." "No General Strike."

How trivial was all that nonsense. What would it matter in a thousand years, or eternity, or to-morrow as far as he was concerned?

The little house in Holland Street had its blinds pulled down. No answer came when he rang the bell. No answer when he had pressed the knob six times. The chatty Edith had gone away, and the house was abandoned.

Within a yard and a half of where he stood, at the corner of the little front room which had been his study, in the desk by the window where he had written the book which no one would publish, was that revolver he wanted. Damn silly to think it was so close and he couldn't get it! He could hardly commit a burglary in Joyce's house, in broad daylight! His luck was out again. God, or Fate, refused him even this little bit of luck!

A young policeman sauntered up Holland Street, stood on the opposite side of the road, and then crossed over.

"Do you want anything?" he asked, suspiciously.

"No," said Bertram. "I suppose the people have gone away."

"Looks like it, with the blinds down," said the policeman.

"Yes."

Bertram sauntered slowly away from his wife's house. . . . Not even that bit of luck!

XXXVI

He walked through Kensington Gardens, where the trees were in their first glory of green, through Hyde Park, where the flower-beds were filled with tulips, down Piccadilly, with its tide of gleaming cars, until in the centre of Trafalgar Square he met Janet Welford. The chances of meeting her were about seven million to one, but he knew that he was going to do so. Or perhaps, when he met her, it seemed by some trick of his subconscious mind, the realising of expectation.

"Hullo!" she said, dodging a motor-omnibus and jumping onto a "save-my-life." "What's the matter?"

"What makes you think there's anything the matter?"

She tucked her hand through his arm and told him his face looked like a haunted man's. She commanded him to take her to tea somewhere. She had a craving for a chocolate éclair, or even two.

It was at table in a tea-shop imitating a Tudor house that Bertram told her of all the tragedy that had befallen him since his visit to Ireland, ending in the rejection of his book, which seemed a small thing to put with the death of his mother, but was a death also-of hope and courage.

"I'm down and out," he said.

"Watch me eat éclairs!" was her unsympathetic answer.

He knew that it wasn't heartlessness, but only her way of dealing with trouble. A touch on his hand, an "I'm sorry!" a silence, with understanding eyes, had been her comment to his narrative about Digby and his mother, and it was sympathy enough. But to his "down and out" she put up a refusal, by way of mockery. It wasn't in her philosophy to accept any cry of "down and out," not even from a man blinded in both eyes, with his hands up to his face, and pitch blackness in his soul. Not once but many times she had heard such a cry from one of "her men," as she called them, and had refused to recognise even his misery, and in a week or two, by some spell she had, heard him laughing now and then. She put this to Bertram now.

"I'm not going to say Fortune hasn't dealt you a bad hand lately. You've been handed some of the worst cards in the pack, I'll admit, but there's no need to sit down and grizzle. Empires have fallen, crowns have toppled to the dust, whole nations are starving, little old England is at the crisis of her fate, and I'm in debt to my dressmaker, so where do *you* come in? Don't think you're the only pebble on the beach. Don't imagine that fate is persecuting you with a special grudge" (he had thought that!) —"when there are millions of hearts bleeding with greater agony than yours, and millions are carrying on mighty plucky, in spite of odds against them. Look at that girl with the fluffy hair and the red eyelids. She's playing rag-time in a tea-shop for all she's worth, though she's having hell from a mother-in-law, and keeping a shell-shocked husband and two children."

"How d'you know?" asked Bertram.

"I don't know," said Janet, calmly. "I'm only making a supposition. If it isn't that, it's something else. You can see she's been crying all right."

Her eyes roved round the room, with its panelled walls and sham oak beams, and "antique" furniture, made at Maples. There were several "couples," and two parties of four. Ruthlessly Janet diagnosed their secret troubles. The thin-faced man, sitting opposite a sad-looking woman, with untidy hair, was suffering from a fear-complex. He was "something in the City," and afraid of losing the job which kept a little home at Streatham, the wife with untidy hair, and five children. He was in debt to his butcher. He had a hard struggle to pay the last instalment on his furniture, bought on the hire system. He was dodging his income tax, and the chief clerk had told him that the firm was on the rocks, owing to the slump in foreign trade.

"How on earth do you know all those things?" asked Bertram again.

"I've studied life," she answered. "There's nothing I don't know about it. See that elderly man with the flabby face, weak mouth, and puffed eyes? Next to the painted flapper?"

Bertram turned slightly in his chair, and said "Yes."

"That's a frightful case. He's the manager of a picture palace. That little girl plays the piano for eight hours a day for two pounds a week, at Croydon, except one day a week-to-day-She keeps a drunken father on that, and pays the rent of eighteen shillings, and ten shillings a week for her little sister's schooling. The manager is a wicked old devil, and hates his poor drudge of a wife. Of course it wouldn't do to refuse his invitations to tea, and other things. It's not easy to get a job in another picture palace, even if one does play the piano blindfold-right notes or wrong-and use the rouge-pot ruthlessly. Plucky kid, I think! Look how she pretends to be merry and bright, poor child!"

"Ever seen her before?" asked Bertram.

"Never. But it's something like that."

She said Bertram had no idea of the amount of human courage in a city like London. The heroism of fighting men in war was nothing to the grim, enduring heroism of husbands nagged by their wives, wives bullied by their husbands, men struggling to keep on this side of destitution, women fighting with all the strength of their souls to keep "respectable" in underpaid jobs, young girls starving themselves on milk and buns in order to dress well enough for a chance in the marriage market, and all looking on the best side of things, refusing to surrender, holding on gamely.

"Doesn't it prove that the game's not worth the candle?" asked Bertram.

"The game of life?"

He nodded.

She caught hold of his hand, and said, "That's blasphemy! That's cowardice! Play the game, whether you lose or win. Stick it out to the end. And forget yourself by helping the other fellow. It's only selfishness that despairs. It's damned egotism that makes a man sit down and whine. There's so much to do, so many to help."

Bertram drew a deep breath. He'd been sitting down and whining. He'd wanted to quit before he'd played out the game. He'd been within a yard and a half of the coward's white flag-the worst surrender.

Janet went on talking, wise things, foolish things, fantastic things, and ate not two éclairs, but four (just to make him marvel) and made him laugh heartily at her description of the last meeting of the "Left Wing," which had broken up in wrath and violence because of a vote against the General Strike. One of the girls had slapped the face of one of the young men, and called him "a crawling Pacifist." He had responded by calling her a "Blood-stained Bolshevik." It had all been great fun.

At the sound of his laughter, Janet smiled with a whimsical look.

"You see life's not so black, if one keeps a sense of humour!"

She proposed an evening at the theatre, after a little dinner in Soho. It was a good dinner, and a merry piece. Bertram laughed most because of Janet's laughter.

Afterwards, when they stood together on the kerbstone hailing a taxi in St. Martin's Lane, Janet put a hand on his arm, and said, "Where are you going now?"

"To my lonely little room."

"No," she said. "That's not good for you. Is your father home?"

"He's gone over to Belfast."

"Well, come home with me, and help to make some hot cocoa."

"Is that a good idea?"

He was startled by the invitation at that hour of the night.

"Doesn't it seem good to you?"

"Wonderfully good! But what about-scandal and all that?"

She laughed gaily, so that the commissionaire outside the theatre turned to smile at her.

"Scandal? I'm immune against it. It never worries me, —especially when I've souls to save."

"Are you saving mine?"

He was afraid he might lose it.

"By the scruff of its neck."

They drove to Battersea Park, and she gave him her hand up the long flight of stone steps to her fourth floor flat, where she stopped and panted a little before fumbling in her hand-bag for her latch key.

The flat was in darkness, but she switched on the lights and the electric fire.

"Ever made cocoa?" she asked.

"Never."

"Well, you've got to learn to-night."

He learnt, and found it easy, and good when made.

She lit a cigarette, and dropped into a low chair and told him to take the cane chair opposite, and put on his pipe, if he liked.

It seemed a thousand years since he'd gone looking for a revolver in Holland Street. Yet his tragedy hadn't been turned into comedy. His problems were the same. His future was hopeless. His book had been refused. Joyce was in Paris with Kenneth Murless. Young Digby had been killed. His mother was dead. Strange that he felt happier, almost cheerful, certainly glad of life again. Loneliness was the worst thing in the world-to him.

He no longer felt lonely. Janet's comradeship was wonderfully good. It was splendid of her to open the doors of this little sanctuary and let in a shivering soul to its light and warmth.

She spoke of his book for the first time, and denounced the publishers as silly sheep.

"Keep it a year," she said, "and they'll all be clamouring for it. 'We want the Truth about the War!' they'll cry. 'We can't get enough of it! We hunger for it!' "

"Meanwhile what am I to do?" asked Bertram.

"Leave it to Janet Rockingham Welford," she said. "That girl has planted men in the strangest places, inspired them to noble and saintly deeds, led them to heights of fame and fortune. Don't worry, for you've come to the right lady, the fairy godmother of the down-and-outs."

"I believe you can do anything you want," said Bertram.

"All but a few things."

"What are those?"

She shook her head and smiled, and kept her secret.

So they talked until two o'clock. Then Janet put her head on one side, listening to the distant boom of Big Ben across the river.

"Mercy me! Two o'clock of a May morning and I promised to be at St. Dunstan's at ten!"

She pointed to the sofa, and said, "If you're sleepy, sleep. I go in there, to my virtuous couch."

Bertram rose, and took hold of her hands and spoke with emotion.

"You've saved me to-night. You've given me courage again. You've been the best of comrades."

He drew her hands towards him, and would have kissed her, but she said "Not to-night! . . . After midnight I take no risks."

She released herself from his hands, slipped away, turned at the door with a ripple of laughter, and went into her room.

"Good night, Sir Faithful!"

She spoke those words as she shut the door, and locked it.

Bertram lay down on the sofa, and in a little while slept, and dreamed not of Janet, but of Joyce. He dreamed that he was searching for her in a wood, and could always see her ahead of him in distant glades, but could never get close to her.

XXXVII

A note came from Bernard Hall of *The New World*, asking Bertram to go and see him at his office. He greeted Bertram with that coldness which was but an outer crust concealing the flame in his heart, flame of passion against the injustice of life, its tyrannies and cruelties, its immense unconquerable stupidities.

"Take a seat, won't you?"

Bertram took a seat in a room strewn with papers and books in careless disorder. A middle-aged woman with grey hair smoothed back in the Quaker style, came in and out with proofs, typewritten letters, cards from visitors, which the editor of *The New World* put down in the general litter on his desk.

"I shall be engaged for half an hour, Miss Doe. They can either wait, or call again."

Bertram wondered if he were to have the privilege of that half hour, and what the reason might be.

Bernard Hall stared at his paper knife for a moment, and then looked at Bertram moodily.

"Janet Welford tells me you're at a loose end, more or less."

So it was Janet who had arranged this interview! Bertram felt embarrassed because of that and his face flushed a little.

"Considerably more than less," he answered.

Bernard Hall smiled, icily, and then his face resumed its habitual mask of melancholy.

"Miss Welford and Christy have both spoken highly of that war book of yours. I'm not surprised you can't get it published. People want to forget that time of madness. They're getting a little ashamed of their own insanity. My job-and yours, I take it-is to force them to remember, so that it shan't happen again very soon."

"Quite so!" said Bertram.

Bertram Hall stared at his paper-knife again, as though its long blade symbolised some mystical thing.

"It's going to happen again," he said presently, "unless we can get some sense into the heads of the average man and woman. The politicians are just preparing the way for a new war, worse than the last-in twenty or thirty years from now. I'm inclined to think they'll succeed. The only chance against it is the intensive education of peoples towards the international idea. We must try and link up with all active brains in Europe who are working for peace and commonsense. There are quite a number of them, but with scattered forces, powerless at the moment against the tremendous strength of reaction and militarism."

Bertram wondered again what all this had to do with him. He was interested, but perplexed that Hall should spend half an hour on a busy afternoon to talk broodily about the state of Europe.

"The trouble is," said Bernard Hall, "that what used to be called the fountain of Truth is walled round by the Enemy and kept under strict control. Its waters are carefully and systematically poisoned before they are allowed to flow into the open fields."

"I don't quite follow," said Bertram.

"I mean the distribution of news in the European Press. There's a conspiracy against Truth. It's almost impossible for public opinion to form any kind of verdict based on actual facts. Newspapers nowadays use facts merely as the raw material of propaganda. They're manufactured to suit the policy of the proprietors, or the purpose of Government. By suppression, or alteration, or over-emphasis, or the trick of false perspective, by scare head-lines and editorial comment, they're made to convey exactly the particular idea which the newspapers desire to suggest to its readers. Who knows what is the actual state of things in Germany, whether she is on the brink of bankruptcy, or getting rich? What's the mental state of the German people, after their tremendous defeat, their blood-bath, the downfall of their pride? Are they cherishing the hope of revenge, worshipping the old gods, or working out some way of salvation? France-what about France? Is Poincaré France? Or Paris? What are the people thinking? Do they really want to invade the Ruhr and force another war for unborn babes-as sure as Fate. . . . Do you know, Pollard?"

"No," said Bertram.

"Well, why not find out?"

He had come to the point of the interview. He had an idea that Bertram might wander around a bit in Europe-the old battlefields, Paris-not Paris of the boulevards, but Paris in the back streets, the little shops, the student quarter, the intellectual clubs-then Germany, among its peasants, in the back blocks of Berlin, in middle-class households. Then Russia, if he liked. He could link up with Christy in Moscow, write different kind of stuff, not statistics or high politics, but the human side of things, how the people were living-and dying-what they ate, how they dressed, what was in their minds. He could pick up a bit of Russian, or find people who spoke something else. He might get a glimpse or two of the real truth.

It seemed that Bernard Hall had been impressed by Bertram's article on "The Mind of the Men," and one or two other things he had sent in. That was the kind of thing he wanted. No profound analysis of the European situation-it was in flux, changing from week to week-but intimate sketches of life; things seen; things heard; the common thought; wayside conversations; little flashes revealing the heart of folk.

"Does the idea appeal to you?" he asked.

It appealed to Bertram enormously. Here was his way of escape, from the depression of life without an object; from the immediate problem of earning a "living wage," perhaps from other troubles which had borne down on him, like Joyce's abandonment. It would give her more time to make up her mind about "one thing or the other." It would give him more time to think things out, without desperate conclusions based on boredom, loneliness, futility, and introspective brooding. Here was objective work. He would be looking out upon the world, not inwards with nagging irritation. It would lift his mind, broaden it, re-vitalise it. It would help him to adopt Janet's remedy for gloom and despair-interest in the other fellow's welfare and sympathy beyond selfishness.

Bernard Hall spoke about "terms" —a share of expenses, articles paid for at a fair rate, no particular number laid down, but one a week if possible. It was good enough, enormously more, as a chance, than he could have hoped.

"When can you get off?" asked Hall.

"To-morrow morning."

Bernard Hall smiled for the second time during the interview.

"Not such a hurry as all that."

So it was fixed and Bertram shook hands on the understanding. As he was leaving, Nat Verney, the Miners' leader in the House of Commons, came in and gave him a friendly nod.

"Good article of yours, Pollard, 'The Mind of the Men,' I agreed with every word of it."

"How's the Lock-out?" asked Bernard Hall, and Bertram noticed that he avoided the word 'Strike.'

Nat Verney laughed.

"You read of my evidence before that private meeting in the House of Commons? Most of the members were bowled over by the facts I gave 'em, and admitted the strength of the men's case, for at least a compromise. That's how it's going to end. A good old British compromise! The wicked thing is that it ought to have begun with that. But the owners didn't give us a chance. Just flung an ultimatum at our heads with a 'Take it or leave it!' Well, we damn well left it!"

"What about the Triple Alliance?"

Verney shrugged his shoulders.

"They've ratted. Timid as rabbits. There won't be any General Strike, or Social Revolution. The Government has won that trick. But they look pretty silly with their Army Reserve and Home Defence. Not a single case of violence, except among soldiers who looted a village through sheer boredom."

A shadow seemed to pass from Bernard Hall's face.

"I'm relieved to hear all that, Verney. I'm for evolution, not revolution. If you'd challenged the Government by 'direct action,' there would have been bloodshed and chaos, ending in the utter defeat of Labour."

"Perhaps you're right," said Verney. "I'm not one of the Reds, anyhow. I've no patience with those who want to destroy at all costs, without a notion of how they're going to build up out of ruin."

Bertram left the two men talking. He had heard enough to know that the Strike, or Lock-out, or whatever one liked to call it, was going to end in compromise. After all, he'd been right in backing the men! None of those awful things had happened which had been prophesied on the one hand by the Duke of Bramshaw, Lady Ottery, and their set, on the other by the parlour Jacobins of the "Left Wing." The miners had gone on whitewashing their cottages, sowing seeds in little front gardens. The Unemployed in London, growing in numbers, because of industry closing down, had not invaded Mayfair, except with collection boxes and banners.

The Government and the Mine-owners had admitted at least half the men's case after an ultimatum far too brutal in its original terms. England was not going to break out in civil conflict just yet, or ever, if the men were given anything like a fair deal. English character remained the same as he had seen it in the trenches, solid, steady, without passion. It had always chosen the middle of the road.

Well, he would soon be out of England, wandering among other peoples, studying their problems and psychology. Perhaps he would get as far as Russia, and link up with Christy in Moscow! Extraordinary adventure! What was it old Christy had said, at the top of his stairs?

"If you're not cut out for disloyalty-and it needs a special temperament-cut and run when loyalty's over-strained. It's the safest way . . . and Moscow's an interesting place."

Queer words! He hadn't understood them at the time. Now he seemed to see a special meaning in them. They referred a little to Joyce, and a little to Janet. His loyalty to Janet was getting overstrained. He was being tempted to disloyalty, perhaps to Christy as well as to Joyce. Janet had put a spell on him. That night in her flat was not very safe for a lonely man, abandoned, temporarily or otherwise, by his wife. It was too cosy there, making cocoa over an electric fire for a girl whose laughter and wisdom and comradeship were given generously. The chance of other nights like that, and of comradeship closer and more enduring, might overstrain loyalty to breaking-point. He was human, and pretty weak at that. "Cut and run," old Christy had said. For him there would be torture of conscience in disloyalty. "Sir Faithful," Janet called him. At least he wasn't cut out for the part of Lancelot.

"His honour rooted in dishonour stood,
And faith unfaithful kept him falsely true."

He remembered words he'd spoken once to Christy. "I believe in loyalty." He had said them sincerely then, before temptation had come, testing him under heavy strain. But there was something in him still which forbade, under pain of self-torture, easy ways of escape which many men chose in such a case as his-new love for old, a kind mistress for an unkind wife, excuse for divorce, the usual routine.

What forbade him? What did he mean by conscience? Not religious scruples, for he had no certain faith. Not rigid principles of high morality, for he was tolerant of other men's personal arrangements in this affair of sex. But by heredity, environment, upbringing, his mind was hedged round with restraints and secret laws. If he broke them, he would break himself. He could only be disloyal to such laws within himself by being an outlaw to his own code. Joyce had gone away from him, but he must be faithful in body and soul to his pledge of loyalty to her, or suffer hideously in self-esteem.

Perhaps that was egotism again, the need of self-pride, the prick of self-conceit and not of conscience. All very difficult! Who could get down to the hidden springs, even in his own soul? One could only know the effect of their working, by experience of mental states resulting from thwarted instincts or acts opposed to instincts. One could balance the profit and loss of obedience to the inner law and disobedience. Obedience was generally more profitable, however difficult to resist the lure of disobedience. When the lure was too strong in its spell, Christy's advice was "Cut and run!" Not heroic, but safer. . . .

When he told Janet that he owed her the best chance of his life, his voice broke a little.

"When are you starting?" she asked, and when he told her that he was crossing to France the very next day, she exclaimed, like Bernard Hall, that there was no such burning hurry. But he told her he was in a hurry to "make good," as the Americans say, and that if he stayed a few more days in town he might have to seek escape from loneliness again in her little sanctuary, which would strain her patience, and his virtue.

That seemed to amuse her mightily, and she mocked him as a modern St. Anthony, and liked his flattery (she said) of her poor beauty.

She sent her love to Christy, if Bertram had the chance of meeting him in Moscow.

"If I don't hear from you at least once a month," she told him, "I'll abandon my blinded men to rescue you from Bolshevists!"

"Then I'll never write till you come!" he said.

They talked, mostly nonsense, until he rose to say good-bye.

"There's a chance," said Bertram, "that I mayn't see you again."

"Good Lord!" she cried, in sham alarm. "Are you going to make another war?"

"No, but there's the usual risk from one street to another. A falling chimney-pot, a typhus bug, or some other way of accident. Anyhow, I want to tell you now that I'm eternally grateful for all you've done for me, in lovingkindness. Wherever I am in the world, or beyond it, I'll never forget my dear comrade."

She let him take her hands and put them to his lips, when she answered him.

"Sir Faithful, I'm not good at serious speech, and don't much believe in it, except at odd times, as a concession to human weakness. But I've liked your company, sir, and I'm sorry we can't be closer partners-because of fate and other things."

"Perhaps one day —" he said, and didn't end his sentence.

She shook her head, as though understanding his unfinished words.

"You'll go back to Joyce. That's best for you. She's the Beatrice of your *Divina Commedia*."

He didn't dispute that. It was the truth, as far as he knew it in his own heart.

"At least our friendship is eternal," he said in a low voice.

"Absence is the ditch of forgetfulness," she said lightly, and then quoted a French verse he had heard before, in war-time, when a French girl had sung it in an old inn at Cassel, on the way to Ypres.

> "*Partir, c'est mourir un peu,*
> *C'est mourir à ce qu'on aime.*"

Before he went away, he asked her a question in which she understood a subtle meaning.

"About Christy, what shall I say to him?"

Janet laughed, with a touch of extra colour in her cheeks.

"Tell him he needn't have gone as far as Moscow. The Superfluous Woman is a stay-at-home, and very happy with her blind boys."

She came out onto the stone landing with him, outside her flat.

"It's not midnight yet," he said. "Will you risk it?"

"Without a qualm of conscience," she answered, and gave him her lips to kiss.

"Good luck, *mon ami!*" So she called into the well of the great staircase, as he stumbled down.

"My heart's thanks!" he answered back from a lower flight.

" '*Partir, c'est mourir un peu!*' " she said in a laughing way, yet a little sad too, he thought.

He spoke the second line:

Some people came out of the flat on the second floor and tramped down the stone stairs noisily, and he had no more chance of farewell with Janet Welford.

"Cut and run," old Christy had said. Well, he was doing so. As Joyce said, "It must be one thing or the other."

Next morning he crossed from Folkestone to Boulogne.

XXXVIII

Folkestone-Boulogne!

It was not three hundred years ago, but only three, that those words, and that cross-Channel passage, meant the way to roads which began very pleasantly past green fields and French villages-with roofs on their cottages, and towers to their churches-through long avenues of poplars growing tall and straight, past cornfields or ploughed fields, stretching away, hedgeless, to the horizon line, until presently those roads became filled with deep holes, and the fields were no longer green, but bare of vegetation as though blasted by some curse of God, and the trees were lopped and gashed, and the cottages had become unroofed, and the churches had lost their towers, and then, at the end of the roads, no house stood, no wall of any size above a rubble of bricks and no man walked hand-high above the ground, but all life was hidden in holes and ditches, and death alone was visible, where unburied bodies lay beyond a line of sand-bags and twisted wire.

To Bertram, all that seemed, for a few moments, as he stood on the quayside at Boulogne, three hundred years ago, and then not three years ago, not three minutes, but still going on.

He was back from seven days' leave. The purple-faced Major with the megaphone could assuredly shout out "All officers back from leave to report to the A.M.L.O."

Eight hundred soldiers, or more, who had been as sick as dogs, would stagger down the gangway, with tin hats, rifles, gas-masks, packs, silent, grim, sullen, because they were going back to the "bloody old trenches."

A line of cars would be drawn up for staff officers from G.H.Q. With luck one might get a lift in one of them part of the way and do some lorry-jumping for the rest of the way, instead of waiting for the night train, so cold, and slow, and crowded and dark.

A convoy of ambulances would soon arrive, with the usual crowd of badly-wounded —the fellows with Blighty wounds-and one would see their muddy boots, soles outward, when the flaps were drawn back. Surely the war was going on, for ever, and ever, and ever, as it had seemed to those who enlisted in 1914 or afterwards. . . .

No, all that was finished! It was merely a dream and a memory. Bertram saw the last representative of the British Army which had poured out here in tides —a dapper young sergeant, in khaki, doing some job with the customs officers or the French police. All else had vanished, even the A.M.L.O. with his megaphone!

With this realisation, Bertram felt as though he were the sole survivor of the war, the only man left alive from that great massacre. None of those people around him had had anything to do with it. In the smoking-carriage where he took a corner seat, were two prosperous-looking Jews with big cigars, two American business men, too old to have been in the last push, an elderly Frenchman, who bought *Le Matin* and the *Cri de Paris.*

Along the corridor, and in other carriages were groups of people going to Paris, or beyond Paris to other parts of Europe, where the sun was shining and life "gay." They were "smart" people, still able to afford the pleasures of life, in spite of the downfall of foreign markets, stagnant trade, unemployment, high taxes. They had forgotten the war and its agonies.

No one in his carriage bothered to look out of the window as they neared Amiens, where one could still see on a far hillside a line of earthworks, which had been thrown up hurriedly as a last line of defence after the Germans had broken through on March 21st and come very close to the old city-as close as Villers Bretonneux on the high ground outside.

Bertram did not travel as far as Paris, though he was tempted to go as far, because Joyce was there. It was at Amiens that he left the train, as the beginning of his wanderings through the old places of war, to find out what the people there were thinking, how they were living, according to Bernard Hall's instructions.

A crowd of ghosts walked with him up the rue des Trois Cailloux-the Street of the Three Pebbles. They were the Comrades of the Great War, who had crowded that street when great battles were being fought, year after year, in the fields of the Somme. He remembered them mostly on rainy days. It seemed always to be raining in Amiens, in war time. The officers wore trench-coats plastered with mud and chalk. The men staggered under their packs. The rain beat down on their tin hats.

French *poilus-Fusiliers Marins, Chasseurs*, infantry of the line, Zouaves, sloped up and down, staring into the shops, drinking *porto blanc* and fouler liquids in little drinking dens strictly against the law.

English Tommies walked with little French girls down the narrow side streets, went with them into dark old houses up cut-throat alleys.

Australian soldiers slouched around with hard, lean, leathery faces, looking for trouble and often finding it.

Crowds of Jocks with muddy knees, wet kilts, tin hats, slanted over Harry Lauder faces, wandered about in a grim mirthless way.

Staff officers motored into the town from Army Headquarters, or Corps, or Division.

Cavalry officers rode in and put their horses in the back yard of the Hotel du Rhin.

Officers of every battalion of the British Army surged along the narrow street-the Street of the Three Pebbles. They were down from the line, while their Division was in reserve, or were passing through on their way to the line. Here, in Amiens, were shops, pretty women, restaurants, cock-tail bars, civilian people, children, roofed houses, —the last outpost of civilised life this side of the filthy fields, and lice, and shell-fire, and sudden death.

Their ghosts walked with Bertram now. He stood at the corner of the rue Amiral Courbet. It was there that he had stood one night, talking to a French girl. It was very dark, for there was no lamp allowed after daylight. She flashed a pocket lamp in his face, and revealed her own, white, with red lips, and black laughing eyes —a pretty witch for a young man down from a battlefield for one night of life.

"*Comment ça va, mon chou? La vie est triste, n'cst-ce pas? Il n'y a qu'une consolation, un seul moyen d'oubli. Un peu de rire, un peu d'amour! Qu'est-ce-que tu en penses? Veux-tu?*"

A sad life, she said, and only one consolation, one way of forgetfulness. A little laughter, a little love. What did he think about it?

He'd thought a lot about it. He was twenty, then, in 1916. A boy, but doing a man's job, and with no life insurance for even another week, or another day, up there, beyond Amiens, this side of Contalmaison still in German hands. He agreed with this girl who had come up to him out of the darkness. A little laughter, a little love. Worth having before the next attack. Worth grabbing at on a rainy night in war-time, and perhaps the very last night on earth. Who could tell? Yet something had made him refuse the offer, some fear, or law, or mental prohibition. His mother had whispered a warning to him about "bad women." His two sisters, Dorothy and Susan, adored him in those days, believed him spotless. He had been brought up in a certain code, which had become part of him, inescapable without stricken conscience, despite the smashing of mental and moral foundations by the earthquake of war.

"*Rien à faire!*" he had told the girl, not roughly, poor kid, but decidedly. Nothing doing.

"*Mais oui, petit officier!*"

She had grabbed his belt, pulled him towards her, kissed his face, wet in the rain, with her wet lips.

It was here, at this very corner, in July of 1916!

Bertram walked down the next turning to the right, leading to the Cathedral. On the other side was a gap in a row of houses newly roofed. It was boarded round. There, in that gap, had been "Charley's Bar," the great cock-tail resort of thousands of young officers who drank quickly because there might not be much time between them and death.

Some of them were still alive, but not many of those who fought in the Somme battles. Izzard was one of them still alive, that fellow in the funny shop at Ottery. He had drunk like a fish in this place before it was knocked to bits by an air bomb in that March of '18. Bertram had drunk with him, eggnogs, and champagne cock-tails. They had both been thoroughly "blind" on more than one afternoon, and slept themselves sober in the Hotel du Rhin before dining at the Godebert in the rue des Jacobins, where Izzard and he had flirted outrageously with the pretty Marguérite, but without much success as she was coveted by Staff officers, and Brigadiers, and even a Major-General.

It was to the Hotel du Rhin that Bertram now went, still walking with ghosts and ancient memories.

The last time he had been there its stairs and passages were strewn with broken glass, and with several other officers he had sat in a cellar listening to houses falling with tremendous crashes, while a fleet of Gothas overhead played merry hell all through a night which was the blackest in the war.

His machine-gun company had been cut to bits outside Villers Bretonneux. Christy had been wounded in the lung and taken away by the stretcher-bearers. The Germans had made a clean break through and there was very little up the road to bar their way to Amiens. Bertram had been ordered to join up with another crowd for a last stand somewhere near Boves. The crowd had gone missing, it was impossible to search for them at night, and the air-raid over Amiens was the worst thing he'd seen in that way.

It had begun at seven-thirty in the evening, with two explosions outside the windows, smashing them, and filling the dancing-room with splinters. The lady manager was there, doing accounts with a young staff officer. She had yellow hair, and two bright spots of colour on her cheeks, and wonderful courage. Her face was pale beneath the bright spots of colour, but that was her only sign of fear. Joseph, the waiter with the shrill voice and high-pitched laugh, disappeared in the direction of the cellar. The other waiter-what was his name? —an old fellow, with side-whiskers, wandered about cursing the *sales Boches*.

A frightful and fantastic night, with dead men and dead horses in the street outside. Now like a dream! Since then, Amiens had tidied up its streets, re-built many of its houses-though not the great gap between the rue des Trois Cailloux and the rue des Jacobins.

An orchestra was playing in the Hotel du Rhin. American tourists and French commercial travellers were feeding in the room where Bertram had sat down on that night of tragedy, with three mayors who had lost their towns, and officers who had lost their Divisions, wondering how long it would be before the head of a German column marched into Amiens. An orchestra fiddling jazz tunes to American tourists!

But there, miracle of miracles, was the lady manager with the yellow hair, and Joseph, the shrill-voiced waiter, and the old boy with the side whiskers! Bertram went up to the lady manager, and greeted her with emotion, as one whom he had known in the wonderful years, and as one who remembered.

"Still here, Madame! You remember me, perhaps? That night of the air-raid, and other nights!"

She shook hands with him, and pretended to remember his face, though thousands of young officers had passed through this hotel in the years of war.

"What memories, monsieur! Unforgettable to us, though others have forgotten!"

"Amiens is almost restored," he said.

"There's still much to be done."

"How strange it must be for you, now that there are no British soldiers in France! This hotel used to be stuffed with officers of ours."

"We get tourists to see the battlefields. English officers come up like you, and say 'Do you remember me, madame?' Sometimes I'm tempted to say, 'Do you remember the agony of France in those years of war?' "

"Why that, Madame? We cannot forget."

She shrugged her shoulders and smiled bitterly.

"Your Lloyd George forgets. He makes friends with the Germans. He wishes to let them off their punishment. He will let them get strong again, so that one day they will come back and crush us."

Bertram laughed.

"He wants peace in Europe. He wants to prevent another war. Anyhow, England doesn't forget the heroism of France nor her sufferings."

"*C'est bien!*"

She bent to her table, and added up a column of figures.

In the yard an American tourist enquired how long it would take to drive to Château Thierry.

That night Bertram met another woman whom he had known in Amiens in the years of war. It was the chambermaid, and she remembered him.

"Certainly you were one of the young officers who used to stay here in the war?"

He shook hands with her, and said, "I'm the officer whose socks you mended once. You told me about your lover, Jean, who was killed at Verdun. We talked long that night."

Yes, she remembered him, his very face, those socks she had mended, that talk.

"*Tiens! Quel plaisir!*"

She was glad to find that he was still alive. A middle-aged woman of plain features, she had not been much of a temptation to young officers down from the line. Yet some of them, deprived of womanhood, for months on end, had made amorous advances even to her, which she had repulsed with loud laughter, in a heavy-handed way. She had mothered some of the younger men, in a peasant way, and had given them good advice about the girls who lured them in the streets, with their flash lamps, like that one at the corner of the rue Amiral Courbet. Her lover, Jean, a butcher, had been killed at Verdun, and she had wept a little in Bertram's room, and then laughed, and said she supposed men were made to be killed that way, like sheep to be eaten. "*C'est la vie.*" It was life and war, which would last as long as the Germans were part of the human race.

Now she leaned on her broom, talking to Bertram about the changes since the war. Prices were high. It was hard for poor people to live. The bourgeoisie were making plenty of money, but the Government was ruined, she was told. The Germans evaded their payments. Anyhow, no German gold came to the people who were trying to build up their cottages again in the battlefields. She had a cousin at Lens. A mother of six. They had no water, no gas, no stone for building, no money for reconstruction. Three years after war they were still miserable. Victory had not brought happiness to France, nor safety. The Boches would come back again one day. It would begin all over again. A pity they weren't all killed when the French and English had the chance! Now the English hated the French, and loved the Germans, for some reason!

"What makes you think that?" asked Bertram.

"It is true, is it not?" asked this woman, Jeanne, quite simply.

She was surprised, and incredulous, when he told her that she was mistaken, and that the English loved France still, and desired to help her.

"What gives you the idea that England hates France?"

She said she read *Le Matin*, which told her so. It was the same in the *Journal d'Amiens*. Everybody spoke about it-especially *les garçons*, who were always talking politics. She didn't understand these things, but she picked up her news from the others. It was public opinion. No one could go against public opinion. *C'est formidable, l'opinion publique!*

XXXIX

For several weeks Bertram wandered about the old places, mostly a-foot, or getting lifts in country carts, once or twice taking a train which crawled from Arras to Lens, and from Bapaume to Péronne.

He had wayside conversations with peasant men and women, young farmers who had been *poilus*, commercial travellers from Paris and Lille, mayors of towns wiped off the map, but now on the sites of their old *mairies* in wooden huts, superintending *la reconstruction* which, so far, didn't seem to amount to very much.

He passed the night in wooden *estaminets* in fields where once British youth had been swept with fire year after year-Ypres, Hooge, St. Julien, Dickebusch, Souchez, Neuville Vitesse, many other places haunted surely by boys he had passed along the roads.

The trenches had silted in. He wandered about, and poked about with his stick, trying to find some of his old dug-outs, and though he had known every inch of this ground, every hummock and hollow, could not find them, for the most part, only one, indeed.

He found a dug-out in which he had lived, not far from Bourlon Wood, by the ruins of Havrincourt Château. The earth had silted there too, but he borrowed a spade from a friendly young farmer near by, and unearthed the wooden steps, and cleared out the entrance, and went inside. The farmer gave him a bit of candle, and would have come inside with him, unless Bertram had said, "Wait a few minutes. I want to be in here alone!" The man understood with the quick sympathy of the French for sentiment like that.

It *was* sentiment, but also more than that. This was a ghost chamber of tragic memories, the unburying of the dead past. The candle burned straight with a thin flame. By its light Bertram found a wooden table, and two chairs, made out of boxes. It was Bill Huggett, who had knocked them together. On the table were things which had belonged to Bertram-an empty tin of John Cotton tobacco which Joyce had sent him, a cracked mug which he had found in Havrincourt Wood, an old envelope addressed to him.

"Major Bertram Pollard, D.S.O., M.C.
    Machine Gun Corps, B.E.F."

It was in Joyce's handwriting. Good God! Fancy finding it here again, moist and muddy as the walls had oozed about it and earth had dropped! How eagerly he must have opened it when it came! Certainly he had kissed it before opening it. Now Joyce was his wife, away in Paris or somewhere, without him.

He sat very still on one of the boxes, with his elbows on the table, as often he had sat in this hole at the end of '17. Christy had come down the steps to report the state of things outside. Old Fritz was putting up a bit of a barrage. Bourlon Wood was soaked with gas. He had told the men to keep their masks handy. A counter-attack was expected within the next twelve hours. A man had just had his leg blown off in Beer Alley.

Bertram's soul lived again in that time. The smell of the dug-out, that thin candle flame, these oozy walls, this table, were no more real than that dead past, yet as real. The past was present. The present was past. There was no difference. All that he had seen in war, the death of many good men, the agony of the wounded, the stench of death, the comradeship of young officers, their laughter, Christy's tears when his nerve broke, his own fears of fear, the heroism of common men, the endless slaughter, the waste of youth and life, came back to his mind, as drowning men are said to see all their life as in a mirror. Was it all going to happen again? Bernard Hall thought so, unless some divine change happened in human nature by "intensive education"! Jeanne, the chambermaid, thought so! Nearly all those French people with whom he had talked along the wayside believed that after a few years, fifteen, twenty, twenty-five, *les Boches* would come back again for vengeance.

As the candle flickered and shortened in a pool of wax on the table, Bertram, sitting there with its feeble light surrounded by darkness, heard a voice speak to his soul, very clearly, as once before. They were the words his mother had spoken on her death-bed. "Bertram, work for Peace. Promise me —"

He raised his head sharply. Had he heard those words only in imagination, or had they been spoken to him? He had heard them clearly, with distinct utterance, yet it must have been only one of the memories brought back in that dug-out.

Yes, he would work for peace, so that boys now young needn't live in holes like this until they were gassed to death or blown to bits, or buried alive. He would work for Peace, as far as he could understand the chaos of life, as far as he could write words of warning, and conciliation, and commonsense, and truth anyhow.

The candle guttered out. He struck a match, picked up the envelope in Joyce's handwriting, and groped his way up, and out.

The young farmer was waiting for him, and stared at him a moment, with a queer smile in his eyes.

"A droll life in those days. With good moments, and many sad, eh? Sacred Name! I laugh sometimes when I think of the blood, the death, the lice, the mud, the *ordure* of it all."

"Would you go through it again?"

The man shrugged his shoulders.

"To save France one would go through it again. Not willingly. But what else? When the Germans attack again, France will fight again."

"You think they will attack again?"

"Naturally. They will want revenge. When they have renewed their strength, they will come back. It is human nature, monsieur."

"Can France stand another war?"

The young peasant farmer stared across the field to Bourlon Wood, so quiet now, so safe.

"Not alone. But we have Poland, Serbia, Czecho-Slovakia."

"England?"

The man looked uncertainly at Bertram.

"Monsieur can tell me, perhaps."

"What do you think?"

The young Frenchman shrugged his shoulders again.

"England does what pays her best. Industry, commerce, count with her most. It's the English character. Hard bargaining, eh?"

Bertram reminded him how many men Britain had sent to France, in time of war, how many bodies of her youth lay still in French soil. Was that hard bargaining? Or self-sacrifice, for honour's sake?

"The *Boches* were England's trade rivals. Their Fleet was a menace to *Grande Bretagne*. Is it not so, Monsieur."

Bertram sat with him on a hummock of earth, shared some sandwiches with him, and tried, in simple phrases, with an emotion that he felt, to assure this peasant who had been a *poilu* of France, that England had a soul above shop-keeping, that her share in the war had been not only enormous in sacrifice, but heroic in ideal.

The man listened to him with patience, but also with amusement.

"Monsieur is an idealist! After experience of war?" That was strange. He himself was a realist. Nations, like individuals, would fight for self-interest, to save their skins, their land, their women. They would fight to get revenge, to kill people they hated, because of pride, and more because of injury, to capture their trade, or their territory. It was natural. It had always been like that. It would never change.

Bertram saw in this young farmer the type of French manhood, the very soul of France. Through centuries of history, men like this, on this soil, had fought for their land and their women, for conquests, for pride in France. They had been invaded, harassed, and ravaged. They had lived always between the plough and the sword, first one, then the other, turn and turn about. Peace was only an interlude, either when France was weak, in defence, or when France was strong, in aggression, in contraction or expansion, as an Empire or Republic.

The French mother rocking her babe in the cradle knew in her heart that one day this man-child would march away to battle. It was in the songs she sang to send it to sleep. The boy knew that when manhood came he would leave home for the barracks, to learn soldiering as he had learnt farming. So it had been in the time of the Valois, in the reign of Henri IV., before Burgundy was France, before the Revolution, all through the Napoleonic era, ever afterwards, till 1918, with brief spells for recovery, the binding of wounds, the growing of another generation of boys. "*C'etait toujours comme ça. Ça ne changera jamais.*" It was always like that. It would never change.

Bertram glanced sideways at the man; thirty-five, perhaps, with a strong, hard profile, ruddy skin, fair moustache. A Frank of northern stock. Teutonic rather than Latin, though, perhaps, with a strain of Latin blood. The typical *poilu* of Picardy, Normandy, Artois.

"France cannot afford another war," Bertram said; "it would bleed her to death. Must there always be conflict? Why not make friends with the Germans?"

The young farmer laughed loudly, and spat.

"Friends with the *Boches*? Does one make friends with a hungry tiger? If one can't kill it at once, one digs a ditch round one's house and keeps one's gun ready. So I have heard! There's still another way to treat a tiger. Cut its claws and cage it. That is our way with Germany now."

"If the tiger escapes and grows its claws?"

"There is still the gun."

"If the gun gets rusty?"

"Then the tiger gets its meal. He's a fool who lets his gun get rusty."

"If it breaks, and he has not money to buy another?"

"That is unfortunate! The tiger wins."

He was a fatalist. Also he assumed that the German by nature was a tiger. Was that true? Bertram thought of all the German prisoners he'd seen in time of war, some he had helped to capture-simple, straw-haired young peasants, who hated war, and loved peace, and the arts and crafts and labours of peace, not soldiers by instinct and passion, like the French, but soldiers by coercion, by discipline, by sentiment; brave, efficient, obedient, but without fire. They were not "tigers," as far as he had seen them, but rather sheepish fellows. It was not utterly impossible that they might abandon the hope of revenge against France, if France would abandon her passion of hate, her uttermost demands of punishment and payment, her pound of flesh.

It was useless to argue with this peasant-farmer, though he had a clear intelligence, and, like most Frenchmen of his class, a surprising gift of words.

"England is a good friend," he said, at the end of this conversation. "There must never be cause of quarrel between England and France. The very dead would rise out of these fields to protest."

It was here, by Havrincourt Château that English and Scots had advanced on a day of November in 1917, with Tanks leading the way towards Cambrai. Now it was quiet in the fields, and birds were singing, and no smoke clouds burst in Bourlon Wood.

The young Frenchman shook hands with him and smiled.

"*Au revoir, mon camarade! Comme vous-même, je n'aime pas la guerre. Mais, que voulez-vous? Il vient quand il vient!*"

He had no love for war, but when it came, it came! Terrible philosophy, upon which no peace could be built, no forward step taken by educated humanity. To this peasant, perhaps to all his kind, war was as inevitable as natural calamities, like rains and droughts, earthquakes, and thunderbolts. And the German was still the German-the Blonde Beast. *Les sales Boches!*

XL

The hostility-suspicion, even, —of the French people regarding England was to Bertram terrible. They were very friendly to him, all those people whom he visited in their huts or walked with over old battlefields. Some of them were even emotional, as one old woman in an *estaminet* along the Arras-Doullens road with whom he had been billeted for a time, and who flung her arms about him and kissed him on both cheeks, and wept a little, and laughed, and cooked a chicken for him. But when they spoke about England, it was with doubt, or resentment, or anger; now and then with passion.

He couldn't get to the root of their grievances. They talked vaguely of England crossing the path of France in Syria. In what way? They didn't know, but said: "*On dit dans les journaux* —" It is said in the papers!

They believed, many of them, that the value of the franc was deliberately made low by the artful jugglings of British financiers. They were certain that "Loy-Zhorzhe" was pro-German for corrupt and sinister motives, that British diplomacy was jealous of French victory, and intrigued everywhere to secure a new balance of power in Europe, so that French supremacy should be weighted down by the restoration of Germany.

In any case, England desired to thwart France of the fruits of victory, and was always manœuvring to let Germany off her debts, to prevent France from seizing German industrial cities if Germany defaulted in her payments.

It was idle for Bertram to argue that Lloyd George and the British people were afraid that if Germany were pressed too hard, beyond her power to pay, beyond human nature, she would seek to escape by force, would nourish desires for revenge which would lead ultimately and inevitably to another war. Germany would form an alliance with Russia, or break into such revolutionary chaos that the peace and recovery of Europe would be retarded for more than another generation.

He put these ideas to a French priest as they sat together in a little wooden presbytery near the ruins of a church on the west side of St. Quentin. They had met in a cemetery where British and French soldiers lay buried side by side.

Bertram, standing bare-headed there by the grave of one of his own comrades, was greeted by the priest, a tall, middle-aged man with a bronzed, clean-shaven face, and the scar of some wound down his right cheek.

"You are an English officer, perhaps?"

"Yes, *mon père*, in the old days."

"Ah, you helped to fight for France! It was a good comradeship in those days. I was a soldier also, a captain of artillery, with the '*Cent-Vingt.*'"

He invited Bertram to his simple *pot-au-feu*, with a cup of coffee afterwards, and a *petit verre*.

It was over that cup of coffee that they argued about French and British policy, and then that Bertram defended the British point of view.

"Why do your English Liberals hate France so much?" asked the priest. "I cannot understand. It is to me incredible!"

Bertram denied that English Liberals hated France. He tried to explain, in faulty French, the "Liberal" idea in England. It was a belief that another frightful war could only be prevented by allowing Germany to recover, and dealing with her so generously that she would not desire vengeance. English Liberals believed that the whole philosophy of Europe must be changed, and that people should rise beyond the old "Balance of Power," with secret or open alliances dividing Europe into groups. The peoples of all nations wanted peace. It was only the old diplomacy that prevented the fulfilment of their desire, and a general brotherhood of European democracy.

The priest struck his fist on the table so that the coffee cups jumped.

"All that is illusion," he said, and he almost shouted the words. "It is hypocritical nonsense. Peace can only be secured by keeping Germany crushed and weak. England is treacherous to

France by making secret overtures to Germany. It is a betrayal of the dead. An outrage to France."

Bertram lit his pipe, and smoked in silence for a moment, astonished and distressed by the violent passion in this priest's voice, by the flash of fire in his eyes.

"*Mon père*," he said, "you speak like a soldier, and not like a priest. Surely you of all men should believe in the forgiveness of enemies-wasn't it ninety times nine? —and the blessings promised to the peacemakers."

"I spoke as a Frenchman as well as a priest," was the answer. "I have seen the flower of French youth swept down by the *sales Boches*. I have seen the beauty of their mother, France, blasted, as in those fields outside. I have seen our women outraged by the brutality of the enemy. It is because of these things, and because I believe in the justice of God that I demand the full punishment of an infamous people. I warn you, sir, that if Great Britain endeavours to thwart that divine justice, France will regard her also as an enemy."

"The dead listen to us, *mon père*," said Bertram, simply. "Outside this window their bodies lie together. It is too soon for any Frenchman to speak of England as an enemy."

"It is too soon for England to behave as such," said the priest.

For several hours they talked, this Frenchman and Englishman, these two soldiers of the Great War, this priest and layman. At the end of that time, Bertram knew that no words in any language or with any eloquence, could ever reconcile their opposing views. The priest believed in "the sword of France" as the means of peace in Europe. Bertram believed in reconciliation, the progress of commonsense, the education of democracy, the spirit of peace in the hearts of common folk.

"Illusion!" said the priest again. "Illusion! In the heart of man, and especially in the heart of Germany, is hatred, evil, greed, brutality, fear, rivalry. So it has been. So it will always be, despite the grace of God, and the teaching of Jesus Christ. We have to guard against these natural passions. We have to uphold justice by force. We must never be weakened by a craven fear of war. Worse than war is cowardice or dishonour. Worse than hatred is the betrayal of friendship. May England be true to France!"

"May France remember England's sacrifice!" said Bertram, "and our dead that lie in her soil."

The priest answered his farewell in a friendly way, gripping his hand first, as a comrade, and then giving him a priest's blessing. But when Bertram trudged away from the presbytery to a wooden *estaminet* a mile away, he was enormously distressed in spirit. This priest, Jeanne, the chambermaid, the young farmer near his old dug-out, a commercial traveller from Paris, the Mayor of Arras, scores of friendly people he met along the old roads of war and on the old battlefields, had talked in the same strain, used the same kind of argument, lamented the ill-will or the "treachery" of England; or if not of England, then of "Loy-Zhorzhe," who seemed to them not so much a human personality as an evil power.

What hope was there for peace in Europe, if France pursued her policy of force, to crush Germany and keep her weak? What chance for the "Comrades of the Great War," lounging about Labour Exchanges in London, marching in processions of unemployed, with banners saying, "We Want Work"?

There would be no work until Great Britain could sell her goods in the markets of Europe. Those markets could never buy if Germany were thrust into such ruin as that of Austria. Germany, perhaps allied with Russia, would struggle like a wild beast. The "sword of France" would not be strong enough to keep her weak for ever. Then France would call to England again. Would the roads have to be tramped again by battalions of boys from England, Scotland, Ireland, going up to the fields of death?

This thought came to Bertram as he went up a road past the ruined village of Barisis. The moon had risen in a pale sky, still blue, and its light silvered the wooden crosses in a military graveyard. Row by row they stood above the neatly ordered graves. For scores of miles, for hundreds of miles, across France, the moon illumined cemeteries like this, crowded with French and British dead.

"God, give us Peace!" said Bertram, aloud, as he bared his head in salute to old comrades with whom he had trudged these roads.

An immense fear invaded his spirit, and a kind of shudder shook him, for he seemed to hear again the march of youth advancing to another Armageddon in these fields-the last youth of Europe.

He was glad to get into the warmth of the wooden *estaminet*. An enormously fat Frenchman greeted him jovially.

"Monsieur is hungry, beyond doubt! My wife has cooked an excellent chicken."

The wife, a pretty, thin-faced woman, with merry black eyes, addressed him as "*mon capitaine*" and spread a napkin as a cloth on a deal table.

She had been in St. Pol during all the war. Did he know St. Pol, not far from Hesdin —? Yes? Then surely he must have known, among English officers who had been friends of hers, *le capitaine* Jenkins, *le lieutenant* O'Mally, *le commandant* Stuart? She had *un très bon souvenir* of the English Army. Sometimes her husband was jealous when she praised the English officers so much!

"Without cause, I'm sure!" said Bertram, with a smile.

The woman laughed, and her black eyes danced.

"In time of war there are many temptations!"

She teased her preposterously fat husband, and he looked annoyed, and said, "*Tais-toi, Yvonne!*" She made a little face at him, behind his back, and when Bertram went to his bedroom after dinner, she lighted his way with a candle, there being no gas in the house.

"*Merci, et bonne nuit, madame!*" said Bertram, politely, taking the candle from her, and putting it down on a wooden chair by the bedside.

She looked at him with a queer, wistful smile, and spoke in broken English.

"I am not married in time of war. You understand? English officers like me very much. Take my hand, try to give me kiss-what you say? —flirt! My big, fat husband not like me talk of those days. But I like remember! You will give me English kiss for old remembrance, eh?"

She held her face up, after glancing at the half closed door.

Bertram gave her a kiss. Why not? It was good to find some one who remembered the British Army with pleasure and affection. She kissed him six times in return, and then, with her finger to her lip, ran out of the room, as a big voice shouted:

"Yvonne! *Qu'est-ce-que tu fais, toi?*"

That night Bertram dreamed that it was Joyce who kissed him.

XLI

The thought of Paris pulled Bertram so strongly that he could wander no longer in the old war zone, and getting back to Amiens from Bapaume, took the train to the Gare du Nord. He had written some articles for *The New World*, photographic and phonographic, things seen and heard, without comment or moral, and some of them had been published, as he knew, not from seeing them —*The New World* was not sold in Paschendaele or Hooge! —but from a note written by Bernard Hall.

"Your stuff is admirable, and much quoted."

There was endless material in the "reconstruction" of Picardy and Artois-the human "stuff" which Hall wanted. Bertram had only to sit down to table in any little *estaminet*, mostly built of wood, amidst a group of huts, in this country of ghosts (as it was to him) to hear in the casual conversation of peasants the aftermath of war's enormous tragedy to France.

Young peasants, once soldiers of France, told tales of hair-raising horror about the trenches of Verdun, or Vermelles, or any part of the battle front, with a simplicity, and matter-of-fact remembrance, beyond all eloquence or art in tragic effect. Some of them had been prisoners in German camps, and their long servitude, monotonous in starvation and misery, had been worse than trench-life.

Women who had been caught behind the German lines, in Lille, Valenciennes, elsewhere, told of their years of anguish, and inflamed again the passion of the men who listened. Reference to death recurred in casual discourse with continual iteration. "Before Jean was killed," "since my man's death," "when my boy fell in the assault on Souchez," a score of times in any half hour of gossip over a flask of *vin ordinaire*.

The loss of homes and fortunes, the difficulty and illusion of this "reconstruction" which was used as a spellword by the French Government, as though the word alone would rebuild houses and churches and flourishing farmsteads, the sadness of women bereft of fathers, husbands, sons, brothers, lovers, by the immense slaughter of French manhood, and the abiding hate of France for Germany, were revealed to Bertram with intimate and distressful detail, as he sat in the corner of any tavern, or talked with any group of men and women in field or market-place.

It came to his mind that here was material for a new "Sentimental Journey" which might live in history because of the tales of Armageddon, but he renounced the idea for himself, beyond his brief sketches for Bernard Hall, because of his desire to get to Paris. It was not the lure of Paris in June, nor that joyous anticipation which had belonged to "three days' Paris leave" in the old days of war, but the urgent, irresistible, almost sickening desire to see Joyce again.

During this time of loneliness, for he was alone with his soul despite his wayside conversations, some fretfulness of spirit passed from him. He seemed to see things with more clarity. His thoughts struck deeper into the essential meaning of life. Contact again with the devastation of war, the sharp realities of the immense heritage of woe left by those murderous years, his conversation with the ghosts of youth, crowding about him in those little forests of wooden crosses, in those quiet fields where the noise of death had once been very loud, seemed to kill the nagging of his own selfish instincts, to rebuke his egotism.

How trivial was the failure or success of his own life! What did it matter in the balance of history, in the destiny of peoples? He had no right to life at all, except by a fluke of luck, or the grace of God. So many of his friends lay here in French soil, as young as he, and younger. That he was alive, glad to hear the lark singing again above these fields (even as they had sung above the noise of gunfire), with the warmth of the sun in his face, was so much to the good, after all, that he could pay back for that only by service and the dedication of life to things beyond himself. He might, by some small grain of truth, by the force of mere desire, by written word or spoken word, help the chance of peace, so that these fields need not be strewn again with dead boys. To that attempt he was dedicated. It was the meaning of his future life, if it had any purpose.

After the mental storms of the last few months, the quarrel with Joyce, his mother's death, the tragedy of Susan, and of Digby, he seemed to have aged by twenty years in understanding and experience. A little by Janet Welford's help, and perhaps more than he could estimate, he had risen above the weakness of self-pity, the most miserable disease, incurable, if allowed to go too far.

It had been all foolishness and pettiness, —that quarrel with Joyce. She was hardly more than a child, even now, and he had dealt with her as though she were a woman of mature views and settled philosophy. He had taken her too seriously. They had both been too serious about their "opinions" —as if they mattered!

In his tramp across the war zone, the vision of Joyce as she was when he first knew her, and dreamed of her, here in France, came back to him-her flower-like beauty, her grace, her elegance, her courage, her vitality. He wiped out all his quarrel with her. He believed, with increasing certainty, that after this separation, and his change in character-he felt that he had both changed and strengthened and become better balanced —a meeting between them would end in reconciliation and understanding.

He regretted his answers to her letters, so harsh and humourless. He would go to her in Paris, and say, "My dear, I want your love again. I have dedicated my life to love-and peace, which is the fruit of love. I am your faithful serving-man. What stands between our happiness together?"

At night, lying on a truckle bed in the *"Fleur des Champs"* or the *"Estaminet des Poilus,"* he yearned for Joyce with the home-sickness of a boy away in a cheerless school. Her physical presence seemed to be with him. He was aware sometimes of the perfume of her hair, he could almost feel the silky touch of those "bobbed" curls. He spoke her name, waking in the morning, in day-dreams, and saw her walking with bare feet across the grass that grew so green now over the battlefields.

Even his jealousy of Kenneth Murless abated, and died out, extinguished by this larger sense that had come to him. Kenneth had been her playmate as a child. His comradeship had been above suspicion, except in the mind of that other Bertram, with nerves on edge, and petty egotism all alarmed.

It was in this mood of exalted emotion that Bertram stepped out of the Gare du Nord and drove in a rattle-bone taxi down the dreary length of the rue Lafayette to the heart of Paris and the Hotel Meurice.

Bertram made his way through a group of Americans with a quickening pulse. His eyes roved about this entrance hall, expecting to see Joyce at once, waiting for his coming, as it were. It was one of the tall American girls who gave him a start and made him take a pace forward with the word "Joyce!" on his lips, though unuttered. She was a tall, slim girl, with glistening gold hair, in a cream-coloured French frock, such as Joyce would wear in a Paris June. She turned round to say a word to a friend, and he had a sense of disappointment.

At the desk he enquired for Lady Joyce Pollard, and as an afterthought, for the Countess of Ottery. The clerk glanced at him doubtfully-he was wearing an old grey suit and a soft hat-and then informed him that both ladies had left Paris the day before.

"Where have they gone?" asked Bertram.

He was profoundly disappointed now, and cursed himself for not having written or telegraphed from Amiens to announce his coming. His hopes had been so high and soaring about his meeting with Joyce that this check was intolerable.

The clerk shrugged his shoulders and smiled.

"How can I tell, monsieur? Paris is the gate to all the Continent!"

"Surely they left an address?"

The clerk looked up in a book. No, the ladies had not left any address. He condescended to send for the Hall Porter, a superb person in a claret-coloured uniform. The Hall Porter himself condescended to inform the rather shabby-looking Englishman that "Madame la Comtesse d'Ottery" and Miladi, her daughter, had departed by automobile to Amiens. He understood they proposed to visit the battlefields in the British war-zone.

Bertram could obtain no further information, and when he walked down the rue de Rivoli, the serenity of mind and exalted sense of sacrifice which he believed he had acquired during lonely nights and days, departed from him abruptly, for a few minutes at least, and he was furious with Fortune for having played him such a scurvy trick.

He had just come from Amiens. Joyce had just gone there! If he had only known that she wanted to visit the battlefields, he could have shown her every yard of earth that was hallowed by the struggle of British manhood-made her see with his eyes the way of battle, taken her to Ypres where her brothers had died, pointed out the line of old trenches beyond which he had once stared into No-Man's Land, led her into the very dug-out where he had found her letter.

On such a journey they would have come together again, gone hand in hand and heart to heart, understanding the immensity of that tragedy of death which made their own lives in debt for ever to the youth that died. No such luck! By twenty-four hours he had missed Joyce, and this chance.

He had the idea of taking the first train back to Amiens, and tracing them from there, but he reflected that in an automobile they would be lost to him, and that his best chance of quickest meeting would be to await Joyce's return to Paris. He would be able to find out her plans from Murless, at the British Embassy.

Bertram dumped his one bag in a small hotel in the rue St. Honoré-he couldn't afford the Hotel Meurice-and walked to the Embassy in the Faubourg St. Honoré.

Kenneth Murless, to whom he sent in his card, kept him waiting for ten minutes, and in spite of that self-rebuke which had softened his feelings so recently towards Kenneth, this delay strained his temper and aroused his old sense of hostility, according to the natural law which makes all men hate those who keep them in antechambers, even as Dr. Johnson hated Lord Chesterfield and dipped his pen in venom to take vengeance.

The door opened, and light footsteps crossed the polished boards. Bertram turned and saw Kenneth Murless, and was aware that, for just the fraction of a second, Kenneth had a startled look, almost a look of fear. It passed instantly into a welcoming smile.

"My dear Bertram! Fearfully sorry for keeping you waiting. The Ambassador is as garrulous as an old maid this morning."

So he made the *amende honorable*, holding out his hand to Bertram with the friendliest gesture. Then he sat on the edge of a Louis Quinze table, and offered Bertram a cigarette.

"Where's Joyce?" asked Bertram, abruptly.

Kenneth did not seem quite sure at the moment.

"Wafted away to a château in Picardy, I believe. Yes, I understand she's staying a while with the old Marquis de Plumoison and his charming daughter, Yvonne, to say nothing of Jérome, the young and handsome Vicomte."

These names meant something to Bertram. Once, in time of war, he had been billeted for two months outside the Château de Plumoison, and with kind permission of the old Marquis, had shot rabbits in the park. He remembered Yvonne de Plumoison, and her kindness to young British officers like himself. Most of them had fallen in love with her for a week or two.

"What about Lady Ottery?"

"Gone for one night only, en route for merry England, where your worthy father-in-law is suffering from that vulgar complaint, influenza. But, my dear fellow, don't you get the family bulletin?"

"I've been wandering," said Bertram. He flushed deeply at Kenneth's question, and couldn't tell whether it held an underlying sarcasm, or was asked in simplicity. Perhaps Joyce hadn't told Kenneth how hideously they had quarrelled that night at Holme Ottery, nor how complete had been their estrangement. It would be like Joyce to keep her own counsel, and put a gay face upon their separation. And yet she was so intimate in friendship with Kenneth that if any man knew, he would. In any case he must have guessed, known, indeed, without guessing, that "something" had happened to bring Joyce to Paris without her husband.

"Come and dine with me to-night," said Kenneth. "I'm entertaining a few friends at the Griffon, a chic little place round the corner."

"Not in this rig-out," said Bertram, glancing at his shabby clothes.

Murless pooh-poohed that reason.

"Any old dress does nowadays. Besides, I'll introduce you as a literary man. You'll be adored by the women."

He congratulated Bertram on his essays in *The New World*.

"You've quite a touch! Guy de Maupassant has a rival."

Again Bertram suspected irony, but Kenneth looked at him in his friendliest way, disarming hostility, and his next words were kind.

"I was deeply shocked to hear of your mother's death; and Digby. Please accept my sympathy."

Then he gave Bertram another piece of news, striking in its unexpectedness.

"By the way, your sister is in Paris. Poor pretty Susan."

By that word "poor" he revealed his knowledge of that tragedy in Mountjoy Prison. He had met her in the Tuileries gardens, with another girl. He had raised his hat to her, but she had looked through his body for a thousand miles.

Bertram was astonished, yet a sense of relief came to him at the news. It was better for Susan to be in Paris than in Dublin. Safer. But how to find her? Kenneth could give no clue, and Bertram, having come to Paris to find Joyce, was in the strange case of a man who had missed his wife and lost a sister.

He accepted Kenneth's invitation to dinner because of that loneliness, and sense of futility, but he hadn't left the Embassy more than half an hour when, by a fluke of chance, he came face to face with Susan in the Place de la Concorde. She was just entering the "Metro" when he saw her, and grabbed her arm.

"Susan! What luck to find you!"

The last time he had met her came back to his mind in a flash-that day in Sackville Street, when her hair was unkempt and her eyes were red and wild, and her frock was wet and muddy after an all-night vigil. Now she was neat and pretty again, but the memory of that night had not passed from her face. In her eyes was still something of its pain.

"Hullo, Bertram!" she said, as simply and unemotionally as though they had left each other only an hour ago. As he drew her on one side to avoid the stream of people pouring into the Underground station, she showed sufficient interest in his way of life to ask what he was doing in Paris. He answered her vaguely, and asked the same question.

"What are *you* doing?"

She, too, was vague, and said something about propaganda work, for Ireland. The French were sympathetic. They believed in Liberty, and they hated England, she was glad to say.

"They don't seem to like us," said Bertram, sadly, but he didn't argue with that "glad to say."

"When can I have a real talk with you, and where?"

She gave her address, at a number in the rue de la Pompe, Passy, and told him that she was living with Betty O'Brien, who, like herself, had abandoned England since Dennis's martyrdom. Betty was staying with her uncle, Mr. Mahony. Any time after nine he would find a little crowd in their rooms. Irish exiles, French Liberals, Russian Communists, some of the people in France who most loved Liberty.

"A rum crowd!" thought Bertram, but to his sister he said, "I'll come to-night at ten, if that's not too late?"

"Any time before midnight, or afterwards," said Susan, smiling for the first time. "They're all talkers. You'll learn a lot, if you're not too aggressively English."

"Joyce thinks I'm not English enough," he answered, and at the name of Joyce Susan's black eyes flashed, and her mouth hardened. She remembered that scene with the telephone-the prelude of tragedy.

"*Au revoir*, then. Until this evening."

She fell in with the crowd of business men, *midinettes*, students, Americans, school-girls, who passed unceasingly through the little iron gates which led down to the "Metro" tubes.

Bertram lunched alone at a *terrasse* restaurant, on the other side of the river in the Boulevard St. Michel. A French girl sat opposite, at the same little table, and entered into conversation.

"*Anglais?*"

"*Oui. Vous voyez!*"

"*Pas Americain, alors!*"

"*Moitié Anglais, moitié Irlandais, pour le dire précisément.*"

She told him that she preferred the Irish half of him. For the English she had lost her love, on account of that monster, "Loy-Zhorzhe."

Bertram groaned a little, and laughed a little, and begged her not to discuss politics.

She expressed the opinion that nothing mattered in life, except politics, because they dictated life. It was on account of politics that she paid three francs fifty for a bad *déjeuner*, instead of one franc seventy-five as in the good days before the war.

Before she had obtained three francs fifty worth of vile food, he learnt that she was a stenographer to a music publisher in the rue des Saints Pères, that her brother had been killed (like all the others) at Verdun, and that she had a lover who was a clerk in the Crédit Lyonnais.

She approached the subject of politics again, when she affirmed that Paris had lost its gaiety because of high prices. And high prices prevailed because the *sales Boches* refused to pay their reparations, much encouraged by England and America, for reasons she failed to understand.

"Quite simple reasons," said Bertram. "Because England and America are persuaded that Germany's bankruptcy would be the worst thing for Europe."

"*O, la, la! Je m'en fiche de l'Europe! Qu'est-ce-qu'il y a pour la France qui est tellement épuisée par l'agonie et l'outrage de la guerre?*"

She didn't care a jot for Europe. What did that have to do with France, agonised and outraged by war?

She gave a little gloved hand to Bertram, and thanked him for his conversation, before going back to her music-shop. She forgave him for being half English because he was altogether charming.

That encounter meant nothing in Bertram's life, except relief from half an hour's loneliness, and one more proof among a thousand, of the alarming dislike of England in France after war. What did it portend? It frightened him, and sickened him. Not in that was the spirit and chance of peace to which he had dedicated his brain and heart. How could a bridge be built over this widening gulf between the French and British foundations of faith for the future of Europe?

The question remained unanswered in Bertram's mind, as he wandered about Paris, disconsolate and lonely-enormously lonely now that he had failed to meet Joyce-until it was time to join Kenneth's party at the Griffon.

XLII

He was the last to arrive, and Kenneth presented him to a young husband and wife whose names and portraits, —the Baron and Madame de Montauban-he had seen in many illustrated journals devoted to "Society" news.

De Montauban was a well-known amateur tennis player, he remembered, and he seemed to be an amiable, vivacious fellow, with easy manners. His wife was one of the prettiest women Bertram had seen in Paris where there is no dearth of beauty-fresher, more "English," as he was pleased to think, than the typical Parisienne. Her complexion was almost as Nature had made it, and she had soft brown eyes, with a very charming way with them, but frank and unaffected.

Kenneth's other guests were the Vicomte and Madame Armand St. Pierre de Vaux, both of whom attracted Bertram with peculiar interest. The husband had lost his left arm and part of his left leg at the first battle of the Marne, but crippled as he was, he showed an astonishing gaiety of spirit, and his lean face, with a little black moustache, and dark, luminous eyes, seemed to Bertram like that of D'Artagnan, the adored hero of his boyhood. His wife was a "*belle laide*," plain but elegant, and with adoring eyes for her crippled man whom she treated half as a lover and half as a baby, fondling his hand, cutting up his meat, laughing at his anecdotes as though she heard them for the first time, and rebuking him for raising his voice too loud in a public restaurant. To these attentions her husband responded with whimsical affection, like a small boy with his mother, whom he adores though she tries his patience.

Kenneth was a good host, speaking French perfectly, with a Parisian accent which Bertram found a little hard to follow-as he had learnt French colloquially among the peasants and bourgeoisie of Picardy-and leading the conversation as easily and gracefully as in a London drawing-room. Now and then, Bertram was aware of Kenneth's glance upon him, once or twice met his eyes and saw in them a kind of embarrassment, like that startled look which he had given for just a second at their meeting that morning in the Faubourg St. Honoré. But it was only the faintest hint of uneasiness for some unknown cause, and was no more than a shadow which left no trace in the sparkle of his conversation.

The table was laid for six, with Kenneth at one end and Armand de Vaux at the other. Bertram had the privilege of sitting on the left of Mme. de Montauban, who was next to Kenneth. Opposite were the Vicomte de Montauban, and Mme. de Vaux-admirably arranged according to the convention that husbands and wives must be kept as far apart as possible when they eat in public.

There was a little general discussion as to the impossibility of getting good food in Paris after the war, even at outrageous prices, due mainly to the profiteering of Parisian middlemen. Presently Mme. de Montauban turned to Bertram and speaking English with pretty accent, "felicitated" him on the possession of so beautiful a wife, whom she had had the pleasure of meeting several times.

Bertram's mind winced a little at that word "possession," but he merely asked where Mme. de Montauban had happened to meet Joyce.

She seemed a little surprised at that question, and her glance flickered for a moment in the direction of Kenneth.

"Everywhere in Paris," she answered, with her beautiful smile. "She has made many friends among us because of her love, so very great, for our dear France."

"*Tiens!*" said Armand de Vaux, on the other side of Bertram, "Monsieur is the husband of Miladi Joyce! She is exquisite! An English rose! Monsieur will pardon me if I confess that I fell desperately in love with her!"

"It's impossible to avoid that tribute!" said Kenneth. "Bertram Pollard knows that all his friends are the slaves of his wife's beauty. Isn't it so?"

He spoke in French, and his words sounded *chevaleresque* and romantic, with a lighter touch than they would have had in English. At that "Is it not so?" he looked at Bertram, and their eyes met. Kenneth's smile seemed a little quizzing, as though he knew his friend's quick jealousy.

Bertram felt no kind of objection to Armand de Vaux's declaration of "desperate love," though he was conscious of some secret reaction to Kenneth's endorsement.

"I am glad Joyce is so much admired," he said simply.

Armand de Vaux paid a tribute to English womanhood. Most of his knowledge of English character, as a young man, had been gained from reading translations of Shakespeare during his *service militaire* in the barracks at Belfont. He had fallen in love with Rosalind, Beatrice, and Katherine, above all with Beatrice, who was, he thought, essentially English and Elizabethan. But he believed from better evidence than that of reading, that English womanhood had retained that Elizabethan quality of character-frankness, simplicity, courage, and above all, a playfulness of spirit.

Mme. de Vaux tapped her husband's hand.

"None of your amorous reminiscences here, Armand. Every one knows that you are a monster of infidelity."

"Before marriage I was a romantic," he admitted with simple self-satisfaction. "Since marriage I have been a model of single-hearted devotion. It is still possible, however, that I may one day sow my last peck of wild oats."

This menace caused great laughter from De Montauban, and his wife, and Kenneth rewarded the audacity of De Vaux, in the presence of his wife-who seemed in no way perturbed-by filling up the glasses of his guests with another bottle of Veuve Clicquot, and drinking to the exploits of D'Artagnan —"Twenty Years After."

Mme. de Montauban ventured to accuse Shakespeare of tremendous plagiarism from Boccaccio and the Italian *novelli*, and there were vivacious passages of arms between her and Kenneth, in the course of which they quoted Italian poets at each other, so leaving Bertram for a while outside the conversation, as he was ignorant of that language.

Armand de Vaux had a tête-à-tête with him.

"You fought in France, I have no doubt, sir?"

"The Somme, Flanders, Cambrai," said Bertram.

"And still with both legs and both arms! That is wonderful. . . . You see I lost two limbs in the Great War. I do not regret them. What beautiful memories of comradeship and laughter, and immense valour! The best years of our lives!"

He spoke with absolute sincerity, and with a new light in his eyes, as though seeing with enthusiasm the vision of his fighting days.

"The comradeship was good," said Bertram, "but the price was too great for that. Why not comradeship without war?"

"*Pas possible!* It needs war and the chance of death to bring out the great qualities of men. Laughter is best when it is in the midst of danger as a shield against fear. *Mon Dieu!* how I laughed in those days!"

He told some anecdotes of war. How the "popote" or mess had been destroyed by a German shell when they were ravenous with hunger after a long march to Ablain St. Nazaire; how they had killed a German sergeant-major and two men, luring them into No-Man's Land by driving a lean pig through the barbed wire at dawn; how they had made a camouflage tree on the Arras-Lens road and sniped Germans like rabbits before they spotted it.

He was enormously amused at his own efforts to get wounded. No wound, no decoration, was the custom in the French army, as far as the fighting men were concerned. Of course, at the back of the front, any little cock sparrow at Headquarters or the Base, could cover his breast with ribbons. But in the front line the only chance of distinction was a wound. For a long time he'd had the vilest luck. All his friends were wounded-and decorated. He remained without a scratch, and without a medal. The Colonel regarded him suspiciously, said he bore "a charmed life," as though he indulged in some private Juju to keep immune from shell-fire and snipers' bullets, aerial torpedoes, trench mortars, hand grenades, and the whole "bag of tricks." The situation became serious. He walked in a veritable hail of shrapnel and nothing hit him. He made a home of No-Man's Land at night, leading patrols, but no, the Boche ignored him. One day, in Arras, a monstrous aerial torpedo made straight for him. "Ah, ha, my friend! At last you are going to do my trick!" But the *sacré* torpedo was a dud, and fell at his very feet without exploding! *Quelle mauvaise chance!* What infernal bad luck! However, fortune's wheel turned at last, and in the battle of the Somme, on the right of the British, he lost his arm and leg and gained the *Médaille Militaire*, and the *Croix de Guerre*.

Bertram joined in his gay laughter. This little French aristocrat was not posing, nor indulging in vainglorious boasting. He had loved the adventure of war, and found in it compensations for all its abominations and its tragedy of great death. A thousand years of ancestry had given him this instinct of war. Its spirit belonged to his blood. He was of the same race and quality as Amadis de Gaul, Roland, Bertrand du Guesclin, the Sieurs de Morny, the Knights of Froissart's noble Chronicles. Old Christy would have voted for his death-theoretically-as a "carrier" of the war-microbe, as some people are typhoid carriers, infecting all who come in contact with them.

"Then you don't agree with *Le Feu*, by Barbusse, as a true picture of the war from the *poilu's* point of view?" asked Bertram.

Armand de Vaux "went off," like a trench mortar. He denounced that book-the most terrible picture of war's horror, which Bertram had read before writing his own-as the work of a traitor to France, as revolutionary propaganda of the vilest kind, an outrage upon the valour of the French soldier.

Bertram was silent, not caring to risk a dispute at this table, but pretty Mme. de Montauban expressed her own opinion.

"I had a nephew at Souchez and Notre Dame de Lorette-Pierre, as you remember? He tells me that Barbusse has given an exact picture of those trenches in the winter of '15. The men were not relieved, month after month. They lived and ate and slept and died, in mud and filth. Some of them went mad, and others walked out into No-Man's Land to end their misery by a German bullet. You remember only the amusing side of war, Vicomte! It is your temperament. In my hospital at Neuilly I saw too much tragedy to believe in your romance."

"Bah!" said the Vicomte de Vaux. "Tragedy? Death? They are part of life, in peace as well as war. 'A little laughter, a little love . . . and then good night!' What more can we ask, except a good fight? *Vive la Guerre!*"

Mme. de Montauban laughed, and shook her head.

"That is the language of the eighteenth century. You speak that tongue, I know. You belong to that period. But for us moderns there is no truth in it. War has nearly destroyed our dear France. Another-and we die!"

"We shall have another," said Armand de Vaux. "I shall weep to be out of it, with only one leg and one arm."

"Why shall we have another?" asked Bertram, and a little chill crept down his spine, because of the calm and certain way in which the little Vicomte had made that statement.

But it was the Baron de Montauban who answered.

"Surely," he said, leaning forward a little, to flick the ash of his cigarette into a bowl of flowers, "you are aware that your Lloyd George arranges another for us?"

"Your Lloyd George!" Bertram had heard that phrase from peasants, chambermaids, commercial travellers, shop-girls, the typist-secretary of a music publisher. He did not expect to hear it from a French aristocrat.

Kenneth made a protest, in his graceful way, deprecating unpleasant themes, except when he happened to lead the argument in his best manner as a one-time President of the Oxford Union.

"As office-boy at the British Embassy, I hesitate to listen to accusations against my Prime Minister."

Armand de Vaux laughed heartily at this diplomatic statement, and said he had no more respect for Ministers of France than for Ministers of England. They were all politicians, playing to their respective galleries. As a soldier and a Royalist he despised them as *canaille*.

De Montauban pursued his idea relentlessly, despite this interlude.

"When I say your Lloyd George is arranging another war for France, I mean all that body of opinion in Great Britain which calls itself Liberal. *Mon Dieu!* In their desire to be fair to the Germans-one might as well be fair to his Majesty the Devil! —and in their anxiety to trade again with their former enemy, they utterly ignore the French point of view."

"What is that?" asked Bertram, anxious to discover whether the Baron de Montauban could give him more light than the peasants of the old battlefields.

"We have only one point of view, and one demand," said de Montauban. "Security! . . . Security for France, after her sacrifice and her victory. Where is that assurance?"

"In the '*tapage*' of our '*soixante-quinzes!*' " said Armand de Vaux.

De Montauban shook his head.

"Let us not deceive ourselves. We are not strong enough to fight alone against the *Boche*."

"We have Poland as a gallant ally."

"She will crumple like pasteboard between Germany and Russia."

"Belgium, Czecho-Slovakia, Hungary," said De Vaux.

"We must have England and the United States," said De Montauban. "It was they who made us sheathe our sword and abandon our full and just right of vengeance against Germany in the Treaty of Versailles. We compromised in return for a pledge of security from our allies. That pledge was broken before the signature was dry on the Treaty. The Americans refused to ratify the pledge of their President. It was our first betrayal. Since then, by a sentimental illusion of world peace, all our rights have been betrayed. The Germans have been encouraged to evade their reparation payments, though without them France is bankrupt. When we threaten to march into the Ruhr to enforce those payments, the Liberals of England cry 'Shame' on us for provoking the poor dear Germans. What will be the end of it? It is almost in sight. The Entente will be broken between England and France. Germany will ally herself with Russia, with whom also the English Liberals are sentimentalising, and France will within the present generation be called upon to defend her soil again, without Great Britain by her side. It is inevitable. It is certain. It is the Great Betrayal. That is why we hate your Lloyd George, and all he stands for."

"The English people are loyal to us," said Mme. de Montauban. She turned to Bertram, and laid her little hand on his arm.

"We are sure that the real heart of England beats with us, after so much common sacrifice, so much agony together. Is it not so?"

"It is true," said Bertram, "I thank you for having said so, Madame."

He found himself speaking emotionally, with a kind of passion in his voice, which he tried to control.

"Since I've been in France, wandering about, I have heard nothing but the French point of view. I agree with it a good deal. I am a lover of France. But there's another point of view."

"Yes?" asked De Montauban, politely, but with a hint of sarcasm.

"Yes. It's the English point of view. That of the common man, the 'Tommy' who fought in France."

"Yes?" asked De Montauban again.

"I know it pretty well. You would like to hear?"

"Tell us!" said Mme. de Montauban.

"It's just this. He doesn't believe in kicking a man when he's down, even a German. And he does believe that another war will happen if France presses Germany too hard. He doesn't want another war, because he has two million comrades out of work as a result of the last, and the trade of England is ruined already. He wants peace, and he thinks the way to get it is by a union of European peoples, forgetting hatred, and no longer grouping into different Alliances, defensive or aggressive. He believes in a League of Nations."

"Then he believes in monstrous illusion," said De Montauban, very coldly, and Bertram thought of the French priest who banged his fist on the table with the cry of "Illusion!"

"Speaking as a soldier," said Armand de Vaux, "I see no safety for France or England, except in the power of their artillery. And I would give the luxury of this very charming dinner to sit in the mud again and hear the *rafale* of the *soixante-quinzes* pounding the *Boche* to bits."

"You're a bloodthirsty ogre!" said his wife, caressing his only hand.

"You're a despiser of my poor little banquet," said Kenneth, ordering some more Veuve Clicquot, and very artfully inviting an interruption of waiters, to change the drift of conversation which abandoned politics for a discussion on the psychology of "jazz," led by the beautiful Mme. de Montauban, in reference to the efforts of the orchestra.

Kenneth had to return to the Embassy at ten o'clock.

Mme. de Montauban and her husband were going to a reception by the Duchesse d'Uzès. It was this lady who rose first, with a smile at Mme. de Vaux who accepted the signal.

The other little parties in the restaurant paid tribute to her beauty with their eyes, as Bertram helped to put her cloak on her shoulders.

She gave him her hand with a charming friendship.

"I understand your English point of view," she said. "It is a little dangerous, I think. The English heart is greater than the English head!"

Then she leaned forward to him, smiling, and spoke in a low voice.

"Do not leave your wife alone too much. She is too beautiful! That is more important than politics-if you love her beauty!"

In another moment she was gone, with a rustle of silk and a gracious smile.

Bertram was alarmed by those words of hers. Were they merely "French" in their general sentiment, or a particular warning? They disturbed him profoundly.

He walked with Kenneth through the Marché St. Honoré as far as the Embassy. Kenneth seemed talkative, discussing those friends of his, as though wishing to avoid other topics.

Bertram broke in across one of his subtleties.

"You've seen a good deal of Joyce lately?"

For just a second-no more than that-Kenneth hesitated in his reply.

"Yes. Longchamps-the Bois-the opera, and so on, in the usual way. It's been beautiful weather lately, don't you think?"

Bertram was silent. He was not interested in the weather.

"You know that Joyce and I have not seen things altogether eye to eye lately? She told you that?"

Kenneth again hesitated before his answer, as though weighing his words with diplomatic caution.

"I was aware of some misunderstanding. . . . But if you'll allow me to say so, I never discuss relations between husband and wife. Don't you think that's a good rule?"

He spoke in his friendliest way, but his rebuke, as it seemed, made Bertram flush deeply.

"I have no intention of discussing my relations with Joyce. I merely desired to thank you for having been a good friend to her during my absence."

Kenneth laughed, in a queer, strained way.

"My dear fellow! No need for thanks. . . . I try to play the game, according to the rules."

He raised his hand with a gesture that was almost a salute, and disappeared into the British Embassy.

XLIII

Mr. Mahony, the uncle of Betty O'Brien, with whom Susan was staying, lived in an apartment on the upper floor of a house in the shabby end of the rue de la Pompe, out at Passy, by "Metro" from the Place de la Concorde.

"*Quatrième à gauche*" —fourth floor on the left-was the direction given to Bertram by the concierge, an enormous man who was wedged with his almost equally fat wife in a little room on the ground floor with a glass window through which he could observe those who came and went. He added to his information by the surly remark that Bertram would find the right door by the abominable noise that issued from it.

"What kind of noise?" asked Bertram.

"The noise of anarchists, monsieur. All talking treason to France and to civilisation. I may consider it my duty to inform the police."

"A prudent idea," said Bertram.

He smiled at the lowering face of the Colossus through the glass window with its dirty lace curtains, and then went up four flights of a staircase which smelt abominably of drains and onions. The plaster on the walls was crumbling off in scabby patches, and the doors to the right and left on each landing needed new paint, badly. The door on the fourth floor to the left had a broken bellrope tied up with a string, and when Bertram tugged it, there was a sound inside like the jangle of a Bulgarian cow-bell. Through a slit in the door came the murmur of several voices, but nothing that could fairly be described as "an abominable noise."

The door was opened to him by Susan, a pale Susan, with no Irish roses in her cheeks, as he noticed when he kissed her.

"So you've come!"

She spoke quietly, with no enthusiasm, but then, at the kiss of the brother who once had been her close comrade, her coldness to him seemed to melt, and putting both her hands on his shoulders and her face against his coat, she began to cry a little, silently.

"What's the matter, Sister Susie?" he whispered, while from the end of the passage came the sound of vivacious conversation.

"Isn't everything in the world the matter?" she asked, and then dried her tears in a comical way with the back of her hand.

"Can't you come out to some café and have a quiet talk? I don't feel like 'company' to-night."

She told him she wanted him to meet Betty's uncle and her good friend, Mr. Mahony, and led him by the hand into a shabbily furnished room, dimly lit by oil lamps, where Bertram saw Betty O'Brien, who rose and gave him her hand, and an elderly man with white hair, a clean-shaven, rather priestly face, and very blue eyes, in which there was a look of humour and benevolence. He was sitting back in a low chair, with broken leather, through which the stuffing protruded, talking in a philosophical strain to three young men, obviously Irish, who were sitting about the room smoking cigarettes. Bertram heard him say something about the need of sacrifice for sacred principles.

"A man who won't die for a principle sins against the light."

"Uncle," said Betty O'Brien, "be hanged to your principles for a minute. This is Susan's brother."

Mr. Mahony rose, and grasped Bertram's hand.

"Susan's brother! Then a friend of Ireland."

"Half an Irishman, and a good friend," said Bertram.

Yet before the evening was at an end, his friendship for Ireland was put to a heavy strain again. Mr. Mahony, with his white hair, and blue benevolent eyes, and the three young Irishmen to whom he addressed most of his monologues, made no disguise of their implacable hatred of England. It was not that they denounced England with any violence of language, but rather the deadly coldness, and the kind of loathing, with which they spoke the very name of England.

Worse than that was their contempt. It was plain that they had the fixed belief that the British Government in Ireland was "on the run." The Irish Republican army was succeeding with its policy of secret warfare. In one week they had killed five British officers and twenty men. They had raided the barracks, seized great quantities of arms, and organised a number of successful ambushes. There were large districts in Ireland into which the Black and Tans dared not penetrate. The British troops were getting nerve-rattled and demoralised. It was obvious by the Government answers to questions in the House of Commons that that was very much the psychological state of "His Majesty's Ministers."

The three young Irishmen, smoking French cigarettes interminably, had all been officers of the I. R. A., and had escaped to France when things had become too "hot" for them. One of them, named O'Malley, a handsome, dark-eyed fellow rather like Dennis O'Brien, but with brighter, more humorous eyes, described his adventures as an escaped prisoner from Mountjoy, where he had been under sentence of death after capture in an ambush near Cork. The Black and Tans had searched the countryside for him, and all the time he was selling eggs in the market-place disguised as a "colleen," and so seductive in appearance that an English officer had given him the glad eye.

Mr. Mahony turned to Bertram and whispered a few words about O'Malley, with a smile of admiration and pride.

"England will never defeat Ireland with that spirit against her! O'Malley is like all the boys-just laughs at death. It was he who executed the British officer who gave the order to fire on the people in the Celtic Football ground-the bloody villain!"

Bertram felt a little cold chill creep down his spine. These people here were the enemies of England. Some of them, like O'Malley, had killed British officers, not in open fighting, but by cold murder, under the name of "execution." And they were proud of their exploits, with bright, humorous eyes, not conscience-stricken, as men with red crimes on their hands, but as men who had done well in the cause of some divine ideal. They used even the name of God with a sense of alliance.

"God is working for Ireland," said Mr. Mahony. "The sacrifice of our boys is not ignored by Him who died on the Cross to save mankind."

Bertram felt the blood surge to his brain at these words. He wanted to stand up and denounce them as blasphemy. To him it was inconceivable that a man like Mahony, a gentleman, a mild-eyed man, a good Catholic, could defend the Sicilian methods of the Irish Republicans in the very name of Christ-who spoke words of peace and pity, who said "Thou shalt not kill," whose Gospel was Love. He half rose from his chair to make a violent and passionate protest, when the words were taken from him by a newcomer, brought into the room by Betty O'Brien.

"Uncle-here is Mr. Lajeunesse."

The man who bore the name of "Youth" was an old gentleman of seventy or more, with a shock of grey hair and a pointed beard, and a delicate, life-worn face. His eyes, surrounded by a thousand wrinkles, twinkled with the light of irony, and it was with irony that he greeted Mr. Mahony.

"I hear you mention the name of Christ, my dear friend! Doubtless you are quoting the Master's words to defend militarism and the right of assassination in special cases? During the Great War, when we murdered each other wholesale, Christianity was of great value to Army Commanders, on both sides of the line. I think the Germans were most successful in using Christ as a propagandist among the troops. But we did pretty well with the same idea. . . . Good evening, Miss Susy! My little Irish rose still blooms in Paris?"

The old man kissed the girl on both cheeks with the privilege of his years, but also with the gallantry of a Frenchman who pays homage to beauty. And Susan's roses deepened.

The three young Irishmen had left their chairs when he entered. They bowed low over his hand and Mr. Mahony addressed him as *cher maître*, and did not resent his irony. It was Eugène Lajeunesse, and Bertram felt a thrill at being in the presence of a man whose books, so wise, so witty, so wicked, so full of tenderness to humanity, and yet so cruel in tearing down the faith of simple folk, had made him famous throughout the world. Alone in France during the War, he had maintained his faith as an international pacifist, and not all the outrages of *Les Boches*, nor all the agony of France had made him swerve from the belief that the war was only one more proof of human stupidity.

He brought with him a young Frenchman, blind in one eye and partly paralysed, it seemed, on one side, so that he walked with difficulty, using a stick, but wonderfully vivacious and good-humoured.

Eugène Lajeunesse introduced him to the company.

"Aristide de Méricourt. You know his name and work? If there is any hope for our poor old Europe, which is *in extremis mortuis*, it lies in the success of this young man and his band of brothers. They are working for international peace and universal brotherhood. What audacity! What sublime hope in a world that is digging new entrenchments of hate!"

"We make a little progress," said the young man with the blind eye. "From all parts of France youth which saw life in the trenches is joining our League against Militarism. The Old Men are becoming afraid of us."

"As one of the Old Men, I am not afraid of you," said Lajeunesse, smiling at his young friend. "I recognise your right to declare a spiritual warfare against all old imbeciles who are preparing for another massacre-the last before cilivisation dies-in the fields of Europe. Gladly would I die to-night to see youth gain its victory over old age, old ideas, old villainies, old hatreds."

"You are not among the Old Men, *cher maître*," said Aristide de Méricourt; "You are Laje-unesse-Youth itself."

The old man laughed, and shook his head.

"I pose as the champion of youth. It is my vanity-to keep young in mind and soul. Alas, I am convicted of senility because of my cynical doubts of youth's adventure. Civilisation is too sick to be saved, and Poincaré, and all the Poincarés and reactionaries of Europe, are determined on its doom. How many men and boys have you in your League against Militarism?"

"Three thousand," said Aristide de Méricourt, with an air of pride. "Our membership is spreading in England, Germany, Italy, even in Austria. We are truly international."

"Three thousand young men pledged to international peace! That is a beginning. It is excellent. But you have three hundred million souls to convert. The odds are heavy, dear child."

"We shall win," said the young man with the blind eye. "Democracy is solid against the spirit of war."

Eugène Lajeunesse laughed quietly, as at a child who talks of killing dragons.

"Let us put it a little to the test. Here in this company of intellectuals are several young Irish-men. Are they for or against militarism-after the war to end war? I have heard something of a little bloodshed in Ireland-or is it only a rumour? They are Catholics and Christians. Beautiful is the simplicity of Irish faith! Have they abandoned the use of Force as a way of argument? Do they believe in Universal brotherhood, among nations and peoples? Or are they using the bomb and the revolver to break away from brotherhood with a nation to whom they are bound in blood, to entrench themselves more narrowly in national isolation? Tell me, little ones. I am an ignorant old man!"

They told him at some length, and with passionate argument. Mr. Mahoney said that the international ideal must be based first of all on national liberty, that universal brotherhood presupposed justice between one people and another.

It was Aristide de Méricourt, who interested Bertram most, for he was the immediate opposite in ideals and convictions of Armand de Vaux who loved the adventure of war and believed that it developed the noblest qualities of man. But there was something strange and sinister in the quiet way in which this cripple denounced the existing institutions of his own country and of western civilisation, the national heroes of France, all the old loyalties of tradition and faith.

Marshal Foch, he said, had "the soul of a grocer." He counted men, battalions, divisions, as so many packets. The sacrifice of human life left him untouched, unperturbed. Poincaré was a stuffed puppet with a squeak. French politicians were corrupt and bought. There must be a clean sweep of superstition-the superstition of the Flag, of the Church, of Patriotism, of national egotism. The democracies of the world must unite against the powers of capitalism. France must link up with Russia for the overthrow of all the forces of *bourgeois* stupidity and tyranny. There must be a revolution in England and the United States, so that Anglo-Saxon democracy might join hands with Latin and Slav. It was the only hope of the world.

"The audacity of youth!" said Lajeunesse. "Once, too, I had those dreams! A thousand years ago!"

"As a Catholic Irishman I disagree with such revolutionary gospel," said Mr. Mahony, but there was benevolent tolerance in his blue eyes for the heresy of the younger man.

Bertram pleaded with his sister for a little private talk.

"All this discussion is very interesting, no doubt, but no good to me. I want to know what you're doing and going to do. I want to tell you Of my own troubles."

"Joyce?" she asked, and he wondered how much she knew of that trouble, his greatest.

They went out to a café close by, and took a seat in a far corner away from a group of men drinking with painted women.

Susan shivered a little, and drew her cloak close about her though it was warm in the café, and oppressive with the smell of cheap wine, black coffee, and stale tobacco.

"You don't look well," said Bertram. "Is anything wrong with you?"

"The price of womanhood," she said. "I'm going to have a baby. The child of a man hanged by the English because he loved Ireland. Funny, isn't it?"

He put his hand on hers, and groaned a little.

"My poor kid! My dear little sister!"

He was stricken by this news of hers, by the awful memory it revived.

Susan spoke calmly, but with a coldness that was worse than tears or passion.

"I'll call him Dennis, if it's a boy. I'll make him Irish in soul and faith, as his father was. And I'll teach him to hate England as I hate it."

Bertram tried to take her hand again, but she pulled it nervously away.

"What's the good of teaching hate?" he asked. "It gets nowhere. It leads only to more tragedy, more blood, more death. I believe in peace, and love."

"Pap for babes!" said Susan scornfully. "Life is war. Peace doesn't exist. We're all savages, and must obey the law of the savage. Strike first and quickest, before your enemy gets his chance. No pity, no forgiveness, no forgetfulness. That's my creed."

"It was not the Master's creed," said Bertram. He told his sister of the words spoken by their mother as she lay dying. "Work for Peace!"

"I'm pledged by the promise I made then," he said. "I'm dedicated to work for Peace."

Susan's eyes filled with tears, but she shook her head and said it was all useless. How could there be peace when the world was stuffed with cruelty? Could there ever be peace between France and Germany? Never in a thousand or a million years. Or ever between Ireland and England, after what had happened, and was happening? Not as long as an Irish boy lived to remember the history of his race.

"I'm dedicated too," she said. "By the blood of the man I married. In private or in public, by spoken word and written word, I've pledged myself to work against England, so that the British Empire will be dragged down from its place, and fall in ruin. I'm only one of England's enemies, and a poor, weak creature, but I can put in a word here and a word there. It all helps, and England already has the whole world against her. France hates her worse than Germany."

"It's madness and wickedness," said Bertram. "You're hysterical, my dear, or I couldn't forgive you for the words you speak."

She flared up at him, and called him a crawling sentimentalist, who tried to make the best of both worlds and stand on both sides of the hedge at the same time.

"You're tricked by soppy sentiment. Just as Joyce has tricked you. Are you still loyal to her, may I ask?"

"I want to be," said Bertram.

She laughed, with a sound of mockery.

"It's a one-sided loyalty, old boy. Joyce has betrayed you with Kenneth Murless. If she's not his mistress, she's a much slandered woman. Every one thinks so in Paris."

Bertram went cold, and stared at Susan with a kind of horror in his eyes.

"Susan! In God's name, what do you mean by that?"

She told him it was none of her business. But friends of hers in Paris who knew that Joyce was her sister-in-law, had taken it for granted that she had "run off" with Kenneth. They were always about together, in the Bois, at the opera, at Longchamps, in Henri's restaurant night after night.

"What else can people think when a woman leaves her husband and comes to Paris with a man like Kenneth?"

"She came with Lady Ottery," said Bertram, "and what your friends say is a damned lie. If they say so to me, I'll beat them into pulp."

Susan laughed again, in her mocking way. "That's the primitive man. Not peace and love this time, when it touches you so closely! You'll beat any man to pulp who slanders Joyce-or tells the truth, maybe. But you can't forgive an Irishman who hates England, not for slandering his country, but for outraging her, trampling on her face, murdering her children! Nor a Frenchman who wants to beat Germany to pulp! Where's your logic, Bertram?"

He sat silent, staring at a puddle of coffee on the marble-topped table. What Susan said was true enough. She had found the weak spot in his armour. His "dedication to peace" only held good as long as it was in the abstract, and impersonal. This accusation against Joyce, that word "mistress" coupled with Kenneth's name, put the instinct of murder in his mind. If he believed the story he would go to Kenneth and shoot him like a dog. Fortunately it was absurd. He could afford to laugh at it. He laughed now, harshly.

"Extraordinary how some women, and most Irish, have the spirit of vendetta. Why do you hate Joyce so much that you want to kill her reputation?"

Susan rose, and left the café table.

"Let's go before we make a public brawl. It's true I hate Joyce. I remember a scene over a telephone one night when she threatened to betray my man. But I hate her now because she's betraying you, in heart if not in body."

Bertram took his sister back without a word, to the apartment house in the rue de la Pompe. There he left her with a gruff "Good night!" She had wounded him horribly with a poisoned shaft. Her words tortured him. He thought of her as a female Iago who had slandered another Desdemona. And he was Othello, refusing to believe, yet with foul suspicion gnawing at him, and making a madness in his brain.

Joyce and Kenneth! No, a million times no. And yet, deep down in his subconsciousness had been that very toad of evil thought. Ever since Joyce had written to him, telling him she saw a good deal of Kenneth in Paris, he had tried to kill this base and frightful thought which now Susan had stated as a well known belief. "Every one thinks so in Paris."

At nine o'clock next morning he took the train to Amiens and, at the Hotel du Rhin, hired a motor-car and drove to the Château de Plumoison where Joyce was staying.

XLIV

He remembered this old château of Picardy. It lay to the right of the cottage where he had been billeted for a few weeks in 1917. He had hardly thought of it since, because that memory had been effaced by more exciting and deadly adventure. But now, as he passed up the dirty village where cocks and hens clustered across the roadway and peasant women stared at him from doorways where once British soldiers had lounged during Divisional rests between long spells in the line, he remembered the way past the pump, and then a sharp turn to the right by the *estaminet* of "*La Véritable Coucou*" —that comical name came back to him now with intimate remembrance-and so to the long avenue of poplars leading straight through the park to the old white house with its pointed roofs.

The Vicomte de Plumoison had given the run of the place to any British officers in the neighbourhood, and Yvonne, his daughter, had invited them to "five o'clock," as she called her tea-parties. She was not very beautiful, though an elegant little lady, but it was paradise enough to sit with any lady in any drawing-room, after long terms of servitude in the lousy trenches, in exile from all beauty. . . .

He turned through the iron gates and walked slowly up the avenue. Somewhere in that white house was Joyce. His heart beat at the thought, with sickening kind of thuds. He was passionate to see her, to take her hand, to draw her close to him, and be assured of her love after all this foolishness of separation and estrangement. A word from her, a straight look out of her eyes, would be enough to kill that toad of evil still alive in the slime of suspicion, in those base and primitive instincts of the male beast which lurk as a heritage of cave-man ancestry in all human brains.

Janet Welford had spoken a true thing when she said, "Joyce is the Beatrice of your *Divina Commedia*." In the time of his greatest bitterness against her, when he felt most injured by her ill-temper with him, she had been his vision, and in his heart, inescapable. His loyalty had been strained, but was stronger than all his weakness, and now, as he went towards her, the thought of this girl who had given him her beauty so generously in time of war, so recklessly, perhaps, fevered him.

He quickened his pace, and instead of going straight up the avenue, took a winding path which led to the back of the château by the trout stream. Perhaps it was some mental "wave-length" which impelled him to do that instinctively, and without conscious purpose, because, as he made his way through a little glade, he saw Joyce a few yards away from him.

There was a stone seat there, which he remembered. It was underneath a grass bank with a little hollowed place in which stood a statue of "*Notre Dame de Lourdes*," —painted blue and white, amidst tall growing ferns. He had once stood there talking to Yvonne de Plumoison with a group of officers. Joyce was alone. Her hat lay on the seat by her side. She had a book on her lap, but she wasn't reading. She was weeping. At least there were tears in her eyes when, at the sound of his footsteps on the path, she looked quickly towards him, and then sprang up with a cry of surprise.

He called her name, and went forward hurriedly, with tremendous gladness in his eyes. She looked as he had thought of her so often. As she stood there, waiting for him, the sunlight, shining through young leaves, touched her hair, giving it a glory. She wore a green frock, cut low at the neck, and looked like the Rosalind in Arden Woods.

She let him take her hands and kiss her, but did not answer his passion with any warmth of greeting, so that almost in a moment he was chilled, and saw that she had become pale in his arms.

"Here's a seat," she said. "Let's sit and talk."

He sat beside her, holding her hand, and was struck by its coldness.

"I've been longing for you," he told her. "Dreaming of you o' nights."

She said something about his letters. They didn't suggest any passionate longing, she thought. He hadn't bothered to join her in Paris when she asked him.

He asked her to "wash all that out." He'd been a blithering idiot. It had all been a question of jangled nerves-the wrong perspective-egotism. He'd been thinking things out during his loneliness. He'd killed his miserable ego. All he wanted now was to make her happy and to serve her. They'd made a mistake in taking things too seriously, arguing about trivialities as though they mattered. They'd allowed "politics" to strain their relations! It was inconceivable, looking back on it. What kids they'd been! He had grown up at last. No more of that sort of nonsense. Tolerance was his watch-word. He'd come to understand that a plain getting on with life mattered more than theories and minor differences in points of view. Love was the only thing worth while.

"Do you mean that?" asked Joyce. "Do you think, honestly, that love over-rides everything?"

"Every damn thing," said Bertram.

She gave him a queer glancing smile.

"It's a dangerous philosophy. Sometimes it leads to peculiar complications!"

"How do you mean?" asked Bertram. "To me it simplifies the whole riddle. The love of a man for his mate, through thick and thin, fine weather and foul, 'in sickness and in health.' —D'you remember the old words in St. Mary Abbot's?"

"Yes. I remember. I was a baby then. We were both babes, as ignorant of life as those tits."

She pointed to two little birds fluttering about the branch of a tree where they sat.

"But with the same share in the eternal scheme of things," said Bertram. "You and I went to St. Mary Abbot's under the same divine impulse as those two tits set up housekeeping in the tree-top."

"Yes," said Joyce, "I suppose it's over-civilisation that has spoilt the game."

"Is the game spoilt?" asked Bertram.

"It's hard to play according to the rules, sometimes. And if we keep to the rules the fun goes out of the game. It's just duty. Mostly disagreeable, and sometimes intolerable."

Bertram laughed so that the two tits were frightened and flew away from their branch. He took Joyce's hand and put it to his lips.

"We seem to be talking in parables and conundrums. Joyce, let's be human. Are you glad I've come back to you? Are we going to wipe the slate clean and start fresh and fair down the good old highway of married life? Say a word of love to me! Put your arms around my neck, and whisper what I want to hear."

Joyce's face flamed with colour for a moment, and then paled again.

"I can't!" she said. "Something's happened to put things all wrong-worse than before-between you and me."

He stared at her, and knew that Fate, or Luck, or God, was going to hit him another blow between the eyes. What did she mean? That "Something's happened —"?

"For Christ's sake," he said, "what do you mean?"

"It's about Kenneth," she answered in a low voice.

That name, after what Susan had said, after a night of dark agony, after a fight with frightful suspicion in which old base jealousies had surged up from the darkness of his mind, was like the jab of a bayonet in his brain.

"What the hell has he got to do with it?" he asked, very quietly.

Joyce touched his hand, as though asking for patience and understanding.

"You'll get angry, I know. But I can't help it. These things just happen. It's as though we hadn't any control over them, or over ourselves. I've always thought of Kenneth as nothing more than a good friend —a nice boy. We've known each other since we were kids. He understands me better than any one in the world. We speak in shorthand, as it were-the same code of thought and all that. He didn't seem to mind when I married you. He thought it was good fun. It made no difference to our friendship. He's perfectly straight and clean. He'd no idea at all, until a few days ago, that he loved me-in another kind of way. We found out quite suddenly, by accident. We were laughing-playing the fool, as usual. We were in a boat together on the lake in the Bois-you know-by the Île des Châlets. Suddenly he looked up at me with a kind of surprise in his eyes. And something seemed to fire a spark between us. I leant over him and kissed him, and he said, 'What's up with us?' —in a frightened way. We found out then that our old friendship had changed. For the first time I knew the meaning of love. —Never like yours and mine, Bertram. Kenneth and I were made for each other from the time we were babies together. It's just that. Unfortunately we've only just found out. . . . I'm frightfully sorry, Bertram. But there it is, and nothing can alter it now."

She had spoken all this quietly, in a matter-of-fact way, but now she began to cry again, with her hands up to her face.

Bertram had sat very still, with his head bent during her monologue. A greyness crept into his face, giving him a dead look. He was dead for a little while. Joyce had killed the spirit in him by those words of hers. He had nothing to say to himself. Not even anger stirred in him, nor self-pity. All that came into his mind was a kind of numbness, and one name reiterated. Kenneth! Kenneth! Kenneth Murless!

Joyce took her hands down from her face, and wiped her tears away with a handkerchief. Then she spoke again in the same quiet tone.

"Kenneth and I want to play the game. He's fearfully sorry about you. He likes you immensely and thinks I've given you a rough deal. That's true. I've been beastly to you, but I didn't know all the time that it was Kenneth I wanted. You've been jolly good to me, Bertram. I see that now. But it's impossible to live together after what I've told you. What are we going to do about it? For the moment I've cut and run. It was Kenneth who asked me to do that. 'You'd better cut and run,' he said. 'We've got to play the game.' So here I am waiting until you think things out. I haven't told Mother yet."

Bertram was still silent, still rather dead in his heart and brain. But one phrase used by Joyce startled him a little. "I've cut and run," she said. Where had he heard that before? It was something that had happened to himself. Some time or other, from some one or other, he too had "cut and run." It was old Christy, who had advised it. "If you're tempted by disloyalty," he said, "you'd better cut and run." Queer, that Joyce should have been given the same advice. Rather funny! Damnably funny!

He laughed at the comedy of it. He stood up from the stone seat and laughed loudly and harshly, frightening the birds again, a jay in the boughs near by, which flew out with a kind of echo of his laugh and a quick beat of wings.

"Good God in Heaven!" he said. "So you haven't told your Mother yet? I wonder what the Countess of Ottery will think of it. Her sense of propriety will be a little shocked. She too will want to play the game according to the rules. I don't know this kind of game. Perhaps it's up to me. I guess the rules will oblige me to give you an excuse for divorce. I rather fancy that's the way it's done in your set. I commit a technical sin. I indulge in a perfectly painless act of cruelty. You institute proceedings for restitution of conjugal rights. Isn't that one of the rules? I refuse on a post-card. Then you divorce me. The newspapers print your photograph-the beautiful Lady Joyce Pollard obtains her decree. I seem to remember that sort of thing. . . . Joyce! Oh, my dear wife! Joyce, my beloved!"

It was quite suddenly, at the end of his monstrous irony, that he broke down and wept, and pleaded with her weakly, in a stricken way.

Several times Joyce said, "I'm sorry, Bertram! I'm frightfully sorry!"

She too was weeping now, and her slim body shook with sobs. Under the trees there in the little glade of a French château, this man and wife, so English, so young, so good to see, if love had been between them, made a pitiful picture.

"You've been very good to me, my dear," said Joyce again. "I'm sorry-for everything."

He went towards her, and took her roughly and drew her close to him.

"Joyce, this is frightful. It can't happen. It's just illusion. You're my wife and I'm your lover. Let's go away together, and forget all else. That baseness with Kenneth. It was just a moment of madness. Weakness. I understand! I've been tempted like that!"

She drew herself out of his arms.

"It's not like that. It's Kenneth I belong to; and he to me. One can't go against revelation."

He told her that she was murdering him. He'd suffered hell already because of their separation. He'd been tempted by sheer weakness and loneliness. Did she intend to send him straight to the devil?

She said something about his going to "a nice woman." She couldn't complain of that. He would find some one more patient with him, more in tune with his ideas.

It was that which angered him and broke down any kind of restraint to which he had clung.

"You're hellishly immoral," he told her. "God knows how far you've gone a header with that swine Murless. If there's truth in what people say of you in Paris, I'll wring your neck and blow his brains out."

She stiffened at that threat.

"I've told you we intend to play the game as far as possible. Kenneth has played up like a gentleman. I hope you won't behave like a savage."

"I *am* a savage," he said, "when it comes to this sort of thing. It is the primitive right of man to make sure of his mate. D'you think I'm going to connive at your sin? To play the *"mari complaisant?"* Not in your life!"

"Don't mediævalise," said Joyce. "We're in the Twentieth Century."

"Human nature doesn't change," he answered. "You're my wife, and I'll hold you, if I have to fight for you."

"You can't hold me," she said. "I've escaped. You can hold my dead body, but not my living heart. Kenneth has that. From the beginning of things, as I see now, he and I were meant for each other. You were an accident that intervened. It was my mistake, and yours. And I've paid for it already, pretty badly."

An accident that intervened! That was how she spoke of his love. That was his position between Joyce Pollard and Kenneth Murless! The phrase slashed his soul, and stung him into a mad rage. The man who had come into this glade with love in his heart for this girl with gold hair and slim white body, strode towards her now with clenched fists and a fury in his eyes. He meant to do her bodily harm, and she saw that in his eyes. But she stood very straight and still, and did not flinch as he came close to her, but smiled with a strange disdain.

"As you like," she said.

It was a kind of invitation to hit her, even to kill her, if he thought well of that, as for a moment he did. But, as once before when he had raised his hand against her, he was disarmed by her prettiness, and the fury passed from him.

Down the avenue came the sound of voices, speaking French, and through the trees Bertram saw Yvonne de Plumoison and her father, as he had seen them walking arm-in-arm in time of war. On the other side of the old man was Lady Ottery with her hand on the arm of Yvonne's brother.

Bertram took hold of Joyce, and kissed her twice on the lips, with passionate brutality, and then released her, flinging her away from him so that she fell on the grass. He hadn't meant, then, to be as rough as that. He made his way through the glade, and turned a moment to look back. Joyce was standing again with her face towards him. He raised his hand with a tragic gesture of farewell, to which she made no answer. Then he walked back to the great iron gates through which he passed, and so towards the village, and so towards life without the hope of Joyce, in loneliness and desolation of soul, worse than he had known.

XLV

He left Paris without calling on Kenneth Murless for the purpose of indulging in violence. What was the good? To blow Kenneth's brains out, or to punch his head, would not bring back Joyce. She had dismissed him for ever out of her heart and life. He walked alone upon the road and all that he had felt in loneliness before was nothing to this certainty of eternal separation. She was dead to him, and he to her.

He made one last foolish, futile effort to pretend otherwise by writing her a letter in which he implored her to wait a while at least before she took the step from which she could never return.

> "Wait six months," (he said). "My loyalty is yours for that time, or longer, and perhaps before the end of it you will realise your horrible mistake-this midsummer madness that possesses you. . . ."

Stuff like that he wrote, but knew the hopelessness of it, and did not wait in Paris for an answer. She wouldn't answer. She had told him all there was to know. As she had said once before, when as yet the "something" that had happened had not happened, it was "past argument." Perhaps-almost certainly-throughout her married life her subconsciousness had known what she knew now consciously. She had been more at ease with Kenneth than ever with him. She had preferred his conversation, his sense of humour, his point of view. There was a secret code between them which he had never learnt. He had been "out of it," after the first few weeks of sentiment and passion.

He reasoned all this out with astounding calmness of mind, between bouts of astounding rage and anguish, in the train from Paris to Berlin. He was quietly and deliberately rude to a young British officer in his carriage who tried to enter into conversation on the way to Cologne, where he belonged to the Army of Occupation. The boy was surprised by his gruffness, and shrank back into sulky silence, staring at him now and then with furtive eyes, until Bertram apologised, and said, "Sorry for being uncivil. I've got the devil of a toothache. You know —a jumping nerve!" One doesn't tell a travelling companion that one has the devil of a broken heart, aching horribly.

"Oh, Lord," said the boy, "what infernal bad luck! No wonder you don't want me to jaw to you! There's nothing worse."

He offered Bertram a brandy flask and said "it helped sometimes." And Bertram, to satisfy him, took a good swig which at least had the effect of sending him to sleep after a wakeful night. It was an uneasy sleep, and he wakened once crying out the name of Joyce. Fortunately the young officer was dozing, or pretending to doze. He left the carriage at Cologne, and hoped Bertram's toothache would be cured by the time he reached Berlin.

A nice boy, like thousands who had been as young as he at the beginning of the war, and now had been four years, six years, even seven years, dead. How extraordinary was that! Bertram had been barely nineteen when he first joined up, in 1914. Now he was getting on for twenty-six, and felt as old as fifty. Well, he'd crammed in all the experience of life-war, marriage, failure, complete and absolute tragedy.

What was life? Nothing but some kind of service, where he could be of use somewhere. Service to boys younger than himself, like that kid on the way to Cologne. He might help, by a hairsbreadth in the balance of fate, to save their lives from another massacre. That would be worth doing. He was dedicated still to his work for peace. But first he must get peace within himself. Not easy, with this conflict tearing inside him. He must get some kind of wisdom, serenity, quietude of resignation before he could work for peace in the world. He would "chuck" thinking about his own wound, and plunge into the study of the world after war. That was the only line of sanity.

Berlin ought to be interesting. He would meet his sister Dorothy there, with her German husband. He would get to hear things and see things. It would be strange to walk about among the Enemy, without being killed.

Not long ago the Germans were "They." During the war that was always the word used. "They" are putting up a strafe along the Menin Road. "They" are very quiet to-day. "They" are rather active on the Divisional Front. It would be damn funny to meet them in shops and restaurants, perhaps in private drawing-rooms —men, very likely, who had potted at him when he'd shown his cap a second above the parapet, or fired the five-point-nines which had rattled his nerves in a rat-haunted dug-out. . . .

Bertram could not get a room in any hotel in Berlin. There was a waiters' strike, and all the hotels were closed and picketed except the Adlon, which paid what the strikers demanded, clapped the difference on to the bills, and did a roaring business with every room booked weeks in advance, and crowds of Germans, Austrians, English, and Jews of all nationalities, clamouring for admittance at any price, and bribing the head clerk with thousands of marks, to get their names on the waiting list.

It was the outside porter of the Adlon who saved Bertram from a night in the streets, by giving him a card to a private lodging-house somewhere near the Grossspielhaus, where he was able to obtain a bed-sitting-room in which all his meals would be served.

His landlord came in repeatedly to study his comfort, to explain the working of the electric light, to ask whether he desired *helles* or *dunkles* beer, and to carry in his tray with the *Abendessen*. He was a tall Prussian of middle-age who had been a *Feldwebel*, or sergeant-major, with the Second Prussian Guards, after keeping a small hotel in Manchester. He spoke very good English, and lingered to talk while Bertram ate a well-cooked steak.

"You were an officer in the English army?"

Bertram nodded. "In France, all the time."

"I also. We were opposite the English at Ypres, Cambrai, the Somme, in '16. I used to hear your men talking in the trenches. Sometimes I called out to them, and sometimes they answered back. 'How deep are you in mud, Tommy?' That was in the winter of '16. 'Up to our bloody knees,' said an English Tommy. 'That's nothing,' I answered, 'We're up to our waists.' 'Serve you bloody well right!' said the English boy."

He chuckled over the reminiscence, but presently sighed deeply and said:

"The war was one long horror."

"What made you begin it?" asked Bertram.

The man shrugged his shoulders.

"It was a war of Capital. We were all silly sheep."

Bertram went on eating, and wished the man would go. He wanted to be alone. But the man stood by his chair and was anxious to talk.

"I suppose they still hate us in England?"

"They're not fond of you," said Bertram.

The man sighed again, noisily.

"I was very happy in Manchester. . . . You will find no hate against the English in Germany. Not much. We know you believe in 'fair play.' Not like the French!"

"You don't like the French?"

The man's face suddenly deepened in colour, and there came into his eyes a look of rage.

"The French? They've put every insult on us. Make us eat dirt. One day we'll go back, and wring their necks-like this!"

He put his big hands together, and gave them a convulsive twist while he made a noise in his throat like a man choking.

"I thought you'd had enough of war," said Bertram.

"Not against the French. I'd march again to-morrow to make them feel the German boot in their backsides."

"Then it would happen all over again," said Bertram. "The lousy trenches, the gun-fire, the massacre of men."

"With a difference," said the man, in a low voice, as though hiding, or half-revealing a secret thought.

"What kind of difference?"

"The French won't have the English on their side next time. *Nicht wahr?*"

Bertram swung round in his chair.

"If the Germans think that, they're making the hell of a mistake. For the second time."

"*So?*"

The man had a scared look, as though he had said too much.

"Your dinner was good. It was good meat, *nicht wahr?* Better than in the trenches!"

He laughed in a guttural way, desiring to wipe out a bad impression.

That night Bertram set out to find his sister Dorothy, the Frau von Arenburg. By a queer coincidence in names, she lived in the Dorotheenstrasse, somewhere across the Wilhelmstrasse, at the corner of which was the British Embassy. Unfamiliar with the geography of Berlin, he lost his way, and found himself in the Leipzigerstrasse, so that, in halting German, he had to ask for the direction from a passer-by. It was a tall young man who listened very patiently to his bad German and then spoke in excellent English.

"If you will follow me, sir, I shall be very happy to guide you to the address."

"Very good of you," said Bertram.

"A pleasure, believe me."

By the way he fell into step it was easy to see the man had been a soldier, and by all his bearing, an officer.

"You are a stranger in Berlin, sir?"

"My first visit," said Bertram. "I arrived to-day."

"*So?* You will find people friendly to you as an Englishman. We admire your sporting instincts, if I may say so without offence. You have chivalry to your enemy."

"I hope so," said Bertram, coldly, thinking of the propaganda of hate in some part of the English press, yet resenting a little this praise of England from a German officer.

"In the war your men bore no grudge after the fight. I was a prisoner after Cambrai, in '17. Your 'Tommies' gave me cigarettes when I was captured, and I was generously treated. I am pleased to acknowledge that."

"Our prisoners were not well-treated in Germany," said Bertram.

"Perhaps that was so, here and there," said the officer. "We hadn't much food to spare. We were all on half-rations towards the end."

"There was great brutality in some of the camps," said Bertram.

"Doubtless some of our prison commandants were brutal. We have not yet reached the stage of the English in good humour. I admit that, in spite of our *Kultur*!"

He laughed frankly, and then halted.

"You are now in Dorotheenstrasse, at Number 20. Good-night and good luck."

He saluted ceremoniously, but Bertram held out his hand and thanked him. The action seemed to touch the young man.

"It's kind of you-to shake hands! We don't like the English to think of us as Huns. We are not so bad as that."

"A war name!" said Bertram. "Now it's peace between us."

"Peace and good will," said the young man. "We cannot say that of all our late enemies."

He hesitated for a moment, as though wishing the excuse of talking further. But as Bertram was silent, he saluted again, swung on his heel, and strode down the street.

After all it was a vain walk to Dorotheenstrasse, because when Bertram rang the bell of his sister's house, the *Mädchen* who answered the door gave him to understand that the Herr Baron von Arenburg and the *gnädige Frau* were away in the country, and would not return until the following afternoon.

It was a disappointment. Bertram felt like all men alone in a strange city, very lonely in its crowds. And his loneliness was deepened by a sense of spiritual desolation, and personal abandonment, because of Joyce.

He was surely, he thought, one of the loneliest men in the whole world that night, and then fought against the self-pity which threatened again to overwhelm him. "Keep a stiff upper lip, my lad!" he said to himself as he wandered about the well-lighted streets with these Germans on every side of him, seeking amusement in the *"Wein-stube"* and dancing halls.

They seemed happy. There was no visible sign of penury here, or of unhealed wounds of war, as in London where unemployed men went begging of the theatre crowds and there was a general air of depression and anxiety of many faces. These people were alert, cheerful, apparently prosperous. The only reminder of the agony they must have suffered was a blind man in soldier's uniform who sat selling matches with a drooping head and pale, sad face. Now and then the passers-by dropped a coin in his tray and he said *"Danke schön!"*

Bertram pushed through a swing door into a place where music was being played. He couldn't wander about all the time. It was partly a drinking-place, and partly a dancing-hall. The open space for dancing was surrounded by little tables all crowded with men and women drinking wine out of long-necked bottles. In the gallery an orchestra was playing jazz tunes, with a terrible blare of instruments. Every now and then men and women rose from the tables and joined the dancers until they were all densely wedged in one moving mass, jazzing up and down gracelessly.

Bertram took a seat at a vacant table, and ordered some wine to pay for his place. He sat there, staring at the dancers and the people at the tables. Some of the girls were astonishingly pretty in the German type, with blonde hair and blue eyes. There was one who reminded him of Joyce, and he felt a sharp touch of pain at the thought. She had the same kind of gold-spun hair and slim figure, but her face was painted, which was not a habit of Joyce's, and it was plain to see that she was a girl of "easy virtue" by the way her eyes roved around the group of men, with inviting smiles. She sat alone, smoking a cigarette, with her elbows on the table. The men were mostly of a repulsive type. There were several of them with shaven heads, or so closely cropped that they were nearly bald, as he had seen Prussian officers when, as prisoners, they had thrown away their shrapnel helmets.

Other men here were foreigners, a few English, a group of Americans, a number of Jews of unguessable nationalities. The women mingled with them, drank with them, ogled them, and they did not resent these German *houris*.

Bertram had never seen such dancing. It was perfectly respectable, but grotesque because of the stiff way in which the Germans interpreted the modern steps with a kind of mechanical jig.

The girl like Joyce-horribly like her-came round to Bertram's table and sat deliberately in front of him.

"English boy?" she asked.

"English," he said.

"You do not drink your wine. Shall I help you?"

"As you like."

She poured herself out a glass of Niersteiner, and touched Bertram's glass and said "Prosit!" before taking a sip.

"Why are you sad?" she asked.

"Is it a gay world?"

She shrugged her bare shoulders.

"For the English it should be good. They won the war."

"I'm not so sure," said Bertram. "Berlin seems full of rich people, all drinking and dancing like this."

The girl looked round on the company, and made a grimace of disgust.

"Foreigners mostly in these places. Jews. Profiteers," —she said the word *Schieber* for the last class. "This isn't Germany. It's the same hell as in other great cities of the world, London, Paris, New York."

"You know London?"

"Very well. I was there as a dancer before the war. At the Empire. How's dear old Piccadilly?"

"Still there," said Bertram.

He wished to God this girl would go away. The line of her neck as she turned her head reminded him of Joyce again.

"I'd like to get back to London," she said. "Here one must be wicked or starve to death. I have a sister who's good. She's a dressmaker. She earns sixty marks a day, sewing on buttons and hooks. It costs her more than that to buy a chemise. She goes to bed when she gets her underclothes washed, once a month. Now she had tuberculosis from *unternährung.*"

"What's that?" asked Bertram.

"What you call under-feeding. Starvation is another name for it. All the good people suffer from *unternährung.* My mother died from it in the war, when none of us had enough to eat, whatever our virtue. You English made us suffer like that. Your blockade."

"Yes," said Bertram.

"It was rather cruel, don't you think? After the war you kept the blockade up until Peace was signed. You made war against our babies and killed thousands, so that we should be starved into surrender. That wasn't what you call playing the game."

"The war game," said Bertram. "You would have been harder with us if you had won."

"That's true. War is perhaps as cruel as peace. Most men are devils, and women she-devils."

"Some of them are pretty decent," said Bertram. "If they get a chance. The ordinary crowd."

"You are not cruel," she answered. "You are kind. You have kind eyes, and you talk to me as though I were a good woman. I would love you very much if you would let me. What do you say, English boy?"

"I must be going," said Bertram.

She made a protest, holding his arm, but he called "*Ober!*" and paid for the wine, and rose from his chair. She held out her hand, and he gave her his.

"I expect you're too good to live," she said, with a queer little laugh.

"I ought to have died before," he said, "but I missed the luck. In the war."

"Learn to laugh," she said. "Laugh at the cruelty of life, like I do."

"I expect you know its cruelty," he said, with a little pity in his voice.

"Down to the bottom of hell," she answered, and laughed again.

"Well, good-night."

"*Gute Nacht, hübschen!*"

She bent down suddenly and kissed his hand.

He went out of the dancing hall strangely perturbed. As the girl had bent her head to kiss his hand, the glint of her hair was a terrible reminder of Joyce. Yet this girl who was "bad" had been kinder to him than Joyce! That was a frightful thought. And Joyce was bad too, in a different way. She'd transferred herself to Kenneth with less temptation than this German girl who sold her love to escape *unternährung*, which was starvation.

His passing out of the hall was blocked by a group of people at the entrance. Something was going to happen, and Bertram was forced to stay and see it. Nothing worth seeing, except as a study of human anatomy in acrobatic eccentricity.

A girl made her way through the little crowd to where a man dressed as a sailor waited for her. She wore a red cloak, but dropped it on the edge of the dirty floor, and took the sailor's hand. For five minutes he whirled her about like a rag doll, flung her over his head, held her wrist and swung her from him, round and round, with frightful rapidity, hurled her backwards, and caught her before her head was smashed against the polished boards —a kind of Apache dance intensified in brutality. Several times the girl came down on her toes from a flying spin and smiled and kissed her hands to the groups of wine-drinkers who applauded and clinked their glasses together as a sign of approval. At the end the girl came to the edge of the dancing floor, picked up her red cloak, thrust her way through the group at the entrance, who said *"Schön! Schön!"* and then collapsed on to a wooden chair half concealed by a curtain in the passage. Bertram saw her face, which was dead white. She was sitting back with her neck over the rail of the chair, gasping like a dying creature.

Bertram spoke to a man in a kind of uniform like a commissionaire.

"Is she all right?"

"She will recover. She goes to another hall presently. She does that five times a night, and is well known in Berlin."

"How much does she get for that?"

The man laughed in his throat.

"Enough to keep her alive. About as much as the price of a bottle of wine. Women are cheap."

Bertram thought of some words spoken by the German girl who had kissed his hand.

"War is almost as cruel as peace."

Terrible words, spoken with tragic sincerity and a painted smile.

It wasn't true. He had seen the cruelty of war, not only in the fighting line and in the fields of the dead, and the wounded, the blinded and gassed, but in villages where women saw their little homes go up in flames, fled from the approach of the Enemy, wept for those who had been caught before escape was possible, led the life of refugees through years of misery and squalor and hopelessness. War was not an alternative cruelly to that of peace. It was an additional cruelty. It didn't stop the private vices and cruelties of men and women. It created more vice, more disease, more starvation, more of that hell into which the girl like Joyce had fallen. . . . But peace, after all, was cruel! And life, anyhow, at its worst and at its best. All one could do, it seemed, was to acquire a little courage, a sense of humour, a touch of charity, and make the best of a bad business, or with luck, which wasn't his, a little private paradise.

XLVI

He found his sister Dorothy at home next evening, waiting for him excitedly, having had the message he had left with the *Mädchen*. He was surprised by her emotion at seeing him, not having realised what this would mean to a girl who had been exiled in the enemy's country through the war, and had seen no one of her kith and kin till now, three years after the ending of war. She took hold of him, laughing and crying at the same time, held him at arm's length to see the change in him, drew him close again, and kissed him with rather overwhelming joy.

She had changed more than he had imagined. Two years older than himself-she was twenty-eight now-her coiled brown hair was already touched with grey, and her beautiful face-she had always been the beauty of the family-bore visible traces of some past anguish. In an indefinable way also, she had become German. There was something of the *"Haus-Frau"* about her, not only in her style of dress but in her look and her way of moving.

She told him she had a million questions she wanted to ask, and first of all of her father, and of her dear mother and of poor Digby and Susan, and then of himself and Joyce, whom she had never seen —"funny that, Bertram!" —and then of England, and Ireland. Poor, tragic, rebellious Ireland!

"A big order!" said Bertram. "It would take a month to tell you all that, and most of it is tragedy."

"You shall tell me for a month. I want to hear everything, through the war and afterwards. Once I was starved for food-we lived on next to nothing in the two last years of war! —but now I am more starved for news. I ache for every detail of it!"

But intimate talk was checked awhile on Bertram's side by the appearance of Dorothy's husband, the Baron von Arenburg. He was a soldierly-looking fellow of about thirty, with easy manners, and a fair, good-natured face, with grey eyes and a little yellow moustache. He shook hands with a firm grip, and said he was delighted to meet Dorothy's brother, "whom she adores!"

Bertram knew something of his record during the war, through Dorothy's letters to her mother. He had been with the cavalry in East Prussia, in the great sweep back under Mackensen. Most of the time he had been on the Russian Front, and was only in the West in the last phase of the war, when the dismounted cavalry were thrown in to stiffen the retreat in September of '18, to the end. "War prolongers!" as the German infantry called them, derisively and with hate.

Bertram noticed that he kissed his wife's hand on entering, with a kind of gallant reverence, surprising, he thought, in a German, though afterwards he saw it was the usual custom.

At dinner the conversation was desultory. Bertram hedged on most of the subjects which might lead him into deep water. To enquiries about Joyce he answered vaguely that she was staying with some friends in France. To Dorothy's questions about the purpose of his visit to Germany he answered that he was "writing a bit" —in a journalistic way. He wanted to study the conditions in Germany, the spirit of the people, and so on.

Dorothy and her husband exchanged glances. This seemed to them exciting news. They were glad, they said, that at last some one had come from England to tell the truth about Germany. The English newspapers told nothing but lies. The falsity of the picture they drew was positively frightful —"utterly grotesque," said Von Arenburg.

"In what way?" asked Bertram.

Dorothy told him "in every way." They pretended that Germany was getting enormously rich, that the people were not taxed, that the German mark was being forced down deliberately, in exchange value, in order to capture the world's trade, that Germany was making munitions of war and training secret armies, that the Revolution was a sham, and the plea of poverty a colossal fraud.

"Is none of that true?" asked Bertram.

Dorothy laughed, the old, full-throated laugh which he remembered in the old days of home life.

"Lies, lies, lies!" she cried.

Emotionally, vehemently, she protested that the middle classes in Germany were so impoverished by the downfall of the mark that even now they were on "short commons" and unable to buy clothes, especially underclothes or boots. So far from escaping taxation, they were ground down with taxes-even small incomes equal to sixty pounds a year in England. The mark fell because every time Germany had to pay her monstrous indemnities she had to purchase foreign money at gold rates, and then print enormous new issues of paper money.

The whole thing was mad. Germany, after four and a half years of war which had ruined her utterly, was expected to pay back the losses of all her enemies, and all their war-pensions, and all the cost of the Army of Occupation. Not even the United States, which had all the gold in the world, could pay such fabulous sums.

"It's only fair that Germany should pay for the ruin she made," said Bertram stolidly. "I was in France during the war. I saw the destruction of her cities and villages and farms and harvest fields. Wiped off the map."

"We're ready to help France to reconstruct all that," said Dorothy, and Bertram winced a little at that "we." He shrank from this sister of his identifying herself with her husband's people. "What we cannot do is to pay for pensions and all the other ridiculous charges."

"Germany is bound to go bankrupt," said Von Arenburg. "Nothing can prevent that, and when it happens, Europe will be dragged down with us."

"France wants to push Germany into the mud," said Dorothy. "Nothing will satisfy her but a march into the Ruhr to seize the industrial cities and strangle Germany's chance of life."

"We shall try to escape-by way of Russia," said Von Arenburg. "It will cause another war within a generation."

"And then the breakdown of civilisation in Europe," said Dorothy. "Dear God! I can't believe that England will allow it. England's generous, in spite of her cruelty at times."

"Cruelty?" asked Bertram.

"The blockade," she said. "It was cruel to starve German babies-after the Armistice-to force the Treaty of Versailles."

Some one else had said that. It was the girl like Joyce in the dancing hall-the little prostitute — It seemed to be a general belief. Was there any truth in it?

"For her own interests, England must prevent it!" said Von Arenburg. "She needs world-markets for her goods. She must work for the recovery of Europe."

"Even if France insists on her right to Shylock's pound of flesh," said Dorothy. "France is the enemy of the world's peace."

Bertram's face flushed.

"I don't want to argue," he said, "but I know the sacrifice of France. I saw her agony with my own eyes. I've just been in the old battlefields again, among the peasants there. There's only one thing that's in all their minds —a dread of another war. They're still not sure that one day Germany won't come back again, and re-light the red fires. They want nothing but security, and they don't see it, except in keeping Germany weak."

"They're going the wrong way to work to prevent another war," said Dorothy. "There's not an insult, a petty provocation, a threat of ignominy, that they haven't heaped on Germany since the signing of Peace."

"One must understand their point of view," said Bertram. "Germany wasn't very tender of French feelings in time of war, when she thought she was winning."

He changed the topic of conversation. His advocacy of France seemed to distress Dorothy.

After dinner, when with a tactful word or two Von Arenburg left his wife alone with her brother, Dorothy revealed her thoughts more deeply, with an emotion which touched him, because he shared her hope.

"It's not that I hate France," she said. "I used to weep for France when German armies were trampling through her fields-during the years of death. But I hate war. Oh, Bertram, you've seen it, and can hardly tell what you've seen, because no words can tell it all, but I've suffered perhaps more than you. Imagine an English wife of a German husband through all these years! You can't imagine. The torture of a dual allegiance-duty to my husband, pity for the German wounded-for their frightful slaughter-for the spiritual despair of the German people knowing, in spite of early victories, that they were doomed-for they knew it always! Then, on the other side, my love for England, my pride in English courage, my dreams at night because of English armies under German gunfire, with you, my dear, among them, somewhere in those dreadful fields. I'm angry with France now because she seems to prevent the spirit of peace."

"She's not sure that Germany won't seek revenge again. Are *you* sure?"

Dorothy sighed, and seemed to think deeply of all that she knew about the German people. Then she told her brother that before the Armistice, and afterwards, the German people had revolted against the war, and militarism. They were all "Wilsonites." If in defeat they'd been treated generously, they would have risen with immense, overwhelming emotion to new ideals of world peace. But the Treaty of Versailles seemed to put them in chains and doom them to an eternal servitude of debt to the victor nations. Then the attitude of France had been so harsh and so provocative that gradually the German people had hardened again in spirit, and the old venom had come back. The ideals of world peace were abandoned by French policy which sought only the ringing round of Germany with hostile states to keep her down under the menace of armed force. Now hatred for France smouldered in every German heart, and the future was black.

"I'm afraid!" she said, "I'm afraid!"

They were the words which Christy had once spoken in his rooms in London, on a journey back from Central Europe.

Her eyes filled with tears, and then she brushed them away and smiled.

"Let's forget all that to-night. Tell me about my dear ones, living and dead."

For hours they talked of their mother and father, Susan and Digby, their old home life, and old friends; and it seemed as though the War had stricken every one, and utterly changed the world they had known when they had lived together under the same roof. It seemed as though they were survivors from a great earthquake. Then Bertram told Dorothy of his own tragedy with Joyce, and she cried out with grief that English womanhood should so forget its old code of virtue.

"Something seems to have changed in the soul of England!" she said. "What is it, Bertram? Have they all broken under the strain of war?"

"It smashed the old traditions," he said. "Some of them wanted smashing, but the process is painful-and some of the best things got broken with the worst."

XLVII

In the company of his sister and her husband, Bertram saw a good deal of the inner life of Germany, and polished up his knowledge of the language sufficiently to carry on conversation with the people he met.

There was much that he came to admire in German character, and there were times when he reproached himself for having forgotten "the Enemy" so completely that he could shake hands with a German (so violating an ancient vow) without any sense of physical repugnance, and even discuss the war in a friendly way with men, like Von Arenburg, who had been responsible for the death of British soldiers, and among them his own best comrades.

He used to wonder sometimes whether that were not treachery to his old standards of loyalty and honour, and was conscience-stricken because he accepted hospitality, kindness, even friendship, from these people. But he found it impossible to keep up the old "hate" against them. Even in war-time that spirit of hate had been behind the lines rather than in the trenches. The "Tommies" had given cigarettes to their prisoners after the heat of battle. German officers had been treated civilly by British officers, if they were at all well-behaved, and within a few days after the occupation of Cologne, British soldiers had clinked beer mugs with the fellows who had once lain behind machine guns, mowing them down. That was the real spirit of chivalry, a lesson taught by the common man, obeying some instinctive decent law of nature, to neurotic and morbid-minded people who watered the roots of hate and cultivated its poisonous fruit with unceasing care.

Only by some friendly pact with these people could Europe have peace. Bertram could see no chance of peace if they were to be treated for ever as moral lepers. It was ridiculous to regard them as moral lepers.

How could he take that view when he moved among their crowds in the Opera House, in pleasant beer gardens outside Berlin to which they flocked in the evenings, by the lakeside and in the woods of the Grünewald? These young Germans with their girls, drinking light beer, eating ices, chattering to the music of the band, playing with little flaxen-haired children, did not behave like moral lepers. They were good-natured, decent, smiling folk, the girls wonderfully neat and pretty and plump, in cheap frocks, the men shabbily dressed, many in their old war tunics dyed and re-cut to civilian styles, but scrupulously brushed.

Von Arenburg, who had a certain sense of humour, limited by a Prussian outlook, used to ask Bertram what he thought of the "Huns" in assemblies like that. "Do they behave like barbarians? Do you see them eating their babies?"

"No," said Bertram; "but I find them enjoying themselves, obviously well-fed, not badly dressed, and spending quite a lot of marks on their evening's amusement. What about this German poverty, that you keep telling me about?"

It was Dorothy who tried to explain. These people in their home lives stinted and scraped to enjoy an evening's pleasure like this. They lived in overcrowded rooms, stiflingly hot in summer. To go to a beer garden in the evening was essential for very life and health. It cost but a few marks for light beer or a pink ice. Look at the girls' frocks, so clean, but so cheap. Look at their boots, made of paper and sham leather.

Bertram was not satisfied with these explanations. It seemed to him in Berlin and the other towns to which he went, that the German people were marvellously prosperous after the war. It was true that in exchange value German paper money was slumping away at an alarming rate, and that every time it dropped prices were higher in the shops. But wages seemed to rise also, and people seemed to get more paper money every month, which, in Germany, had still a fair purchasing power.

He wandered round the great stores, like Wertheim's, and was startled by the amazingly low price of everything manufactured in Germany, and there seemed nothing they didn't make. Translated into English figures, at the current rate of exchange, they were a mockery of English competition. At such prices they could beat us in every market of the world, and, so it seemed, were doing.

Von Arenburg pooh-poohed his argument.

"It's all illusion," he said. "I admit the feverish activity of German trade and industry. It's the genius of our people, inspired by a desperate desire to avert their ruin. But nothing can do that so long as the Allied nations do not release their stranglehold. We sell below cost price. To buy raw material from abroad we have to pay the difference on the mark. We're bleeding to death. Presently the crash will come, and Europe will shudder in all its members."

Bertram was not good at arithmetic. International finance was a mystery to him. He could not find any clue to this economic mystery of the German people, bankrupt (they said) yet prosperous, capturing world trade (as they admitted), yet "bleeding to death."

More within his power of observation was the mentality of these people, and in patient listening at luncheon tables and dinner tables, where he met the Junker crowd and the "Intellectuals," in conversations with shop-keepers and peasants, he tried to discover the drift of thought in Germany after defeat.

Largely the peace of the world depended upon their outlook on the future. Had they liberated themselves from their old militarism? Were they preparing to march forward as a free democracy in a commonwealth of nations, away from the darkness of the old War-Gods in this Jungle? Or were they again worshipping those ancient gods with secret rites and propitiations?

It was hard to tell among Dorothy's friends. They revealed how deep the agony of war had been in their souls, how sharply the wound still hurt. These German ladies, very charming, some of them, had lost fathers, husbands, brothers, lovers, sons, even in more appalling numbers than the death-rate of England. Whole families of the German aristocracy had been wiped out, and in the humbler classes it was the same.

They cursed the war, and the Army commanders, and the politicians. They said they had been "betrayed" by the conceit of Ludendorff, by the folly of the Supreme War Council, by the spirit of Bolshevism among the troops on the Russian Front who had been bitten by that frightful microbe. They protested against the "cruelty" of the Versailles Treaty, and asserted their faith in Wilson's "Fourteen Points" which had never been fulfilled. That was another betrayal, not only of Germany, but of all the hopes of the world.

Yet never once in any company did any German, man or woman, acknowledge the guilt of Germany in having started the war. Russia had "moved first." England had hemmed in Germany. The German people had been ringed round by enemies. And in spite of all those enemies, the German armies had never been defeated. It was the home front that had broken down, by sheer starvation.

Never defeated! Bertram challenged that belief, with some violence, at one of Dorothy's afternoon "at homes."

Among the ladies were several ex-officers, two Generals of Rupprecht's Army, so long opposite the British, in Flanders.

It was General von Althof who made the statement, with simple sincerity.

"*Gott sei dank!* Our brave Armies were never defeated, from first to last."

"That surprises me," said Bertram, with an ironical smile; "I always thought the German Armies were broken to bits. First on the Marne, in July '18. Afterwards like brown paper on August 8th. They could never hold a line again. When the end came they'd lost hundreds of thousands of prisoners, thousands of guns, and the whole war-machine was destroyed. Otherwise there was no need to sign the Armistice, the greatest surrender of any nation in the history of the world, surely?"

It was not a courteous way of speech; not kind. But Bertram was becoming rather tired of this calm forgetfulness of what had happened in history, and he disliked the type represented by General von Althof, one of those hard, bald-headed Prussians, with a mind as narrow as a Brazil nut.

Von Althof became red about the gills, and then very pale.

"Doubtless, as a young regimental officer, you regard local successes as great victories. That is a common error, not difficult to understand. As a General of the German High Command, I repeat, sir, that our glorious Armies were never defeated in the field of battle. The Armistice was forced upon us by revolution at home, and the broken *morale* of a hungry people."

"There can be no argument about it," said one of the younger officers. "It is an accepted fact."

Bertram made a considerable argument about it, until checked by Dorothy, who was visibly distressed.

General von Althof departed with suppressed rage, after a stiff bow to Bertram, and the other officers took their leave later, so that only a few ladies remained.

One of them was the Fräulein von Wegener, a pretty blonde, who seemed to be Dorothy's greatest friend.

She crossed over to Bertram, sitting by his side, and her eyes were alight with amusement.

"Of course I don't think our Armies were defeated —I'm German! —but I adore the courage with which you attacked Von Althof. It made me tremble all over! I have never seen any officer disagree with a General. It isn't done in Germany. You reminded me of St. George and the Dragon."

Bertram's rage had subsided, and he felt guilty of a social misdemeanour in having raised such an argument in Dorothy's drawing-room.

"I behaved like the Dragon," he said. "Breathing out fire. A disgraceful incident!"

"I love sincerity," said Fräulein von Wegener. "And I hate Generals."

"How's that?" asked Bertram. "They seem to be highly respected in Germany, in spite of their-well, let's call it failure to achieve absolute victory."

The girl laughed, with a pleasant, musical, mirthful sound.

"Their self-conceit is *kolossal*! But they've been found out. The German people have no more use for them."

"You think that?" asked Bertram, doubtfully.

"The people," she said, and then lowered her voice. "Not the little crowd in drawing-rooms like this. . . . I go among the working folk, in children's clinics-for charity, you know. They hate war and all its stupidity. Never again, they say."

"Not even against France?"

She hesitated, and seemed embarrassed for a moment.

"Not even against France, if she gives us a decent chance."

She spoke of Dorothy, looking across at her with admiration.

"Your lovely sister has made me a Pacifist. She's a saint. She has converted me from all my wicked ways."

"You were very wicked?" asked Bertram.

"In idea," she said, smiling. "Full of naughty passion, and intolerance, and rebellion against God. Now I'm getting good. I have a new philosophy."

"What's that?" asked Bertram.

"Love of humanity," she said.

"It sounds good," said Bertram. "But I seem to have heard of it before, and it's a little vague."

He came to know more of her philosophy, even more of her love of humanity, because Dorothy invited her often to the house, and to the Opera, where she was placed next to Bertram, and to picnic parties in the Grünewald, where she looked her prettiest in muslin frocks "made by my own little fingers" (she told him), and to evening concerts in public gardens outside Berlin.

Anna was her name, and because of her close friendship with Dorothy-they were almost like sisters, it seemed-she insisted upon Bertram calling her that and forgetting the *gnädiges Fräulein*. She called him Bertram, after demurely asking his permission. He found her amusing. She had a playful sense of humour and teased him because of his English shyness. For England, in spite of being German, she had a romantic admiration, and she confessed to him that the manners of Englishmen seemed to be adorable, because of their courtesy to women.

"My manners are atrocious," said Bertram, "as you may have observed."

She did not agree. She thought he had the look of a Lancelot in Tennyson's "Idylls of the King," which she read with exquisite delight.

It was impossible for Bertram to ignore the fact that she flirted with him ardently, and that her eyes worshipped him. He was not annoyed. He liked it. He liked the little curl that played about each cheek, and her milky skin, and her laughing voice, and pretty, plump figure. She was what Christy used to call, in his dry way, "a cuddlesome thing-and highly dangerous."

Bertram did not find her extremely dangerous, though he acknowledged to himself that a little care might be necessary at times, if he wished to avoid temptation. There was no need why he should avoid temptation, being a free man, now that Joyce had flung him over, but always there was that trick of conscience in him, or self-imposed repression, which had held him back from easy amour, which meant no more to other men he knew than a passing adventure, without consequence. In any case, this girl was of high caste. A love affair would mean marriage, and he was not as free as that, nor so inclined.

There was a moment of danger one evening in the Grünewald, that wonderful woodland within a tram journey of Berlin. Dorothy and her husband had wandered away, hand in hand, like two lovers of the humbler class who came here also for their picnics and pleasure parties. Anna and Bertram sat together in a little bower, hidden from the passers-by, where they had all had tea together an hour or more ago. Birds were singing in the boughs above their heads, and Bertram sat with his back to a tree, listening to the pleasant twitter and watching the light play through the leaves. Anna sat on the grass, a yard away from him, with her muslin frock spread out and her straw hat by her side. The breeze played softly with the little curl on each cheek, and she was like the princess in a German fairy-tale.

"Bertram," she said presently, "you are very silent. Talk to me, and tell me pretty things."

"Silence is good," he said. "I like looking at your prettiness."

"*So?* Now that is what I like to hear you say!"

"I've said it."

"Say it again. Do you think me pretty?"

"Wonderfully beautiful!"

"No, not that. That's insincere. Dorothy is beautiful. I'm only a *hübsches mädel* —a pretty maid. Do you like me, Bertram?"

"Very much."

"You don't hate me because I'm German?"

"I've finished with hate."

"Do you love me a little?"

He laughed at her audacity.

"What do you mean by love?"

"I can only tell by what I feel."

"How's that?"

"I feel that I want to be with you always, and to go where you go."

She was on her knees now, and moved a little way towards him, and dropped down on the grass with her elbows up, and her dimpled chin in the cup of her hands.

Bertram was startled. This was going a little too far, perhaps. It had reached the danger point.

"I'm afraid if you went where I am going it would be to unpleasant places. I'm off to Moscow next week."

"To Moscow! And next week! Let me come with you, then. With you I should feel safe, even in Moscow."

The idea amused him. It would be pleasant enough to have Anna as his travelling companion. It would be a cure for loneliness. But it was out of the bounds of possibility, and not within his code of honour, or mental liberty.

"My passport is only for one," he said. "And it has taken me a month to get."

"Wait another month and get two!"

"*Nicht möglich!* Let's join Dorothy and her husband."

"Cold Englishman!" she said, and sprang up with a vexed laugh.

"Not cold," he said, taking her hand. "Only prudent. Or cowardly."

They walked away, through the wood, hand in hand, as Dorothy and Von Arenburg had gone before them. Anna held his hand tight, and presently looked up at him with coaxing eyes and a childish pout.

"If you're going so soon, we may as well begin to say good-bye."

The meaning of her words was plain. She wanted him to kiss her, and under a tree there the place was good and discreet. He rather liked the idea of kissing her, but for a little warning that it could not end there, if he began. She called him "cold Englishman." He was not that. He was too easily fired, and knew that if he once let a spark touch his passion, it might blaze into something like a bonfire. He didn't want to make a blaze with this little German girl. So he compromised-the middle of the road again! —and raised her hand to his lips, very gallantly, but without ardour.

"Pooh!" she said, and taking her hand away, put it round his neck and pulled his head down and kissed him, and then with a laugh ran from him towards Dorothy and her husband, who appeared down one of the glades.

It was on the way home that evening that he told Dorothy of a telegram he had received that morning from Bernard Hall of *The New World*. His passport had been arranged with the Soviet authorities. Christy was waiting for him to go down the Volga in the famine region. Bernard Hall wanted the truth about the famine.

Dorothy received the news as a tragic blow.

"I can't bear you to go away!" she cried. "Stay here, Bertram. Give up the visit to Russia. It's more dangerous than ever. Stay with us in Germany, and make your home here."

"My home?" he said, with a sudden pang of self-pity, "I have no home, now Joyce has left me."

Dorothy answered him in a low, emotional voice.

"There are good women in Germany. One of them loves you already."

"Meaning Anna von Wegener?"

"You have guessed?"

She was astonished at the rapidity of his intuition, and surprised, and rather hurt, when he laughed.

"It wasn't a difficult guess. She doesn't let concealment 'like a worm i' the bud, feed on her damask cheek.' "

Then he spoke seriously to this sister who had always been his comrade.

"I'm still haunted by the thought of Joyce. I pretend I've done with her, cut her image out of my heart and soul. But that's bunkum. She comes into my dreams at night, and stands between me and the sunlight. I can't play about with other women-or do more than play-until I've cut out Joyce, and the wound is healed."

She pressed his hand with a sympathy that was good to him.

"Explain to Anna," he said, "or she'll think I'm heartless."

Perhaps she explained well enough. Anna von Wegener was very demure next time she met Bertram, and only showed by her blush that she remembered the scene in the wood. She was with Dorothy and Von Arenburg at the Schlesische Bahnhof when Bertram took the train to Riga.

"I shall pray for you all the time," said Dorothy. "Don't stay too long in that frightful country."

"Take care of your health, my dear fellow," said Von Arenburg, grasping his hand.

"Remember your friends," said Anna.

They waved hands to him until the train disappeared.

For a long time he sat motionless in his carriage, thinking of that chapter of life in Germany, and of the new page he was about to turn. He might never come back from Russia. Disease, starvation, crime, all kinds of danger lurked in that unknown country. It was cut off from the outer world. No letters passed, unless smuggled through or sent under official seal. He doubted whether he would get any news while he was there. Perhaps he would never hear the end of the story of Joyce, his wife. It would be strange never to know, until he passed to that place where, perhaps, everything was known, even the secret workings of the heart.

By his side was a bundle of letters from England, and some copies of *The Times*, forwarded to Dorothy's address. He opened them, but left most of them unread. They were just trivial letters from acquaintances and tradesmen. *The Times* interested him more. The King had gone to Belfast to open the Northern Parliament. He had made a speech, pleading for forgetfulness and forgiveness. There was talk of a Truce —a Treaty of Peace. At last! Thank God for that! . . . British trade returns were still going down. Unemployment was going up. There were the usual lists of births, marriages, and deaths. . . . Deaths! His eyes fell on four lines of small print.

> *Murless*, on the 19th of this month, at the British Embassy in Paris, the Honourable Kenneth Murless, of pneumonia. Aged twenty-seven.

Bertram read the lines three or four times before the meaning of them fully reached his consciousness. He uttered a sharp exclamation, startling the German folk in his carriage. In his mind was a strange mingling of pity for Joyce and gladness for himself.

Kenneth had died not much more than a month after the dinner at the Griffon. Perhaps Joyce had not gone to him so soon. . . .

That was a rotten way of looking at things. What a tragedy for Joyce! And for Kenneth, that very perfect gentleman, who had tried to play the game "according to the rules!"

XLVIII

The journey to Riga had not been too bad, except for examination of passports and luggage at odd times of the day and night, at unexpected frontiers. This happened each side of "the Polish corridor," which had been made by the Treaty of Versailles like a wedge driven through Germany to Danzig. It happened again on the frontiers of Lithuania and Latvia.

An American in the train called it the "Get-in-and-get-out-express." It stopped for six hours at Eydtkuhnen on the border of East Prussia, and there was time to walk about and see something of the devastation made by the great Russian drive in the early years of the war. Here were still the blackened ruins of farmhouses and barns and peasants' cottages, but German industry had built up the villages again, very neat and pretty under their new red roofs, wonderful in contrast to the poor attempts at reconstruction in the war zone of France.

Bertram had to wait four days in Riga before he could get a train to Moscow. The Soviet agents there were unhelpful and rather insolent. The stamp of the Moscow Executive Committee on his special passport did not seem to inspire them with any zeal. They informed Bertram that he might have to wait three weeks for a train-or longer. The thought seemed to amuse them.

Three weeks in Riga! The idea was affrighting because of its boredom. In three days Bertram had exhausted the interests and amusements of a city that seemed dead all day and only wakened to life at one in the morning, when the night cafés and dancing-halls were filled with a company of Letts, Poles, Russians, Finns, and Germans, drinking large quantities of *schnapps* in quick gulps until their eyes watered and their noses reddened, and they became quarrelsome with their women and each other in a medley of languages.

In one of these cafés Bertram sat opposite an American who opened a friendly conversation.

"Staying long in this City of Departed Glory?"

"Not longer than I can help. I want to get to Moscow, but the trains don't work."

The American asked his business there, and raised his eyebrows with a smile when Bertram said, "Journalism. I want to find out the truth about the famine."

"Well, there's a famine, I'm told," said the American. "You might call it a famine, without much exaggeration. About twenty-five million people starving to death, more or less. I'm pushing up some food. A relief train is going to-morrow with the first supplies. That's my job. I'm A. R. A."

He pronounced the letters as though they spelt a word —"Ara." They conveyed nothing then to Bertram, though afterwards he came to know them as the greatest hope of life in Russia for the starving children from Petrograd to the Volga Valley, and the Russians spoke of "Ara" as though it were God. It meant the American Relief Administration.

"Any chance of a place on that train?" he asked.

The American smiled again.

"I expected that question. Is your passport all right for Moscow?"

Bertram showed it, and the American nodded.

"Any objection to lice?" he asked.

"I don't invite them to dinner," said Bertram, "but we were on speaking terms in the trenches. 'Chatty,' the men used to call it."

"They'll give you the glad hand in that *train de luxe*."

"Then I can get a place?"

"I'll fix you up. Better take supplies with you. Cheese. Biscuits. A kettle. Enamel mugs. Candles. Blankets. There's not a restaurant car, nor a *wagon lit*."

He smiled grimly, and Bertram knew why on the next night when he boarded the train to Moscow. It was nearly midnight, and the station was dimly lit, and after stumbling over grass-grown rails, Bertram found a train in darkness, except in one or two carriages where candles had been lighted and put on the window ledges. A number of Lettish porters staggered along under heavy bundles, and there were more of them in the corridor of the train from which a frightful smell met the open air. The carriages were wooden compartments, stripped of all upholstery, with plank beds, and they seemed to be entirely occupied by Americans and Russians who were quarrelling with each other for vacant possession. There was a jabber of both languages rising into violent oaths of the choicest brand from New York, Omaha, Kansas, and Kentucky. One voice rose higher than all the rest, with a bull-like bellow.

"For Christ's sake! If all you Tavarishes don't get out of this bug-box, I'll get the Cheka on to you and have you minced by Chinese torturers!"

The owner of this voice, as Bertram saw in the candlelight of one carriage, was a young man of Herculean build, in a felt hat, Garibaldi shirt, riding-breeches, and top boots. To make clear the mystical meaning of his words, he seized one of the porters, lifted him up as though he were a sack of potatoes, and flung him at six others massed in the dark corridor. It had the effect of clearing a space and creating a moment's quietude.

"Who the hell are you?" asked the genial giant, peering at Bertram and putting a flash-light close to his nose. "Do you belong to this outfit?"

Bertram mentioned the name of the American who had "fixed him up." It was an ordinary name, but produced an immediate and softening effect.

"Good enough! You're the young guy who's going to the famine districts? Glad to meet you."

Bertram found his hand in an enormous fist, and recovered it in a limp and boneless state.

"My name's Cherry," said the young giant. "I'm from Lynchburg, Virginia. I do the courier stunt for Ara, from Riga to Moscow. I also boss this train, and make it move. When it stops, I make it move again. Sometimes. If I get out and push. I inspire terror among Tavarishes. When they play tricks I treat 'em rough. When they play straight I'm full of loving-kindness. It's the only way to get anything done by these lousy Tavarishes."

"What's a Tavarish?" asked Bertram.

"A Comrade," said Cherry of Lynch, Virginia. "It's a nice way of saying Bolshevik. Call them Tavarish all the time. It makes them feel good. Human equality and all that punk. Have you brought any bug-powder?"

"No."

"I'll lend you some. Otherwise you'll be eaten alive."

But for Cherry, Bertram would have reached Moscow even more of a wreck than he did. In spite of the powder, he was attacked by many different species of insect as he lay on an upper plank, with Cherry beneath. He saw them crawling in legions up the wooden walls. They ambushed him beneath his blanket, sent out scouts and advance guards and then attacked in mass formation. The nights were torture. In the day time the enemy retired to their hiding places.

The train was crowded with Russian and Lettish couriers, all in charge of heavy packing-cases and sacks. Next to them, four to a carriage, was a contingent of young Americans, going out as clerks to the headquarters staff of the A. R. A., in Moscow. Certain mysterious young men who talked to each other in low voices, were pointed out by Cherry as Russian Soviet officials belonging to the secret police of the Extraordinary Commission, known as "the Cheka," because each letter of that dreaded word formed the initial of the full Russian title for this organisation.

There was no heat in the train, and it was cold after crossing the Russian frontier in the rainy season of early autumn.

Bertram's cheese and biscuits, which he had bought in Riga, became utterly distasteful to him after two days, and he yielded to Cherry's insistent invitation to share his bully beef, pork and beans, tinned butter, and fresh bread. It was Cherry, also, who taught him how to get the one source of comfort available on Russian journeys —a plentiful supply of hot water at every wayside station. The pass-word was "kipyitok," and this was yelled by Cherry to the *provodnik*, or guard, of the train, who filled the passengers' kettles so that they could make tea in their carriages.

The Russian frontier was at a place called Sebesh, the other side of a long stretch of flat, barren, abandoned country which seemed to be a kind of No-Man's Land. The train was immediately boarded by a number of hairy men in sheepskin coats and fur caps, accompanied by two soldiers of the Red Army. Bertram felt a thrill at his first sight of Bolsheviks and Red Soldiers. His mind went back to the atrocity tales of Countess Lydia and her sister, and other refugees from the Russian Terror. These men who pushed their way down the corridor were agents of that terrible new social code and faith which had declared war upon all civilisation based upon individualism and private property, and proclaimed Communism as the new gospel which mankind must accept, whether they liked it or not. Those soldiers represented the power by which that code was enforced upon one hundred and fifty million people. It was their Army which had defeated Koltchak, Denikin, Judenitch, Wrangel, and all the counter-revolutionary forces-financed, armed and equipped by the Allied Powers-which had invaded Russia, laid great districts in ruin and flame, hanged many peasants to the branches of trees, and retreated in disorderly masses from the relentless pursuit of "the Reds."

The two soldiers escorting the hairy Bolsheviks were not formidable in appearance. They were both about eighteen, with puffy, pale faces, and a hang-dog, under-fed look. They wore long grey overcoats, reaching to their heels, and curious cloth caps, shaped like Assyrian helmets, with stiff peaks behind, and in front the Red Star, five-pointed, of the Soviet Republic.

"See how these Tavarishes love me!" said Cherry.

Certainly the small group of Bolshevik officials who came to examine passports and baggage, greeted Cherry with a kind of forced amusement, in which, as it seemed to Bertram, there was a hint of fear. Perhaps it was due to the vice-like grip with which he insisted upon shaking hands with them; and the bear-like way in which he thumped them on the back.

"*Dobra den, Tavarish!* How goes it, old face-fungus? *Kraseeva*, eh? Fine and dandy, what? Well, *dos vidanya*, you darned old hypocrite, and don't you come poking your nose into my car. *Niet! No pannamayo?*"

He fondled the head Bolshevik's beard, patted him playfully on both cheeks, gave him a mighty dig in the ribs which took his breath away.

"That's how I treat 'em," he told Bertram. "A touch of good humour works wonders with them. Look at those two young murderers! Laughing like hell! It's the first time they've laughed since I came this way before."

The two young soldiers regarded him with eyes of wonder and admiration, between guffaws of laughter. When he stepped down on to the platform, a group of Russian porters and peasants gathered round him, listening to his oration in American and Russian, gazing at his mighty girth with astounded smiles. He towered above them, and occasionally pushed at a man's chest, and pummelled a Russian boy with ogre-like playfulness.

Six hours at Sebesh.

"Come and see the flight from the Famine," said Cherry. "It'll take away your appetite for my bully beef. Cheap for me!"

He strode down the rails for five hundred yards and halted before a long stationary train without an engine. It was divided into a number of box-like cattletrucks, from which, as they drew near, came a pestilential stench through half-opened doors. In the dirty straw of each of the trucks squatted a group of human beings, men, women, and children. They were hunting vermin in their rags. Some of them lay curled up in the straw, sleeping, or dying. Perhaps dying, thought Bertram, for even those who were sitting up had a grey, haggard, deathly look, as they stared out at him with deep-sunk eyes, in which there was no interest, no life, no spirit.

"Letts," said Cherry, "on their way home from the famine districts. They've been dying all the way. Hunger, weakness, typhus. Look at that girl. Typhus, beyond a doubt."

The girl was lying on the grass by the side of the train. Her head turned from side to side. Her face was flushed and puffed.

"It's the vermin that gets 'em," said Cherry. "They're eaten up with it."

A tall, bearded peasant, clothed in rags tied about him with bits of string, came up to Bertram and spoke to him in English, with an American accent.

"Say, mister, can you change a hundred thousand roubles into German marks?"

Bertram laughed, and was astounded.

"A hundred thousand roubles! I'm not a millionaire."

"No need to be," said Cherry. "It's worth about six shillings in English money."

He took some dirty bits of paper from the bearded peasant, and gave him some German notes.

"There you are, Nunky. How do you come to speak the American lingo?"

"I worked in Detroit," said the man. "Before the world went wrong."

"Where do you come from?"

"Ufa."

He turned and pointed eastward.

"Three thousand miles."

"How long on the road, brother?"

"Five months. I am nearly at the journey's end. Across the frontier."

"How is it in Ufa?"

The man looked at Cherry with tragic eyes. He spoke in simple, Biblical words.

"In Ufa there is great death. The people have no food. The mothers are glad when their children die, because it is sad to hear their weeping. I am one who escaped in time. God has forsaken Russia."

"I guess that's a sure thing," said Cherry.

Back in the train to Moscow the American boys were singing negro choruses in harmony, and queer rag-time songs from the Winter Garden, New York. Cherry went into their carriage, and led new choruses, and college yells, with his enormous hands. Spasmodically, hour after hour, until late at night, these songs broke out, while Bertram lay alone on the wooden plank above Cherry's bunk, with his thoughts travelling faster than that slow-going train which every hour or so panted like an exhausted monster, reduced speed to a crawl, made one or two ineffective jerks and tugs, and then came to a dead halt. There was no more fuel. The provodnik and his comrades descended and searched around for logs of wood. Cherry stimulated their energy by shouts and curses, and roars of laughter, and back-thumpings, and general noises of encouragement to make them "get a move on." One hour, two hours, three hours-once fourteen hours-passed before the train lurched forward again with an immense rattle of wheels and wood.

Bertram stared out of the window for hundreds of versts, at the flat, dreary, monotonous panorama of Russia. It seemed lifeless and abandoned, except at wayside stations where groups of peasants stood about the wooden sheds, staring at the train as though it were a miraculous advent. Away from these stations there was but little sign of human life. Now and then Bertram saw a *droschke* driving along a road which led to some distant village of wooden houses with a white-washed church rising above them. A woman gathering faggots with one hand while she carried a baby in her shawl, raised her head and looked at Bertram as the train halted near her bundle of sticks. It seemed to him that she had some message for him in her eyes. She drew her shawl on one side, and showed her child, a little wizened thing, monkey-like.

At another place a peasant was kneeling before a wayside *ikon*. He knelt with his head bent and his beard on his chest, and crossed himself again and again.

An immense melancholy came out of this Russian landscape, and darkened Bertram's spirit. In imagination, without knowledge, by instinct only, he was stirred by the sense of travelling through a country of despair and immeasurable misery. The silence of the countryside was intense and brooding. No sound of laughter, of human gossip, even of human toil, came from its woodlands or open fields. There was no clink of hammer on anvil, no rhythm of an axe at work, no shout of ploughman to his team. The peasants in the wayside stations seemed to have no work to do, no object in life, except to stand and stare with gloomy eyes. "God has forsaken Russia," said the man from Ufa. The vital energy of life itself seemed to have burned low in these people.

Away back in the train an American chorus rang out.

> "Just hear that whistle blow!
> I want you all to know
> That train is taking my sweet man away
> From me to-day!
> Don't know the reason why,
> I must just sit and cry —"

Nigger melodies, Russian forests, the chug-chug of the train, Cherry's boisterous voice, the sad eyes of a peasant woman with a sick child, a line of bugs crawling up the carriage wall, the smell of a Latvian cheese, the melancholy of life, the isolation of the human soul, the death of Kenneth Murless, the mystery of Joyce, the typhus-stricken girl lying by the railway line, the endless monotone of this Russian landscape, the puzzle of his own life, made up the incoherence of Bertram's thoughts on the way to Moscow.

Kenneth's death would make no difference, except to Joyce. No difference to Bertram. He had left Joyce forever. She had finished with him, and he with her. Perhaps she would go back to Holme Ottery for a time, until the American took possession. What did it matter where she went? He must cut her out of his mind. It was only a year's habit, and weak sentiment, that made him think of her so much, with a dull ache of pain. . . . How long to Moscow, on this abominable journey? Damn those bugs!

XLIX

Moscow-and old Christy! Bertram saw him on the platform amidst a group of Red soldiers, bearded porters, and *droschke* drivers in fur caps and long blue coats. He was wearing the same old grey suit in which Bertram had last seen him in London, with the addition of a sheepskin waistcoat. His lean, ugly face was twisted into a humorous smile as he saw Bertram.

"Welcome to our city!"

"God in Heaven!" said Bertram. "This is a grand meeting."

For some reason, inexplicable to himself, the sight of Christy was like finding a solid raft after shipwreck.

"Follow me, and don't rub shoulders with your fellow men," said Christy.

He led the way from the platform into the station hall. It was a great place with white-washed walls and filled with such a stench of human filth that Bertram felt like vomiting. The great floor space was entirely covered with the heaped-up bodies of men, women, and children. They lay piled up on sacks and bags, and across each other's legs and arms, in a tangled mass of sheepskins, rags, and mangy fur, all brown with mud and dirt as though they had been dipped in the slime of Flanders, as Bertram had known it in war-time winters. It was nightfall, and they were settling down to sleep, restlessly, so that there was a heaving of bodies, and a tossing of arms. Some slept with stertorous breathing. Children wailed. Girls who were almost women lay in the arms of bearded men. One man lay dead among the living, as Bertram saw at a glance, not unfamiliar with death. His head was thrown back on a bit of sacking, showing a thin, turkey-like neck with loose wrinkled skin. His eyes were wide open and glazed.

"What's all this?" asked Bertram.

"Refugees from famine," said Christy. "The end of the journey. To-morrow they go into camp. Apart from typhus, they're all right now."

Bertram breathed deeply of fresh air when they emerged from the station.

"Can I get into a hotel?" he asked presently.

"Can you do what?"

Christy laughed quietly at the question.

"This is Bolshevik Russia! The Carlton doesn't function at the moment. There are no hotels. The *Narcomindjel* provides you with a billet, if they like the look of you."

"Who may they be?"

"The Soviet Foreign Office. East side Jews from New York deal with us, mostly. Not bad fellows, if you're civil."

"Supposing they don't like the look of me?"

Christy smiled grimly.

"You'll get another kind of billet. With bars to the windows."

"Any chance of that?"

"Not now. Bolshevism is busted. They want help from the outside world. That's why they've let me stay and let you come. Things are changing pretty rapidly. I'll tell you all about it presently. First the Foreign Office, and Mr. Weinstein."

He hailed a *droschke*, spoke a few words of Russian-amazing fellow! —and Bertram found himself driving through Moscow at night, with Christy by his side. Moscow-or some fantastic city of a dream after a goblet of absinthe? The moon was up, and shone brightly down upon a vision of white palaces, red walls, turreted gateways, tall bell-towers, and clusters of pear-shaped domes, all golden and glistening in the white moonlight. Under the gateways were deep caverns of blackness, and high walls with fan-shaped battlements flung black shadows across broad squares all flooded with the moon's milky radiance. The *droschke*, pulled by a lean and wiry horse, lurched over cobbled roads like a boat in a rough sea, and pitched into holes and pitfalls which more than once brought the horse to its knees. Under a gateway, very narrow, with a turret overhead, a red lamp was burning, and there seemed to be an altar in the little chamber at the side, glinting with gilt candlesticks. The driver pulled off his fur cap, and crossed himself.

"The shrine of the Iberian Virgin," said Christy. "A thousand years old, and more powerful than Lenin in the peasant mind!"

There was a great open square on the other side of the gateway, below a steep wall of red brick. At one end of it was a fantastic church, with a twisted dome painted in all the colours of the rainbow. In the high wall were arched gateways, lit by hanging lanterns, guarded by Red soldiers whose bayonets flashed like quicksilver. At one angle of the wall was an open staircase of red brick, leading to a high turret. Each of its steps was clear-cut by a light behind, with strange theatrical effect. Beyond seemed an endless vista of golden cupolas, surmounted by shining crosses, above white walls, all glamorous and shadow-haunted.

"The Kremlin," said Christy. "From that high tower-old Ivan Velike-Napoleon saw Moscow burning, and read his doom in its smoke and flame. We're passing through the Red Square. Every stone of it has been wet with blood. Those walls have looked down on a thousand years of human cruelty-not ended yet. . . ."

"A cut-throat looking place," said Bertram, and shivered a little. There were few people about. There was no sound in the city except the klip-clop of the lean horse, and the footsteps of sentries pacing under the Kremlin walls.

"It holds the biggest drama in the world," answered Christy. "What's happening here is going to alter history everywhere. Peace or war, perhaps civilisation itself, is going to be decided by the brain that is working at this hour of midnight, beyond those walls. The ruthless brain of a fanatic who is also a realist. He experiments with human nature like a vivisector with guinea-pigs, without compassion, in the interests of science. To prove or disprove a theory."

"Lenin?"

"Lenin. . . . Genius or maniac? Damned if I know!"

The Foreign Office, which Christy called by its incomprehensible name, was in a big block of buildings at the corner of an open place beyond the Red Square. A young soldier in an overcoat made for a bigger man, so that the sleeves came below his hands, barred the way with his rifle at the foot of a staircase, until Christy said, "Tavarish Weinstein."

At the top of the staircase, Christy plunged down a corridor, turned sharply to the left, knocked at a door, and opened it without waiting for an answer. It was well past midnight, but at a desk heaped with papers, a man sat working. He was a delicate-looking man, past middle age, with a pointed beard and moustache, like a French painter. Like such a type, also, he wore a jacket of brown velveteen. He looked up at Christy's entrance, and Bertram saw that the pleasant aspect of his face was spoilt by "crossed" eyes.

"Good evening, Mr. Weinstein! This is my friend, Bertram Pollard of *The New World*."

"Glad to meet you, Mr. Pollard. A tiring journey, I'm sure."

He shook hands with Bertram, with a limp, soft touch, and spoke in a gentle, tired voice. As chief of the propaganda department of the Soviet Republic, he did not come up to Bertram's expectations of a leading Bolshevik. He might have been the editor of *The Ladies' Home Journal*, or one of the most respectable members of the Royal Academy. He did not even look like a Jew.

"You purpose to visit the Famine region of the Volga?" he asked Bertram, and then, in a melancholy voice, said something about the tragic conditions in that part of Russia. The Republic was doing its best to cope with them. But it was very difficult. They needed foreign help. From England and the United States.

"We have nothing to hide," he said presently. "Go where you like, see what you like. Write what you like. We only ask you to tell the truth. So many lies have been told about us. Incredible! We welcome the truth. We wish the world to know."

"My friend Pollard is a glutton for truth," said Christy, with just the flicker of a wink at Bertram. "Where are you going to billet him, Mr. Weinstein? With me, I hope?"

"Certainly. You are comfortable?"

"Luxurious, even."

"That is good. We like to treat our guests well."

He rang up a number on the telephone, and spoke rapid Russian. Then he turned to Christy again.

"It is settled. Sophieskaya, 14. They have prepared a room for him. Good evening, Mr. Pollard. I shall read your articles with interest, I am sure."

Christy led the way out of the building, and asked Bertram to get into the *droschke* again. They drove across a bridge, turned at right angles along the bank of the river. On the other side was an astonishing view of the Kremlin again in the white moonlight, with great blocks of darkness between its churches and palaces and towers.

"An 'Arabian Nights' Dream!" said Bertram, in a low voice.

Christy did not answer him directly.

"That fellow Weinstein is not a bad fellow. As gentle as an invalid lady at Bournemouth. As subtle as a Chinese mandarin. I don't think he'd hurt a spider, willingly. But of course he'd vote for the death of any counter-revolutionary, man, woman, or child. That's fear. Fear is the father of cruelty. Well, here we are."

The *droschke* driver pulled up his horse with a clatter of hoofs. Two soldiers standing by a sentry-box came forward with a lantern, and held it up to Christy's face, and Bertram's.

"That's all right, my children," said Christy. "Now for a hundred thousand roubles."

"In Heaven's name, what for?" asked Bertram, still ignorant of Russian money.

"To pay the *isvostchik* —meaning the cabby. Hear him howl when I give it him."

Christy was right. The man wailed and whined, raised his hands to heaven, called upon the moon as witness, flung his fur cap on the ground, spat on the mass of paper which Christy had given him.

"*Skolka?*" said Christy.

The man renewed his loud plaint, until one of the Red soldiers struck him on the chest with the butt-end of his rifle.

"I paid him forty thousand roubles too much," said Christy. "He wanted fifty thousand more. Such is the greed and dishonesty of man!"

"What's this house?" asked Bertram, staring up at a great mansion with a classical façade. "It looks like a palace."

"That's exactly what it is," said Christy. "This is where I live. Nothing less than a palace for dear old Christy! An English aristocrat must have his four-poster bed and Louis Quinze suite."

He went up a flight of steps and pulled a chain. There was the loud jangling of a bell, and presently a great rattling of bolts.

"They keep us under lock and key, so that we don't escape without paying our bill," said Christy. "You'll find these Bolsheviks bleed the Western capitalist."

The door was opened by a pretty, sleepy girl, with a shawl round her head. She greeted Christy with a smile, a yawn, and a German "*Güten Abend.*"

"Don't be frightened at anything you see," said Christy. "What you don't see is much more alarming."

The first aspect of things was not frightening. Bertram found himself in a great and splendid hall, panelled in richly carved oak, with gilded decorations. Beyond was a wide flight of stairs, leading up to a corridor hung with tapestries. It was at the corner of the corridor that he had his first shock. From behind a curtain, or through some door which he had not seen, six figures appeared in single file, utterly silent. They looked like Chinese mandarins in wonderful robes of cloth of gold. Their pig-tails swung as they passed.

Christy turned round and winked at Bertram, and then led the way through a noble salon, all gilt and brocade, in the Louis Quinze style. Round the walls were portraits of men and women of the old régime, in white wigs and flowered silks. Immense candelabra, like those at Versailles, were suspended from a ceiling painted with cherubs and naked goddesses.

At the farthest door another unexpected figure stood motionless. It was a Turkish soldier in a red fez, and embroidered sash round blue baggy breeches. Christy passed through the salon, and led the way down another corridor where Bertram was startled again by a man suddenly opening a door, looking out, and shutting it with a bang. In that brief glimpse Bertram had seen an Indian prince, as he seemed, in a high white turban, and robe of cream-coloured silk.

Further down the corridor, another door opened, and a man came right out into the passage. He wore a flannel shirt and pepper-and-salt trousers, with his braces hanging down. His feet were bare, and he was carrying a wine-bottle in one hand and a wet sponge in the other. He looked like a respectable butler in a good English household, retiring for the night. As he passed Christy, he crossed himself with the wine bottle, and squeezed a drop of water out of the sponge on to the polished boards.

"*Le diable est mort!*" he said, with great joyfulness.

Christy passed into another room, which was an almost exact reproduction of the Louis Quinze salon. A grand piano was open, and a young man without a collar was playing "Three Blind Mice," with one finger.

"This way," said Christy.

He pulled back a heavy curtain, opened a door, and led Bertram into a room which might have been a king's study. It was panelled with oak, and furnished with oak chairs and tables, elaborately carved with Gothic decoration. A marble Venus stood on a high pedestal in the corner of the room, and on one of the tables was a bust of Napoleon. A figure of St. George and the Dragon in coloured marble inlaid with gold, was in front of the window, which looked across the river to the Kremlin.

On an enormous hearth, with iron dogs, some big logs were burning.

Two candles were alight in beer bottles, next to the bust of Napoleon, and in the centre of the room was an iron bedstead and a tin bath.

"Here we are," said Christy. "Home at last!"

Bertram was silent for a moment, looking unutterable things. Then he asked a series of questions, quietly but firmly.

"Tell me, have I gone raving mad? Or is this a real house in Bolshevik Russia? Who were all those strange people? Or did I only think I saw them?"

"It's quite all right," said Christy, soothingly. "I know how you feel, because I'd the jim-jams myself when I first came here. This is the Guest House of the Soviet Republic. It is also infested with the *Cheka* or secret police, who will take down anything you say as evidence against you, as the London Bobbies say, if you speak too loud, and unwisely of dangerous things. It used to be the palace of the Sugar King of Russia. It's one of the few houses in Moscow which was left untouched by the Revolution."

"Those Orientals?" asked Bertram.

"A mission from the Far Eastern Republic."

"That fellow with the wine bottle and the wet sponge?"

"An American newspaper correspondent. Jemmy Hart. One of the best."

"And the dreamy fellow playing 'Three Blind Mice'?"

"Kravintzki-one of the bright spirits of the Cheka. His signature is necessary for all executions. That's why he plays the piano with one finger."

"I don't follow that."

"Not to tire his wrist."

"Well, now I know!"

He took hold of Christy's arms and squeezed him tight.

"It's good to see you again, you ugly old chameleon. Let's sit and talk. I've a thousand things to tell and to ask. Since you left me I've been through the Slough of Despond, and the Valley of Doubt. I'm carrying a dead heart in my body. I'm in darkness, and can't see a ray of light ahead."

"Well, you're a cheerful kind of blighter to come to Moscow!" said Christy, with a grin. "You won't find any rosy hope in the Volga Valley! Nor any blaze of light 'twixt Moscow and

Petrograd. But let's talk in front of the fire. God, how good it is to talk! How good and useless, except to one's own soul!"

All through the night in a Guest House of Bolshevik Russia, they talked as only men can whose friendship is proved. Bertram spoke a little of Joyce, and learnt that Christy's wife was dead. They were both lonely men, and glad of this comradeship.

L

Moscow by day was more squalid, but more cheerful, than Moscow by night.

The Kremlin as seen from Bertram's "billet" in the Sugar King's palace was still magnificent and glittering under the sun's rays, but lost some of its mystery and fantasy as he had seen it under moonlight. The streets were no longer deserted, but crowded with every type of Russian life, with Asiatics among them, as they existed after a revolution which had destroyed one of the richest, most luxurious, and most corrupt aristocracies in Europe.

In Europe geographically, but Oriental in character and race. It did not need Christy's remark, "This is the East and not the West, which explains a lot," for Bertram to see that. Many of the people in the streets of Moscow were Eastern types, Slav and Tartar, and Semitic. The typical peasants of Moscow had blue eyes and straw-coloured hair, but the flatness of cheek-bone did not belong to Western physiognomy. Some of them were Mongolian in the slant of their eyes, in the blackness of their hair, and the sparseness of their beards. They wore shaggy goatskin caps brought far back behind their heads, with a mass of mangy hair, —distinguished from the fur cap of the usual Russian peasant. Men from the Caucasus, wearing the astrachan fez passed by, with Cossacks of the Don in long black coats, square cut across the shoulders and falling to their feet.

These crowds were tramp-like in their way of dress, careless of rags and broken boots. It was difficult to distinguish any difference of class or caste among them, except that Red Army officers and officials were smarter than the rest, with top boots more weather tight, and fur caps less shaggy. In the coldness of early autumn, when the first snow began to fall, every one in Moscow was muffled up to the ears with shawls or bits of fur, and those who had no boots swathed their legs around with wrapping over sandals or clogs and seemed warm enough, and well enough shod for the mud and slush.

There was no visible sign of hunger in the faces of the passers-by, and the children especially looked fairly plump and healthy, surprisingly well.

"There's no famine here-yet," said Christy. "There's an old proverb, 'All things roll down to Moscow.' It holds good now. This is the seat of the Administration. It's stuffed with Soviet officials. They've a call on the supplies of the country. And the kids get first serve. It's fair to say that."

Christy was scrupulously fair to the Soviet Republic, and Bertram thought he erred on the side of generosity. He accused him even, though not seriously, of having been "converted" to the black cult of Bolshevism.

But Christy in that long night talk had been illuminating, and impartial. He had studied the Bolshevik theory and practice, as he had seen it working, with a penetrating vision. Theoretically, he thought there was a lot to be said for the Communist idea. What was it, after all, but an endeavour to carry out the commands of Christ to His apostles who had "all things in common"? It was a fanatical revolt against the crimes of Capitalism and Individualism-Sweated Labour, Profiteers, Warmongers, the blackguardism of Trusts, the corruptions and cruelties of Caste.

"We can't deny these things," said Christy. "We can't pretend that all is well with Western civilisation. As we know, Pollard, it stinks with iniquity!"

The Soviet system was simple-in theory. In return for service to the state, the citizen would receive food, shelter, clothing, education, all the elementary needs of life, and even its arts, graces, and amusements. Service to the state was recognised by the membership of a Trade Union. Once a man had his "ticket," whatever his class of work-it applied, of course, to women too-he drew his ration of food, clothes, and so on, received his opera and theatre passes, was entitled to all the culture and gifts of the state.

"Very much like a soldier in the British Army or any other," said Christy.

The Soviet Government was made up of a body of men elected as the Central Executive Committee by a series of Soviets starting with the villages and sending one of their members to a big and more important body. They elected members in their turn to still more important groups, until finally the Central Committee was reached.

"Very indirect," said Bertram.

"Precisely. Not democratic. A weak point in the system. The Central Executive is as far removed from the people as the Greek tyrants."

Theoretically, however, the idea of common reward for common service, thought Christy, was the ideal towards which mankind had always been groping.

"And actually," said Bertram, "how has it worked?"

"It hasn't," answered Christy. "It's failed to work, hopelessly. It's landed them all into an unholy ruin. They admit, with reservations, their own ghastly failure."

The chief cause of failure, beyond any doubt, was the resistance of the peasant to the system of requisition. To ration every citizen, it was, of course, necessary to commandeer the peasant's labour and produce. All that he produced over and above his own needs belonged to the State. Red soldiers went down to his farmstead to remind him of the fact, and to collect his grain, potatoes, flax, butter, vegetables, eggs, poultry, and milk. The peasant said, "Why should I sow that others should reap?" He concealed his produce, bartered it secretly for jewels, furs, trinkets, any old thing, with city folk who didn't find their daily ration enough for daily life. When caught, he was shot or imprisoned. When many had been shot, the others ceased to sow, undercultivated their fields, —even burnt their grain!

This peasant revolt against Communism broke the country, already ruined by war, revolution, and counter-revolutionary armies. The Central Executive could not get their supplies to ration the city folk. Factory workers, not getting food, abandoned the factories for the fields. No more engines could be made or repaired. The transport system broke down. It became more difficult to convey food to the cities. They disintegrated. In Petrograd there were three million people at the beginning of the war. There were now seven hundred and fifty thousand. All industry had ceased. No spades, ploughs, reaping machines could be replaced. The whole machinery of Russian life had collapsed. Now the Famine on the Volga threatening twenty-five million people with starvation, had hit the only class which was comparatively comfortable, the peasants of Russia.

"How much is the famine due to Bolshevism?" asked Bertram.

Christy pondered.

"It's due to the drought. Last year and this. An act of God, as men say, though I don't believe it, if there is a God, and He is kind. But its severity was increased by the System. The Bolsheviks requisitioned the peasants' reserves to feed the Red Army defending Russia against Koltchak, Denikin, Wrangel, and the rest. There were droughts and famines in Russia before. The peasants expected them, and kept reserves of grain for a lean year. Now there are no reserves. In that way Bolshevism is responsible for the famine. But in no other way. Let's be fair."

"You're too damned fair," said Bertram. "How about the atrocities-the inhuman cruelties-the Chinese tortures?"

Christy lowered his voice. They were talking in the palace of the Sugar King, infested with secret police.

"I've no personal knowledge. The *Cheka* keeps its secrets. There have been many executions-in batches. Men and women, without mercy. Perhaps in Eastern Russia Mongols have done the dirty work. But I'll say just this-to be fair again. All Governments, especially in time of Revolution, are ruthless against those who challenge their authority and seek to overthrow their power. So it would be in any country in some degree. These people hold their place against hordes of enemies, within and without. They proclaimed the Reign of Terror against all plotters and counter-revolutionaries. Fear made them cruel. Fear made them kill the Czar, as the French killed poor old Louis and Marie Antoinette. Now there are no more counter-revolutions, and the Terror has abated."

"Why have counter-revolutions ceased?" asked Bertram.

"The people are sick of bloodshed. The game's too dangerous. And Russia is so stricken that even the last of the old régime, who still linger on in holes and corners, believe that the overthrow of the Soviet Republic would be the last blow to the life of Russia. At least it functions. It makes a train move, now and then. It gets some supplies from the peasants. It sends some seeds to the Volga valley. It works. . . . And it has abandoned Communism."

"What's that?" asked Bertram, astounded.

"The whole thing has been scrapped by Lenin, its chief, author and organiser. On October the eighteenth he 'blew the gaff' on the whole show, confessed the utter breakdown of the Communist system-for the reasons I've given, and some others. 'We've suffered a terrible defeat on the Economic front,' he said. 'The only way by which we may save ourselves is by a strategic retreat on prepared positions. He's restored private property, to a great extent, and the right of private trading, as you'll see. He has abandoned rationing, and re-established money for wages and payment. The kind of money I paid to our *isvostchik* last night-the *droschke* driver! Four hundred thousand roubles to the English pound. One has to carry a carpet-bag instead of a purse."

"God!" said Bertram. "An awful mess!"

"The worst mess in the world. The greatest tragedy in modern history. Another experiment in human progress has ended in disaster to a hundred and fifty million people. Famine has stricken them, and will creep even to the edge of Moscow before the winter is out. Pestilence sweeps them like a scourge. And Lenin, in the Kremlin, is trying to think of some way out of ruin. I think he's found a way, which at least he will try."

"Tell me."

Christy lowered his voice still further.

"Alliance with Germany. Red soldiers in exchange for railway engines. Arsenals in return for economic aid. A threat of war to France and Poland, with all the Continent afire, unless Europe comes to her aid. International blackmail."

"That's Hell," said Bertram.

"If it happens," answered Christy. "You've just come in time to see the transition from Communism to Capitalism. You'll find it interesting before you get down to the Famine. This city is a melodrama, if you keep your eyes open."

Bertram kept his eyes open, and his ears. Building on Christy's outline of information, he was able to fill in the details of Russian life from personal observation, and plunged into it.

LI

He saw something of the melodrama of Moscow in the Trubnaya Market, which had been opened again, owing to Lenin's new law allowing private trading. Until that time, all private barter had been forbidden under severe penalties, yet it had gone on secretly between city folk and peasants and, as Bertram found afterwards, there was hardly a man or woman in Moscow or Petrograd, outside the class of Soviet officials, who had not been imprisoned for this "crime." Now it was done publicly, and legally.

Bertram walked through the market which covered a great square with dilapidated houses, pock-marked by bullet-holes, on each side. There were rows of wooden booths with room enough between them for three people to walk abreast, all crowded with peasant folk in their sheepskins. They were selling the produce of their little farmsteads, and the food made a brave show in the capital city of a famine-stricken land. Bertram saw plenty of meat, butter, cheese, and bread. For those who had paper money in big enough bundles, here was nourishment enough.

There were other people besides peasants. Standing on the outer edge of the wooden rows, were long lines of men and women-mostly women-who, he saw at a glance, were not peasants. Some of them were in peasant dress, but their faces could not disguise a heritage of education and gentility. Others wore the clothes of the old régime, of bourgeoisie and Western fashion-black dresses, frayed and worn and grease-stained, leather boots, down at heel, or broken at the toes, hats which had come originally, perhaps, from smart modistes in the Nevsky Prospekt, or even from Paris, a bit of lace at the throat and wrists.

These ladies, for they were that, stood in the market-place holding out the last relics of their former state-ermine stoles, fur tippets, embroidered slippers, fine linen, old boots (less broken than those they wore), cloth jackets, silk petticoats, trinkets with glittering stones, gold lockets, rings, lace, embroidery, perfumes, combs, hair pins, brooches. Some of them seemed hardly able to stand, and were thin and weak and haggard. Bertram noticed their hands, delicate and finely shaped, but grimed with dirt of hard work and lack of soap. Gipsy hands of patrician women. They avoided his eyes when he looked at them. They seemed startled by his own appearance, knew him instantly as a man of the class that was once theirs, and shrank from his scrutiny.

One girl, younger than the others, flamed scarlet at his glance, and turned her head away with visible distress. He did not look at her again, in order to avoid this hurt to her pride, and indeed he had a sense of shame in walking down the lines of those women, scrutinising their faces, witnessing this public humiliation of their pride. Yet he had an intense wish to get into conversation with them, to find out their way of life. They were the last of the old régime within the frontiers of Russia, less lucky than the Countess Lydia and her sister, and all the crowds of émigrés who had escaped in time. What stories they would have to tell! What agonies they must have suffered before arriving at this market-place!

He stood in front of an elderly woman who was holding out a little tray on which was a gilt crucifix. She had a thin face, with grey hair almost white, beneath a little black bonnet. He asked the price of her crucifix, speaking in French, and at his question her hands trembled so that she could hardly hold the tray.

"Why do you speak to me in French?" she asked, replying in the same language.

"I guessed you spoke French. And I don't know a word of Russian."

"You are not French?" she said, looking timidly into his face.

"I'm English."

She answered him in his own tongue.

"I thought so when I saw you before you spoke. How do you come to be in Russia? Few foreigners come here now."

"I'm a newspaper correspondent. I've come to write about the Famine, when I can get as far as that."

"There is misery to be found without going so far," she said. "There are many who are hungry even in Moscow. I am one of them."

"May I buy your crucifix?"

She glanced nervously on each side, and spoke to him in French again in a low voice.

"We are being watched. It is very dangerous for me to be in the market place. They do not like my name. Perhaps you would be good enough to go."

He was aware of a young officer of the Red Army standing three paces away, watching and listening.

"*Au revoir, madame.*"

He turned away, stared into the face of the officer, and went further down the line.

The girl who had flamed scarlet at his glance was still there, and gave him a strange, wistful, lingering look which startled him. Then, as he drew near, she left her place in the line, and went to the lady with whom he had been speaking and whispered to her.

These people were frightened, in spite of the "New Economic Laws" which permitted private trading. They had come out into the open, but were not certain of this new liberty. Perhaps they had been trapped in some such way before.

After wandering about the streets and markets of Moscow for a long morning, Bertram became conscious suddenly of hunger, and he puzzled as to the way in which he could satisfy this desire. It was a long tramp back to his Guest House, across the river, and it would be more amusing to find an eating house of some kind. Christy had told him that two had just been opened in a street called the Arbat, the only two in Moscow —a city of two million people-which once was crowded with restaurants as luxurious as any in the world. He hailed a *droschke*, and by good luck made the *isvostchik* understand the name of the street, paying him a hundred thousand roubles from a wad of paper advanced by Christy, for the short drive.

The man seemed satisfied, touched his fur cap, and said, "*Spaseeba, tavarish.*"

A few shops were open down a long street of houses which had all been shops, by the look of them, but were now mostly empty and boarded up, and falling into ruin. The newly opened places had a few objects of merchandise in the windows. A pair of top boots, marked at a million roubles, adorned one window-front. In another were three fur caps, a guitar, a German pipe, and a wicker cradle. A motley collection of household goods-including a leather arm-chair, a broken bedstead, some rather good rugs, a cloisonné clock, and a rosewood piano-was the greatest display of "stock" which he could observe through any window. In most cases there was nothing but what could be seen at a glance. The "private trading" in Moscow was not yet magnificent. He discovered the restaurant by the sight of an uncooked leg of mutton, baldly displayed in one of the windows, and by the words, "Angliske Restaurant" written in Russian characters above it.

When he entered, he saw a bare room set out with wooden chairs and tables, with here and there a piece of furniture of the Louis XV. period, and on the walls some gilded mirrors of the same style. A woman, shabbily dressed, and wearing carpet slippers, but with an unmistakable air of elegance, was stirring something in a pot over a wood fire. At the back of the room was a long counter, on which stood some tall bottles, a samovar, and some coffee cups, and behind it, on a high stool, sat an elderly man with silver hair and a little white beard. He was peeling some potatoes, while behind him, with her hand on his shoulder, was a girl of sixteen or so, as poorly dressed as Cinderella, but as pretty, in a dark way, with large brown eyes.

Bertram was aware of three pairs of eyes upon him, studying him intently, with surprise and suspicion. The woman who had been stirring the pot, advanced with her ladle, pointed to a table, and spoke in Russian.

He answered in French, and asked politely whether he might have something to eat.

"You do not understand Russian?" she answered suspiciously, in French.

"No, not a word, alas! I'm English-just arrived in Moscow."

"English!"

She spoke the word in his own tongue, with joyful intonation.

"Why do you leave happy old England to come to this miserable land?"

"To help the starving people of Russia, if I can," he answered.

"That is brave of you," she said. "There is much danger in Russia, and no kind of comfort."

She called to the white-headed man behind the counter. "Nicholas, Katia, here is a gentleman just come from England!"

They came from behind the counter, and the elderly man clasped Bertram's hand.

"I used to know England well, and love my memories of it. I was a painter in those days. We lived in Cheyne Walk, Chelsea. Katia was a baby then."

The girl took Bertram's hand, and dropped a curtsey like an English debutante.

"I remember England, just a little. It seems like a fairy-tale now!"

They served him with some soup called Bortsch, and afterwards cooked a piece of meat for him with some of the potatoes which the elderly man had peeled; and while he was eating, the lady talked to him rapidly, emotionally, as though relieving the pent-up thoughts of agonising years.

It was a tale of misery. Her husband, now peeling potatoes, had been a painter at the Imperial Court, and known to be a personal friend of the Empress. He had been arrested by the *Cheka* and thrown into prison, where he was kept without trial for eighteen months, half-starved, in a foul cell crowded with men of good class. Many times he was examined at night by the Extraordinary Commission, mostly young lads who tried to bully him into admission of counter-revolutionary acts. Each time he believed he was being taken to execution, like others in the cell who were taken out and shot. For some reason they had spared him. Perhaps because he was an artist, and they pretended to reverence art, though they had no reverence for life. She and Katia had been turned into the kitchen of their beautiful house, which for a time had been used as a billet for Red soldiers-rough country lads who stabbed their knives into her husband's canvases, used the tapestries to wipe the mud off their boots, and were unspeakably filthy in their habits. She had been very much afraid for little Katia. Those young soldiers had been rough with her, as they were with peasant girls. . . . She and the child had starved many days. They would have starved to death unless they had sold, secretly and at great risk, some of the jewels they had hidden. They sold them to peasant women for potatoes and cheese. Now the peasant women were hungry themselves because of the drought! She had worked at the hardest toil, chopping wood, shovelling snow, dragging sledges to Government stores.

"Look at my hands, monsieur!"

She showed her hands, coarsened and begrimed, like a gipsy's.

Then she had been arrested for the crime of private trading, and imprisoned for six weeks. All that time she had thought only of Katia, left alone with the brutal soldier-boys. But God and His angels had guarded the child. Two months after coming out of prison her husband was liberated, without explanation or excuse. Just pushed out of prison with the words, "*You can go, tavarish!*" That was happiness beyond words, to be together again, in spite of poverty and starvation and coarse toil.

"We have suffered less than others," said the lady. "We have been lucky. My friends have been worse treated by the cut-throats and robbers who rule our unhappy country."

Her husband whispered to her.

"Hush, my dear. For the love of God —"

A look of terror came into his eyes, because two young men came into the restaurant and sat down at a table near the counter. The lady became as white as death for a moment, lest they had overheard her words. But they called for plates of Bortsch and talked together in low voices, paying no heed to those who served them. They were unshaven and dirty, with long over-coats and top boots, caked in mud, and the Red Star of the Soviet Republic in their caps showed them to be officials of some kind.

There was no more conversation from the lady. She went into a little back kitchen. Her husband, once painter to the Imperial Court, peeled more potatoes. Katia added up some figures on a slate, glancing over at Bertram with a little smile about her lips and in her timid eyes.

There seemed to be no sense of freedom, no respite from fear in Soviet Russia. Those women in the market place had been scared when he approached them. This little family dared not talk a word before unknown men of their own city.

LII

"I'm off to Petrograd for a couple of days," said Christy one night in the Guest House. "You'd better come while you're waiting for a train to the Volga district. I've fixed it with Weinstein. Here's your pass."

This visit to Petrograd gave Bertram another impression of Soviet Russia, broadened his outlook on the tragedy of a great people, killed something more of the petty selfishness of his own trouble.

He said something of the kind to Christy on the train journey through endless fields sowed with rye six months from another harvest time.

"I find Russia makes one forget one's ego. It's like seeing the end of the world-the death of civilisation. It's absurd for the individual to whine about the loss of a collar-stud, or a pretty wife, in the midst of an Empire's ruin."

"A nice cheerful way of looking at things!" said Christy, with his usual irony. "Heaven knows how gay you'll be by the time you get to the Volga Valley."

"These people seem to be down to the bed-rock of primitive existence," said Bertram. "Nothing matters except food and shelter, and escape from death. All the rest is so much 'jam,' as my batman used to say. It simplifies things, as war does."

"An easy process of simplification," said Christy. "Another war, or another drought in Russia, and a great part of Europe will be simplified off the map."

There was a great silence in Petrograd. Heavy snow had fallen, and lay deep in the streets, except where gangs of men and women had shovelled a passage-way for sleighs which drove slowly with a tinkle of bells. The Neva was frozen over, and standing on one of the bridges, Bertram stared at the panorama of the city, magnificent with its vista of palaces, churches, vast galleries, and great blocks of stone buildings which had once been the offices of the Imperial Government and of world-wide trade, but grim and black under snow-covered roofs.

The silence of Petrograd was strange and fearful. There was no sound of labour in the great factories across the river. No smoke came from their chimneys. There was no throb of engines, or clang of iron. Nothing moved on the quaysides. The immense buildings with sculptured façades on the side of the city were deserted of all life. No man or woman went in. None came out.

Along the Nevski Prospekt once, as Bertram knew, the greatest highway of luxury in Europe, most of the shops were boarded up like those in Moscow, and nothing was being sold or bought. But there were people there, a sense of life, in contrast to the deadly quietude in other streets. With fur caps pulled down, and sheepskin coats tucked up about their ears, and with snow-shoes over their boots, they were dragging hand sledges over pavements covered with frozen snow so slippery that Bertram found it hard to walk without staggering or falling. The sledges were laden with sacks of potatoes, logs of wood, or frozen meat, and some of them were escorted by Red soldiers, as though this treasure might be attacked on its way.

Bertram was aware of some difference between these sledge-draggers and snow-shovellers of Petrograd and the population of Moscow. They were not peasants, but city folk of the old bourgeois class. Their clothes still showed traces of fashions that had passed. Some of these women, and young girls, dragging heavy loads, had frocks of a style that would have looked well in Paris, or Berlin, or London, before they had been torn, and grease-stained, and mud-splashed. Elderly men, clearing the roads, wore "bowler" hats, and coats with astrachan collars, and looked like bank managers, or clerks, once respected in merchants' offices, who had come down in the world to the level of the doss house.

Some of the younger Russians wore their rags with a kind of swagger and cheerful unconcern, only intent on keeping warm, by bits of sacking used as shawls round the neck, or by wearing seamen's jerseys under their black jackets. Even in Petrograd youth had not lost all its spirit of gaiety, and Bertram heard a laugh now and then from young folk who went hurrying by, arm in arm. But the general impression of the faces he passed was haggard, mournful, and anxious. Christy gave an explanation.

"This city is running short of food. Moscow, with its crowd of Soviet officials, has first call on supplies. These people we pass are wondering if their next meal will be their last."

"I want to talk to them," said Bertram. "If only I knew a bit of Russian! I want to see inside their lives."

"Try them with French, or German, or English," said Christy. "Some of these people shovelling snow used to spend the season in Paris, Berlin, London."

It was a woman selling cigarettes outside the station whose life was revealed to Bertram.

She leaned against a wall, coughing, in a thin dress that was no proof against a temperature of forty degrees below zero. She was a middle-aged woman, with a thin face and sallow skin through which the cheekbones showed. Bertram asked her in French for ten of her cigarettes, and paid her ten times too much, in filthy paper.

"You've given me too much," she said, in a weak voice, "and I have no change."

Her French was more perfect than Bertram's.

"Never mind the change," he said. "It's cold for you, standing here."

"Soon I shall be dead," she said. "Are you French?"

"No, English."

She stared at him with a kind of wonderment.

"Once I was a governess in England."

She mentioned the name of an English family, unknown to Bertram.

"You have been here during the Revolution?" he asked.

"Since the beginning of the war. My husband was shot when Kerensky went. He was an officer, and his men killed him, like so many others."

"You are alone now?"

"I have a little son. He is dying of hunger. I cannot earn enough to feed him. Sometimes I have thought of killing him, but have not the courage."

"That is terrible!" said Bertram. "How can I help you?"

"Why should you help me?" she asked, in a harsh voice. "What am I to you? I am only one of millions who starve in Russia."

He gave her a bundle of paper money, and she stared at it with dazed eyes, and gave a little cry, not of joy, but of anguish. Perhaps this charity from a stranger only sharpened her sense of misery, made more poignant her knowledge of inevitable death.

Bertram raised his hat, and moved away, joining Christy again.

"It's useless, old man," said Christy. "I began like that. But I've chucked it up. How much did you give her?"

"Five hundred thousand roubles. Surely that will help her a little?"

Christy shrugged his shoulders, and laughed.

"In this city one pays a hundred and twenty thousand roubles for a pound of tea. Eighty thousand roubles for a pound of bread. Sixty thousand roubles for ten cigarettes. What can you and I do in private charity? It's merely pandering to one's own sentiment."

"One can't leave a woman like that without giving her something. One's coat, if one has nothing else."

"Useless, Major. Useless. There are millions like her, as she said. We can do better than that. Our job is to tell the truth about the agony of these people, so that the outside world may help in a big way. Poke up the conscience of all our Pharisees who pass by on the other side, while Russia lies bleeding in the ditch."

He took Bertram to a camp for refugees from the famine districts of the Volga.

"You saw some of these on their way in the cattle-truck trains. This is the end of the journey for some of them. I'm told it's worth seeing."

It was called a "camp," but the refugees in the place to which Christy went-there were many others round Petrograd-were housed in the old Imperial Barracks-an immense white-washed building on four sides of a hollow square. It was worth seeing, as Christy said, but not pleasant to see. Outside the thermometer told forty degrees below zero. Inside there was no heat except that of human bodies lying huddled together on bare boards. There were thousands of peasants with straw-coloured beards and blue eyes from Samara, and Saratoff, and other places which soon to Bertram were to have a frightful significance. They had with them their women folk and children who squatted about in the barrack rooms or lay sleeping in tangled heaps like those in the station at Moscow. A meal was being served from the kitchen-thin potato soup, and a square hunk of black sour-smelling bread, provided by the Soviet Republic for these people of the sun-burnt valley, once the richest granary of Russia. The soup was ladled out to those who lined up in queue, with mugs and bowls, but Bertram saw that many did not take their place in the line. They lay on the bare boards, flopping their heads from side to side, or very still, with glazing eyes.

"Typhus-dysentery-weakness," said Christy, after some words in German to a Russian doctor.

The doctor was a black-bearded man in a white surgical coat. He had grave, thoughtful eyes behind his glasses.

"We do what we can," he said, in German. "But the food is hardly enough, and there are no medicines, no soap, no change of clothes, no fuel for heat. Disease is spreading. But we do our best."

Passing through the courtyard with Bertram and Christy, he pushed back a wooden door, and beckoned them to look.

Inside was a great pile of dead bodies, thrown one on top of the other, men, women, and children, mixed up together in a huddle of death, with brown, claw-like hands protruding from the mass of corpses, and faces staring upwards, and here and there a bare limb revealed in its skin and bone. They had been tossed on top of each other, like rubbish for the muck-heap.

"Two days dead," said the Russian doctor.

"The End of the Journey," said Christy, in a low voice to Bertram.

Bertram was sick for a moment in the corner of the yard. This stench of death was worse than a battlefield.

LIII

By favour of a Soviet official with whom Christy was on terms of friendship —"a very mild type of Bolshevik, like so many of them," he explained-they were allowed to visit the Port of Petrograd.

"Is it worth while?" asked Bertram; "I want the human side of things. I want to know how people are living, and suffering in this frightful country."

Christy answered with a touch of rebuke.

"We're not here for melodrama. This Port will tell us why people are *not* living in Russia. And why there's unemployment in England. It was one of the gateways of the world's trade."

It was a mournful place. They stumbled over cables concealed beneath the snow, and wandered in solitude past docks and warehouses, empty of all shipping and merchandise. Out in the snow lay numbers of ploughs and reaping machines, brand-new in their crates.

Christy inspected them, and read a word.

"Düsseldorf. . . . That tells a tale. Do you remember what I said about a Russo-German alliance?"

"Why are they left rotting in the snow?" asked Bertram.

"No means of transport, and Oriental inefficiency," said Christy.

Further in the Port were three tramps flying the Swedish and Danish flags, and one wide-decked vessel with one funnel called *Tyneside Lass*, from Newcastle.

Christy was excited by that.

"From little old England! What's she doing? Let's go and see the Old Man!"

At the top of the gangway was a young skipper, who looked surprised when Christy hailed him in his own tongue.

"Glad to see you, gentlemen," he said, with cheery greeting. "Come into my cabin and have a spot. It's biting cold."

He mixed a stiff dose for each of them, and raised his own glass.

"Cheery oh!"

"What are you carrying to Petrograd?" asked Christy.

"Railway engines. All German. From Hamburg. My owners have a contract to carry eight hundred. Four at a time. It looks as if I'll get frozen in, this trip."

Christy looked over to Bertram, and raised his eyebrows, before asking another question.

"How do the Bolshies pay for German engines, skipper?"

"Some gold. Mostly diamonds and furs."

"Sound business for Germany," said Christy. "How do you get on with the Bolshies?"

The young skipper shrugged his shoulders.

"The officials keep civil tongues. They'd better. The stevedores are poor lousy bastards. Can hardly lift a cable without breaking theirselves. Half-fed, and no guts. Start work at eleven, and take two hours to get the cranes working. Well-meaning enough. Some of 'em speak a bit of English. There's one that was Professor of Biology, or some such thing, before the war. I gave him a slab of cheese, and he wept tears and kissed my hand. I've no use for this Bolshevism. It don't seem to do a country any good, though there's some that think so in Newcastle."

He wished them good health, and waved his hand to them from the top of the gangway as they went back through the snow.

"Major," said Christy, using the old title as though they were still in Flanders' fields, "those railway-engines from Hamburg give me furiously to think. Here's the key to Russia's way of escape. Perhaps Germany's also, if France puts the screw on too hard. What about the Treaty of Versailles-German indemnities —a French invasion of the Ruhr-if Germany allies herself with Russia? Russia and Germany *contra mundum*! A formidable combination, by the Lord!"

"Don't you jump a bit too far ahead?" asked Bertram. "Four railway engines in a Tyneside tug don't seem to justify a prophecy of world war."

"Remember Owen," said Christy calmly. "Reconstructed a Megatherium out of one tooth. These four railway engines, with seven hundred and ninety-six to follow-and those ploughs lying in the snow-mean that Germany is getting her foot into Russia, doing business, preparing to do more. For Russia's sake I'm mighty glad, but it mustn't be left to Germany alone. If that happens, there's going to be Hell to pay."

Bertram was silent on the way back. Christy had the gift of seeing far ahead, and his prophecies were rare, and never rash. The individual did not interest him very much. He thought more of the actions and reactions of peoples, of mass movements, economic laws, world balances, the ebb and flow of trade, the undertow of passions, and political chances.

That night they went to the Marinsky Theatre, and lost their way in the snow. With his few phrases of Russian, Christy asked the way of a young lad in the uniform of a Red soldier, and was answered in very good English.

"If you come with me, gentlemen, I shall be very glad to show you."

"Are you English?" asked Bertram.

The boy laughed, and said his father was English, but now dead. His mother was a Russian lady. She taught languages, especially English, to students who came to her at night after their day's work. She received three thousand roubles a lesson, and was never home till past midnight, and then very tired. He chattered cheerfully as he strode over the snow in heavy boots, a little fellow, with bright eyes and a lively sense of humour. Yet it was not a merry tale he told, though fantastic.

"I was an important person for a time. They made me President of Arts and Sciences. I gave lectures to working men at night, on the origin of art, evolution, and elementary biology."

"How old were you then?" asked Bertram.

"Sixteen," said the boy. "Now I am eighteen."

He looked no more than fourteen.

One day he was arrested for counter-revolutionary opinions. Some working-man had discovered that his father was an "aristocrat," or objected to his discipline in class. Anyhow, he was denounced, and kept in prison for nine months. His poor mother had nearly died of grief.

Then he was liberated, luckier than others who had been shot in batches for the same suspicion. Now he was an office-boy in a Government department.

"It's been perfectly rotten," he said, using English slang with a foreign accent.

He halted outside the Marinsky Theatre, and saluted, and then shook hands.

Bertram tried to slip some money into his hand, but he shook his head.

"My father was an English gentleman," he said simply.

There were tickets for sale in the theatre, according to the "New Economic Laws," but it was plain that most of the people had passes, and it was explained to Christy by a young Jew who spoke French, that it was a "Trade Union" night.

It was a performance of "Carmen," magnificently staged, and well played, but to Bertram and Christy the audience was of more interest than the performance. The immense and splendid theatre was packed with "the proletariat." Nearly all of them wore the Russian blouse, belted round the waist, or the Red Army tunic. The women were dressed very much like an audience in one of the poorer suburbs of London, but here and there a few had ventured to put on a bit of "finery" —a little lace round the neck and wrists, a trinket or two. In the Imperial box sat a group of men with black hair over their foreheads, like women's "fringes," and grimy hands. Above their heads the Imperial Eagle had been covered with the Red Flag of Revolution.

Bertram thought of the pale-faced Czar sitting there with the Empress and their beautiful daughters, with high officers and ladies of the Court.

Then, by some curious association of ideas, he thought of Joyce, as he had sat with her in the boxes of London theatres, so beautiful, so exquisite in her evening frocks. The Emperor and Empress and all their family had been murdered. Joyce had disappeared from his life, by some act of revolution which had murdered *him*, killed his spirit, stone dead.

The body of Bertram Pollard sat in the stall of the Marinsky Theatre at Petrograd, but it was not the Bertram Pollard of Holland Street, Kensington, or "Somewhere in France." He had changed. He was a different man. This visit to Russia was changing him still further. It made all other things seem trivial and insignificant-the things he had made such a fuss about. Ireland! It did not mean much to the world in progress or reaction. That guerrilla warfare was a Chinese cracker compared with the frightful things that had happened here in Petrograd. The Social Revolution in England-Holme Ottery up for sale! How laughable, how negligible, compared with the utter extinction of the Russian gentry!

Petrograd and Moscow put things in a different proportion. The agony of these people made private troubles, heart-breaks, love affairs, strangely small. Those dead bodies in the barracks-they too put things in a different proportion, made life itself of but little account, individually. What was this new sense of proportion going to mean to him?

Perhaps he would find the meaning at last for which his mind had been groping, like a man in a dark room. Perhaps he would get outside himself in service to these people who were so immensely stricken.

"A hundred thousand roubles for your thoughts," said Christy.

"I'm wondering what I'm here for," said Bertram.

Christy glanced at him sideways.

"To learn a bit of life. Perhaps to light a little lamp in the darkness of a human heart. Anyhow to see 'Carmen' jolly well played!"

The young Jew who had spoken to them before, came up during the entr'acte, when they joined the crowd in the *foyer*, a strange, shaggy-haired, pale-faced crowd, very cheerful on the whole, and enjoying their evening.

"What do you think of it?" he asked.

"Magnificent," said Christy. "Who are all these people in the audience?"

"Soviet workers of one kind or another."

"Communists?" asked Christy.

The young Jew smiled, and shrugged his shoulders.

"Are we still Communists under the New Economic Laws? We've gone back to private trading, private property, money instead of rations, foreign capital, if it can be got."

"Do the people like the new way?"

"It's like a weight lifted off their shoulders! They're beginning to breathe again."

He lowered his voice.

"I'm in a Soviet office. But like most Jews I believe in trade, barter, property. All the same, the Revolution did some good. The workers didn't get free seats at the Opera in the time of the Romanoffs."

He looked at them with shifty eyes, afraid that he was talking dangerously, yet wanting to talk.

"Bread and circuses are all right," said Christy, "but circuses without bread are poor fare."

The young Jew couldn't follow this allusion, and looked mystified.

"Was the Revolution very terrible in England?" he asked.

"What Revolution?"

"The English Revolution."

"It hasn't happened yet," said Christy. "It won't happen."

The young Jew was incredulous.

"We have read a lot about it in *Prahvda*. That's our Soviet paper. All your people are starving, are they not?"

"They were pretty well fed when I left them," said Christy, laughing.

The young Jew did not believe him, by the look in his eyes, but the curtain was rung up again, and they left him.

"They all think there's been a bloody revolution in England," said Christy. "They get no news except the stuff published for propaganda purposes. The outside world is a mystery to them."

"It will soon be to us," said Bertram. "I've heard nothing since I left Riga. For all I know England may have been sunk beneath the sea. Or Ireland."

"No such luck," said Christy, making the obvious gibe.

They went back through the snow with the audience of the Marinsky Theatre, to the music of sleigh-bells. That night they slept at a place called the International Hostel, which was another kind of "Guest-house," mostly inhabited by Soviet officials of high rank, and by German traders. Most of the night was spent in catching bugs.

LIV

Back in Moscow, Bertram made enquiries as to the means of transport to the famine-stricken districts. They lay two thousand miles east of Moscow, in the Volga Valley, and the chief rail-heads were Kazan, Simbirsk, Samara or Saratoff. If he could get as far as Kazan, he might, with luck, find a passage on a boat down the Volga to the other places. But he would have to look quick about it, as far as the river trip went, because the Volga would soon begin to freeze.

Mr. Weinstein of the Foreign Office was not hopeful of an early train.

"I think, perhaps, your best chance would be to link up with a party of gentlemen from the A. R. A. for whom a special train to Kazan is being provided this week or next."

A special train! It sounded incredible! But Bertram knew already the mighty power of "Ara" in Russia. Had he not been fixed up by its influence from Riga to Moscow? Had he not seen the inspiring work of Mr. Cherry of Lynchburg, Virginia, with Bolshevik officials and railway porters?

The first food ship had arrived in Petrograd from New York. Groups of young Americans were already in far outposts organising committees of Russians for the administration of food relief. They had already started soup-kitchens for starving children in Petrograd and Moscow, and were pushing out supplies to Kazan and the Volga Valley with a rapidity that took away the breath of Russian officials to whom the word *Seichas* —immediately-meant the day after to-morrow, or the week after next.

The Director of "Ara," the American Relief Administration, learnt that word first from his Russian dictionary, and used it with terrible persistence to the Soviet authorities of transport, to Russian station-masters, to foremen of gangs, to engine-drivers, and any other people he could find who had something to do with getting an engine to move and trucks to follow it. He taught the word and its meaning to young Americans from the Universities of Harvard and Yale and Columbia and Virginia, who, after a glimpse of war, had volunteered for Russian Relief as the next best chance of getting in touch with life-and death. They too used that word *Seichas*, with a Western meaning and added American interpretations such as, "For the love of Mike, why don't you get a move on, you sons of bitches?" —even to high Soviet officials, and lesser authorities.

By some miracle, astounding to the Russians themselves, trains began to move from Riga to Moscow, from Moscow to the Volga, laden with food supplies for the starving children. Although in the whole of Russia there were only two thousand five hundred engines standing together, though mostly immovable, instead of seventeen thousand five hundred which moved before the war, the best of them began to get steam up, pulled out with long train-loads of trucks, did actually get somewhere, in spite of break-downs, lack of fuel. Oriental methods of delay. "*Seichas, you Tavarishes!*" said the Americans, at any kind of delay, and by that mingling of cajolery and terror which was the method of the genial Cherry, were getting some kind of efficiency into the utter chaos of Russian railways.

All these things Bertram learnt from Jemmy Hart, the American journalist, whom he had met on his first night in Moscow at the Guest House, when he appeared in his flannel shirt and pepper-and-salt trousers, with a bottle of wine in one hand and a wet sponge in the other. He had been imprisoned as a spy by the *Cheka* before the arrival of the A. R. A. Then he was let out, and treated as an honoured guest of the Soviet Republic. Hence his "billet" in the Guest House. He was on terms of familiarity with Lenin, Chicherin, Radek and other high powers, to whom he behaved as one old poker player to other experts of the artful game, with cheery cynicism, ready to call their bluff, or to double the stakes if they revealed a weak hand.

"These fellows cringe, if you treat 'em rough," he told Bertram. "When they start their highfalutin about 'the Dictatorship of the Proletariat,' ask them why they look so well fed when twenty-five million people are starving to death. Mind you, I'm not a counter-Revolutionary! I'd rather back these Bolsheviks, crooks as most of them are, than see fellows like Koltchak and Denikin trying to get Czardom back on to the necks of these poor, lousy, simple people. . . . So you want to get to the Volga? Well, come along to the Colonel and I'll fix you up. I'm going too."

The Colonel was a West Point man, with a hard, handsome, masklike face, which became human and friendly when he smiled. He was not a waster of words or time, and after a few enquiries as to Bertram's mission, agreed to give him a sleeping berth in the special train which was being provided for himself and his staff. It was due to start in a week's time. Allowing for the Russian translation of the word *seichas*, that meant two weeks at least. He would raise Hell if it was longer than that.

"You'd better have a yarn with our Doctor Weekes," he said. "What he doesn't know about bugs, typhus, dysentery, plague, and dirt, needn't worry you in this country. He'll tell you how to skip between the bad bacilli. It's worth while."

He shook hands with Bertram, and closed the interview. It was good enough. Bertram need no longer worry about Mr. Weinstein and the Soviet Foreign Office. Under the wings of "Ara" he would be carried to the Volga and find out the truth about the Famine.

In the Trubnaya market a Russian girl spoke to him in English. He recognised her as the girl who had flamed scarlet when he looked at her in the line of barterers, and afterwards looked into his eyes.

"You spoke to my mother the other day," she said. "She was afraid because a man was watching. Now she is a little ill, but would be most glad if you would have the kindness to call on her. It is long since she has spoken to an English gentleman."

Bertram said he would be glad to call. This girl's face, with her dark eyes and looped hair, would make it interesting. In any case, he was in Russia to learn the inside of life, if he could get so close. Here was a chance of knowledge.

"How shall I find your mother?" he asked.

"It is difficult," she said, smiling in a friendly way. "We do not live in the big house that was ours. But if you will meet me at any time you say, at the corner of the Arbat, where the houses were burnt down, I will take you to our home. Perhaps after dusk would be safest."

"At seven o'clock, or eight, if you like," said Bertram.

"At seven, then. My mother used to be Princess Alexandra, in the old days. My father was Prince Alexander Suvaroff. Perhaps you remember him at the Embassy in Paris? Now he is very old and weak, and broken."

"And *your* name?" asked Bertram.

"Nadia."

"Mine is Bertram Pollard."

She asked him to repeat it, and said, "I shall remember. It is very English."

"You were angry with me when I looked at you in the market-place," said Bertram.

"No, not angry. Ashamed. That was foolish. There should be no pride left in Russia. We are all on the same level now."

He wanted to talk with her, but she seemed uneasy lest they should be seen together, and slipped away from him among the crowds of peasants in the market-place.

That evening, before seven o'clock, he stood at the corner of the Arbat, by the burnt ruins of some houses. His feet were deep in snow, and heavy flakes were falling. He stamped up and down to keep his feet warm, until presently a woman's figure, snow-covered, with a fur cap tied under the chin, stood beside him.

"Good evening," she said in English. "You are a little early, I think."

"And you also, mademoiselle.

"I was so afraid of keeping you waiting in the snow."

"That was my idea too."

"Come!" she said.

They walked together up the Arbat, and then the girl touched his sleeve, and turned down a narrow sidestreet, and again out of that.

"It is not far now."

Presently she stopped in front of a dilapidated building standing back in a courtyard filled with bricks and rubbish. She opened an iron gate, and crossed the courtyard.

"You will see that we do not live in luxury, sir. You must excuse our gipsy way of life. Now we are here."

She went down a narrow corridor smelling of bad drains, and pulled a heavy curtain aside from a doorway which had lost its door. Inside was a square room with uncarpeted boards, dimly lit by an oil lamp, and barely furnished. . . . An elderly man with a white beard and moustache sat in a low chair made out of packing-cases, and lying on a truckle bed, covered with a patchwork rug, was the lady to whom Bertram had spoken in the market-place.

"Here is Mr. Pollard, mother," said the girl, as she held the curtain for Bertram to enter.

"How kind and good of you to come!" said the lady. "I so wished to speak to you the other day, and yet I was afraid! We have been through so many terrors that now we tremble at any unexpected thing."

Bertram bent over the truckle bed and kissed the delicate hand that was held up to him. Some instinct of chivalry or sentiment made him pay this homage to a lady of the old régime, lying in this dirty little room, without a relic of her former state.

"Father," said the girl, "this is the English gentleman."

He did not look like a prince, as he rose from his packing-case chair. He looked at first glance like a dirty and dissipated old fellow who had been sleeping on the Thames Embankment. His trousers and frock coat were all baggy, and patched, and grease-stained. His hands were encrusted with dirt. But he greeted Bertram with a dignity that no poverty could take away.

"It is a pleasure to meet an English gentleman again. I knew England well before the war. You will excuse our poor apartment. We are reduced to ruin, and but for my dear wife and daughter, I should have no courage left."

He held Bertram's hand with a lingering grasp, and then glanced at his own with a sardonic smile.

"We have no soap at all, and it is hard even to get water for washing purposes. We can, however, make you a little tea, if you will give us the pleasure of drinking it with us. Nadia, there is enough tea for us all?"

"Yes, father. I will make it."

"For four years," said the old man, "we have lived on bread and tea, bread and tea, bread and tea. It is hard to keep one's courage on such a diet!"

"It is better now that we can sell a few little things in the market place," said the lady. "Is it not so, Alexander? In spite of the *Cheka* we managed to hide a few treasures!"

"My dear," said the old man, "one never knows who may be listening."

He glanced nervously towards the curtain.

"It is safe to speak in English," said his wife.

"You must have suffered terribly," said Bertram.

"It is not to be put in words," said the old man. "I marvel that I have not gone mad."

They tried to put into words the story of their suffering, and told Bertram enough to let him imagine the rest. They had been turned out of their palace, like all the others, and the Prince had been put into prison before he had a chance of escape. Nadia had escaped. She was in Paris when the Revolution burst out, and very rashly, said her father, made her way back into Russia at a time when thousands were in flight from the Red Terror.

Dressed as a peasant girl, she had come back to Moscow on a troop train crowded with Red soldiers.

"It was for love of us," said her mother, stretching out her hand and touching the girl's arm. "God will reward her. We should have died without her."

"It was my duty, little mother," said Nadia, bending down and kissing her mother's forehead. "Not for a second have I regretted coming back."

"In spite of all our misery!" said the old gentleman.

Nadia turned to Bertram with a smile.

"My father and mother make too much of my coming back. Even without them I should have returned. I am a Russian. This is my country. With the Russian people I suffer, and if need be, die. I am sure all English people would do the same."

Bertram thought of the Countess Lydia and her sister, and of all the Russian émigrés in London and Paris, living in luxury, dancing, gambling. Not doing much on behalf of their own folk, except in support of counter-revolutions and invasions, plots and intrigues for the overthrow of the Bolshevik régime, which had only increased the ruin and agony of the Russian people, and intensified the Terror. He marvelled at this girl who had come back into the midst of that Terror when the others had all been escaping across the frontiers.

He looked at her now, as she heated the samovar, in a shabby frock, in boots that would have been slung over a garden wall by any English tramp, yet moving with elegance and a natural grace. She had taken off her fur cap and jacket. Her black hair, falling in a loop about her ears, framed her white face like a Helleu etching. She had very "liquid" eyes, with long dark lashes, and a broad forehead, like most Russian women, but with sharper cheekbones than the Slav type, and thin red lips. About twenty-five, he guessed, and delicate from what the Germans called *unternährung* —semi-starvation. She was aware of his eyes upon her, perhaps read the admiration in them, and a faint blush crept under her skin.

"How long did you remain a prisoner, sir?" asked Bertram.

The old man raised his hands.

"Two terrible years. I did not wash all that time or get a change of linen. It was worse than death. I used to smile when the *Cheka* examined me, and other prisoners wept before I left the cell, because they thought I was to be taken out and shot. 'In the next world,' I used to say, 'I shall not need a change of linen.' "

"I think they pitied my husband," said Princess Alexandra. "He had been a Liberal always, and very generous to the poor."

"I was a friend of Tolstoy," said the old man. "I corresponded with Kropotkin. I was even a little of a revolutionary, believing in the need of liberty in Russia. Alas, the Revolution has killed all the liberty we had, and the tyranny of Lenin is worse than that of Ivan the Terrible."

He spoke the words in a whisper, leaning towards Bertram, with his hand to his mouth.

Nadia handed Bertram a cup of tea, and then sat on a stool by his side.

"My father has abandoned all hope for Russia," she said. "That is natural, after so much suffering. But because I am young, I still believe that out of all this agony some good will come. Russia has been purged by fire. There was great corruption in the time of the Emperor. The Court was very vicious-you have said so many times, father! —and young people of the rich class were lazy and luxurious. Not one of them did any kind of work. From babyhood they were petted and spoilt. They thought of nothing but gaiety and sensuality. Now we younger people who stayed in Russia have learnt to work, and to weep. We have been hungry with the people. We have made our hands as coarse as theirs. We shall be all the better for it, perhaps, and help to build a New Russia on nobler lines, some day. Do you not think so, darling mother?"

The old lady's eyes filled with tears.

"I belong to the Past. All my memories are there. I dare not look forward to the future-My poor Russia!"

"Our poor Russia!" echoed her husband. "In the hands of those who are murdering the very souls of our people by their evil propaganda."

Nadia spoke again, very gently, to avoid any hurt to her father and mother.

"The soul of our people will never die. It is a great, simple, and generous soul, as I know now by working among the peasants. Presently this régime will change. It is already changing. It will become moderate. Russia will get new liberties. There will be a greater happiness than before."

Suvaroff shook his head.

"Russia is famine-stricken and diseased. For the sins of those who rule us, and for our own sins in the past, we shall perish as a civilisation."

"Never!" said Nadia, bravely. "Russia will live with greater glory, more enlightened, with a people worthy of great liberties. It is my faith. Without that I should die."

There was a moment's silence, as heavy footsteps strode down the stone corridor, and suddenly the curtain was drawn back. A young man stood there, in the uniform of the Red Army.

For a second or two Bertram was startled and afraid. There flashed into his mind the thought that perhaps his visit here had led to trouble for this little family of the old régime. He was relieved when the old lady smiled and said:

"My son! . . . Come in, Alexis. We have an English visitor."

The young man saluted, and then shook hands with Bertram, and spoke in perfectly accurate English.

"Delighted to meet you, sir. My father and mother told me they had asked for the honour of a visit from you."

He sat on the edge of his sister's stool and put his arm round her waist affectionately.

"Well, Nadia!"

The old lady seemed to read the thought passing through Bertram's mind.

"You are surprised that we have a son in the Red Army? It is either that or death for our young men."

The boy, Alexis-he seemed a year or two younger than Nadia-looked down at his uniform with a smile.

"It's not only fear of death that makes me wear these clothes. I'm a Russian. I help to defend my soil from all invaders. Does not honour and a decent code of patriotism require that, sir?"

He asked the question of Bertram, who did not answer.

"We think," said Prince Alexander Suvaroff slowly, and with a touch of embarrassment, "that England, and other countries, made a mistake in supporting the attacks of men like Wrangel and Denikin. Bad as the Bolsheviks are, as God knows, the leaders of the White Armies were, perhaps, equally corrupt. My son expresses the thought of the younger generation."

"It is mine, certainly," said Nadia.

The son only stayed a few minutes. He had just called in to have the pleasure of meeting the Englishman, and to kiss his father and mother. Soon after his going, Bertram rose to take his leave.

"But you will never find your way back!" cried Princess Alexandra.

"I will guide him to the Arbat," said her daughter.

In spite of Bertram's protests, she put on her fur cap and coat again, and waited while he said good night to her father and mother. The old man rose again from his packing-case.

"If you would call upon us now and then, it would be a charity, sir. We know nothing of the outer world."

"With pleasure!" said Bertram.

He kissed the old lady's hand again, and at this sign of regard and sympathy her eyes moistened.

"You have seen the old régime in their poor hovels," she said. "The others are like us or worse."

"I have seen their courage," said Bertram.

"Many of my friends have starved to death," said the Princess. "It is Nadia and Alexis who have saved us. My daughter is a medical student. They still get rations, and she brings home most of them to us. Without that we should not be alive. . . . Come again, dear sir!"

"But not in the daylight," said the old man, with a hint of fear. "My name is still a cause of suspicion and dislike."

Out into the snow again Bertram walked with Nadia. Once she stumbled over a snow-drift in the courtyard, and Bertram said, "Take my arm, won't you? It's safer."

She laid her hand on his arm, and said, "You are very kind."

"I marvel at your courage," he said, presently.

She answered with a kind of surprise.

"Without courage, what is life? I am young. It is only the old who are afraid of new adventures."

She told him about her medical studies at the University of Moscow. All the classes were at night, because the students worked during the day to supplement their rations.

"You take yours home," he said. "How do you manage to get enough to eat?"

"A very little does for me," she said. "I am strong."

She had finished her studies now, and was fully qualified. Her ambition was to go to the famine district and join the medical staff at Kazan who were fighting the typhus. They had asked for her, but it was difficult to travel.

"How will your father and mother manage without you?" he asked, and she told him that Alexis had just been promoted to the Red Army Staff. He would be able to get better food for them, and protect them, because of his service to the state.

"I am going to Kazan," said Bertram. "Why not come in the same train, if I can help you? The Americans are running it, and they would welcome your help."

She was excited by the possibility, and begged him to speak a word for her; and then, believing she had asked too much of him, pleaded for forgiveness for putting him to so much trouble.

"It is my eagerness to do some work for Russia which makes me forget my manners," she said.

He put aside the idea of trouble, and had only one doubt in trying to get her a place in the train to Kazan.

"They tell me typhus is a scourge there, and very dangerous."

"Of course," said the girl. "But you are going, are you not? You are not afraid, because you also want to be of service to our poor people. Why, then, should I who am a Russian, be afraid to go?"

He found no answer to that, but thought only of her devotion to her people and her unselfishness.

He said something about "self-sacrifice," and she answered by words that he afterwards remembered.

"It is the only way of happiness, don't you think?"

"I don't know," he said, "I'm an egoist."

She refused to believe that.

"You have come out here to help poor Russia. Even at the risk of your life. That is not egoism."

"Mixed with egoism," he said. "To acquire knowledge for myself. To kill boredom. To heal what I'm pleased to call a broken heart! Infernal selfishness-all that!"

"You have a broken heart?" she asked, with great surprise.

The snow was falling on them at the corner of the Arbat where they stood, and they both wore white crowns and mantles, but paid no heed to it, because of this talk.

"I call it that in a romantic, sentimentalising way. My wife ran away from me not long ago. It hurt damnably. Wounded pride, perhaps. One never knows."

"I am sorry," she said gravely. "You loved her very much?"

"Enormously, for a time. I was very young."

He laughed uneasily. The old wound still hurt.

"Love is difficult," she said. "So it seems, from novels I have read, and people I have met. I have had no experience myself. . . ."

"How is that?"

"Hunger, poverty, and terror do not seem to encourage the love instinct, except in a brutal way. Anyhow, it has left me alone. It is no doubt a pleasant thing. Something one ought not to miss in life."

She spoke without any embarrassment or self-consciousness, but as a child, simply, before the mysteries of life. Yet she was not a child, but a woman who had lived through bloody Revolution and great brutalities. Her simplicity in regard to love was not through ignorance, but inexperience.

"I should be glad to love you," she said, "if it would help your broken heart at all. It would be very nice for me."

She made this astonishing offer with the same simplicity and sincerity. It was as though she offered to bind up some wound.

The snow was heavy upon them, and in whirling flakes around them. He could hardly see her face or figure. They were alone in a world of whiteness in the ruin of Moscow.

"It's good of you," he said. "I shall be glad of your comradeship."

"It is the same thing," she said. "Comradeship-love-service together-understanding. That would be good to have."

"The best things in life," said Bertram. "The only things worth living for."

"You think so too? Well, then it is a promise between us?"

"A hope," he said.

She told him she must be going back, and held out her gloved hand. It was wet with the snow, when he put it to his lips.

"You are very kind," she said.

She turned from him, and in a moment was lost to him in the whirl of snowflakes.

"Extraordinary!" said Bertram to himself, aloud, as he groped his way across the Arbat Square in the direction of the Kremlin's great walls. He felt less lonely, though he was alone in Moscow.

"It is the same thing," she had said, "comradeship-love-service together-understanding."

Comradeship. Well, even without love, it would be good. He needed it enormously, from a woman, as well as from Christy. Why from a woman? Why had Janet Welford's comradeship been so much better than any man's? Perhaps women understood better, with more tenderness for the weakness of men. Or was it just the lure of sex? Impossible to tell. Why bother to find out? Why not accept life without analysis, as simply as Nadia's offer of love? It was the second time he had been offered woman's love since Joyce had gone from him. The pretty German girl had wanted to go with him, and he had laughed at her, and played the prig. Was he always to refuse the chance of human affection, woman's tenderness, his spiritual and physical hunger for such companionship? A voice whispered in his ear, "Loyalty to Joyce! . . . Loyalty! . . . Loyalty!"

"No," he said, answering this call of conscience, "I've been loyal long enough, by God! And now I'm absolved."

LV

He invited Nadia to dinner one night in the little restaurant in the Arbat, and she accepted with the permission of her mother and father, who saw no harm in it, but only a little danger from secret police.

Nadia laughed at that peril. She was under the protection of "Ara," she said, and the *Cheka* could not touch her. That was true. Bertram had taken Dr. Weekes to the gipsy-like room in which Prince Alexander lived with his family, and he had been shocked by their dire poverty. He knew their name in Russian history, and their former palace in Petrograd, now used as a soup-kitchen by the American Relief.

A cheery young American of the South, with a slow, drawling speech and quiet manners, he was a man of delicate physique who seemed to have worn himself out in service to a suffering world. He was chief medical officer of "Ara," and had devoted himself to the hunger-stricken and diseased children of Austria, Germany, Poland, and Armenia since the ending of war. Nadia had lit his eyes with enthusiasm for her courage. "Some girl," was his verdict, and his word was enough to secure her appointment as interpreter and woman secretary on the "Ara" staff.

"There's a heap to do for a girl like that in Kazan," he said. "Our boys there are clamouring for interpreters and secretaries. But I fancy I've got a special job for her, where her medical training will count. We'll see about that later, when we get to Kazan."

So that part of the programme was fixed. She was to travel with them to Kazan, with two other ladies selected by the Colonel for office duty in that city, and she was very happy at the thought, in spite of the tragic nature of the adventure ahead. She had the zeal of Dr. Weekes himself who was restless until he reached the famine district.

"My job is with typhus," he said. "I've declared a Holy War against it. It's my personal vendetta. Where typhus is worst, there I go. One day, of course, it's going to get me! But that's the fortune of war, and meanwhile it's a good game."

Nadia had the same kind of philosophy, it seemed.

"I want to help Russia. The best way I can help is to make use of my medical training where the people suffer most. There's a dreadful dearth of doctors, and the poor peasants are hopelessly ignorant of the most primitive rules of health. I can teach them, wash them, help them to kill their lice."

In the restaurant of the Arbat, Bertram was received with friendly greetings from the husband and wife, and Katia. They were amazed and delighted to find Nadia with him. The elderly man with white hair and a pointed beard kissed her hand respectfully, as the daughter of Prince Alexander Suvaroff, but Katia flung her arms round Nadia's neck and kissed her on both cheeks.

"You know this English gentleman, then!" cried the lady of the restaurant. "Doubtless you were old friends in England before the war!"

"Not old friends," said Nadia, "but good comrades now."

"Do not use that word comrade!" said the lady. "It has been debased. *Tavarish! tavarish! tavarish!* I am sick of it!"

"In English it is better," said Nadia. "It has its old meaning still."

She and Bertram sat at a little table in the corner. Katia waited on them delightedly, kissing Nadia's neck, or hair, or hand, every time she came to the table. And Nadia was joyful because a white cloth was spread on the table, and there were cut glasses for their cider, which was the only drink, and plates without a crack in them.

"It is like a fairy-tale," she said. "Not for four years have I sat down with snow-white linen to the board."

Bertram wondered that she could endure so long a time of squalor, after her life in great mansions, surrounded by luxury from childhood. Did she not sometimes crave to escape from it to Paris or London, like so many others?

She shook her head.

"I want to see this through," she told him. "It has been a great adventure of the soul. Terrible, but educating. You have been a soldier. You know what our men called 'the front line spirit?' I have been in the front line, the danger zone, and have nothing but contempt for those who fled to safe places in the war. Except the old and feeble, and the very young."

A great adventure of the soul? Yes, there was something in that. Life at its bleakest and barest like a Polar expedition to which men like Shackleton and Scott had gone so blithely. For him also, this Russian visit was to be a great adventure of the soul. Perhaps with this girl who offered him her love! Queer that! It wouldn't be bad to "see it through" with her. He had no other call now, no kind of human tie elsewhere. Why not see it through in Russia as well as anywhere in the world? It was cut off from the rest of the world almost as completely as Robinson Crusoe's island. A shipwrecked country of a hundred and fifty million people, with himself among them!

They talked of the Bolshevik régime. He denounced it as the greatest tyranny on earth, the most brutal type of Government ever devised by evil minds.

She shook her head at that.

"Not quite so bad. They have done some good. They have taught the people to read and write-millions of them. They have fed the children first-always."

Bertram was amazed at her tolerance.

"Surely you don't defend these people?"

"No," she said, "but I understand them. They have been cruel, but through fear. They were afraid of counter-revolutions, plots of every kind. They stamped out their enemies lest the Revolution should be defeated and Czardom brought back. So it was in France, under Robespierre, was it not?"

"This Communism!" said Bertram. "It seems to me an outrage against human nature. It attempts to crush the individual instinct which is the strongest thing in life."

"Yes," she answered, "that is true, I am sure. But the individual must subordinate his instincts to the good of the Commonwealth. One must not forget that Communism was killed by the peasants-and alas, they too were greedy and cruel when they had the only source of wealth."

"Is there any hope at all for human nature?" asked Bertram.

She looked at him with surprise in her dark eyes.

"Do you doubt it? Oh, surely not! Out of all our ignorance and agony some knowledge will come for the future race. You and I are learning. Others will know because of our endeavours, and our failure, and our love. I am glad to think that."

"How wise you are!" he said, without irony. "I am bewildered by life, and without any certain faith. You seem so sure!"

"I am Russian," she said, laughing. "We talk and talk on abstract ideas. We do nothing worth doing. *Nichevo!*"

Katia came up again, and sat beside Nadia. A party of young men came into the restaurant and sat talking quietly, and drinking coffee. The ex-painter to the Imperial Court was washing up dishes behind the counter.

"I must learn Russian!" said Bertram.

Katia clapped her hands.

"Nadia will teach you!"

England seemed a million miles away. Joyce was in another planet. Nadia's black eyes were very kind to him.

LVI

It was a six days' journey to Kazan, and seemed interminable. The "special train" was not so magnificent as its name, but exactly similar to the one from Riga-in discomfort, and in lice. The American Colonel arrived with a young man acting as a kind of A. D. C., and with Dr. Weekes, two other young men of the American Relief Administration, a Russian officer of the Red Army, detailed as interpreter, the two Russian ladies appointed as secretaries, and Nadia. Jemmy Hart, the newspaper correspondent, joined up with Bertram, and two officers of the *Cheka* accompanied the party, nominally as police protection, but really for political espionage.

Christy came down to the station to say farewell. He revealed a hint of anxiety about Bertram.

"Don't take too many risks, Major."

He had an idea that he might not stay much longer in Moscow. He would leave Russia to Bertram. Probably their next meeting-place would be Berlin or London.

In his casual way he mentioned an exciting item of news.

"Janet has come out to Berlin. I may go and see her there."

Janet Welford in Berlin! What was she doing there?

"Having a look round," said Christy. "Getting a background for a new novel. . . . There's another reason."

He mentioned the other reason in a "by the way" kind of tone.

"I asked her to meet me there. Now that my wife's dead, there's no reason of consanguinity, affinity, or spiritual relationship why these two persons should not be joined in holy matrimony. If Janet's willing, which is very doubtful."

"Well, here's luck!" said Bertram.

He spoke the words heartily, and gripped Christy's hand, but, at the back of his brain, as it were, was a sense of envy. Envy of Christy, his best friend! Inconceivable, that-and yet there was the thought nagging at him. Janet had been very kind to him in her rooms at Battersea Park. She had once made his heart thump by a cry of regret that they had not met and married before Joyce came along. What were her words? He remembered them.

"A pity, Sir Faithful, that you didn't marry me instead of Joyce! I understand you better. And you were my first Dream Knight, in the days when you kissed me in Kensington Gardens."

He leaned out of the carriage window, and gripped Christy's hand again.

"Give my love to Janet. Tell her that I've killed self-pity. She'll understand!"

"Take care of yourself!" said Christy, and then sloped away from the Kazansky station, with his pipe in his mouth.

The journey began, and continued, day after day, with many halts in the middle of Russian forests and the open countryside. Snow lay heavily on the branches of fir-trees, and thick on the ground, so that a traveller's eyes tired of the white monotony. Every twenty versts or so they reached a Russian village, with its low roofed wooden houses, surrounded by high stockades. Peasants were shovelling snow to make pathways to their village. They gathered in the station yards to stare at the train, kept back from too near approach by soldiers of the Red Army who looked half frozen and half starved. In many stations were refugee trains without engines, with snow up to the axle wheels of their closed trucks, in which families were densely crowded, lying together all hugger-mugger, for warmth's sake. It seemed as though they had been there for months. There was no apparent prospect of these trains ever moving. Those who died were buried in pits by the railway track. Across the flat snow-fields there were here and there processions of men, women and children, crawling like ants on the march, black against the whiteness of their way. They, too, were refugees from Famine-without much hope ahead, thought Bertram, remembering The End of the Journey, in Petrograd. He wondered how many would lie down to die in the snow.

"They are wonderful in endurance," said Nadia, to whom he put the question, as they stood together in the corridor, looking out of window. "In every village they pass they get a bit of bread from those who can ill spare it. So they live from place to place. Those who are strong."

He had many talks like this with Nadia in the corridor, or in her compartment, with the two other ladies, belonging, like herself, to the old régime, once ladies in waiting of the Imperial Court. The Colonel of the A. R. A. had provided food for the party, mostly tinned stuff which Dr. Weekes and Bertram, appointing themselves cooks, heated up in enamel saucepans over tins of solid alcohol. It made the time pass, and was more comforting than cold food.

At night, in the darkness of the corridor, Nadia stood by his side, and sometimes they held hands, like children when the lights are out.

They talked of the mystery of life and death, the chances of world peace, the future of civilisation. Strange topics of conversation between a young man and woman! But travelling through Russia after war and revolution, they seemed the only subjects worth discussing.

Dr. Weekes joined them, and told stories of his experiences in Armenia and the Balkans-tragic tales of widespread famine, disease, death. He, too, balanced the possibilities of Western civilisation. Disease, unless checked by international effort, might wipe it out in Central Europe. It had already made deep tracks in fields of child life. Another war, anything like the last, would so weaken Europe, apart from its own massacres, that plague and pestilence might do more destruction than Attila and his Huns in the old days of the Roman Empire.

"You and I," he said, turning to Nadia with his slow smile, "are two of the most important people in the world. We're disease-killers, apostles of sanitation. But the odds against us are millions to one."

"The fewer men, the greater share of honour," said Nadia.

She had a surprising knowledge of literature, Russian, French, and English, and, better than such knowledge, a keen intelligence and candour of outlook which made her opinion astonishing for so young a woman.

But Bertram admired her, not for her cleverness of opinion, but for her spiritual quality and entire absence of self-consciousness. Delicate as she was, the daughter of an aristocracy to which physical labour had been abhorrent, she stooped to dirty work with a sense of beauty in its labour, and Bertram was horrified to find her swilling down the filthy lavatories before the rest of the travellers had stirred from their bunks.

"For God's sake," he said, "leave that to the *provodnik*. It's his job, not yours."

"It's a job he neglects," she said, smiling. "As one of the medical staff of 'Ara,' cleanliness and sanitation are in my department. The smell from this place is terrible."

"All the more reason for you to avoid it," said Bertram.

She shook her head.

"In the Famine district there will be worse smells and worse dirt, and lice everywhere. If I wanted to avoid them, I should not be here."

"You are wonderful!" he said.

"A simple Russian woman," she answered. "Why do you think me wonderful?"

There were other people in the train who thought her wonderful when Bertram told them of that early morning act. The Colonel and Dr. Weekes were filled with admiration.

"By God," said the Colonel, "if all the Russian people were like that young woman, this country wouldn't be plague-stricken with Bolsheviks and bugs!"

At night, in their candle-lit carriage, the Colonel and the Doctor, and Jemmy Hart, the newspaper man, and the Colonel's A. D. C., or "pup," as Hart called him, played poker with Russian roubles. They gambled fiercely, raising the stakes by tens of thousands, with a limit of a hundred thousand, as though possessed of untold wealth. But at the end of the long evening's play, no one had lost or gained more than a few dollars in American rates of exchange.

During these poker games Bertram went into the dusky corridor again to stand by Nadia. They were left alone, for the other two Russian ladies went early to their bunks. The train crawled slowly, or halted for hours while new fuel was stacked in the engine. The moon rose and flooded the white landscape and the snow-capped farmsteads and the laden boughs.

"Russia is like a dead body under its white shroud," said Nadia.

"It seems as lonely as an undiscovered land," said Bertram.

She asked him to tell her a little of his life, so that she might know him more. He told her only of the things that had happened, the war, his marriage, the death of the child, Digby's murder in Ireland, his mother's death, his separation from Joyce. He was not good at self-analysis, and too much of an Englishman to attempt it. Yet she seemed to understand more than he told her.

"Russia does not hold all the unhappiness of life," she said. "You have crowded too much suffering into a few years. It has wounded your spirit. You feel broken, and perhaps a little resentful of Fate. So much bad luck after the strain of war!"

"I'm not whining," said Bertram. "Your courage through more dreadful things rebukes my cowardice."

"You are not cowardly," she told him. "I think you will be very strong and brave when your wound is healed. You have the eyes of leadership. One day you will help to lead your country in thought or action."

He laughed at her, but she was sure.

One thing she said in those night talks as the train went crawling through the white wilderness, gave him a glimpse of a spiritual passion in her soul.

"I hated ugliness, and pain, and dirt. As a child these things were all hidden from me. As a young girl I was surrounded with beauty and illusion. Now I want to get deeper and deeper into the misery of the people. I want to be with them in their pain and their filth. I want to share their worst agony. It is to pay back to them by the suffering of my body and spirit for all the cruelties of my ancestors. If you will read Russian history, you will find my father's name-though not my father-attached to acts which kept the peasants enslaved, and brutalised them. The old régime is suffering now for the sins of its fathers. It is right that we should be punished."

"I don't believe in that doctrine," said Bertram. "We should be punished for our own acts, perhaps-though we are the children of heredity-but not for the crimes of those who gave us life."

"It is the Law," she said. "The Greeks knew it. Fate pursues us. It is in the Christian faith. The sins of the fathers shall be visited upon the children."

"It's unfair," said Bertram. "Damned unfair."

"Alas, it is true," she said. "We must do good for our children's sake."

"I had a child who died, as I have told you," said Bertram. "Sometimes I'm glad. The world is too cruel."

"Not too cruel for those who have courage," she said.

She spoke of her desire to have a child.

"Perhaps, if we love each other, you and I may have a child, dear sir. That would give me great happiness."

Bertram was profoundly moved by those words, spoken with such simplicity.

"I am a stranger to you," he said. "You do not know my weakness and my character."

"I knew you," she said, "when you looked my way in the market place."

That night they clasped hands in the darkness of the corridor.

"My Russian comrade!" he said to her.

"Dear friend of Russia and of me," she answered.

LVII

The city of Kazan was buried in snow, frozen hard, and glittering on its surface as though strewn with myriads of diamonds. It was a little Moscow, more Oriental, less ruined by street fighting, strangely beautiful with its gilt-domed churches and Russian mansions, and wooden hovels, all canopied in snow. It had been a rich city before the Revolution. Many great nobles had had summer houses here. Its market received the wealth of the Volga and merchandise from the Far East. A third of its population was Tartar, and under the Soviet régime it had been made the capital of a new state called the Tartar Republic, subject to Moscow, but with a certain independence for local business.

The Tartar type was striking, in its contrast to the blue-eyed, yellow-bearded peasants amidst whom they dwelt, and Bertram, staring at the tall, lean men with Mongolian cheekbones, leathery skin, and straight black hair, thought of Ghengis Khan and his hordes of men like this, who had swept across Europe in the Middle Ages to the very gates of Vienna.

Kazan was now on the edge of the famine. Hunger was creeping about the city itself, though even here there was meat to be had in the market for those who had money to buy it. The peasants along the Volga valley were killing the last of their cows, for lack of fodder, and the flesh was sent up to Kazan by the last boats that could make the journey before the Volga froze. After that there would be no more meat, as now there was no grain, no milk, and but small stocks of bread and potatoes. Soviet officials were still getting rations direct from Moscow, but that system was to be abandoned, except for a favoured few, owing to the "New Economic Laws" which had been framed mainly because the means of rationing had broken down.

The Colonel of the A. R. A. and his party were met at the station with sleighs by four or five young Americans, in heavy fur coats and Tartar caps, remarkably cheery, in spite of the frightful picture they painted of the local conditions. They had established the first food kitchens in Kazan, and had pushed out the first relief to the villages beyond.

"What's the situation?" asked the Colonel.

Cyrus Sims, a young man looking like a Bolshevik bandit, until he pulled off his shaggy cap with ear-flaps and revealed a good American head, typical of Harvard, gave a few preliminary facts to "put the Colonel wise," as he called it, before an interview with the President of the Tartar Republic.

"The situation, sir? Well, briefly, these people are waiting for death. They can't see any escape, except by our help, which won't amount to much for some time to come, as you know. We've undertaken to feed fifteen hundred children within three weeks from now. Sounds good. There's a child population in this state of one million seven hundred thousand, all hungry, and mostly starving. Child population, you understand, sir! Of course we're not going to feed adults. They'll die. The Volga's trying to freeze. Another week or two and no boats can pass. That'll mean sleigh transport to the starving villages. We shall want three thousand five hundred horses to feed those fifteen hundred babes. And the horses are dropping dead along the roads. No fodder. Certain supplies have come down from Moscow by Soviet authority. Potatoes mostly. They're rotting on the barges."

"Why, in God's name?" asked the Colonel.

"Same reason, sir. Dearth of horses for sleigh transport."

"We shall have to get a move on," said the Colonel. "Keep the horses alive. There's lots of fodder to be had if we raise Hell. . . . Are you well billeted?"

"Sure," said the young American, resuming his disguise as a Bolshevik bandit, and tying the ear-flaps of his Tartar cap under his chin. "Better come along, Colonel, and get warm."

The whole party was crowded into sleighs, and set off in a procession, with a merry jingling of sleigh-bells. Dr. Weekes and Bertram had Nadia for their fellow traveller, and the doctor pulled the rug over her and packed the straw about her feet.

"It's as cold as Calgary," he said, "and that's the coldest place I know."

"In Russia," said Nadia, "our blood is a mixture of fire and ice."

"That's a darned queer mixture," said the doctor. "Unknown to chemical science."

"It's the secret of Russian history," she answered.

Peasants halted on the foot-walks to stare at the passing sleighs. Their faces were haggard, and their eyes looked dead.

"There is hunger here," said Nadia. "In Moscow we haven't enough to eat, but here they starve."

The sleighs halted outside a marble-fronted house with many windows, and Nadia gave a little cry of surprise.

"I know this house! It belonged to my father's brother. I was here as a child, with my mother and Alexis. My uncle was the Governor of Kazan, and very kind to me. They shot him dead in the street one day."

Bertram looked at her, and saw how she was stirred with the remembrance of old days before the agony of Russia had touched her life. For a moment her dark eyes filled with tears, but when she stepped down from the sledge, taking his hand to help her, she spoke brave words.

"How lucky I am to be with those who have come to rescue Russia!"

There were log fires burning in all the rooms of the house, and little camp beds in most of them.

"A good billet," said the Colonel. "You boys know how to grab at luxury."

"Not much luxury, sir, and plenty of bugs," said the young man named Sims, who was in command of the "outfit" at Kazan. "This place was used for refugees, until we came. It's still a menagerie."

"Work for me," said Dr. Weekes. "I'm the world's light-weight vermin-killer."

The Russian ladies were invited to lunch, but a special billet had been arranged for them in a house near by.

"A good scheme," said the Colonel. "We don't want any scandals for the Hearst Press. And I can see you boys have already fallen in love with my Princess."

"She's a peach," said one of them. "But we're too busy for amorous dalliance, Colonel."

The Colonel winked at Bertram.

"You see the virtue of the A. R. A.? Marvellous, don't you think? Almost incredible!"

Perhaps his cold clear eyes had perceived the comradeship of Bertram and "his" princess. If so, he was discreet, and made no personal remarks, and it was by his suggestion that Nadia was asked to go with Bertram and Dr. Weekes to inspect the hospitals and homes for abandoned children in Kazan.

"You'd better take the Princess with you, Doctor. I've faith in a woman's eyes, and anyhow, I'm going to put her in charge of the local committee for child-feeding, so she must get about and see things. You'd like to join them, Pollard?"

It was Nadia who acted as interpreter, and it was by her side, getting courage from her, that Bertram went into places which made him cry out to God in his heart, and filled him with horror, and turned his stomach so that he could hardly prevent himself from vomiting, as he had done in the barrack yard at Petrograd.

The children's homes seemed worst of all. In the first of them were fifteen hundred who had been abandoned by their parents.

"Why abandoned?" asked Bertram.

Nadia bent down to one child, a girl of twelve or so, stark naked, and so emaciated that all her ribs were visible beneath the tight-drawn skin. Word by word she translated the child's monologue, told with the gravity of an old woman.

"She says her father belonged to Lubimovka. Once his barns were filled with grain and he had twenty cows. When the drought came, the standing wheat was burnt black in the fields. Red soldiers came and took the grain from the barn, all but a very little. Then the cows died, one by one. There was no food in the house. This little one had six brothers and sisters. Three of them died, because they had no food. The mother wept very much when they died. The father did not weep, until one day he took his children for a long, long walk away from Lubimovka to the town of Tetiushi. Then he said, 'Wait here a little while, my children. Perhaps God will send his angels with food for you.' And then he wept, and walked away. They waited a long while, and he did not come back. And God did not come with His angels. So they lay down to die. It was little Anna that died. The two others were fed by the market people in Tetiushi, and then put on a train that came to Kazan. So they were brought to this house, with many other children who were like themselves. They had bread once a day, and potato soup. They would be glad to have some clothes, because it is very cold."

Nadia turned to Bertram, and her eyes were shining with tears.

"This little one knows why her father abandoned her. It was because he loved her, and could not bear to hear her crying out for food when there was nothing in the house."

"Why are these children naked?" asked Bertram. "They will perish of cold in this house. It's an ice-well."

Nadia spoke to a sad-eyed man in a linen coat.

"He says it is the only way of keeping down typhus. When the children come in their clothes are crawling with vermin. He takes off their clothes and burns them. But there are no means of replacing them."

"Surely they could make fires in the house?"

Nadia shook her head.

"It is impossible to get fuel."

"There are great woods around Kazan."

"There is no means of transport for the timber."

"Men could haul it."

"The men are weak, he says, and despair makes them lazy. And anyhow, he could not pay for their labour."

They walked through room after room, all crowded with children. Their heads had been shaved, and in their nakedness they lay huddled close together, so thin, with such deep-sunk eyes, that they were unlike children of the human race, but like a tribe of white monkeys, clinging to each other for warmth in a frozen world. They did not play, or chatter, or laugh. They were utterly silent, with drooping heads, and a terrible old sadness in their little sunken eyes. Because there was no fuel, there was no hot water, and because there was no hot water, there was no cleanliness. A frightful stench pervaded the rooms. Some of the children lay in filth. . . .

"To-morrow I shall come here and do some work," said Nadia. "The good man means well, but he has no energy."

Dr. Weekes made some notes in a little book.

"Blankets. Clothes. Soap."

He whispered a warning to Bertram.

"Don't brush against the door-posts as you pass. They're alive with vermin."

They passed into another room, where there was row after row of children lying on the bare boards, in a kind of feverish sleep, with their heads flopping from side to side.

"Typhus," said Nadia.

Among the children was a girl of about twenty, in a cotton frock. She lay amidst a group of them, with one arm over their naked bodies, sleeping, with a flame of colour on her face.

Nadia spoke to the man in the linen coat, and then turned to Bertram and Dr. Weekes.

"It is the Countess Narishkin. She was a nurse here. Yesterday she developed the typhus fever. There is no kind of hope for the poor child."

She knelt down on the bare boards, and put one arm under the girl's head and raised it a little, smoothing her hair back.

"Princess," said Dr. Weekes, sternly, "you know enough about typhus to avoid unnecessary risks."

"That is true," said Nadia. "For the sake of others."

She rose from her kneeling position, laying the girl's head very gently on the boards again.

"I have some medicine," said the young doctor, "I will give her an injection this afternoon. But I'm afraid —"

He looked at Nadia, and she said "Yes," understanding him.

That afternoon, using their sleigh, they went to twelve such homes for abandoned children, and in each of them were the same scenes of stricken childhood, and in each of them the same amount of fever, of vermin, of filth, and of stench.

"God!" said Bertram, at last, "It's too awful. Can you bear to see any more, Nadia?"

She put her hand on his arm.

"It is only the beginning of the things we shall see. It makes you suffer, dear comrade! That is good. You will write such pictures that the world will be moved to tears and charity. They will forgive the sins of Russia because of all this agony. By your words of truth and pity you will help to save those little ones."

"I'll try," said Bertram.

It was a dedication.

In the great hospital of Kazan, once famous in the history of medical science, they plunged deeper into human misery. It was crowded with men and women suffering from every kind of disease, but mostly from typhus and dysentery caused by vermin and hunger and weakness. Whatever their disease, the patients lay huddled together, not on beds, for they had been burnt for fuel, but on the bare boards. They had a few blankets, but not many, which covered four at a time, two lying one way and two the other. There was no heat in the stoves.

Dr. Weekes questioned the chief medical officer, who looked in a dying condition, utterly pallid, and with hardly the strength to walk about his wards.

"Have you any drugs?"

"Very few!"

"Any anæsthetics-chloroform-morphia?"

"None."

"Any castor-oil?"

"A tiny drop."

"And disinfectants?"

"No."

"Any soap?"

"Not for two years."

"Any bandages, cotton wool, surgical dressings?"

"None, sir."

"My God!" said Dr. Weekes, and it was the first word of dismay that escaped his lips.

In ward after ward they saw the huddled victims of pestilence and famine. Their clothes had not been burnt, like those in the children's homes, and they were hunting vermin ceaselessly in their sheepskins and rags. It was difficult to give a guess at the age or class of these people. Young girls looked like old women. Young men had the worn, wrinkled look of extreme age. They were all reduced to a dead level of misery and squalor, and dirt; though among them, said Nadia, who spoke with many, were women of education and even of learning. She went about among the beds. Some of the women lying on the boards, raised themselves a little and kissed her hands.

A strange scene happened downstairs, as they were leaving. The news had gone round among the nurses that an officer of "Ara" had come to inspect the hospital, with means of help. Twenty of them suddenly came clamouring round Dr. Weekes, all crying together, all stretching out their hands to him, like a Greek chorus, with burning eyes in white faces. It was almost dark in the passage there, and Bertram was alarmed by those women's eyes and by the almost savage anguish of their voices.

"What do they say?" asked Dr. Weekes, turning to Nadia. "What's their trouble, anyhow?"

"They say they are starving. They implore you to send them bread. How can they nurse the sick, they say, when they are so weak and famished? Only last week two of them died of dysentery, caused by hunger. Soon they will all be dead, they say, unless they get some food."

"Tell them," said Dr. Weekes, "that the A. R. A. will send them food, though we are here only to feed the children of Russia."

He turned to Bertram with troubled eyes.

"I think the Colonel will stand for that pledge. We can't let these women starve."

It was Nadia who translated the promise to them, and as though she were the Lady Bountiful who had been the means of rescue, they pressed round her, kissing her hands and her dress, until she laughed and protested, and pointed to the doctor as their champion. He hurried out with deep embarrassment, because one of them seized his hands and tried to kiss them.

That night, as a strange contrast to those scenes, Bertram went to the opera of Kazan with the Colonel and his little crowd. They were playing Boris Goudonoff to a crowded house of young Russians, who were warmly clad, and, in appearance, well fed.

"How is it possible that these people have enough to eat, and enjoy themselves," asked the Colonel, "while millions are starving all around?"

"They enjoy themselves," said Cyrus Sims, "but they're all hungry. There's not a single man or woman here that's had enough to eat to-day. But they come to the opera as the one little gleam of light and joy and colour in the monotony of misery."

"I cannot believe it," said the Colonel. "Those people aren't hungry. I guess they're Soviet officials who have hoarded up secret stores."

"Some of them, perhaps. But there's not much chance of that. They've been rationed as Soviet workers until a week ago. Now the rations are cut off, and they're tightening their belts."

"It's a new *bourgeoisie*," said the Colonel. "The Bolsheviks declared war on the old *bourgeoisie*, and then set up a new one of their own. There's no more equality in Soviet Russia than there is in the United States."

Bertram agreed with him, but that night he had to admit, after an amazing invasion of the A. R. A., that the glamour and glitter of the opera only concealed the sharp tooth of hunger. It showed itself naked and unashamed when the door was opened to a ringing of bells and a party of opera singers desired to know if they might invite themselves to supper with *Messieurs les Américains*?

How could a party of young Americans, six thousand miles from home, refuse to share their bully beef with art in distress?

"Come right in!" said Sims, in command of "the bunch."

They came right in, six ladies and three men, including the Prima Donna, who was a Persian lady, with a wonderful voice, enormous black eyes, and a ferocious appetite. The American boys brought out their tinned beef and biscuits, their cheese and butter, and made a picnic meal with hot cocoa. The Russian ladies of the opera, speaking but a few words of French and German, which was their only conversational link with their American hosts who had picked up a smattering of those languages, after two years in Europe, made no concealment of their delight in the presence of this food. They fell upon it like harpies, and it was the beautiful Persian girl who devoured the last of a Dutch cheese with her big black eyes raised in ecstasy.

One of the Americans produced a gramophone, and turned on a jazz tune, and initiated the Persian lady into the mysteries of the fox-trot, while she screamed with laughter. The others, still roving round for stray biscuits, laughed up and down the scale.

Bertram slipped away to his camp bed in a little salon which had once been the writing-room of Nadia's uncle, Governor of Kazan in Imperial Russia. Those dancers in the next room were like the merry ladies of the Decameron, surrounded by plague.

He looked out of his window to the white night, with a moon above the snow. It was very quiet in Kazan, with its houses filled with naked children, and starving people, where typhus prevailed.

LVIII

In the house where Nadia was lodged with the two other Russian ladies, Bertram was able to have some private talk with her before taking the boat next morning down the Volga.

"I've come to say good-bye," he said. "For a few weeks at least. Afterwards —"

She looked up at him with a smile, as she sat sewing at a table. She was making herself a linen coat such as doctors wear in the wards.

"Afterwards, my friend —?"

He was silent for a little while, thinking deeply of many things-of all his life, and the meaning of it, and the hope of it.

"Perhaps it's too soon to talk of afterwards. When I come back we will arrange something."

"What kind of thing?" she asked.

"Our life together," he said simply.

She rose, and let her linen drop, and took his hands.

"I will be your good comrade," she said. "For a little while, if you like. For ever, if you like."

"I want comradeship," he told her. "I'm lonely, and I hate loneliness. I think we could do good work together, for children, for peace, for ourselves. I'll be a faithful servant to you, Princess!"

"Not mine," she said, smiling. "I'm no Princess, but a serving wench. I'm Communist enough to believe in equality between a man and his woman. We will serve God together!"

"I don't know much about God," said Bertram. "I'm a hopeless infidel. But I'm spiritual enough to adore the goodness in you. Your courage! Your self-forgetfulness."

"Where love is, there God is also," said Nadia. "That's Tolstoy, but it's true, I think. We will find God together, in love for each other and the world."

"I've made a hopeless failure of love once," said Bertram. "I'd be glad to get a second chance."

"You shall have the chance, dear sir," said Nadia. "You are one of the great lovers of the world. How proud I am to be your handmaid! I will help you to do your work for poor humanity. Every word you write shall be a light to my love for you. You will make the world know the truth, and I shall have a share in it by keeping you well, giving you comfort in spirit and body, making for you that little private paradise of which once you spoke to me."

"You promise me good things," said Bertram. "Better than most men get, and more than I deserve."

"I promise myself better things," she answered. "I am selfish in thinking of so many sweet gifts that will come to me with you. Happiness in Russia! I think I shall be the only happy woman."

"You make me a little afraid," said Bertram. "You will find me out as a poor fellow."

"No, I have found you out as a kind, brave gentleman."

"Something happened to us in the market-place at Moscow!" said Bertram.

"It was God's hand that turned your head my way and let me look into your eyes."

"It was luck," he said. "God, if you like!"

"Love, anyhow," she answered.

He stood looking into her eyes, and his were thoughtful.

"My love," he said, "is not a boy's first flame of passion, body and soul on fire. That was given to my wife, Joyce. In a way it's hers now, because it belongs to the past which was hers and mine. I shall come to you in a different way, Princess. Not as an ardent boy, but as a man who's seen the brutality of life, and come through agony, and perhaps has a better understanding of himself and of human nature. But what love I have in my heart, and a comradeship of utter loyalty, devotion, and humility, shall be yours until I die, if you'll let me live with you so long."

"We shall arrange our life together," she said, using the words he had spoken. "Our loving comradeship has no ignorance. We have both seen life's misery and been touched by it. We shall have the wisdom of love, so that it is more precious."

LIX

The boat was the last to leave Kazan to go down the Volga. There was already ice in the river, and the wooden piers were being pulled in. The Russian skipper was anxious to get back on the return journey, lest the boat should be ice-bound.

It was not a bad boat. There was room on board for three hundred passengers, and many little cabins in the first class. In the old days it had been a pleasure-steamer for Russian gentry, and the well-to-do *bourgeoisie*, when the summer shone upon the broad waters of the Volga. There had been wine parties on summer nights in the panelled saloon, and under the awnings on the promenade decks. Gipsies had sung the Volga song and their own weird melodies to Russian aristocrats with their pretty mistresses, in this ship of pleasure. Now all its paint had gone, and its decks were dirty, and its cabins foul.

Incredible filth was in the cabins. Bertram and Dr. Weekes made a brief inspection of them and then beat a hasty retreat. Insects of every species crawled up the panels, swarmed in disgusting orgies under the mattresses, made dwelling-places in the very wash-basins. For months, according to the skipper, this had been a refugee ship, transporting thousands of people escaping from the famine. On every voyage dozens of dead bodies had been thrown overboard. Typhus had raged in the ship. Specimens of all the vermin of Southern Russia had mingled in this floating menagerie, and bred and multiplied.

Dr. Weekes was frankly scared.

"A death-ship!" he said.

Yet, with generous courage, he gave Bertram the only clean place for a sleeping berth. It was the table in the dining saloon, which seemed to be free from vermin. Bertram refused the privilege, and would not accept until the young doctor shared its table space. Jemmy Hart, the newspaper correspondent, was with them. He cursed Russia, Bolshevism, and bugs with untiring eloquence, and with rich imaginative efforts. They brought with them sufficient tinned food, it seemed to Bertram, to provide a battalion with two months' rations, but before the return journey they were on half rations and hungry.

Hungry, though for a time Bertram lost his appetite and never wanted to eat another mouthful of food again until he died. How could he sit down to a meal of pork and beans, good white bread, and American cheese, after days among people who had but a handful of grass between them and death, who watched their children die, one by one, and lay down themselves to die, with nothing of any kind to eat, though they had garnered filth and eaten that until it was gone.

For a day and a night the boat steamed slowly down stream, between the low-lying banks of the Volga, rising steeper as they travelled south. On each side of them was a white desolation, immense, monotonous, unbroken, except now and then where distant villages lay buried in snow. No smoke came from them. No peasants came down to the landing-stages. No sign of human life appeared.

"It's a great white death," said Dr. Weekes in a low voice. His fur cap and heavy astrachan collar were covered with snow as he stared from the bridge across the countryside.

"Better dead than alive in this country," said Jemmy Hart. "That Bolshevik vermin made a merry game of me last night."

They tied up at Tetuishi, and went across the landing-stage, up steep snow banks to a little town perched on a hill. A few Tartars wandered about the market place, gaunt and shaggy. There were lines of booths, like those in Kazan and Moscow, but there were no soldiers and no buyers, and no merchandise. From a Red soldier sitting inside a sentry-box, with his rifle between his knees, blue-lipped and blue-nosed, and as starved-looking as a stray dog, they found out the whereabouts of the President of the Tetuishi Commune. It was Jemmy Hart who acted as interpreter, having learnt Russian in its prisons.

The President was a dark, liquid-eyed man, with shaggy black hair. Sitting behind him, in his office, were three or four other men of the Soviet Committee, with moody, melancholy eyes. They looked like respectable mechanics at a Baptist meeting, and not like "the bloody Bolsheviks," as Jemmy Hart called them in their presence, relying on their ignorance of English with an American accent.

Jemmy asked for sleighs and horses —*seichas*! Immediately. He spoke in the name of the A. R. A., to which they bowed their heads, as at the name of God. Certainly. They would have a sleigh and two horses —*seichas*. It was four hours before they arrived, and during that time, between Jemmy's explosions of impotent wrath, the President of Tetuishi imparted information regarding his district.

It had been a rich granary before the droughts of 1920 and 1921. It had exported a surplus of two million poods of grain. Now the last harvest had only given sixteen hundred poods of grain. The people had very little to eat. In some villages nothing to eat. They were dying in great numbers at Spassk, and in other places to which he pointed on a map which hung behind his desk. The Soviet Government had sent down some barge-loads of potatoes. Owing to the lack of horses it was difficult to transport them to distant villages. It was a great tragedy. Many poor people were doomed.

He spoke in a quiet, kind, melancholy voice, not agonising, not pleading for help, but accepting on behalf of his people an inevitability of death.

The horses came at last, and with Dr. Weekes and Jemmy Hart, Bertram drove across the snow-fields to the nearest villages. The Tartar driver shouted to his lean nags and they went at a great pace over the hard snow, through a frosty wind which slashed Bertram's face like a whip.

They halted outside the high stockade which surrounds all Russian villages, to keep in the cattle and keep out the wolves.

"Let's walk in and see the best and the worst," said Dr. Weekes.

A broad roadway divided the village into two. On each side were neat houses of unplaned logs, squarely built, under sloping roofs, heavily laden with snow. Steeply the snow was banked up all round them.

Not a soul stirred in the village. From one end to the other, there was no sign of life. No dog barked. No cattle stood in the yards or sheds. There was no crowing of cocks or clucking of chickens.

"Is everybody dead?" asked Dr. Weekes, and his voice was startling in the melancholy silence of the place.

"No," said Bertram, "I have seen faces at the windows, but hardly human."

He glanced at the window of a cottage close by, and Dr. Weekes looked in that direction. Three little faces were staring out at them, gravely. They were like monkey faces. They were like the faces of the abandoned children in Kazan.

"Let's go in," said Dr. Weekes.

He knocked at a cottage door, and after a moment or two it was opened, and on the threshold stood a tall peasant, with a flaxen beard and blue eyes.

Jemmy Hart spoke to him in Russian, and he bowed, and made a gesture, with simple dignity, inviting them to go in.

The room into which they went was spotlessly clean, and newly scrubbed by a woman who stood shyly on one side and then crossed herself, in the Russian fashion when strangers pass the threshold. The three children who had stared out of the window came and clung to her skirts.

Jemmy Hart talked to the man, and then turned to the others.

"He says they are starving, like all the others."

"Ask them if they have any food at all," said Dr. Weekes.

"The man says 'some dried leaves.' "

"Let us see."

The woman went to a cupboard, and brought out a small wooden bowl, in which was some fine, brownish powder.

She showed it to Bertram, and then began to weep very quietly.

"That is all they have," said Jemmy Hart.

"What will happen when that is gone?" asked Dr. Weekes. "Have they any hope of getting food from the local Soviet?"

"He says there is no hope, because there is no food. They are waiting, he says, for death."

Dr. Weekes took one of the children in his arms, and felt its body.

"It won't be long, I guess," he said very quietly.

"The man says he will take us to see some of his neighbours," said Jemmy Hart.

They went with him into another cottage.

An old woman was there, with a child in her arms. She lifted up a cloth around its body, and showed a little skeleton figure, with a strangely distended stomach.

"Starvation," said Dr. Weekes. "They swell out like that in the last stage."

The old woman talked with passionate grief, to which Jemmy Hart listened with his head bent.

"She says this child belongs to her son. His wife died a week ago, of dysentery. There was no more food in the house. He walked away into the snow, and has not come back."

A group of women gathered in the farm-yard next to this old woman's cottages. In some way they had learnt that strangers had come-perhaps with rescue. They pressed round Bertram, plucking at his coat, crying out to him, weeping, yet with a kind of anger, as though fierce with despair.

One of them brought out a bowl filled with bits of black stone, as it seemed, or lead. She took out a bit of it, and flung it on the ground, and then raised both arms to heaven and gave a loud wailing cry. The other women spoke to Jemmy Hart, and seemed to explain.

"It's clay," said Jemmy. "They dig it out of a hill called Bitarjisk. It's sold for five hundred roubles a pood. They powder it up and mix it with water and swallow it. It has some nutritive quality, I guess, but these women say it bursts the bowels of their little ones."

The tall peasant who was their guide, elbowed his way through the women who clung to Bertram and his companions with shrill cries. He led them to another cottage, and bade the women stay outside.

Inside it was very quiet and cold. For a moment there was no sign of any life here. But from a pile of rags on a wooden bench against one of the walls, a man rose to a half-sitting posture. He was nearly naked, with but a tattered shirt over his body. His chest was bare, and showed deep hollows below the bones of the neck, and his arms were like withered sticks, and his legs had no flesh on their bones, but only a scabby skin. He was bleeding from the mouth, and there were bloody rims round his eyes. He seemed to Bertram like Lazarus risen from the tomb.

There were other living people in the room. Bertram heard a faint stir above the stove where, on the shelf above, Russians sleep in winter. A woman lay there with a little girl. They raised their heads feebly, and let them drop again. They were nearly dead, it seemed. At the far end of the room, on the window seat, with his head back against the framework, was a young lad-eighteen, perhaps-with a fair, handsome face, and blue eyes. He did not move his body, or alter the position of his head, but his eyes stared at the strangers in his father's house. He was still alive, but too weak to raise a hand or stir a limb.

Jemmy Hart bent down to the man, and spoke to him. For a time he was silent, and seemed to have lost the gift of speech. But presently he spoke some words in a whisper.

Jemmy translated them.

"He says death has been long in coming. They have been waiting like this, day after day, and still live."

The peasant who had been their guide spoke to Jemmy, who told the others.

"This man was rich once. He owned many fields and a herd of cattle. The drought burnt his harvest up, and all his cattle died. He sold his clothes for food. He has nothing in the world. There are many like him."

"For Christ's sake," said Bertram, "give him this!"

He handed Jemmy all his money —a great wad of roubles.

The old man stared at it, and muttered something.

"What does he say?"

"He says money is no good. There's nothing to buy."

The peasant guide spoke again.

"This man says it's true," said Jemmy. "Money is no good in this village, because there's nothing to sell, and nothing to buy. It's the same in Tetuishi, and that's the farthest any one can go without horses. Your money is just waste paper, old lad."

Bertram was pale to the lips.

Then there was nothing to be done for these people. No power on earth could help them. They were waiting for Death to cross the threshold, as their kindest visitor, and Death tarried.

They went into other villages, and it was the same. The women clamoured about them, believing they had come from some great power, with rescue, and they had none at that time, though later they would get food to the children, or to some of them. Young girls, beautiful as all the peasant girls in the Volga valley, lay dying in cottages and barns. Lads on the threshold of youth's adventure, waited patiently and quietly for death, with those who were old enough to die. The children did not even wail in their hunger, but crawled about the floors with swollen heads and grave wondering eyes. In some of the barns where once rich stores of grain had been, now lay unburied bodies. . . .

"I can't stand much more of this," said Bertram. "War is a merry game to famine!"

That night, on the vermin-haunted ship, he could not eat, but saved some bread and cheese for people he would meet on the morrow, in other villages further down the river.

"Nothing but an enormous act of world charity will save these people," said Dr. Weekes.

"I'm afraid it won't happen," said Bertram. "People are fed up with tragedy. The war deadened them. All the appeals for devastated Europe-Austria, Hungary, Poland, Armenia-have led to reaction and boredom. Russia comes too late in the day."

"Charity will use its hatred of Bolshevism to close its heart-springs to the Russian people," said Dr. Weekes. "They'll say, 'Why in Hell should we help Soviet Russia to feed its Red Army'?"

"And charity isn't enough," said Jemmy Hart. "Not the private charity of dear old ladies. The nations of the world must save Russia-and mighty quick, or it will be too late for the people we saw to-day."

"And those we shall see to-morrow," said Bertram.

They sat up late in the saloon, on the table, with their legs up to avoid the crawling things.

"What's going to happen to this sad and bad old Europe?" asked Jemmy Hart.

For hours they discussed his question.

Dr. Weekes had a fine and spiritual outlook on life. He deplored the attitude of his own country, which he accused of selfish indifference to humanity.

"We're betraying Christ," he said. "We're the Pharisees of the world. 'Thank God that we are not as these men are-publicans and sinners.' We're up to the neck in self-righteousness. We came into the war a damned sight too late to suffer the agony of those who fought first and longest. We cleared out of Europe a damned sight too quick. Back to Big Business. A hundred-per-cent Americanism. God! I'm ashamed of my own folk!"

Jemmy Hart would have none of it.

"We're the Tom Tiddler's ground of all the beggars of Europe. We fill the hat every time. I guess we'll stuff food into Russia, while swearing by all our gods that Europe can go to hell."

"Russia is the key of world peace and economic recovery," said Dr. Weekes. "These people must be saved, for our sake as well as theirs. We want them to buy our goods. We want their grain and oil and minerals and timber and flour. There won't always be drought in Russia."

"What about the Red Army?" asked Jemmy Hart. "As long as it stands to arms, Poland stays mobilised. As long as it threatens Poland, France presses Germany for the last gold mark, because France pays Poland."

"Precisely that," said Dr. Weekes. "The nations must present an ultimatum to Soviet Russia. 'We'll feed your people, make your trains run, re-start your industries, in return for certain conditions which we impose. Down with the Red Army. No propaganda. Recognition of pre-war debts. That or nothing.' "

"Would Lenin accept?" asked Bertram.

Dr. Weekes nodded.

"He knows the game's up. He *must* accept to save his people. But we must act together, or he will drive wedges between us and play Germany against France."

So they talked. But in their silences they thought of the peasants who were dying in the snow-bound villages beyond the river banks.

Day after day they went down the river, tying up at landing stages, driving over the snow-fields, going into the land of Famine, until Bertram said, "I've seen enough. The horror is getting on my nerves."

"I agree," said Dr. Weekes. "We have enough to report. Mine will go to the A. R. A. Yours to the world. With Jemmy Hart's. Your opportunity is greater than mine. If you write the things we have seen, you'll make men and angels weep."

"If I write what I feel," said Bertram, "it will make them sick."

"If I write what I know," said Jemmy Hart, "my best friends will denounce me as a Bolshevist!"

It was in the city of Samara, crowded with refugees, abandoned children, typhus-stricken families, and starving peasants, that Bertram wrote the Truth about the Famine.

Every word he wrote was an appeal to the world for mercy and pity on behalf of these people. As his pen travelled over the white pages of his writing blocks, he had before his eyes the vision of women wailing over their starving children, of straw-bearded peasants with the agony of death in their patient eyes, of boys and girls he had seen lying down to die in each other's arms. He wrote with a Biblical simplicity, but Dr. Weekes who read what he wrote, wept frankly and unashamed, and said, "It's God's truth, Pollard! You'll make the English-speaking peoples see the things you have seen, and feel the touch of the pity that's in your heart. I envy you your gift of words."

The boat was ice-bound at Samara, and it was by train that Bertram went back with Dr. Weekes to Moscow, with all his narrative. It was a four days' journey, and like the Russian journeys he had made, filthy and fatiguing. During those four days and nights he thought always in his waking hours of that lady, Nadia, to whom he was returning after his work for the people she loved. Through all this time, indeed, on the Volga and in the villages, her words were with him, her spiritual comradeship gave him courage and endurance, the gift of her love lightened even the darkness of all that horror. He was going back to the best woman he had ever known, utterly unselfish, "saintly" in a gay and beautiful way, yet human and gracious as one of Shakespeare's women. She would be his companion along the lonely road. She would keep his courage to the sticking point. She would be, perhaps, the mother of his children. The image of Joyce was fading from his mind. She belonged to a different age, and a different world —a thousand years ago, a million miles away. He could think of Joyce now without a pang, without anger, even, and without jealousy. He was sorry about Kenneth Murless. It was hard on Joyce that Kenneth had died. Not a bad chap, after all! A gentleman in the old meaning of the word. With Nadia as his mate, he could wish Joyce all happiness. That pretty child! That spoilt darling of an ancient caste, now passing into history with other ghosts!

With Nadia he would walk in the middle of the road, as he had tried to walk with Joyce. No longer was he lonely.

It was the Colonel with his young "puu" who met them at the station in Moscow. Sims was there too, and some of the other boys.

"Glad to see you back," said the Colonel. "It seems an age since you went. Thought you might have turned Bolsheviks and gone to rule the Far Eastern Republic!"

"Any news?" asked Dr. Weekes.

The Colonel pondered.

"Devilish little. Odd bits. There's a Treaty of Peace between England and Ireland."

"Thank God for that," said Bertram.

"Upper Silesia has been divided by the League of Nations. The Germans are howling in agony."

"I guessed they would," said Dr. Weekes. "Any local news?"

The Colonel pondered again.

"Sims left his heart behind him in Kazan, with that Persian *prima donna*. Sad business!"

"A libel, sir!" said Sims.

The Colonel thought again, and a grave look, not of mockery, came into his face.

"One tragic thing that makes us all sad. Our Russian Princess-you remember her? —Nadia-died a week ago. Typhus. A most devoted and beautiful young lady. I hate to think of it."

"I'm sorry," said Dr. Weekes, in a low voice.

Bertram said nothing.

He walked alone again.

LX

He did not stay long in Moscow. He took the train to Riga, and posted his articles across the Russian frontier. Then he went on to Berlin, with a "wire" in advance to Christy.

Christy met him at the station, and not only Christy, but Janet Welford.

"Sir Faithful!" she cried, using her old nickname for him. "By my halidom, but I'm glad to see you! After all this age of time."

She took his hands, and gave him her cheek to kiss. Then a grave look came into her eyes, and the merriment died out.

"You're not looking too well. Anything wrong with you, friend?"

"A bit chippy, that's all," said Bertram. "But enormously glad to see you again. Have you fixed it up with Christy?"

She blushed and laughed.

"We've made a kind of contract, subject to alteration."

She took his arm, and spoke gravely again.

"You're ill, my dear."

"It's nothing," he said. "A chill!"

It was more than a chill. It was typhus. That night they put him to bed, fever-stricken. The vermin of the Volga had done their work. Janet Welford sat with him in a room that Christy had hired, and several times he spoke her name, without knowing she was near. Once he spoke another name which she had never heard before. "Nadia" —it sounded like that. But in his delirium he talked incessantly of Joyce. The image of the girl who had been his wife came back to him. They were married again. All else was blotted out.

"Joyce, darling! How beautiful you are! The ideal beauty! That was old Christy's phrase. Joyce! . . . Joyce. . . . Is breakfast ready? What a kid you are! Why, Joyce, sweetheart, aren't you ready yet? I've been waiting for you. I'm always lonely without you. Even for a second. Joyce . . . Joyce . . . Joyce. . . ."

Janet Welford bent over him.

He looked so young in his fever, with flushed cheeks and tousled hair. A boy again.

"Loyalty," he said. "I'm nothing without loyalty, Joyce. It's all yours." He seemed to be arguing with her, trying to make her understand.

"The middle of the road. That's where I am. Between the extremes, Joyce. A damned lonely place."

A German doctor came with Christy.

"It is very dangerous," he said. "This is Russian typhus. He must be removed to a hospital. In the morning. The authorities insist on it in cases of infectious fevers. To-night I will send you a nurse."

"No," said Janet Welford. "I'm nursing him to-night."

"At the risk of your own life, *gnädiges Fräulein.*

"I'll take the risk, doctor."

Christy was anxious, helpless, gloomy.

"Turn and turn about," he said. "I'll take the night watch, my dear."

"No," she said again, "this is my work. Lie down till the morning, and be good."

Early in the morning she came out of Bertram's room.

"He keeps calling for Joyce. She ought to know. Can you send her a telegram?"

"Holme Ottery," said Christy. "That ought to find her. But she doesn't deserve it."

"No woman deserves such love as his," said Janet; and Christy saw that she had tears in her eyes. He knew that he was only second in her heart, and that Bertram held first place. She made no secret of it, and spoke frankly to him.

"I love every hair of his head, my dear. You won't be angry when I tell you that?"

"Not angry," said Christy, "nor jealous. I have your friendship, and it's good enough."

"My friendship for ever," she said, "and more loyal because you know about this boy, and understand."

"Need you send for Joyce?" he asked. "Perhaps if he gets well —"

She shook her head, and knew what he meant to say, and did not dare to say.

"No. That would be a dirty kind of trick, and I've kept clean, so far. All through the night he has kept calling for Joyce. She's still in possession of him, and I've no claim."

"In London," said Christy, "he had to cut and run from you."

He was arguing against his own hopes and chance.

"Yes," said Janet, "I could have had him then. But it would have been stealing. Breaking his loyalty. I'm not like that."

"He's been too damned loyal," said Christy. "My lady Joyce chucked him as she would a broken toy. Why send for her? Perhaps she won't come, anyhow. The little bitch!"

"We'll give her the chance," said Janet, and she wrote out the telegram.

"We'll play the game, for Bertram's sake," she said later. "It may be the last thing we can do for him. Another visitor may come before his wife gets here."

"Is it as bad as that?" he asked.

"You know what typhus means. It burns quick. Oh, my dear, I think my love is dying!"

She wept a little, and Christy leaned over her and put his hand on her shoulder and said, "Courage!" She took hold of his hand and held it tight.

"Old Plesiosaurus! You're a good friend in distress."

"But not a lucky lover!" he answered gloomily.

"When we set up house together," she said, "you'll marvel at your luck!"

She laughed in her old gay way, even though her eyes were still wet with tears, and Christy was comforted by the promise of her words, and worshipful before this woman whose spirit was so honest and so kind. Her love for Bertram made no difference to him. Her comradeship was gift enough.

Together they went each day to the hospital where Bertram lay. The German doctors would not let them go into his ward, because of infection, and their reports were not comforting.

"*Sehr krank! . . . Gross gefähr. . . . Es geht nicht wohl.*"

Bertram was very ill. He was in great danger. It was not going well with him.

It was Janet who remembered that Bertram had a sister in Berlin-the beautiful Dorothy, now Frau von Arenburg. A note from her brought Dorothy and her husband to Christy's room, infinitely distressed by the grave news. They haunted the hospital and Von Arenburg interviewed the doctors, and in his rather Prussian way impressed them with "the enormous importance" of Bertram's recovery to the friendly relations between England and Germany.

Anna von Wegener sent immense bouquets of hot-house flowers which were never allowed to enter the sick man's room, and other German ladies whom Bertram had met at his sister's house were prodigal with fruit and flowers. But Bertram, lying there in delirium, knew none of this kindly remembrance from those whom he had called "the Enemy."

"It is the crisis," said the German doctors one day. "If he lives through the night —"

"Let's pray a bit," said Janet to her friend. "We're both infidels, but God will understand."

"I don't believe in prayer," said Christy. "I'm a blasphemer and a heretic."

"So is all humanity," said Janet. "But in time of trouble we cry out to God, in spite of disbelief."

"It's our cowardice," said Christy. "It's the dark of the mind. The primitive savage before the Ju-ju of his fears and hopes."

"Children crying for help to the Eternal Father," said Janet. "Something like that, though I can't get the hang of it."

They went together into a church somewhere off the Wilhelmstrasse, and kneeling side by side, Christy and Janet bent their heads and stayed in the silence and the gloom before an altar with twinkling lights, and in their queer way prayed to the Unknown God for Bertram, their friend.

"What was your prayer?" asked Janet, when they came out.

Christy smiled.

"Not much of a one. I said, 'Oh, God, where in God's name are you? Why have you made such a mess of this bloody old world?' Then I kept on saying, 'Oh, God! Oh, God!' until my mind went into a kind of coma, very restful."

"Fine," said Janet. "A real confession of faith."

"What was your prayer?" asked Christy.

Janet could hardly remember her prayer. She had offered her heart to the Unknown God, and said many times, "Dear God!" and then, "Dear Bertram!"

"We're weakening," said Christy. "This is nonsense. It's a disgrace to the intellect."

"No," said Janet, "I'm strengthened. I believe God will like this little visit. I believe it's a good thing to do."

"Anyhow, it won't do God or Bertram any harm," said Christy.

He spoke in his sardonic way, but he, too, felt strangely comforted and puzzled at the meaning of it.

When they went back to the apartment house where Christy had rooms, they found Joyce there waiting for them. Neither of them had seen her before, and by a glance they tried to take the measure of this girl who was Bertram's wife. She was very pale, and looked ill, but wonderfully young and elegant, and exquisite.

"How is my husband?" she asked, and that word "husband" seemed strange on her lips, because of her youthful girlish look.

Janet told her that he was pretty bad.

"It was good of you to wire to me," Joyce said. "I am deeply grateful to you."

"He called to you many times on the night he was first so ill," said Janet.

A little mist came into Joyce's eyes.

"I don't deserve his remembrance. I've been rotten to him," she said, humbly, and that humility and that confession softened their hearts towards her.

"He's been very loyal to you," said Janet. " 'Sir Faithful,' his friends call him."

"I was disloyal," said Joyce. "Perhaps he told you?"

She looked at Janet Welford, and her face flamed with colour. Perhaps in some way she guessed that Janet had been Bertram's best friend.

Janet nodded.

"Things happen like that. Perhaps they can't be helped. It's good if one gets a chance to patch things up. Life's mostly patchwork."

"When can I see him?"

She saw him that night. His fever had left him —"Our prayers!" said Janet-and the German doctors allowed Joyce to sit for a little while by his bedside. He was sleeping when she went into the ward where he lay alone, but presently he awoke and opened his eyes, and looked at her.

"Hullo, Joyce," he said, in a kind of whisper. "I'm not dreaming again, am I?"

"I've come back," she answered, and she put her arms about him and wept, so that her tears fell on his face.

He was silent for a little, while looking at her with a faint smile.

"Do you mean back for always?" he asked presently. "As man and wife?"

"If you'll have me," she said. "Do you forgive me, Bertram, for all my beastliness?"

He took her hand, and stroked the back of it with his finger-tips.

"How beautiful you are!" he said.

"Do you forgive me, dear heart?" she asked again.

"Hush," he said. "There's nothing to forgive. We were both kids."

A little later he spoke again.

"I am sorry about Kenneth. Very rough on him and you."

She bowed her head, and was very white.

"It was best like that. It has let me come back."

"I knew a girl who died-in Russia —" said Bertram. "One day I'll tell you. Not now. How's England and Holme Ottery?"

"England's still there. Holme Ottery's sold. I've a little house close by. We'll go back and live there. It's ready for our home-coming."

"Home-coming!" said Bertram. "How good that sounds! I've been wandering alone since you left me, Joyce. Always damned lonely."

"I'm with you now," said Joyce. "Body and soul, Bertram. The past is dead, and I'm changed."

He put his arms about her, and drew down her head until it lay upon his breast.

"Let's begin again," he said. "We're young enough."

THE END

www.ingramcontent.com/pod-product-compliance
Lightning Source LLC
Chambersburg PA
CBHW060412310726
48976CB00003B/1032